Prince ra

Dearest Nülifer,

Enjoy reading this ♡

xx

Enjoy

All the best

2021

xx

Nazahah Zahid

DEDICATION

To all the children in Syria, whose cries have gone unheard for
too long. And to my husband, whose supportive
encouragement meant the world to me whilst writing
'Princess Mira'.

PREFACE

Are you listening?

When I tell you that the streets of where we called 'home' were once proudly paraded on by our mothers and our fathers, our sisters and our brothers, and by our neighbours, who all personified the benevolence and propriety of my warm-spirited nation?

Are you there?

When I tell you that my children, my sisters and my brothers all danced to the melodic fusion of bazaar stallholders selling their favourite treats after school, inducing the subtle scent of rose and pistachio-flavoured Atayef and vanilla cream-filled basbousa?

Are you still listening?

When I tell about how every home was adorned with beauteous calligraphic portraits and the fragrance of freshly baked ka'ak ambled for hours throughout the weekends? And hospitality and companionship were the two vocal aspects of our upbringing which made us who we are today.

Are you enlightened?

When I tell you about how, despite the presence of rejuvenated shopping malls, the comfort of the antediluvian souks and bazaars were still cherished by us for their crowded alleys, cheers of children playing ghommemah and the passionate dialogues between stallholders and bargaining aunties.

Are you fascinated?

When I tell you that every Muslim, Shia, Sunni, Christian, Jew and Druze conversed with immense dignity, respect and devotion, all annexed to the humbleness of each other's pure friendship? The sound of poetically authored fairy tales by the cities' 'Hakawatis' was devotedly heeded by the children amongst the neighbouring streets, who all assembled in rows around the storytellers for hours, embedded into a different dimension of tales, adventure and utopia.

Are you captivated?

When I tell you about how my progenitors taught us the ponderous calibre of personal and spiritual evolvement that taught us that Islam had not one iota of comparison to the loathsome illustration now exploited amongst our generations?

Are you still listening? To the sound of roaring bombs launched on my brothers, who shriek in agony as they flee from the nightmare from which they cannot awaken? Are you there, listening? To the howls of my sisters, who whimper in torment as they remove the shrapnel from their naked, defenceless bodies? Are you still listening? To the way my mother's lament and desolation keeps her awake at night, finding her child's face on every child, except their face is right there, amongst the behemoth mountain of dead, distorted bodies? Did you hear her, the sorrow in her voice, when she hysterically ran to every person her eyes met and asked grievously, "Please, have you seen my son?"

Are you still listening?

Did you listen?

5

CHAPTER ONE

Aleppo 2010

Alone. Even the word itself seems empty, desolate even, but being alone was often what Amira revelled in. It wasn't that she was lonely, but that she found serenity and calmness in being alone within her own company.

"But Amira, how can you say you like to be lonely?" laughed Baba.

"Let me tell you something Amira, my princess," he continued, playfully. "We, as humans, we aren't designed to be alone. You hear me? The worst thing in life is ending up alone with no one around you. Is that what you want? To push everyone out? To be isolated forever?" said Baba, staring directly at Amira, who sat gleefully across the dining table from her father.

Amira loved debating with her father. It was something she cherished about her relationship with him. Baba was a good-humoured, light-hearted man, who loved amusing both his children with his humoured advice and often canny sayings. Really, this is why Amira idolized every moment with her father because she simply found a peace of mind and composure in his royal presence.

"Oh my god, Baba," Amira giggled innocently, clapping her hands in hilarity, "I never said I like being lonely, now did I?" she chuckled, as Baba peered at her pure, honest face through his reading glasses.

"All I'm saying is that there is a sense of fulfilment in being alone sometimes, a sense of contentment in your own presence. Rumi even said it, Baba! 'Do not feel lonely, for the whole universe is inside you'." Amira gawked at her father, who was now folding up the newspaper he was reading and removing his reading glasses.

"Yes, yes, bring out Ustadh Rumi again; seriously Amira, there's just no winning with you, is there? Always wanting to defeat your poor old Baba." Amira skipped towards her father and embraced him graciously, and planted a kiss on his warm temple and turned to face him. "Of course, Baba, that is because I am Amira, the princess, although the way I always win at everything, you should have called me Malika, the Queen!" flaunted Amira, flicking back the few golden locks of her mane that were drooping over her shoulders, and parading around her father nobly.

"Just like your mother, you are. Go on, leave me ALONE then, so I can enjoy my own presence. Go help your mother with supper," sighed Baba, with a slight grin on his wrinkly face.

With that, Amira picked up her school books from the dining table and headed for her room. As she stumbled towards the door across the dining room, she yelled, "The entire universe is inside you, Baba!" She snickered and hurried up the stairs to her bedroom.

Amira had always been a fan of poetry and she had loved everything about fictional and expressive poetry for as long as she could remember. This was mainly due to her father, who although he hated to admit it, loved writing poems in his spare time. "These poems, they're just silly scribbles, Amira, don't waste your time on my poems," he'd always say when Amira pleaded to read some of his work. Despite his lack of bravado and self-esteem in his own work, his demeanour towards

7

Amira's profound poetry writing and recitation was beyond cordial and supportive. The more her father beautified the world of poetry, the more Amira fell in love with it. She often wrote poems at night, when she couldn't sleep and would spend hours and hours finding the right poetic stanza or verse to complete each poem. She wrote about anything. Love, life, friendship, war and fictional characters. Quite remarkably, she was pretty talented at writing for a 14-year-old, and maybe that was all down to Baba's passion behind his daughter's striking flair.

Amira bounced onto her bed which was still unmade from the morning and reached out for her favourite book from underneath her duvet. She often hid her most treasured belongings in hiding spots because her younger brother, Adam, would always scurry indiscreetly into her room whilst she was at school and finish a single marker aimlessly drawing on anything he could find; books, homework sheets, walls, anything. Although Amira adored every inch of her 4-year-old brother, she couldn't stand when all her things had been doodled on by a drooling toddler who had no sense of restraint.

She rested one arm on her windowsill and the other on her knee and opened up to where her handmade bookmark, made by Adam, was cushioned deeply into the core of chapter 5. She began reading silently.

'Cities of Salt' by Abdelrahman Munif. Aside from bringing poetry to life, Amira was also an avid reader. This particular book, which she had already read twice, was a favourite of hers. It commences with the impoverished, humble dwellers located in the smouldering desert whose serene and simple life is rattled by the detection of oil by American researchers who have been welcomed into the country. Amira found this novel enticing for two reasons, one being the engrossing narration of how modernization and deviation introduced the development of oil from the community's point of view and the second being the notion of religion being involved as it caused fury and resentment by the locals due to the presence and interference of non-Muslims, which also lead to the increase of materialism, which equally meant there began to be a great diminution of spiritual and mutual values. Besides this, Amira was conjointly interested in such books as they all revolved around the concept of social issues within society and a country as a whole. Such books correlated with what her own nation was encountering more and more every day, with the government ignoring social problems and cordial disputes, so it made Amira feel more knowledgeable in order to engage and understand more of what her nation is experiencing.

She read for 20 minutes or so before something caught her eye from outside the windowsill, which overlooked a small section of her neighbourhood street, 'Shajara Street', which meant 'tree' in Arabic. She looked up from her page, squinting slightly to focus on the group of boys playing football and shouting loudly. She tried to make out what the noise was about until she realised they were arguing over a flat, burst football. Amira was chuckling at the boys' foolish backlash over a burst ball when she saw someone peering towards her direction amongst the chaos. She stared helplessly as if she was bewitched by the tall figure, now smiling at her, showing off one of his dimples. He was taller than the other boys around him and almost towered over them with his hefty arms folded into a cross, and his athletic built almost visible through his white vest. He winked at Amira playfully, as he did almost every time he saw her and turned around to fetch the ball and start blowing air into it. His hair, which was naturally dark, was tied up messily into a small bun, with bits of loose strands sliding down on either side of his head. The vest he wore over his broad shoulders was neither too loose nor tight, but fitting to reveal his slight ab formation in the sunlight. As the sun beamed over the town like a majestic chariot in the clear sky, Amira watched on as the boy began fiddling with the ball.

Amira had known Khalid for as long as she could remember. Her father was friends with Khalid's father, who owned the small bakery three streets away from Shajara Street. Amira's father also employed Khalid, after his 16th birthday, to work for him in his pottery shop, where they handmade and sold intricately painted vases and cups, with beautifully painted drawings of Arabic calligraphy and images of the nation's favourite flower; jasmine. For as long as Amira could remember, Khalid and she had always been present in each other's lives.

"Amira! Are you waiting for your royal knight to formally invite you to dinner himself, huh?"

Amira suddenly lost her trail of thought and shook her head as her mother caused her to lose her momentum of day-dreaming aimlessly. She placed her bookmark into her page and went down into the kitchen. She was greeted with a peppery waft of the freshly baked Kibbeh, which was just one of Amira's most favoured dishes. It was a layer of ground meat, onions and nuts, all sandwiched between layers of bulgur kibbeh and baked to perfection. Amira always loved making the kibbeh patties and lightly frying them and topping them off with some mint-flavoured yoghurt. As it was a Friday afternoon, Mama had made one of everyone's favourite dishes. She had been doing this for as long as Amira could remember, every Friday making a favourite dish for Baba, Amira and herself, then when Adam was born, for him too. For Baba, she made his all-time favourite salad, Fattoush, which was a mixture of lettuce, cucumber and tomatoes, tossed in a tangy vinaigrette dressing with sumac, garlic and crunchy pita chips. Adam loved one thing and one thing only, meat Borek. It's possibly the only thing he ever ate, alongside an occasional spoonful of Mutabbal, which was chargrilled eggplants mashed with garlic, yoghurt and tahini sauce. Everyone loved the meat Borek, a blend of meat and spices rolled into a puff pastry and fried to excellence.

Amira saw her mother fiddling with the plates when she crept quietly behind her and grabbed her by the waist.

"RAHH," Amira bellowed at the top of her lungs. Mama dropped the plastic plate onto the floor and shrieked with alarm whilst clasping her chest. Amira burst into a fit of hysteria whilst Adam scurried across the room also giggling uncontrollably at Amira's antic.

"AMIRA! I SWEAR ONE OF THESE DAYS YOU WILL GIVE ME A HEART ATTACK, YOU IMMATURE CHILD! ARE YOU 14 OR 4!?" howled Mama heatedly, still clasping her chest trying to catch her breath.

Amira cackled louder and her belly began to hurt. She loved to scare Mama when her attention was occupied deeply by something.

"What's all the noise? What's Amira done now?" said Baba, ambling into the kitchen holding his newspaper under his arm.

"Baba! How do you even know I did something, huh? Why am I always the first to blame?" Amira hooted with defeat.

"Because," Baba claimed, now grinning proudly, "you're really the only trouble-maker in this house. Who else is going to be giving your mum scares? Adam?" Amira plumped herself into her usual spot on the floor, around the tawila, a small, slightly raised table on the floor.

"So, Adam ate all the washing-up soap yesterday and burped bubbles for 7 hours, but I'm the trouble-maker; hmmm, ok."

By now, Baba had sat down and Adam scampered after him like a little puppy and plonked himself into Baba's lap. Mama also walked steadily towards the table and sat down, placing the hot plate of crepe-thin Druze pitas beside the other dishes she had prepared. Although Amira's family were Sunni Syrian Muslims, as most of the Syrians in Aleppo were, there was a remarkable amount of comfort with how people got on with each other and respected each other's beliefs. People in Syria were not afraid to befriend and openly welcome one another into each other's lives. They often ate foods from the Druze community as well as from Turkish cuisine. The warm aroma of the Druze pitas made Amira's mouth water as her mother placed them right in front of Amira's plate. Amira made a private gesture to Adam, who was bouncing in Baba's lap, and used her eyes to turn his attention towards the meat Borek.

"It's mine; I'm eating it all," she mouthed teasingly.

Adam looked at Amira's face, which was somewhat hidden behind her curls and masking her clouded amber eyes, then looked down at the bowl of Borek. He started bouncing harder in Baba's lap and motioned his concern to Mama of Amira's taunt by mumbling gibberish. Adam was a mute, well not really a mute, but unable to speak or form proper words or sentences yet, despite being a fully grown 4-year-old boy. He was fully capable of screaming, shouting and making jabbering blather, but unable to even say 'Mama' or 'Baba'.

"Stop it, Amira; why are you teasing him?" said Mama, slightly annoyed. "Because I love him," smirked Amira, winking at Adam buoyantly.

Mama passed the plates around and they began to feast on the vibrant array of dishes. Amira took the kibbeh first, as she always did and chomped a huge bite. Fresh, warm steam escaped from inside the other half of the half-eaten kibbeh. She misjudged exactly how hot it was and panted as the piece inside her mouth burned the bridge of her mouth. Adam sniggered.

"Steady on, it isn't going anywhere, Amira," Mama said out of frustration. "Always first to eat and last to go! Honestly, girl, I'm surprised you haven't put on any weight from the amount you eat daily."

This was true. Amira never put on any weight despite having the appetite of a horse. She was a petite, well-framed girl, with slight curves around her hips and thighs. She had full, plump, peachy lips and faded brown freckles on either side of her high cheekbones. Her button nose was small and perfectly placed in proportion to her thin eyebrows, lips and cheeks.

Everyone said a prayer and tucked in.

"Bismillah," Amira whispered under her breath and began eating.

"Ignorant fools, the lot of them," Baba exclaimed angrily, as the TV blared in the background. "So, the United States of idiots is renewing sanctions against us, saying we support these buffoons who call themselves Syrian Muslims," Baba continued.

Amira sniggered at the way Baba pronounced 'buffoons' and took another bite of her kibbeh. This was a norm in Amira's household now, Baba and Mama always talking politics. She was always captivated by how precisely Baba followed politics and was up to date with what was going on in the world.

"So apparently, we are seeking weapons now?" Baba scoffed, as he slurped his orange blossom water. "We gave Hezbollah Scud missiles too, by the way," Baba mocked. "I tell you something, Sana, no good ever came from the US intervening in anyone's country but their own," Baba voiced to Mama.

Baba despised America. Who didn't?

"What this country needs is a proper leader, a man," Baba said passionately. "Not people like Assad. Since 2000, Syria has been nothing but a shamble," said Baba, now showing a sense of gloom and mourning in his tone.

"Baba," … Amira said, slightly puzzled. "Baba, why don't you like Assad?" Baba lifted his cup and slurped the last of the orange blossom juice and sighed dejectedly, then looked at Amira's innocent face.

"My princess, look at Syria. What do you see? Fear. Scare. Worry. People are scared, Amira, scared to talk, to voice their opinions, to speak up for what's right."

Amira listened attentively as her baba spoke. Baba had a small vein above his eyebrow that widened ever so slightly when he became even a little worked up or passionate about a topic. Amira often saw it during Baba's and her debate sessions. It was fully visible now.

"There's always a sense of dismay, suspicion amongst the people," Baba answered. "But why?" asked Amira, even though she knew the answer but only asked to make conversation with Baba so he would get everything off his chest for the day.

"Dictatorship," Mama interrupted, as she took the last bite of her plate full of Mutabbal. "Indeed, Sana, indeed. Nowadays you can't even say anything against the mighty Bashar Al-Assad without being questioned," Baba mumbled under his breath.

Amira sat silently and watched as her father took a spoonful of his warm soup and tried feeding some to Adam, who as always, babbled something indistinguishable and flapped his arms to move the spoon away from his face. Though this was a daily ritual of Adam's, Baba still tried every time to see if he would succeed in feeding Adam something new.

Mama didn't really have a favourite dish but enjoyed everything she cooked for her family. Mama was very simple but naturally graceful in appearance. Her long, light brown hair was mostly tied in a ponytail and her slim physique was a credit to her healthy eating ever since Amira was born. Her eyes reminded Amira of light brown chocolate truffles engulfed into her face, which was a warm, slightly tanned vanilla. Amira studied Mama's hands. They were moderately haggard and paler than usual, making her dark blue and green veins more noticeable and her nails needed a clipping, but other than that they looked like the normal hands that she had lived with for the past 36 years. She had once worked as a nurse in a local hospital, feeding the ill and changing their clothing and bedding, but gave it up after Amira was born.

Baba finished the last of his remaining soup, turned to the TV and exhaled forlornly.

"It just isn't the same anymore," said Baba sadly. "What isn't, Baba?" Amira asked, now looking at him with sunken eyes and upset as her father sighed.

"Syria, Amira, Syria," and with that, he placed Adam beside Mama and left the room.

▪▪

In her bedroom, Amira cloaked herself tightly in an old patchwork quilt, sat on the edge of her windowsill and watched as the remaining leaves of the trees outside her house danced viciously in the wind. It was a cold, gloomy afternoon in Aleppo, early December 2010. The dismal, wintery sun was the only source of luminosity of the day. Amira was so engrossed in daydreaming that she didn't realise that Adam had walked into her room.

"GAAAAAAAAAA," Adam yelled, in attempt to frighten Amira. Amira pivoted slightly on her bed and faced Adam. She played along with her little brother and ran to catch him. Adam shrilled with the thrill and ran out of the room.

"Amira, please, I have a headache. Stop all the noise," said Mama from next door.

"Come here please, my child." Amira strolled into Mama and Baba's bedroom and saw Mama laying on her bed, distressingly.

"Mama, what's wrong?" said Amira, worried at her mother's sudden pale complexion and heavy breathing as she walked towards her bed and placed herself as close to her mother as possible.

Mama's eyes were sunken and closed. She moved gently as she heard Amira's concerned voice. Her eyelids seemed weighed down. She shuffled like a child and managed to sit up sluggishly beside Amira.

"Amira, my love, why the worried face? It's just a headache, silly," said Mama, as she reached for Amira's hand and stiffened at the sight of fear in her child's eyes.

"Do me a favour, my child, and run to the pharmacy and bring me my medication please; I didn't realise I had taken the last of them yesterday evening."

Amira shot up from her mother's bed.

"Yes, Mama, I'm going right now before it shuts," Amira hastily replied. "My sweet princess, Allah give you every happiness Insha'Allah. Now go quickly before dark."

Amira ran down and put on her suede boots that her Uncle Ahmed, Baba's brother, gifted her for her 14th birthday, along with her light woollen jumper, and tied her mane into a ponytail. She opened Mama's purse and took out 30 Syrian pounds. As she headed for the door, she caught sight of Adam from the kitchen, who was blowing bubbles all over the floor and told him;

"Adam, stay with Mama, okay? And I will bring you choccy, okay?" Adam clapped his hands and with that, he was up the stairs and halfway to Mama's room.

Before she exited the front door, she caught a glimpse of herself in the framed mirror on the wall beside the planted cactus pot. She focused on her face for a second. Her cheeks, now flushed and a deepened rose colour, hid her faint freckles. A single spiralled lock fell down her face; she fingered it and ruffled it in place behind her right ear. She caught her breath after running down the stairs and getting anxious with fear for Mama and left for the pharmacy.

Mama had been ill for 5 years now. She always blamed it on headaches or migraines, but deep down, Amira knew it wasn't as simple as Mama and Baba made out. For 5 years, Amira had encountered Mama numerous times during her worst days of being constantly in bed, vomiting and passing out. Amira hated the thought of her mother going through pain, let alone watching it before her very eyes.

The nearest pharmacy was located approximately 15 minutes away by foot. It was near the town centre, near the fancy restaurants, cinema and parks. Amira always took a risky shortcut whilst going to the pharmacy, risky in terms of safety as there were always groups of boys smoking down the alleyway. Amira reached the alleyway and looked ahead. There wasn't any sign of anyone, so without hesitation, she began pacing down the alley. She walked for a minute before she heard a sudden gravelly clatter, as if someone had thrown a pebble behind her. She turned. The alley also had some intersecting alleys, in which the local, foolish boys always hid and jumped out to scare passers-by. There was no one there. Amira turned back and began jogging faster down the alley. It wasn't that she was scared, but just wasn't looking to be confronted by the local idiots who got off on irritating girls. Again, Amira heard a sound, and this time, she saw a small pebble launched in front of her right leg, flung from behind. She gulped and spun round. "BAAHHHHHH!!" roared a mighty yell. Amira dropped her purse, gambolled back harshly, almost tripping on the pebble and screamed with a frozen look as she stared into the dark, earthy hues of brown in the eyes of her tormentor. It was Khalid.

"KHALID!!!!! IS YOUR ONLY GOAL IN LIFE TO CAUSE ME GRIEF?" Amira yelled as she grabbed Khalid's arm and slapped him twice, angrily.

Khalid guffawed, it was a playful, mocking laugh. His broad shoulders shook in sync with his hiccup of giggles and tears rolled down his cheek. Khalid had an infectious laugh that always made Amira smile and she would end up chuckling, even when she was mad at him.

"Erm, yes, that's why I live Mira, to piss you off every day," said Khalid with cockiness.

Mira is what Khalid called Amira; it had been her nickname since they were young.

"Khalid! You frightened me badly this time, for goodness sake," declared Amira, despite secretly enjoying Khalid's daily teasing. Khalid stopped laughing and placed his arms around Amira and they began strolling down the alley.

"Mira, you scare too easily; besides, how many times have I told you, don't walk down this alley? It's not safe, but you never listen."

Khalid's tone turned somewhat assertive and militant. Amira liked when she saw this side to Khalid, the patriarchal, domineering side to his character. It made her feel as if she was cared for, looked after by Khalid's subtle notions of indirect care that he showed towards her. The truth was, Amira liked Khalid a lot. She had for a while now. Although they grew up together since infancy and were the closest of friends, she felt something more in her heart every time Khalid was close. She was besotted by his charm, his witty jokes, and pranks.

"I had to hurry and go to the pharmacy, so I thought I'd take this route," Amira replied. "Pharmacy? Mama?" Khalid questioned. Amira nodded. "Oh, is…is everything okay, Mira?" Khalid said. "Yes, I guess, just Mama unwell again. Having a bad week, I suppose," Amira responded, dejectedly. Khalid sensed the upset in Amira's voice.

He tried teasing her again.

"Guess what? I wrote a poem for you; wanna hear?" said Khalid, lightening the mood.

Amira already knew he was messing around. He couldn't write a poem if his life depended on it. He always took the mick out of Amira and her poem-writing just to vex her.

"Shush, Khalid!" said Amira gleefully, trying not to show Khalid her smirking face.

"Come on, I spent hours on it just for you, to show you how good my poetry is." Khalid grinned mischievously from ear to ear, causing his dimples to become even more visible under his slight patchy facial hair.

Amira groaned. "Go on, if you must."

Khalid took his hand off Amira's shoulder and fisted his chest and exhaled. Amira looked on, as he ran in front of her to face her and began...

"Roses are red, violets are blue..." Amira rolled her eyes and puffed out. She already knew he was going to say something stupid next.

"You thought this was a love poem, well guess what, the jokes on you," Khalid clapped his hands and tried high-fiving Amira.

"Come on," he said, "that was a good one, and I mean I spent 4 hours on it, finding the right rhyming words. Don't you think, eh Mira?" Amira smiled at Khalid, shyly.

"Okay, read me one of yours, please," Khalid said, now fixated on Amira's lit-up face.

He beamed directly into Amira's hazelnut, amber eyes and smiled. There was always a sense of belonging that Khalid felt whilst around Amira, as did Amira when she was around Khalid. Although neither of them had never really expressed their feelings to one another, they got on like brother and sister, like lovers, like soul mates. The locals always sensed there was something more between both of them, and made indirect jokes. "Where's your Romeo, Princess Amira?" they'd say. "Khalid, Amira not around today?" They both ignored it but secretly, both of them knew what they had was more than just friends.

"No, I'm not reading you anything, because you always make fun of me, Khalid," replied Amira modestly.

"Come on Miraaaaaa, for me?" replied Khalid, now tugging at her arm furiously.

"Fine; don't make your silly comments then, okay?" she replied. "Yes, yes, I won't, I promise," answered Khalid, who had his arms folded and was gazing readily at Amira as they halted in the alley. Amira was quiet for a second, thinking of which poem to recite. She had been working on one about the winter nights in Syria.

She began…" I wrote this one about winter, last week" …

"Everyone knows your connivance, winter,
For all the times you furiously visited,
And left us frozen, even inside our lover's embrace.
Even the wilting trees in the gelidity and cold,
Secretly distinguish themselves under the snow and write,
Passionate, warm love letters,
Every single winter's night.
The skies would be lurid,
And the terrain, white,
Whilst the world seems tranquil,
For the trees every single winter's night.
If I could have a single wish,
It would be to have you near,
To inhale your scent for just a moment or two,
I'd be intoxicated whilst gripping your soft hands,
And share this cherished winter's night with you".

Khalid's chocolate eyes pierced into Amira's. His small grin radiated his face and Amira knew this look. He liked the poem.

"Bravo, Princess Mira, you've done it again. Come here," said Khalid, and pulled Amira close and gave her a quick hug.

Amira felt his sudden warmth. She also caught a whiff of his musky cologne from his neck. She felt a sense of nervousness, a quiver every time Khalid touched her. They had reached the end of the alley when Khalid gave her a high five and with that, he left. Amira started walking towards the side road to get to the pharmacy, and Khalid headed in the other direction. They strolled in completely opposite directions. Amira walked, slowly, catching a glimpse of the sun which was now setting steadily. She could still smell Khalid. She turned. Khalid walked towards his favourite, local hideout spot, 'Basheer's café'.

As Amira looked on, her trail of thought of Khalid wandered from every time Khalid and her had their heart to heart conversations, drank orange blossom juice under their special weeping willow tree in 'Shamsa Park' and watched movies in Khalid's house with his baby brother, Shakil. Amira was so lost in her thoughts that she didn't realise Khalid was now staring at her, smiling. She looked at him, his loving, charming face. She smiled, as he gave her a quick smirk and a cheeky wink, and entered the café.

CHAPTER TWO
Aleppo March 2011

"Everywhere in Syria, all you hear of is corruption, exploitation and malfeasance. It's the norm," complained Baba as he drove past the congregation of enraged protestors and activists.

Amira saw mainly youngsters, a few middle-aged and very few elderly folks amongst the crowd. There were also a few women present. The mob seemed to grow bigger and bigger and began holding up the traffic around the city centre, which meant Amira and her family were glued in the never-ending queue of traffic.

"More and more people are protesting against Assad; I mean, really? Did they not see what happened to those poor boys on Sunday? Think of your mothers; these protests mean nothing in the eyes of the oppressors," Baba grieved, wiping the sweat off his brow.

Amira looked out onto the mob of angry civilians. There had always been regular protesting within Syria, with activists and more common locals who were just fed up of the way the country was run. Their general complaints revolved around the notion of Syria being corrupt, the lack of political freedom under Assad and high unemployment amongst the lower-class citizens, which made up the majority of the Syrian population.

Adam, who was bouncing on Mama's lap, was pointing at a lanky, curly-haired boy who was dressed in the Syrian flag colours with a vendetta mask covering his face and an Arab Keffiyeh scarf wrapped loosely around his neck. He held a banner that read 'BRING BACK OUR BOYS'. The protest was a reaction of Syrians angered as a result of 15 teenage boys, in the southern city of Daraa, being arrested for writing "The people want the regime to fall" on walls across the city. The slogan, which was invented by the birth of the 'Arab Spring', was widely known throughout the country. The military police then brutally tortured the boys which led to many resentful and furious Syrians. Thus, the protesting got bigger and bigger amongst many cities across the country.

"These kids ought to learn from previous events. The governments don't sit there and watch silently at these protestors. They are cunningly planning ways to eliminate," Baba exclaimed, now sounding tenser and more worried.

Amira peered at Baba through his side mirror. His eyes were deeply buried in his face, his hairline was receding slightly and his lips were tightly gripping his fat cigar. The whole family was on their way to spend the day at her Uncle Ahmed's house. He had invited them for dinner before he left for business in Turkey.

When they arrived, Amira saw her cousin, Khadijah, waiting by the front porch. She was a timid, simple girl who, unlike Amira, had deep brown, coarse hair that was rough from the edges. Her timid figure didn't seem that of a 13-year-old's but an 8-year-olds' instead. She was a friendly girl, who was an only child, which is why she constantly looked forward to spending time with Amira and Adam. Baba parked his old, rusting Volvo 240, gifted to him by Abu Saleem, Amira's grandfather, before he passed away. Amira ran to Khadijah and hugged her tightly. It had been a while since they had seen one another.

"Dejah, you missed me, huh?" teased Amira. "Nope," smiled Khadijah. They all met at the front gate and went inside.

Uncle Ahmed was a short, beefy man with an almost invisible neck, a messy moustache the same size as a caterpillar and a short, tangled beard. He worked for a tour guide company amongst the middle eastern countries such as Egypt, Libya, Iraq and Lebanon. On Tuesday, he was set to travel to Turkey for three weeks and accompany a family from the USA as acting tour guide. He enjoyed his job, and every so often, Amira's family would get a chance to try different sweets and desserts from different countries that Uncle Ahmed travelled to. Uncle Ahmed was married to an elegant, diminutive woman with magma red hair that plunged over her small shoulders, slender eyebrows and gleaming skin. Aunty Nabeela had been married to Uncle Ahmed for 18 years. It's weird to think a short, grubby man like Ahmed, despite being a lovely person, had managed to marry someone as glamorous as Nabeela and to think their only child, Khadijah, was an offspring of Nabeela, who was shy, timid and average-looking.

Soon after they arrived, Amira began to smell the pungent, spicy aroma of homemade chicken shawarma being cooked in the kitchen. In a traditional Syrian home, everyone ate together, men, women and children. There wasn't any segregation or split between genders. Everyone enjoyed and honoured one another's company and eating a meal in someone's house was far from formal. Everyone spoke about life, politics, future plans and laughed whilst raising their spoons from serving dishes to mouths.

An abrupt bellow of a cackle resounded beyond the kitchen and through the dining room. Mama and Aunty

Nabeela were in fits of laughter over a recent film they had both watched. Both women had a loving, pure friendship, which grew stronger after Aunty Nabeela experienced two very painful miscarriages and one still-born pregnancy.

"Dinner is ready!" called Nabeela from the kitchen.

Everyone assembled around the floor table and sat patiently, eagerly waiting for the array of food to be spread out before being demolished. Nabeela and Mama entered with two dishes in each hand. Amira's mouth watered as soon as she spotted the juicy, glistening pieces of shawarma meat displayed in a leafy nest of lettuce, tomatoes and lemons. She placed some on her plate, alongside some creamy, homemade hummus, green pitted Zaytuns and half a piece of fresh, crusty za'atar man'ouche, which is a traditional Lebanese flatbread with distinctive, flavourful herbs. Everyone tucked in.

"This is so good, Aunty Nabeela!" smiled Amira, taking a bite of the shawarma that she had rolled inside a pitta bread and drizzled with mint sauce inside.

With a pleased grin, Nabeela raised her thin brows and blushed.

"Thank you, Mira darling, I knew you'd enjoy it."

Amira paused, after chewing on the spicy, perfectly baked falafel, as if her thoughts had stopped altogether.

"Holy, this is divine. You should open your own café, Aunty Nabeela," blurted Amira. Nabeela's cheeks reddened at the courtesy of Amira's compliments.

"I tell you, Ahmed, it was a nightmare getting here. Two hours stuck in traffic; these protests are just getting more intense every other month," Baba muttered as he sipped his green tea.

"Of course, they are!" exclaimed Ahmed. "Look at Daraa! Did you hear about those boys being arrested and tortured on Sunday? Disgusting, I tell you!" blurted Ahmed, with a look of disgust on his face.

Mama and Nabeela were speaking between themselves about the dangers young boys were now facing.

"Nabeela, the other day I went to pick up some vegetables and fruits from Uncle Tahir's stall and a young boy was being escorted into a van by militant police because he got lippy with them." "What did he say?" asked Amira, curiously.

"Oh, something or another about Assad and making Syria a democracy instead of a dictatorship. The usual," replied Mama.

"Funny thing is, these activists, may Allah bless them and their naivety, they are now protesting against Assad's resignation as president, so it's literally erupted nationwide," laughed Baba.

"That man will not resign even if he lives to be a hundred," fumed Ahmed, puffing away on his hookah pipe.

Amira attentively listened to the conversation between her family. It was the same conversation she heard the teachers speaking of in her school, the students in older classes and the local traders in the markets. Later that evening, Amira went to drop off a plate of fresh Kunefe that Mama had prepared for Khalid's family. Amira strolled down the market towards his house. The stallholders were closing up their stalls for Magrib Salah. The market seemed sober, muted almost. Every weekday, eager school children in downtown Aleppo pour into the streets of Amira's home town, Kafr Halab, and set off in hot pursuit of their late afternoon candied fruit fix. Amira's favourite afterschool treat was a slice of Uncle Fahim's glorious semolina and nut cake. Amira, alongside her best friend Maliha, would daily get a slice of his cake and when there wasn't any left, they'd enjoy a few pieces of his homemade pistachio baklava instead. Amira would always bring a piece back for Adam, too.

Amira reached Khalid's house. He lived only 15 minutes away from Amira in a small boxed flat with his father and younger brother, Shakil. Khalid's mother had passed away 5 years ago whilst giving birth to Shakil. She had bled to death. Mama had always been like a mother to both Khalid and Shakil since then.

Amira entered the main gates of the flat, which were rusting and barely standing, and scurried up the stairs. Khalid's door was a molten red colour which Khalid and Amira painted last year from a pot of paint they happened to find outside an old art gallery that displayed paintings and sculptures made by foreign artists.

The door was left slightly open. Amira went in.

"Miiirrrrraaaaa!" shrieked Shakil, with a juice carton in his hand. He skipped towards her and hugged her legs tightly.

Shakil loved Amira. She was like an older sister to him. He was roughly the same age as Adam, so they spent a lot of time together.

"Khalid! I've asked you once and I will not be repeating myself again, do you understand?" screamed a deep, hoarse voice coming from inside the kitchen.

Amira saw Khalid's father, Uncle Hussain, wearing his crummy sleeping rope, that had looked as if it had not been washed for weeks. A giant of a man, he was advancing rapidly through the kitchen doorway, his tanned face almost completely hidden by his shaggy, greasy hair and his chaotic, tangled beard. He walked right passed Amira as if she were invisible. He leapt at Khalid, who was dressed in his camo trousers, white Syrian football shirt and an Arab Keffiyeh scarf wrapped around his neck. Amira had already guessed what the dispute was about.

"Baba, I am 16 years old; I have my own views and beliefs. I don't care what anyone says, I am going to the march and the protest later in Idlib. I'll be back in 3 days. What's all the fuss?" snapped Khalid, angrily, now realising Amira had entered the house and was holding onto Shakil, who was frightened by all the shouting.

"Assad has already killed hundreds of demonstrators and imprisoned many more! You want to be another percentage? Another victim? Another body I'd have to bury?" Hussain was now stuttering his words, forcing to spit them out without crying.

Amira caught a glimpse of Hussain's face. He turned to her in desperation. She could make out from his eyes, glinting like black beetles under his thick strands of auburn hair, that he wanted Amira to intervene somehow and stop Khalid from going to Idlib.

Khalid bulldozed past his father towards the main door and left, slamming it on his way out, causing the planted pots to rattle. Amira looked at Uncle Hussain, with reassuring eyes.

"It's okay, I know where he's gone. I'll speak to him," she consoled Hussain, handing him Shakil and the plate of Kunefe.

"He thinks this revolution and uprising against Assad is a good thing," whispered Hussain, helplessly. "I did too at first, I even went on marches with Khalid, but look, Amira child, just look. The dangers are too frequent now. Every other day there are bombardments, shelling and mortars. Just last week, Muhammed next door lost his brother in these protests."

Amira walked to Hussain and rubbed his shoulder in comfort.

"I'll bring him back, Uncle, I promise," and with that, Amira kissed Uncle Hussain's forehead and Shakil's cheek and left.

Amira knew exactly where Khalid was. Ever since Amira and Khalid were little, they would both meet every Sunday after Quran classes at Shamsa Park. There was a small hill, which overlooked the town of Halab beautifully. They'd spend hours laying on the grass, watching the clouds and guessing their shapes. It was one of Amira's earliest childhood memories and also the place both Khalid and Amira would visit to be alone from the outside world. Khalid had visited this place nearly every evening when his mother passed away, and Amira, she would simply find serenity in investing her thoughts and energy into this special place where she could block off the entire world and be at peace within her own companionship.

As expected, Khalid was slumped miserably on 'their hill', which was a few yards away from their favourite weeping willow tree, throwing small pebbles forcefully down the hillside curve. Amira didn't say anything but motionlessly perched beside him. He continued for a moment, then lifted his head to meet eyes with Amira. They were a murky cinnamon colour in the setting sun.

"Mira, just don't, okay?" Khalid finally uttered, disheartened.

"Khalid, he's just worried. Syria isn't as safe as it was when we were kids," Amira responded calmly.

Even though Amira was slightly angered by Khalid's reaction and him slamming the door causing Shakil to be frightened, she could never stay mad at Khalid, ever. She somehow knew the reasoning behind his reactions, the thoughts he held before he spoke them aloud and the way his mind worked. She knew, deep down, that all Khalid wanted was to stick up for what is right and by going to protests, he felt he was doing the right thing.

Khalid exhaled loudly.

"My Syria. It's mine, my mother's, my brother's, my father's. I want to show everyone how much it means to me," expressed Khalid intensely with a sudden passion behind his staggered voice.

Amira grasped Khalid's hand delicately. Khalid loosened his clenched jaw and tensed muscles in his arms and stared at Amira's concerned, earnest face, a face brighter than the moon, pale and somehow fluctuating around her berry-flushed cheeks. Khalid could get the gist of Amira's distinct features, but none of it cemented in his mind beyond an impression of bewildering artistry and astonishing grace.

He entangled his fingers around Amira's and lifted his hand towards her face. Amira gulped. Khalid's heated palm was now against Amira's flushed skin, inducing a quiver from Amira as she peered into Khalid's eyes. Her long, champagne-stained locks wafted around her shoulders like smoke lingering in the air.

Khalid leaned forward towards Amira's cheek, then her lips. He could hear the drumming sound of her beating heart inside her chest and her soft breathing suddenly augmenting in pace.

"Shhhh," he whispered. "It's me, Mira," Khalid breathed, his eyes closing. In the shade of Amira's face, Khalid could smell the honeyed fragrance of the perfume she sprayed on her neck.

Amira closed her eyes with Khalid's words of warm reassurance and placed her lips against his.

Amira felt safe, although he spoke no words. He kissed her tenderly and ran his lips on her skin towards her ear. Amira tilted her head swiftly as he breathed out onto her burning flesh and beamed into his chestnut, glassy eyes.

"Please don't go, Khalid."

Khalid locked his arms around Amira, pulled her towards his chest and fondled her lovingly. In his embrace, the world stopped still on its axis. There was no time, ticking away endlessly. There was no rain, no wind, no fear. Amira's mind was at peace. She pressed her body, soft and warm against Khalid's. All the years that Amira had idolized the notion of solitude and isolation from the hubbub and bustle of the world, all seemed to have faded into the fervency of Khalid's arms.

"Mira, I'm not going anywhere."

CHAPTER THREE
Aleppo March–November 2011

Bashar al-Assad. The president of Syria. He inherited power in July 2000, a month after his father, military strongman Hafez al-Assad, died. Following the Arab Spring in Tunisia, Egypt and Libya, protests began in Syria last week on March 15, 2011, demanding political reforms, a reinstatement of civil rights and an end to the state of emergency, which had been in place since 1963. Assad's aim was to remain a dictatorship and use deadly forces to crush the dissent and this was the cause of protesting erupting widely across all of Syria. The unrest and rebellion increased rapidly and the repression intensified greatly before Amira's eyes. Opposition supporters took up arms, first to defend themselves and later to rid their areas within Syria of security forces. Amira was in school one day when the teachers were all glued to their radios, listening to Assad's vow to crush and vanquish "foreign-backed terrorism".

"It's all very complicated you see," said Maliha, Amira's best friend.

"My baba told me it's basically us against them."

"Them?" queried Amira.

"Yes, them, the rebels. People like us, who don't want Assad to be in power are fighting against the people who do," replied Maliha.

Amira and Maliha were on their lunch break on a warm, spring afternoon. They were both munching on some leftover kibbeh from the canteen. Nowadays, politics was what everyone spoke of at lunch, break times, at home, in the markets. Amira was aware of the matters of state in her country but chose not to pay too much attention to it as it just revolved around negativity and antagonism. She was very well aware of the clash between government and anti-government fighters. The protesting became more and more apparent in Aleppo as the weeks progressed. There was no central coordination of demonstrations, which sprang up spontaneously and the list of expectations and demands grew expeditiously with revolutionaries hungry about the idea of Assad forcefully resigning, the dismantling of the repressive security apparatus, removal of elite groups from positions of power and the solid introduction of political reforms that would repeal emergency laws and lead to a new, authentically socialist, democratic constitution.

Maliha, who was Amira's oldest childhood friend, was an extreme supporter of anti-government groups. She regularly went on protests and marches alongside her cousins, despite the dangers. One day, she asked Amira to join her.

"Come on Mira! You will love it, I'm telling you, trust me. The adrenaline you get, the rush, it's amazing!" begged Maliha.

They were on their way home from school, both arm in arm, strolling through the market as they did every day.

"I just don't see the hype! Besides, Baba says it's too dangerous now. Every day there are arrests and beatings." Maliha scoffed abruptly.

Then she faced Amira and smiled mischievously.

"What?" said Amira, confused at why Maliha was suddenly smirking.

"Your boyfriend will be there...," replied Maliha, now nudging Amira and leaning over to see her reaction.

"First of all," she declared, "He is NOT my boyfriend, and secondly, he will NOT be there, for sure!" exclaimed Amira, who was suddenly overcome with a sense of annoyance and slight fury at the thought of Khalid going to protests when she had told him not to.

"Okay, okay, easy, girl. Keep your hair on," sniggered Maliha.

Amira hated the thought of Khalid still attending protests. He knew of all the dangers of it and still, he would sneakily go to them without telling her. On a few occasions, she had heard from Maliha that he had gone and didn't speak to him or days.

Later that evening, Amira was immersed in her poetry writing when she heard a pebble hit against her window. She got up from her bed and peered out of her window. Khalid was standing there, holding an ice cream cone, invitingly. Amira gave him a glowing smile and made her way down.

"Just where do you think you are going, Amira?" questioned Mama curiously as Amira sprayed some of her mother's perfume on her jacket.

"Erm... Khalid..., he is outside. Just going to the park for a bit, Mama, I'll be back soon," stuttered Amira.

"Hmmm, people will start talking, Amira; too much mingling isn't good. Now that you're older, you have to be more careful, Mira," lectured Mama.

"Okay, Mama," replied Amira, placing a kiss on her mother's cheek, staining it with light, rosy lip balm.

"Rose and pistachio booza," said Khalid, looking rather pleased with himself as he handed Amira her favourite flavoured ice cream.

"Your favourite, am I right?" he laughed. "You know it is, so why are you asking, huh?" giggled Amira.

She took a lick of the honeyed rose syrup and crunched on fresh pistachios. "So, what's this for?" she quizzed Khalid, who was already halfway through his hazelnut and chocolate booza.

"Nothing, just wanted to treat you, Mira," he replied lovingly.

Khalid and Amira headed for their usual spot on 'their hill'. On their way, they saw a group of three boys who were playing football in the alleyway where Khalid had once scared Amira. They were older boys, 17 or 18 years old. One of the boys who was a skinhead, had a broad physique and his dark, almost black eyes were like cockroaches. He followed, with his beady eyes, Amira's slender figure as she interweaved her way amongst the three boys with Khalid leading the way. The boy gestured his friends and then whistled loudly as Amira passed him.

"What a beauty, eh, boys!" he sneered, his voice musky, echoing on the walls of the alley.

Amira paused.

She gulped a hard boulder down her throat as Khalid turned around to face the bully. Amira could feel her cheeks flushing, ears going bright red and her breathing rapidly quickening. She was not afraid of the bullies at all; they were not a threat to her whatsoever. What she was afraid of was

Khalid's reaction. Khalid had anger issues, and had done since infancy. Anger and resentment would flow through him like fresh, hot lava. In that very look, Amira knew that a vortex of disbelief and utter rage spiralled inside him.

Khalid exploded, and ferocity seized him.

He said nothing to either of the boys; he didn't need to. He curled his fist into a rigid ball and aimed for the front of the boy's nose. His fist hit the bridge of his nose first and fresh blood plunged from him and all over the ground. The boy lay defenceless on the floor, almost blacked out. The other two boys lasted 8 seconds before they ran off from the alley into the market, leaving their ball behind. Khalid lifted the ball, as if it was a prize he had won, took Amira by her hand and ambled over to the boy.

"Khalid?" Amira sniffed, not realising she was now in tears. He didn't say a word, just clamped her hand harder, then finally spoke.

"Anyone speaks to you like that again, you tell me. Okay?" instructed Khalid, authoritatively.

Amira nodded.

He turned to face her, wiped her warm tears away delicately and smiled.

Amira didn't know what to feel. She abhorred Khalid's outbursts and sudden acts of vehemence, but equally, relished his guardianship, care and protection. She felt shielded around him, as if he was always there to curtain her from any evil, harm and upset.

Amira knew that Khalid would always protect her.

"Syria has become a dictatorship without the dictator," spoke Khalid.

They had both reached Shamsa Park and were seated on their usual spot. Khalid rested his head on Amira's shoulder. She rhythmically fingered the loose curls of his hair and hummed in acknowledgment.

"I tell you, if it wasn't for you, Mira, for Baba and Shakil, I'd join the defectors from the military army and battle alongside the 'Free Syrian Army."

The defectors, also known as the military traitors, were a rebel group who aimed to overthrow the government.

"You can't join the Free Syrian Army, Khalid, you weren't in the military!" Amira exclaimed.

"Yeah, so? I'd pretend and still join anyway," Khalid replied.

"No, you wouldn't do something as stupid, Khalid," said Amira timidly.

"Course not," he teased, "I wouldn't ever leave you, Mira."

He kissed her cheek, then took a piece of toffee out his pocket and gave it to her.

"Khalid..." Amira whispered weakly.

"Mmmm?" Khalid responded.

"Maliha was saying that this so-called 'Syrian Civil War' is the next World War Three?" Amira grilled anxiously.

Khalid grunted, "You know Maliha, always exaggerating things. That girl loves to talk."

Amira didn't seem convinced. She had heard the conversations between her mother and father about the formation of the Syrian Civil War. She didn't really delve too much into the recent political drama, out of apprehension. Only the other day, Amira had witnessed the conflict extending and showing no signs of being abolished, and anyone showing any sort of sympathy towards the demonstrators immediately became targets of Assad's regime, thus causing thousands of Syrians to be detained and hundreds killed. Amira had feared Khalid would get too embroiled into current affairs and be tortured as a result. Khalid was passionate about his country, his land and his neighbours. His nobility was what would potentially endanger him if he showed too much allegiance to his state.

In Shamsa Park, there was a graffiti wall, beside the small lake where Amira and Khalid used to feed the ducks. The wall had graffiti of Assad, the Syrian flag, and Hitler standing beside Assad. There were also different quotes and freedom slogans plastered across the wall.

"Let's see if there's anything new," said Khalid, pointing to the wall. Teens always came here and left new graffiti for everyone to see.

Amira and Khalid walked towards the wall to find empty cans of spray paint left neglected on the floor. Khalid lifted the green can and sprayed. Then the red. They were empty. He then sprayed the black can and thick, charcoal paint squirted out the can. Khalid's face lit up.

"Come on!" he chuckled.

Amira suddenly felt a sense of paranoia. She knew exactly what Khalid was planning to do next, and the thought made her panic in fear of Khalid landing himself in a predicament and danger.

"Khalid please, let's go now," asserted Amira.

Her heart thumped inside her chest.

"Quick one, no one is here, Mira," replied Khalid. Amira watched as Khalid walked towards Assad's picture on the wall, shook the can of graffiti paint and clearly wrote the simple word 'KILLER' on Assad's forehead.

"See that? That's what he is Mira, a killer, and everyone will know the truth soon," boasted Khalid, looking pleased with his work.

Neither Amira nor Khalid were prepared for what happened next.

Someone charged at Khalid, like a bull charging at a matador. The sudden stench of blood sprung into Amira's senses. She froze. Aside from the pounding of her heart, no muscle moved. It was as if both Khalid's and the man's voices were underwater, muffled.

The man, who was dressed in a military uniform of camo trousers and jacket, had a gun attached to his belt and handcuffs on the side of his waist. His voice was that of a bear, husky and feared, whilst his clenched jaw was a chiselled, perfect square in proportion to his beastly face.

He smashed his elbow into the side of Khalid's skull, the soft spot high on his temple, leaving Khalid almost unconscious as he was caught off guard. He then struck his heavy palm down the side of Khalid's face, crushing his nose.

Khalid howled in agony. Amira couldn't swallow the pain of seeing Khalid cry in anguish. She leapt onto the man and with all her might, tried pulling him away from kicking Khalid constantly in the abdomen.

"You little cockroach! This will teach you not to graffiti on the walls again, you worm!" yelled the militant with disgust as he pulled Khalid from the floor by his hair. Amira was now shrieking at the top of her lungs and trying hard to cling onto any part of Khalid and shield him.

"LET HIM GO! PLEASE, LET HIM GO, LET HIM GO!" she wailed breathlessly. She tugged at him, scratched him, and then finally, slapped his sweaty, feral face.

The militant bully stood still. He faced Amira. She shuddered at the sight of his repulsive, dark, face.

He was now facing Amira. Fresh, hot tears sprang out from her reddened eyes. She looked deep into the man's rigid, cold eyes. In that moment, Amira already knew she was about to be another victim, another item of prey, another sufferer at the hands of Assad's regime.

"Pretty girl…I almost felt that slap," he hissed at Amira, looking devilishly into her sore eyes.

"Your soft hand against my face has made me forget your foolish mistake," he continued.

"Am... Amir...," croaked Khalid, as he lifted his bloodied, battered face from the ground.

Amira looked at Khalid, lying helplessly and without a moment of hesitation, jumped past the man and onto Khalid.

"Pretty girl, come here and show me you are sorry, princess," sniggered the man as he grabbed Amira by both hands and lifted her off Khalid and threw her to the ground. She groaned in pain.

"Amir...Amira, please, run," Khalid whispered again.

The man threw his gun on the floor, his handcuffs, unfastened his belt, chucked it aside and unbuttoned his uniform trousers.

"Ahhh, Princess Amira? Do not worry, you're going to make up for your mistake and then both of you can be on your way. Very fair, no, princess?" seethed the man, now smirking disgustingly with a look of excitement on his brutal face.

He dropped onto Amira, both his legs on either side of Amira and hands on her shoulders.

"It will only take a minute, princess. Look...," he motioned his head at Khalid, laying there powerlessly.

"You want him freed? Yes? Then just relax, let me grant you both your freedom, Amira Princess," he hooted vehemently, as he lifted Amira's shirt and slid his beefy hand under her vest. Amira felt the man's rough, frosty fingers as he touched her tender skin.

He travelled his hand higher into her vest and pulled back her bra. His hand was now circling around Amira's breast.

"Just stare into his eyes and it will all be over soon," he murmured.

Amira kicked, screamed, yelled and spat at the man. He was too heavy for her to push him off. He grabbed both her hands with such force, causing both her wrists to burn in pain.

"AMIRA! GET UP, AMIRA, GET UP!" Khalid bellowed loudly, as if he had suddenly regained consciousness.

Amira heard nothing after that. She didn't hear Khalid. She didn't hear the birds singing in the sky. She didn't hear the trees rustling in the wind. The colour of the sky darkened to that of the pits of hell. She lay there, motionless. She closed her eyes and felt his hand slithering down her trousers, around her thighs. His vulgar tongue licked at her neck and stubby fingers curled around her hair. Every time Amira shut her eyes, the man bashed her head against the ground severely and demanded she open them.

"LOOK AT HIM! LOOK AT HIM WHILE I FINISH WITH YOU," he spat.

She didn't want to. She shut them repeatedly, for the pain of a cracked skull would have been more bearable than staring into Khalid's eyes and being raped.

Finally, the man pulled off Amira's trousers forcefully to bare her naked legs in the open.

Amira clenched her jaw and slapped her hands onto her face. He began stroking her thighs and hips.

Then, without warning, an impetuous, powerful gunshot deafened Amira. Heated blood splattered all over her legs, arms, hands and face. The man launched on Amira's body and lay there, dead. The sound of the gunshot rent the still, peaceful, evening air. The thunderous outcry of the shot reverberated in Amira's ears and the echo seemed as if it rang far over the hills of Shamsa Park. The man was dead before the gunshot reached Amira's ears.

Amira wriggled her way from underneath the beast, struggling at every tug and pull.

She saw Khalid, standing there, holding the man's gun firmly in his hand. He dropped it to the floor and fell in agony from the kicks and punches he had taken. Amira instantaneously got up from the floor, picked up her trousers from her ankles and ran to Khalid. The weight of the militant had almost winded her as he fell mightily onto her petite body.

"Khalid!" she whimpered, as she dropped beside him, seizing his arms and cradling him into her arms.

She wept onto Khalid as she held him like a baby. He said nothing for a while, and then finally moaned quietly.

"Amira, we need to go. Not safe here. Someone will see us."

"Please Khalid, just wait a while; you can't walk like this. Let me call Baba for help," she pleaded with him desperately.

She was in a state of frenzy and terror that Khalid would collapse. For the 20 minutes they were sitting there in each other's arms, Khalid clutched his abdomen and whined in pain. Amira feared he was injured internally.

"It's getting dark, we need to. I'll be fine, Mira," Khalid insisted. He lifted his head from Amira's arms and tilted his face towards her.

He looked at her swollen eyes and smiled.

"Excuse me, why the face? I'm fine Mira, look." Khalid lightly punched Amira's cheek teasingly.

Amira held onto Khalid and helped him up. He staggered a few times and cried in pain as they made their way slowly down the hill. Amira looked back to where the man was laying, lifeless on the cold grass. He lay there, on his belly, arms on either side of him. She took a final look as they neared the bottom of the hill in Shamsa Park and that was that.

She held Khalid by his arm and helped him walk across the road.

"Where are we going, Khalid? My house?" she asked.

"No, not yours, your family won't be able to see you or me in this state," he replied.

"Then where?" she queried.

"Baba and Shakil have gone to Aunty Maryam's house for 3 nights to look after her children whilst she's in hospital," Khalid answered, struggling to walk even a few steps without falling.

They reached Khalid's house.

"Mama and Baba will be worried and wondering where I am," said Amira. Khalid pointed to the phone as he dropped his exhausted body onto the sofa.

Amira dialled her home number and waited for someone to answer.

"Salam?" answered Mama.

"Mama, I'm just at Maliha's house. We are working on our project together," Amira quickly replied, without even replying to Mama's greeting.

"Amira? Is everything okay? Why are you breathing so heavy? What's happened?" Mama was now sounding concerned and her voice lowered.

"I thought you were with Khalid?" she continued with the questions.

"No, Mama, nothing has happened. I was just playing with Maliha's cat and running around and haven't caught my breath yet. No need to be so worried, Mama."

"Amira, I am your mother. I knew you before you even knew yourself. I know every time a child of mine is suffering or scared," Mama warned. Amira turned back, whilst clutching the phone, to look at Khalid. She looked at him moaning every other minute. She swallowed a thick, rigid lump and exhaled.

"Mama, everything is fine," she said, wiping the tears from her eyes and trying hard not to sound croaky.

"I'll be home soon." Amira hung up and went to the kitchen. She grabbed a bowl, filled it with warm, salty water and found a clean cloth to soak it with.

Khalid's body ached with such pain that his tanned complexion soon became blanched. His natural golden skin had now changed in tone to something so barren, lifeless almost. It scared Amira just to look at him. His eyes close and he buried himself in a deeper place to be able to cope.

Amira sat herself gently beside Khalid and stroked his hair tenderly, as if she were even scared to touch him. She soaked the cloth in the salty water.

"Khalid, let me clean the blood. Look," she said, pointing at the thick blood seeping through his shirt.

"Can I?" Amira asked tensely.

Khalid kept his eyes shut and nodded gently.

Amira lifted Khalid's sodden shirt and carefully tried getting his arms through. He bit his lip tightly and wailed.

"Mira, careful, please," he snivelled.

"I'm sorry, Khalid."

"Get the knife," instructed Khalid, breathlessly.

Amira got the kitchen knife and handed it to Khalid who started pointing towards his shirt. Amira made a small slash in Khalid's shirt and then used her hands to rip open the front of his wet shirt, unmasking his beaten body.

Amira focused on the cuts and bruises forming near Khalid's left lower belly and a large slash on his shoulder blade, then to his forlorn face. Khalid had never shown such weakness and it hurt Amira to see him in such a state of vulnerability and distress like this.

She soaked the cloth in the warm water and placed it tightly against his wounds. Khalid wheezed achingly as the salt water stung his wounds.

"Mira, you're killing me here," he joked, holding back tears to stop Amira from getting upset.

"Khalid, I'm sorry," she soothed. "I'm almost done."

Amira finished up bandaging him and placed a warm, fleece blanket over Khalid, who was now falling in and out of sleep. Amira had made him a cup of warm green tea and given him strong painkillers for the pain. When she was done, she sat there in silence and stared at Khalid. Sharp stinging irritated her sore eyes. Amira was a strong, fierce girl, but once the first tear vulnerably broke free from her eye, the rest followed and chased the previous in a ceaseless torrent. She sniffed away a few more tears into her palms when Khalid suddenly embraced Amira's right hand and held it tight.

"I would've had him," he laughed.

"Naaaa, he just caught me off-guard. If I had seen the bastard coming, trust me I would've had him, Mira," Khalid chuckled, lightening the mood.

Amira broke into a quiet giggle and shook her head at Khalid's puerile joke even at a time like this. She smiled at him and held his hand tightly against her cheek. He pulled her hand towards him, causing her to follow and she rested on his chest, one arm around him and the other tucked away secured on the side of his stomach. She breathed in his scent and closed her eyes. They lay there, together, under the heated fleece. Amira's consciousness began diminishing and ebbing away slowly, and her recollection of the earlier events that had occurred hours ago was gradually coming to an end whilst in Khalid's proximity. Her eyes grew weighty from the arduous effects of the needless upheaval of her mind. They both gave away to sheer exhaustion, total defeat and reality, and slept in each other's arms.

CHAPTER FOUR
Aleppo February 2012

Spring in Syria shows up in her own time, bringing life to the roses and tulips, creating new masterpieces each day and changing the endless portrait of every city that beholds upward at the eternal, blue sky.

Gone are the frosty mornings of glacial illumination slapping the faces of children as they walk to school. Gone are the thick duvets of snow, blanketing the grounds, and gone are the dark, dismal midnights, leaving every street in Syria disconsolate with isolation.

Amira was on a school trip to visit the National Museum of Aleppo, which was located in the heart of the northern city on Baron Street, adjacent to the famous Baron Hotel where tourists often stayed. It was also close to the Bab al-Faraj Clock Tower. The summer sun beat down on her back relentlessly, enforcing fat beads of sweat down her forehead and scalp. Her class were simply walking towards the museum, but to Amira, it suddenly seemed like a major task. Maliha, who was yapping away, as usual, was speaking to Amira about a dress she wanted to buy for her auntie's wedding. Amira, however, was not paying attention to a word coming from Maliha's mouth. Her thoughts were intermingling around so many things, except Maliha.

Mama. Baba. And then there was Khalid.

Mama's illness became worse by the day and had deteriorated more so recently due to current affairs outside in the community. Baba, who worked for decades building and forming a suitable home in the market for his pottery shop, had been raided last week by thieves. All his years of handwork, perseverance and patience, had all gone down the drain. The raid left Baba's shop overturned with pieces of broken pots concealing the hidden ground.

"So, I didn't know whether to wear heels or flats. I've worn my heels twice now; getting bored of them, to be honest," Maliha gloated.

Amira became slightly bothered and annoyed at Maliha's insensitivity to everything that was occurring in Amira's life. Amira was still traumatized from last year's incident with Khalid and the militant whom he killed, and the fact that she was nearly raped and lewdly touched by a man.

Amira never really got over the trauma. She often suffered panic attacks when vivid flashbacks visited her every so often. She tried avoiding Shamsa Park at times, for the memory of the incident brought back too much distress for her.

The militant was found dead in the park by locals and taken away. It gained media coverage for a month or so and was left forgotten after that. Khalid counted himself lucky to have gotten away with such a big crime of killing a police militant, especially under the strict regime. Khalid recovered from his wounds and injuries with no internal issues and was up on his feet well within a week with nothing more than a broken nose, which in time also healed, like his bruises, and left only scars from that unforgettable day.

Maliha continued to speak of dresses, make-up and shoes, and Amira continued to listen, without saying a word, and staring ahead motionlessly as they walked around the museum.

After lunch, Amira's class finished their tour of the museum and headed towards the exit to go back to school. Amira had to collect Adam from nursery today. He had started nursery last week and was enjoying a new atmosphere and being around new children his age. He had also started saying a few new words like 'Baba' and 'Mia'.

Outside the museum, the school bus waited across the street. The class had their lunch in the internal courtyard of the museum which was home to herculean, vast basalt statues of ancient Hittite and Roman mythological personalities. Amira was feeling full after having munched on the lunch that Mama had prepared for her the night before.

Unexpectedly, the sound of boisterous taunting and yelling was emerging from the street beside the museum.

"What's that noise?" Amira puzzlingly questioned under her breath.

Suddenly, a herd of military police dressed in full uniform paraded down the street.

The smouldering fire of intense fury and hatred was festering in the small narrowed eyes of every militant. Amira caught sight of two middle-aged militants who had handcuffed two teenage boys, roughly 16 years old in age. One of the boys had an apprehensive look on his naive face and his cheeks flushed a bright red colour. He wore an Arab keffiyyeh scarf, as did his friend, who had light ginger hair and fierce green eyes. Both boys were harshly dragged by two policemen and they howled in pain as their wrists were cut from being yanked across the floor whilst in metal handcuffs.

Amira's heart sank. She remembered that cold winter's evening, November the 16th last year.

She remembered Khalid's screams, his injuries, and his seeping skin. Her breathing became rapid and shallow and she could feel her rhythmic pulse pounding in her temples. She recognised this dreadful feeling, the same feeling she felt the night Khalid shot the militant, the same feeling she had felt for nights after the shooting when she lay in bed unable to sleep.

She began to panic and the pounding of her heart became louder and louder inside her chest.

Maliha turned to Amira.

"What did they do? Graffiti? They wouldn't dare to confront Assad's men, surely?" Maliha said anxiously with concern.

Before Amira had a chance to answer, one of the policemen raged loudly.

"Come on then boys, say it louder for us all." The man's voice trumpeted like thunder across the whole street.

The vexation in his voice brought a tremble through Amira's body.

"Go on then, say it LOUDER for 'US' all," the man continued, now addressing the people in the street watching.

The boy with the ginger hair looked up from the floor, right into the eyes of his tormentor, and spat out blood onto his face.

"Assad is a FUCKING killer," he unflinchingly roared, with a look of heroism on his tender face, and with that, the Militant police officer who had handcuffed the boys got out his pistol and shot him right on his forehead.

The crackle of the gunshot brought a shiver down Amira's spine and made the hairs on her neck stand on edge.

She stared, frozen, as the bullet punched its way through the middle of the boy's head, causing a cavernous hole in its wake that rapidly oozed with molten red blood and gushed out like a waterfall.

The boy fell to the ground from his knees, leaving nothing more than a pool of blood around him. His friend had now passed out and was being dragged to the police van, alongside his friend, who was dead to the world and forcefully thrown behind the truck into the van, leaving a trail of his blood down the street.

Amira held her breath until she heard screams from her classmates. She tried holding on for as long as she could until she finally let out a scream. She screamed. Screamed till her eyes were full of tears, her heart full of rage and body full of exhaustion and sweat. Then, she heaved and threw up onto her feet and passed out.

■■■

Amira woke up in her sitting room at home. Upon gaining slight consciousness, she sheltered herself in the soft sheets blanketing over her trembling legs. She rubbed the remaining sleep from her nightmare and gazed out onto the horizon from the sitting room window. The flamboyant blaze and lights extended across a clear, blue sky. Although this was a scene another would consider most magnificent and alluring, to Amira, it felt strange, dismal almost.

"Mira?" asked a familiar voice.

Amira looked around to see her baba's smiling face.

"Ahhh, Mira, my princess, you gave us a fright dear. How are you?" he soothed as he stroked Amira's golden curls.

"Baba? I was at the museum…, how? When?" Amira asked puzzlingly, unable to ascertain how she had ended up at home.

"Khalid," Baba replied.

"The shooting at the museum, my dear, it was a terrible thing. Maliha saw you faint and helped you up. But she hardly had a chance before Khalid came to bring you here," said Baba.

"But how did he know that I was there?" asked Amira, troubled.

"He knew you had gone to the museum for your trip, so as soon as he heard of the shooting, he left his home and came to you as quick as he could. He even managed to nick his friend's motorbike," laughed Baba.

"Honestly, that boy," he continued. "He has a heart of gold and the temper of a dragon," said Baba.

"Temper?" Amira questioned curiously.

"He was ready to fight the police who shot the poor boy. I don't know how I managed to convince him to calm down and think rationally, honestly I don't," replied Baba.

Amira got a sudden lump in her throat as she remembered that day Khalid got beaten up and shot the policeman. Khalid joked and teased as he did, as if nothing had ever happened that day that changed his life. The day he killed a man. Amira knew, she knew the real pain Khalid felt when he was alone with his thoughts and the way it might have affected him. She knew him better than she knew herself.

She sat up and was overcome with an intense throbbing in her head. She winced in pain.

"Easy, Amira, rest up," said Mama, who was coming into the room with a mug of hot green tea. "Here, drink this."

Amira sipped the tea and watched her baba, who was frowning at the TV.

"You know why those poor boys were beaten and killed, don't you? And what caused the death of that poor fellow?" asked Baba.

Amira shook her head.

"It's all part of the ongoing civil war," Baba began to say.

"There's all these groups, Islamic groups, rebels, Assad's army, then there's us. Stuck in the middle of this corruption."

There was a frustration in Baba's voice that echoed into Amira's heart and intertwined with her own feelings of rage and frustration over the injustice within Syria.

"The opposition, mainly the Free Syrian Army, and the Syrian government, supported by Shia militants and Hezbollah, and now, even Russia has got itself involved. Everyone wants a piece of Aleppo!" fumed Baba.

Amira listened to the news frantically as it blared in the background.

'10th of February 2012, yesterday, two large bombs exploded at Syrian security force's building in Aleppo and according to the Syrian government and state media, it was caused by two suicide car bombs.' Amira gathered that the blame was pointed towards armed opposition groups, thus spawning hatred amongst the younger generations and leading to more patrols on the streets.

The blasts, which were approximately two minutes apart, crushed the composure of the Muslim holy morning and nearly eleven months without momentous violence in Aleppo.

"Dark times are ahead, Amira," Baba warned, with a look of despondency on his face.

Amira sat back and stared out the window. She was lost in her thoughts and began feeling a sudden rush of anxiety coursing through her.

She thought, 'Fear, dismay and revulsion are universal and pervasive as the moonlight that shines without fail every night upon every cracked street, every alley and every home.'

"I worry, Mira. For you, Adam, us all," Baba went on.

"Aleppo has already become a battleground; Allah alone knows when things will become better for us all."

CHAPTER FIVE
Aleppo July 2014

It was Amira's 19th birthday. She had matured into a slender, stunning woman. Her hair fell chaotically behind her shoulders and reached just above her curvy hips.

Usually, for her birthday, Amira spent the day with her friend Maliha or Khalid. Today, she was spending it with her family at Uncle Ahmed's house. He had recently returned from a trip from Egypt.

Amira wore her best dress, a floral knee-high dress with white leggings. On top, she wore her mother's jewelled cardigan that Baba had bought her for their wedding anniversary. Before they left, Amira patted some rosy blush onto her plump cheeks and a nude lipstick on to her lips. She didn't need much makeup at all. Her features were captivating enough for anyone to do a double-take whilst walking.

Amira felt as if it was just like any other day. She didn't care much for her birthday anymore, despite having done in the past. She saw it as another year of getting older, another year closer to death. The only thing she was looking forward to was seeing Khalid.

On the way to Uncle Ahmed's house, Baba stopped at Khalid's father's bakery to pick up his famous orange cream pastries. Amira anticipated the journey, hoping to see Khalid. Khalid was now 21 years old. He had found a new job in an orphanage just east of Aleppo, working as a sports coordinator. The young boys loved him. He taught them football alongside horse riding and archery. He had worked at Amira's father's pottery shop since he was 16 until it got raided by thieves a few years back. All of Baba's hard-earned money spent and invested in the shop, pottery supplies, clay, expensive handmade paint and sculpting carving tools were wasted in an instant. He now worked with Uncle Ahmed, assisting him on his tours.

"Baaaaaaba! Mamoniaaaaahh," squealed Adam, as Mama fastened him in his car seat.

Amira giggled.

"Yes, yes, Adam, Mamonia for you," smiled Amira, reassuring Adam that he would get his Mamonia semolina pudding from the bakery.

Adam still had difficulty with his speech and no matter how hard Amira tried to help him with his speech and language formation, it seemed almost impossible.

"He will learn in his own time," Baba would encourage Amira.

Adam had started school a few days a week and the teachers also encouraged by saying that every child learns to form their words and speech in their own time. Mama would constantly worry.

"Amira! My princess, what would you like today, huh?" asked Baba, peering at Amira from his rear-view mirror, smiling.

"Hmmmm. I think I'll have a Mansoura pastry, please," she replied.

"And you, my Queen?" teased Baba, now facing Mama and smirking brightly.

"Nothing. I am on my diet as you know already, dear," Mama responded.

"Diet!? Oh, my Allah. My lady, you need no diets, you are the finest woman I have ever laid eyes upon," countered Baba, cheerfully, as he clapped his hands to praise Mama's beauty. Amira chuckled under her breath and smiled at the charm and pureness of Mama and Baba's love.

Baba parked outside the bakery and Amira swiftly glanced into the window to see if Khalid was there. It was a Friday and usually Khalid set off to the orphanage late, after he had read his Friday Jummah prayer.

"Amira, come," Baba said, as he hopped out of his seat. Amira had known Khalid since infancy, yet even after 19 years, she still got goosebumps and a racing heartbeat whenever she saw him.

They entered the bakery and were warmly greeted by Khalid's father.

"Salamu Alykum!" he roared loudly, pleased at the sight of both Baba and Amira.

"Wa'Alaykumus-Salam, Uncle," Amira replied respectfully.

"I'm here for the regular, Hussain. Off to Ahmed's today," said baba.

"Of course, brother, give him my Salam," replied Uncle Hussain.

Amira looked around the shop. No sign of Khalid. Her heart sank slightly.

"What happened to your window, Hussain?" asked Baba, staring at the huge crack in the bakery's window.

"Oh, that happened last week. Government police were here," he replied.

"What? Assad's men did this?" asked Baba, angrily.

"Well, there was a group of youngsters. They were just off Jibril Street where they were simply hanging around," said Hussain, placing a piece of pastry into a paper bag. He continued.

"They got a little loud, as usual, you know how they are, these boys. Well, anyways, they got a little rowdy messing around the fountain and started chanting praise of the Free Syrian army. Before you knew it, a whole load of Assad's men had emerged from god knows where and arrested the lot."

"And the crack in the window?" Baba questioned.

"The police got a little physical, let's say. Dashed a brick right for a young boy, missed and hit the window instead. The lot of them, beaten, bruised, shackled and arrested," Hussain sighed, handing Baba the paper bag of treats.

"Assad's men, who are they tackling? Young boys? Rebels? ISIS? Every day it's a new group, a new lead," exclaimed Baba, frustrated.

"I tell you, brother, that is true. But look, it's as if new groups are being formed every other day in Syria. I mean look at ISIS. They've already established a strong presence in Aleppo and control most of the East," Hussain remarked.

"And Assad's men in the West," added Baba.

Aleppo had become a war zone between the West and East cities, with Assad controlling the west and rebel groups controlling the east.

Amira grabbed the bag of pastries from Uncle Hussain and thanked him.

"There's an extra one in there for you, Mira. Happy birthday, darling," Uncle Hussain winked, impersonating the exact wink and impression Khalid would give Amira. She smiled and said her goodbye and left with Baba.

As expected, the journey to Uncle Ahmed's house was a particularly wearisome and lengthy one. With protesters emerging from every angle of the city centre, it was inevitable that they would reach Uncle Ahmed's house by late afternoon. Amira gawked out her window on the crowds and the protestor's families. Every day, people were being arrested, tortured and imprisoned, yet still, people had the bravery and bravado to march alongside activists and proudly chant against Assad's poisonous regime.

When they finally arrived, Amira was greeted by her uncle, her aunty and Khadijah.

"Just because they lifted the siege of Halab last October, they had us fooled into thinking they wouldn't return. Scum!" snorted Uncle Ahmed, puffing on his pipe.

"Government forces are controlling all of Halab, every street, every corner, every town," he continued as Baba listened, humming in agreement.

"They're continuing their offensives now before our eyes. Shooting down anyone who dares to oppose the mighty Assad," Uncle Ahmed huffed.

Baba lifted his eyes from his plate of candied almonds and looked at Uncle Ahmed with concern.

"Business is slow, Ahmed," he whispered, almost as if he didn't want Amira to hear. She was sitting on the Persian rug opposite him and Ahmed, scribbling poetry into her notebook.

"The closure of airports last year already cost us a lot. Travelling seems more and more difficult now. It's as if no one wants to visit Syria anymore," Baba pointed out.

Since the destruction of his pottery shop, Baba had begun travelling with Ahmed to Turkey, Damascus, Egypt and other neighbouring towns and countries as an acting guide. However, recent airport closures meant it was difficult for both brothers to travel for work, not forgetting dangerous too. Travelling abroad meant often having the need to travel through the main fighting and controlled areas of both rebel forces, Islamist groups as well as regime guards. There were also inter-rebel conflicts and clashes which previously resulted in more casualties and deaths amongst some parts of Idlib, which was a neighbouring city to Halab, Aleppo.

"It will get easier, God willing, brother. Have faith in the one who created you. Inshallah, Allah has a plan for my Halab and for my Syria," Uncle Ahmed recited rather poetically.

"The presidential elections amidst all this opposition boycott amuse me, I tell you! Does it take a mastermind to decipher that it's rigged? Always has been and always will be," he went on.

"Ha! You know what Russia and Iran think, don't you?" Baba laughed.

"The elections are a sense of freedom and transparency," he snickered with a sense of disgust in his chortle.

Amira listened on. She remembered the uproar on the 4th of June when Assad was elected and won with 88.7% of the vote with a turnout of 73.47% of eligible voters. She recalls that day when Khalid was angered by the election and went to a protest near Idlib without her knowing. She found out upon his arrival when his father had an argument with him about it and Khalid smashed his bedroom window out of anger. She soon discovered his bruised knuckles and was furious at his decision to attend the march.

They hadn't really met after that day properly, and secretly, Amira missed him. Khalid was staying clear to avoid Amira's anger at his betrayal of going when he promised her he wouldn't ever go again.

"Amira, child, how is your poetry writing going?" asked Uncle Ahmed, turning his attention to Amira who was focused deeply in the world of poetry.

"Good, Uncle," smiled Amira.

"So, you want to be a poet, eh? Very good, beautiful ambition," he said proudly.

"My girl can be anything she wants, she knows that," Baba boasted fondly with a big grin on his wrinkly face. His eyes lit up at the sight of Amira's smile and sudden sense of shyness.

"CAAAAAAAAAAA," screeched Adam, sprinting into the room with a cupcake in his hand.

"Adam, my ears!" said Amira, as she tried licking the icing from Adam's cupcake.

"Your mother and Aunty secretly made these for you, Amira, for your birthday," whispered Baba, trying not to spoil the surprise in front of both women who were busying themselves in the kitchen.

They emerged into the room holding two trays of vibrant yellow and pink beautifully iced cupcakes with pistachios.

"FOR ME?" Amira jumped up and danced around the women, teasing them with her silly remarks.

"Well, looks like it's all mine seeing as you are both on a diet," she giggled.

They all laughed and ate a cupcake.

"Happy birthday, Amira, my princess, my darling," Mama said sweetly as she held Amira's face and stroked her golden hair.

Just before nightfall that same day, Amira took a plate of cupcakes to give to her neighbour, Baba Mohammed, an elderly man who recently lost his wife and now lived alone. He was a friendly man with a pure white beard that shone brightly under the sunlight. He was loved by everyone. He often helped others, despite being an elderly man himself and struggling to do basic tasks sometimes.

She made her way to his small house which was almost a minute away from hers. She arrived outside his door and knocked louder than normal for him to hear.

Baba Mohammed opened the door, his winter-white hair and beard making him look almost angelic; his eyes were hazel and slightly blood-flecked and his face was timeworn and shrivelled. He broke into a warm-hearted smile and clapped his hands.

"Amira, my dear! Fancy seeing you here, princess." His voice was weak and frail but had a soothing effect to the ears. He gazed at the plate and gasped playfully.

"For me? Oh Amira, come in come in."

"Yes, Baba, it's my birthday today. My mother and aunty made these for me and I saved you some because I know about your sweet tooth," Amira said, mischievously, as she placed the plate onto the table beside Baba Mohammed's chair.

"Come, sit, I have a new poem for you." Baba Mohammed was also a fanatic of poetry and Amira often found herself sitting beside him for hours and hours, listening to his words of wisdom and poems he made up within a few seconds. She looked up to him and had always regarded him as a grandfather figure.

She sat herself on the plump cushion on the floor beside Baba Mohammed.

"Nizar Qabbani," said Baba Mohammed, smirking at Amira. They both loved the quotes and poetry written by the famously renowned writer, Qabbani. He wrote mostly love poems. Whenever Amira reads his poems, all she thought of was Khalid.

Baba Mohammed cleared his throat and began to recite.

"Balqees...Oh princess," he began.

Amira smiled, as she knew this poem. It was a poem heartbroken Qabbani had written for his wife, Balqees, who was killed by a guerrilla bomb in Beirut. This had a devastatingly weighty effect on Qabbani. In this poem, he candidly rebuked and scolded the entire Arab nation for her death.

> *"Balqees...Oh, princess,*
> *You burn, caught between the tribal wars,*
> *What will I write about the departure of my queen?*
> *Indeed, words are my scandal,*
> *Here we look through the piles of victims,*
> *For a star that fell, for a body strewn like fragments of a mirror.*
> *Here we ask, oh my love:*
> *Was this your grave,*
> *Or the grave of Arab nationalism?"*

These were just a few powerful lines from his heart-wrenching poem, written out of despair and mourning for his beloved.

"He was never afraid to stand up against the Arab authoritarianism, was he?" Baba Mohammed exclaimed.

"I like this poem a lot, Baba. It makes me sad to think Qabbani lost the love of his life in such a brutal way." She paused, not thinking that Baba Mohammed's wife also lost her life to cancer, which in turn was also a brutal manner in which you depart this life.

She gawked at his face and felt ashamed for blurting her words out without thinking.

He stroked her head.

"It's okay, Amira, this Dunya is cruel to us all. We are all waiting for the afterlife to finally live," he declared.

Amira listened to his pacifying words in harmony.

"Like Qabbani says, dear... 'The most dangerous heart disease; a strong memory'," Baba uttered.

"You are born alone, die alone and will meet your Lord alone. May we all be reunited in Jannat-Ul Firdaws, my dear, Inshallah."

"Insha'Allah," murmured Amira, contentedly.

"I should be going now, Baba, I have homework to do," Amira said, not realising it was getting darker outside.

"How is school, Amira?" asked Baba Mohammed.

"Alhamdulillah, good, but it's difficult sometimes. There's always conflict near my university. The youngsters have no fear of the government forces patrolling the streets and always start shouting their mouths off against Assad. It just makes life difficult to get past the commotion safely to go home, to be honest," she explained.

"Just stay focused, Amira child, you have a bright future ahead of you, my dear. I can see it," he muttered proudly with a beaming smile across his humbling face.

"I will wait for the day I hear of your famous poems recited in every home, may my Allah let me live to see this day Insha'Allah," Baba Mohammed blissfully declared with exhilaration in his rickety voice.

Amira blushed.

"You will Baba, Insha'Allah."

On her way home, Amira thought of the poem by Qabbani about his wife. The pain he must have felt, losing the love of his life, someone he grew old with, who knew his every secret, his fears, his weaknesses and strengths. Amira, although having loved the feeling of contentment within her own presence of being idle, could not apprehend the sense of anguish and wretchedness one must feel losing the love of their life.

Amira was about to enter the gate of her house when Khalid walked out of the alley beside her. She froze. She felt a muscle twinge inadvertently at the corner of her right eye and her mouth formed a rigid smile. She had waited to see Khalid for days now, especially today, but she was caught off guard. The very faint make-up she wore had been washed off now; the dress she wore all day had been replaced with her scruffy lounge-wear clothing and her hair was tied up in a messy bun. For the first time, Amira felt conscious of her appearance in front of Khalid. Although to Khalid, he thought of this presentation of Amira the purest, most beautiful and natural, Amira still felt unworthy.

"Happy Birthday, Mira," Khalid said, grinning radiantly from ear to ear.

His eyes seemed darker than normal. Amira looked into his eyes and from them came a swift glance of obscure intensity, a gentleness, a sense of familiarity. His hair had messily grown past his ears and he had it up in a chaotic bun with a few curly strands falling down on either side of his ears. Amira gulped and bit her tongue inside her mouth.

"This is for you." Khalid reached for his pocket and took out a small box.

Amira's eyes were everywhere but Khalid's face now.

He moved closer and her breathing became softer as he looked into her eyes giving a wistful look that melted into a smile. There was something about that gaze, that look of his that Amira would never find in another.

"Did you think I'd forget, huh?" he laughed, handing her the box with a red ribbon on top.

"No," Amira said.

She opened the box to see something was wrapped in pink paper.

She beamed a smile as she unravelled the messy wrapping and drew out a dainty heart-shaped necklace. The thin-chained piece of silver had faint engraving on the heart that read four simple letters:

'MIRA'.

"Khalid...This is beautiful," she whispered, overwhelmed by the gift. Subconsciously, they both began strolling towards the side alley.

"This must have cost so much; you didn't have to, Khalid," she said.

"Nonsense, anything for my Mira," he boasted.

Khalid and Amira had reached the alley when Khalid pulled out another gift from his trouser pocket.

"I also got you this, Mira. It's nothing special, but I wanted to get you something that you would use every day and remember me by," he murmured quietly.

Amira opened the long, thin-shaped present and gasped excitedly.

"Khalid! I love it!" she shrilled cheerfully, like a child.

It was a wooden engraved pen that read 'My princess'. She embraced Khalid tightly.

Khalid whispered into her soft hair, "Now you can think of me whenever you write your poems."

"Khalid, I don't need a pen to ever remember you, silly, you are always in my heart," she blushed.

She was touched by his gifts.

"Turn around," Khalid instructed as he took the necklace from Amira's hand.

Amira turned to face the wall of the alley as Khalid gently lifted Amira's golden mane to fasten the necklace around her neck. She shivered at his touch. He placed the necklace on her neck and before she could turn, Khalid brought his face closer to the back of her neck.

She felt his hot breath on her neck and the tender brush of his cushioned lips against her skin. His hand ran through her curls and the kisses were now on her frail shoulders. Amira closes her eyes and all previous thoughts were halted in their tracks.

"Khalid…," Amira breathed.

Khalid's lips moved away from her frame and they both turned to face one another. Khalid stroked Amira's red, burning cheeks and looked deeply into her eyes. Eyes that were filled with love, devotion and adoration.

"You like the gifts, Mira?" he asked.

"I love them, Khalid, you know I do," she replied. "Thank you, Khalid."

Khalid looked down and Amira perceived a sensation of concern suddenly on Khalid's face.

"Promise me, Mira?" he uttered.

"Promise you what, Khalid?" she asked confused.

"That you will never forget me."

Amira raised her brow, surprised at his question.

"Khalid? What's wrong?"

"Nothing, Mira, just promise me you won't, and that you will always stay with me. I can't lose you," he stuttered.

"Khalid! Stop this now. I'm not going anywhere and you know I won't ever leave you," Amira snapped.

"Promise?" he asked again, reluctantly.

"I promise," Amira smiled.

They both left the alley and Khalid walked Amira home. Amira could smell Khalid from her hair, her neck and her hands. His musky scent enveloped her body like a protective whirl of intoxicating drugs that she couldn't get enough of. He gave her a quick peck on her cheek and one of his cheeky winks as she reached her doorway.

Amira watched on as Khalid sauntered across the street and she fingered her necklace.

Little did Amira know, that after this day, life would no longer be the same again. For Khalid, for Mama, Baba, Adam, or for Amira.

Ever.

CHAPTER SIX
Aleppo 2015

The 11th of April 2015 marked the tragic day Amira's neighbourhood was shelled by rebels in defiance against the government-controlled area of the northern municipal of Aleppo. It was an early Saturday morning and Amira's family had just started eating their breakfast when the ear-splitting sound of howling blasts deafened the whole family. The bombing affected the street Maliha lived on, however, thankfully her whole family were okay. Then, hours after the devastating shelling, helicopter gunships aimlessly struck the local market in the town's rebel-held neighbourhood of Maadi in apparent retaliation. The shelling wounded many people and killed up to 15 civilians.

"BAAAAAAAA!" shrieked Adam at the top of his lungs, with fresh hot tears gliding across his petrified face.

"Shhhh, Shhhh, Adam, it's okay, come here," piped up Amira, holding him close to her chest as Mama and Baba left the house to see what had happened.

10 minutes later, Khalid appeared, out of breath, looking for Amira.

"Khalid! What happened?!" Amira demanded, clutching tightly onto Adam who was still crying out of fear.

"Rebels. They bombed the market, where all the police force is located. Assad's men," he replied, panting loudly, almost out of breath as he spoke.

"What? But there's people living here! Are they out of their mind?" yelled Amira out of anger.

"Is everyone okay? Is anyone hurt? Your dad's bakery?" Amira's questions didn't stop.

"It's okay, his bakery wasn't hit by the shells, it was closer to the other end, where Saleem's clothes' stalls are and Uncle Noah's candy shop," he continued, trying to calm Amira down.

"But they're all okay. I don't know if anyone got killed, Amira. You stay here, I'll be back," he rushed out and Amira waited.

Twenty minutes, forty minutes, an hour went by. Amira was still waiting. Adam had managed to drift off to sleep in Amira's arms and she was carefully placing him in his bed when she heard someone entering the house downstairs. It was Mama and Baba.

Amira rushed down. Red hot blood flushed her cold cheeks as she met eyes with her mother.

"Mama?" croaked Amira. She couldn't breathe.

It was as if someone was forcefully choking her, which sent her heart racing. Amira didn't know why she felt like this.

Maybe because she thought something bad had happened, or maybe because the silence in her mother's facial expression made the atmosphere full of paranoia and cold fear.

"Amira, my child, come sit down," soothed Baba with his sedative voice.

"Wha...What's happened, Baba? Please, just tell me," she began crying now, dreading the unknown.

Baba tried holding onto Amira's shoulder to prompt her to sit, but she refused and pushed back.

He sighed.

"It's Maliha," he started.

"She...She's a Shaheed, Amira," Baba muttered quietly.

"What?" Amira stuttered, holding back vomit.

"You're...you're lying!" she shouted. "SHAHEED? WHAT DO YOU MEAN SHAHEED?" she yelled.

Suddenly, a voice from behind Baba spoke.

"Meaning she's a martyr, Mira, she's gone to heaven," Khalid beckoned from behind.

Amira felt her tears burn against her skin; all she wanted to do was curl up into a ball and wait for someone to tell her it was all a misunderstanding, a mistake. But no one would, no one was going to, because Maliha was really gone, dead. A suffocated cry of anguish forced itself up her dry throat and she ran up to her room, slammed the door shut and fell onto her bed. She sobbed for hours into her pillow.

A few hours later, Khalid let himself into her room. Amira took no notice and continued to lay on her bed and watch the ceiling.

"Mira?" Khalid lulled.

"Mira, are you okay?"

Amira wiped another tear from her eye and rolled over.

"Mira, I know it hurts. Please, you need to be strong," Khalid sighed under his breath as he tried consoling Amira, who lay still as a statue.

Khalid held onto Amira's shoulder. Amira had always been extremely embarrassed and conscious of how she cried, but today was the day she gave birth to the enormity of her sorrow and mourning. She clamoured loudly into the palms of her hands with salty tears soaking her sleeves, flooding down her arms and into her clothes. Khalid held back tears as he saw Amira sob like a child and held her close to him.

She sunk into his embrace, unaware that her soaked sleeves were drenching Khalid's shirt. She cried and cried till no tears were left inside her empty soul and Khalid let her. Never had Amira experienced such grief before, nor had she mourned over a close loved one dying. Amira had seen Maliha just two days ago, as they revised for their end of month test. Maliha spoke about boys, make-up and Hammad, the boy she liked and wanted to marry. Everything was as normal as it could be in both their lives. How could she have been killed? How could she have died?

Amira questioned herself repeatedly inside her head. Khalid explained to Amira that Maliha was buying a loaf of bread for her family for breakfast. She was alone in the market when the bomb hit.

"She was found under a mammoth accumulation of rubble, Amira," stated Khalid.

"She couldn't be saved."

Amira lay there, in Khalid's arms, listening to his flat, soul-crushing words as they escaped his lips. This was the first time

Amira had grieved for a loved one. When her grandfather, Baba's father died, she didn't mourn for him as much as she was for Maliha. She was never close to him nor was she old enough to properly understand the loss of a paternal family member. It was all new to her and she didn't know how to cope.

Khalid continued.

"They're still digging out all the other bodies. There's lots of casualties and injured people, with a few also dead," he said to Amira.

"I'm going to help them, Mira. Will you be okay?" he asked.

Amira didn't look up, nor did she speak. She simply nodded in answer and lay back on her pillow.

Khalid kissed her forehead gently and left.

The next day, Amira went outside with her parents. They sluggishly ambled towards the ravaged alleys of where the market had stood only yesterday.

Amira looked around her. Smoke still danced around the demolished buildings and stalls as people walked around the rubble and the smell of rotting flesh made Amira shudder in disgust. Maliha's body had been taken to the local mosque for Ghusl, a special ablution needed to be performed before a body can be laid to rest. Maliha's mother, sister and cousins all performed the ablution on her and she was laid to rest in the graveyard where Amira's grandfather was buried. She was buried early after the afternoon Zuhr prayer, alongside the other victims who had lost their lives. Amira didn't attend the funeral but prayed at home instead. She didn't want all the confrontation, questions and constant talking of Maliha and how young she was. Above all, she didn't want to hear of any more political talk or debates surrounding Assad, rebels and other groups that were all fighting against each other.

Amira saw Baba Mohammed, who was wandering ponderously around the debris on the floor. He held his back with one hand, while the other gripped firmly onto his wooden walking stick. He caught a glimpse of Amira's family. His face was expressionless, vacant almost. He scanned Amira's face, which was puffy and weak, and gave her a dying half-smile. They walked towards each other, then Amira flung her arms around him and wept into his white thobe. His fragrance reminded her of her baba's; a profound aroma of deep Arabian Musk. She sniffed and looked up at Baba Mohammed, who also had a tear in his eye.

"Stay strong, my child, Allah is watching," he said, pointing towards the sky.

"Allah knows, dear child. He is with us all. Whoever kills a person unjustly…it is as though he has killed all of mankind. And whoever saves a life, it is as though he has saved all of mankind," he recited the words of the Prophet Muhammed.

Baba took a hold of Amira as she greeted Baba Mohammed.

"What has happened to Syria?" he urged with despondency, looking directly into Baba Mohammed's eyes.

"What is happening?" Baba continued.

"Aleppo has fallen. Aleppo is falling," Baba Mohammed dejectedly mumbled under his breath to Baba, now trying to avoid eye contact with Amira to protect her from anxiety.

Amira walked on and continued to delve into the lifeless market towards where Maliha would have been trapped. Khalid mentioned she was buying bread so she must have been near the other end, Amira thought. She coursed over the large bricks and ruins and finally made it to the far end of the market. She stood there, inspecting the destruction around her. She gazed deeply into the mess and began reminiscing on the last conversation she had had with Maliha. They spoke about their future, and where they wanted to be in 10 years' time.

"I don't know about you, Amira, but all I'm saying is I'm having a whole football team of kids, with Hammad of course," she joked to Amira.

"Hammad has almost finished his exams and as soon as he is done, he is going to speak to my parents about marriage! Oh my gosh, Amira, I get butterflies just thinking of it all."

A harrowing tear skittered down Amira's cheek. She inhaled a deep breath of dry, muggy air and turned to go home. She didn't want to see anymore. When she turned, she saw Hammad standing behind her. His face, tanned and drained, looked powerfully dominated by an intense sadness and it grew deeper each time he breathed whilst gawking directly into the rubble.

Amira assumed Hammad hadn't seen her as they hadn't made eye contact yet, so she walked right past him before he finally spoke.

"I passed, you know," he whimpered with a tenuous whisper.

"Got my exam results today, I passed. I was going to tell them by the end of this week. I was going to tell them that I wanted to marry Maliha."

Amira looked at Hammad and no longer saw the excitement, desire and fire in his eyes when he spoke of Maliha. All that remained was a vacant, empty soul. He was just a shell of a man now, a man whose soul had died alongside his lover's.

Amira tripped as she hiked over the large pieces of broken ruins along the market alleys and cut her knee. She hissed in pain and went back to where her parents were still talking to Baba Mohammed.

"Amira? What happened to your knee?" Mama asked, alarmed.

"Are you hurt?"

"No, Mama, I just tripped. Can we go, please? I don't want to be here anymore," Amira pleaded.

"Of course," Baba replied.

Amira kissed Baba Mohammed's hand and left the market.

Amira was almost blinded with the scintillating bright spots and all she wanted was the obscurity of her bedroom. Nausea began to overpower her and she desperately held her vomit in. The crushing pain of the migraine pulsated so vehemently around the side of her skull that all she craved was a tight scarf tied around her head to ease the pain.

They were just about to leave the market when Amira took a final look back. In those alleys and in those streets was once the beating heart of Aleppo, where the ancient walls surrounding the marketplace were once home to many, and every day after school, Amira and Maliha drank in the vibrancies, the fragrances and the ambience. All that was left now was a maze of rubble and detritus of the devastation.

Baba Mohammed, who was still standing where he was, had his arms folded. He unlocked them when he caught a glimpse of Amira's face and waved hopelessly at her as she continued to scan the market. She waved back and couldn't even manage a slight smile at him. She turned back and went home.

That was the last time Amira saw Baba Mohammed.

CHAPTER SEVEN
Aleppo 2016

War.

"What is war?" Amira thought.

What is war, but a butchery, a bloodshed and an extermination of our bravest brothers, of our feeble mothers and of our sinless children?

That was what war was defined as in Amira's eyes.

The deceived were misled and blinded into hating one another. The nation was exiled.

It wasn't just a battle between those who were with or against Assad, it was more than just that. Other countries were heavily involved with their own agendas, which only led to the exacerbation and prolonging of the complex fighting within Syria. It was now a much more personal fight. The fostering of hatred, malice and repugnance lived deeply in the hearts of Syrian rebel groups as well as Islamist groups and Assad's regime militants. The divisions between the majorities of the Sunni Muslim majority against the president's Shia Alawite sect led both sides to commit atrocities and tear apart the long-lived communities, dimming their hopes of peace within their nation again. It also gave life to the flourishing of jihadist groups of the Islamic State, known as ISIS and Al-Qaeda. The Syrian Kurds, who also thirsted for the right of self-government, despite not having fought Assad's forces, only added another fuel to further add magnitude to the conflict.

Assad's focal advocates were Russia and Iran, while Turkey, western powers and several Gulf Arab states backed the opposition. Russia had many military bases located within Syria and the launching of an air campaign in endorsement and support of Assad in 2015 was labelled as crucial in turning the torrent of the civil war in the government's favour.

The strikes led by the Russian army were described as a simple act of targeting only terrorists. It was these simple targets by Russia that murdered Baba Mohammed on the 28th of April 2016.

Baba Mohammed had suffered a terrible fall on the 27th of April and was rushed to hospital by a neighbour. After being admitted for the night, Al-Quds Hospital, which was located in opposition-controlled Aleppo, was vigorously hit by four executive airstrikes. Baba Mohammed died, alongside the other patients, doctors and civilians. His body was never found.

The next day, on the 29th of April, Malla Khan Mosque in Aleppo, which was situated in the heart of the government-controlled neighbourhood, was struck with mighty rockets, killing at least 15 people. The Syrian government reported the rebels behind the attack.

Thankfully, no one from Amira's family was killed.

That week, Baba called for Uncle Ahmed and Khalid's family. Uncle Ahmed, Khalid and his father, Uncle Hussain all met at Amira's house.

"Come in, come in," Baba exclaimed at the front door as both families arrived outside at the same time.

Amira was in the kitchen when she heard them arrive. She took four glasses of green tea inside to where they all sat and handed each one a glass.

"Salam, Uncle Ahmed, Uncle Hussain," she greeted them respectfully.

She turned to face Khalid to greet him, but he was looking down into his lap. She could see the dismal frown on his forehead and his eyes were closed.

She placed his cup of kahvah beside him and left.

Mama was upstairs putting Adam to sleep. He had had a very high temperature for days now and was getting worse every day. The pharmacy that Amira went to weekly for her mother's medicine had been demolished and raided by attacks. The only place to get medicine was deeper into the city, which on a normal day a few years back would have been perfectly safe to travel to, however, militants from Assad's army were placed on every corner of every street. It was too dangerous for Amira, or anyone, to travel to with the fear of unexpected rebel attacks and shelling.

Mama was also running out of her weekly medicine and it was creeping up on Amira that without it, her mother would suffer greatly due to unbearable migraines and dizzy spells.

Amira sat at the top of the staircase, listening closely to what was being said downstairs. She took long pauses in her breathing to make sure of being able to hear the men's conversations downstairs.

"We've been speaking about this for months now, Hussain, it is time," said Baba, faintly.

Amira could just make out the conversation and where it was leading to. She had also heard enough times when Baba, Uncle Hussain and Khalid had this conversation informally, but this was the first time she was hearing it in a serious setting.

"Ahmed, meet us tomorrow here at 9 am, pack only essentials, tell the girls the same and bring every identification document you own," advised Baba.

"Same with you, Hussain, only essentials. We won't have space or the capacity to carry too much."

Khalid was quiet and still hadn't said a word since he arrived. Amira started becoming anxious. She twiddled her fingers, as she did when she was apprehensive.

"I have a friend in Turkey. He lives in Alanya. We will settle there, Insha'Allah. We will birth our children in our new homeland, watch them grow, fight with them against any evil and grow old together, my brothers. Syria is finished for us," Baba pronounced woefully.

"There is nothing left for us here anymore, my brothers..."

Amira's heart sank.

The feeling of being pushed out of her homeland because of war made her gut twist inside her stomach. Tomorrow, she was to leave a place that had been her childhood cocoon, where she learnt to ride her first bike, learnt to read, write, learnt to create poetry from blank words and form them into credible masterpieces. It was home, home to her, where she made lifelong friendships and relationships, where she wanted to grow old and become a poet. It was also the place where she fell in love, since the tender age of infancy, growing up alongside Khalid, teasing him, playing hide and seek in Shamsa Park, growing closer and now, migrating together in search of a new home. For now, all Amira could do was bury this anguish deep into the depths of her heart and deal with it later, for she had her family to think about, Adam, Mama and Baba.

"Is there no chance of staying anymore?" Khalid finally spoke.

"Child, look around you. Is this the Syria you want your children to grow up in, to be educated in? Is it?" said his father, Hussain.

"Who is really with us? Iran? Russia? Iran has deployed hundreds of troops and spent billions to help Assad. You really think that this is simply about fighting rebels and terrorists now? It isn't," Uncle Hussain stated.

'The unity that was once shared between every Syrian was exiled and expatriated in the name of war', thought Amira, dwelling on the notion of divisions that were formed before her very eyes.

Syria had become a victim, prey almost, to so much hate and destruction. Now nearing its 5th anniversary since the beginning of the civil war, Amira thought of how the last 5 years had modified into what some would define as 'hell on Earth' now.

Once deemed as a political and military heavyweight in the domain, Syria's affluent anamnesis, life story and highly momentous culture can be described as both elaborate and diverse. For centuries, since the time of the Ottoman Empire, and the split from the empire in the 16th century into a separate administration up until the Syrian civil war, Syria had been a stupendous caldron of different religions practised, different ethnicities living in harmony alongside others and different people from different walks of life all living in an air of friendship, concord and unity. Syria's majority was once Sunni Muslims, while 12 or more percent were Alawite Muslims and 4 percent Druze. Amira had Christian neighbours who were married and she often offered to babysit their children on her weekends when they wanted to go out. Within her town, there were also Kurdish civilians who made up the majority of the population of the northeast of Syria. Living in Syria for her whole life, Amira never had any problems as a Sunni Muslim whilst living around other religions.

Syria vaunted and flourished one of the oldest and most cultivated and Byzantine literacy traditions in the whole world, with an opulent folklore of mystical storytelling that Amira grew up around. Equally, poetry was also widely read, written and vocalised. Films had been produced in Syria since the 1920s and musicals were also very popular in the 40s. Now, all the cinemas, libraries and theatres were shelled by ISIS and other so-called 'Islamist' groups. Amira remembers going to the cinema theatre with Maliha every so often when their favourite films were showing. Now, all that was left were bittersweet memories of eating stale popcorn, drinking orange blossom juice and sneaking in Khalid and Hammad to watch movies with them.

The hustle and bustle of the city that maintained and concealed the life of Syrians were now supplanted with the eerie, grotesque taciturnity of weeping mothers and whimpers of orphaned children.

Now, in 2016, it was estimated that the population of rebel-held eastern Aleppo had been reduced to 300,000, whilst 1.5 million were living in government-held western Aleppo.

The attacks had been becoming a lot more frequent now and for Amira's family, living in Aleppo was no longer possible. Aside from the financial issues that Baba, Uncle Hussain, Khalid and Uncle Ahmed faced, the fear of hunger, poverty and poor housing accommodation were also deemed as obstacles. The government military troops were in constant combat to control and capture rebel-held parts of Aleppo and on the 25th of June, the Syrian Army and allied forces such as Iran and Russia, began their long-awaited North-west Aleppo offensive, with the eventual ambition being to cut off the Castello highway, which in turn would result in the severing of the last supply route for the rebels inside the city, thus entirely encompassing any remaining forces.

"The siege just means normal people like us are entrapped in this shithole. There's hardly any supply of food and water left!" roared Khalid, as he finally unleashed his angrier side.

"What is Assad playing at? What is he waiting for? For rebels to fucking surrender?" Khalid was now shouting with fury.

Amira heard Baba and Mama speaking of this yesterday. It was late July now, and the Syrian government forces had managed to disconnect the last rebel supply line coming from the north, and completely encircling Aleppo. However, within days, the rebels operationalised and launched a grand-scale counterattack south of Aleppo.

"It's a stupid endeavour! An attempt to open a new supply line into rebel-held areas of the city and cut off Assad's side," yelled Baba last night.

The whole campaign was possibly deciding the fate of the entire war.

"My friend in Turkey, he works as an aid worker. He settles refugees from all over the Middle Eastern countries. He will help us, Insha'Allah," Baba explains.

"How will we get there, exactly?" asked Uncle Hussain. The uncertainty and hesitation in his voice seemed insecure to Amira, as if he was doubting the whole idea of leaving Aleppo.

Baba began to explain the breakdown of the route.

"Idlib is first," he began.

"Idlib?! That's the most dangerous place to be right now!" roared Khalid promptly.

"The rebel towns in Idlib, they're also constantly at war with Assad's forces. Just the other day, the marketplace near the centre of Maarrat al-Nu'man was hit by an airstrike. I lost my friend, Naveed, in that bloody attack," Khalid yelled.

His father hushed him as Khalid was unaware of the fact that he was becoming louder and louder.

"Can't we travel from Aleppo to Kilis? It's an easier route to Turkey, isn't it?" asked Khalid.

"Refugees fleeing the regime from Aleppo in hope of crossing over to Kilis in Turkey are just being forced back with bullets and abuse and that is something I cannot risk. And another thing, I don't want to involve our families with smugglers and paying thousands just to cross a border. Everything will be done properly, which is why we will fly out to Turkey instead," explained Baba.

Amira listened on. The more they spoke, the more restless she became. She didn't know how to feel about the whole situation. She was fully aware that the state her country was in was deteriorating daily. She had been a witness to the injustice that had been occurring for years now within Syria, all in the name of war and conflict. September the 6th 2015, a barrel bomb killed 3 people and injured dozens in Ariha, Idlib. Ten days later, barrel bombs unjustly murdered 45 people in the al-Mashhad neighbourhood of Aleppo. The following day, barrel bombs killed 21 people in Bosra and again on the 26th, at least 5 people were killed in Taftanaz. The bombings would worsen each time, with more and more causalities.

Amira remembered the day she sobbed her heart out during October 2015 when she heard of the sickening attack on a school which was educating Palestinian refugees, killing innocent lives. 2016 alone had seen a recent bloodshed and they were prey to all the attacks taking place within Aleppo, Idlib and the surrounding areas. February was a long month, with horrendous attacks on hospitals in Al-Ghariya and East of Ghouta. Amira, like every other Syrian child, was no stranger to the ignorance of what war implanted in the youth of Syria. Rebels, Assad's young military forces, Islamic groups, all blinded by the colour of so-called freedom, oblivious to the shrieks of mothers and children in the darkest and most obscure of nights. To those who had lived their whole lives in Syria, like Amira and her family, they were all either preparing, undertaking or contemplating a mass migration season in hope for new land, new homes and new lives.

Amira sorrowfully listened to the conversation continue downstairs. Her heart sank more each time. She didn't know what she was afraid of. Was it fear? Fear of attacks on their journey to Turkey, or the fear of never seeing her loved ones again? Or was it just the fear of change? The fear of modification to her current life? The fact that she would no longer see her friends again, no longer see Maliha's resting place again, no longer wake up at 7.30 am every day to pray, eat breakfast and leave for school again, no longer visit Khalid in Shamsa Park again, no longer watch movies with Shakil and Adam again, no longer lay in her room and write poems again. The overall dismay and uncertainty of the unknown was the main reason for Amira's anxiety about travelling to a new home and settling. The place that she once considered 'home' was a complete opposite to the word. Though it were just bare walls and empty, sorrowful streets made of concrete and clay, to Amira, there was love there. There was love within the streets of Aleppo, within the towns and within the homes of Syrians.

"Idlib is dangerous, yes, I am aware. But we need to understand the risks and act accordingly," Baba explained to Khalid.

"The whole country is controlled by rebels; Assad and ISIS are dangerous Goddamit! Do we have any other choice?!" Baba's voice was deepened and becoming more aggressive. The atmosphere seemed tense.

"We travel to Idlib, then Lebanon. No other airport is in use, so we will fly from Beirut Rafic Hariri international airport and from there, it's a simple plane to Turkey and we are there. Inshallah, by God's will, we will reach there safe and sound."

Although Amira wasn't in the room, she could smell the bitter scent of pure frustration and uneasiness in the air. She could almost imagine the look on Baba's face, the vein on his forehead widening and fluctuating with apprehension.

"Is Amira awake, Uncle?"

Amira's hammering heart skipped a beat as her Baba replied;

"Amira? She should be...Why?" he replied to Khalid.

"There is something important I want to discuss and I want Amira to join us, please," Khalid responded.

Amira's heart twisted and sank as she heard her father's footsteps getting closer to the stairs. 'What important conversation did Khalid want to discuss? What was so important that he needed her there? Why in front of everyone?' So many questions filled Amira's mind. She quickly ran to her room before her father saw her sitting at the top of the stairs. She stumbled on her books and quickly jumped inside her bed.

The footsteps grew louder and finally, her father entered.

"Amira? Are you awake?"

For a moment, Amira ignored her father and pretended to sleep. But then, she was suddenly overcome with courage to face Khalid.

"Hmm, yes, Baba," she groaned, swallowing the large lump in her throat.

"Come downstairs, sweetheart, Khalid wants to see you."

Amira threw on her robe, fastened it at her waist and quickly tied her hair into a ponytail. She gulped as she dawdled down the stairs. She fingered her necklace that Khalid gave her for her birthday and fidgeted with the chain as she entered the room. Khalid was looking down.

She greeted the room and sat beside her father on the floor.

Khalid looked up, directly into Amira's eyes.

She felt a salty bead of sweat at the back of her neck and she rapidly wiped it away. They focused on each other's eyes. Khalid's dark hues of cinnamon darted back and forth, gleaming under the fire-lit lamp. His eyes held a secret passion, passion and urgency to erupt his feelings to everyone that night. Amira, despite sitting amongst her uncle, father and Khalid's father, continued to be enchanted by Khalid's eyes. She couldn't look away, not for a second. His gaze comprised of unrefined, raw sentiment and emotion. For a moment in time, the troubles of the worldly life were all forgotten whilst she was enthralled by Khalid's bewitching gaze.

Khalid spoke.

"I have been meaning to do this since the day I was old enough to understand the beauty of your daughter's love…"

Khalid motioned towards Baba and then at Amira.

No matter how warm the veins inside Amira's skin were, she couldn't help but completely freeze as Khalid continued to speak.

"She has shown me patience, endurance and guardianship. She has shown me love." Khalid pressed his slender fingers tightly against his forearms and looked up at Amira.

"As soon as we reach Turkey..." he gulped as he spoke to both Baba and his father.

Amira watched his face, then Baba's and then Uncle Ahmed's and Hussain's.

"As soon as we reach Turkey, I want to marry Amira."

▪▪

As the sunlight from dawn greeted the empty streets, the skies were brimming with amalgamated tinctures of toned blooming pinks and lemon yellows. The subtle welcoming of a new, fresh day. To Amira, it was the start of a new beginning. There was something about the prodigious sun that elevated the city. Every morning, the golden sun overlooked the damaged and wounded city and exploded the sky with alluring hues of citrus orange and amethyst purple. Amira caught a glimpse of sheer paradise that quickly faded into the demolition of her city.

Amira was awake at dawn. The restlessness she felt picked and poked at her throughout the ticking hours of the early sunrise. She sat up in her bed and studied the street outside her window. She recalled the memories of her past. She could just about see the side alley in which Khalid always pranked her. Those alleys and streets, and the walls around Amira were undoubtedly a home to not only her, but many others. Now, it was everything but. Aleppo seemed like a foreign, unidentifiable labyrinth, from which people knew no way out except departure.

7.45 am.

Amira's Baba entered her room, surprised at Amira already awake and ready.

"Amira? Did you sleep, my child?" he asked her.

"Baba...I couldn't."

Baba walked towards his daughter and hugged her like a baby.

"Do people think they will be left alone after saying 'We believe' without being put to the test?" Baba recited the words of the Prophet Muhammed's hadith.

"My child, he will never burden a soul more than he can endure." Baba stroked Amira's curls and soothed her with his softening words.

"I'm scared, Baba...I'm so scared," Amira cried into her baba's arms as she exhaled the pain out of her chest.

Baba lulled her quietly.

"I know, Amira, my princess, I know. We have to be strong. It's just me and you who are the strong ones. We need to stay strong for Mama and Adam, my child."

Amira wiped her tears and gave her father a faint, meaningless smile. In this despondency, there was no past or future for Amira, all she was doing was living every moment. She hadn't felt this type of pessimism before, and she hoped for a stronger will-power and resilience against this vanquishing.

"Come, child, get your things together," Baba whispered.

"And listen to me, don't you dare forget to bring your poem book, you hear me?"

Amira managed a feeble simper at her father and replied with her eyes.

"Of course, Baba, that will stay with me forever, wherever I go."

"That's my girl. Now come on, let's get the rest up."

Once everyone had their bags of clothes and belongings, Baba led both Amira and Mama for Salah.

"Allahu Akbar!" Baba delivered with verve.

Amira and Mama followed behind him as he prayed 2 Nafl Salah, asking aid from the Almighty before they set off on their journey. He finished and sat silently for a moment before breaking into a sorrowful supplication. He raised his hands and recited loudly as Amira and Mama stayed quiet with their hands also raised in Dua.

"Ya Rabi, I entrust my life, my children and my family in your supremacy," he began with a shaky voice.

Amira had her eyes closed and could hear her mother's doleful sniffling.

"Ya Allah, you are the Almighty, the one who hears our silent cries. Today, I pray for the innocent lives that have been lost during this carnage, I pray for their loved ones to be safe.

Indeed, you know what lies in every heart, so please aid the poor souls of the orphaned children living in exile, free the oppressed and give directorship and guidance to the oppressors. Protect our children, protect our religion and protect our customs and traditions and make this journey easy for us Ya Rab."

Baba exhaled.

"Ameen."

Uncle Ahmed, Aunty Nabeela and Khadijah arrived first. A few minutes later, Khalid and his brother and father also pulled up outside.

"Salam Ahmed, Hussain, Khalid," Baba greeted them and took them inside.

"We have three vehicles. That's more than enough space for all our stuff. Hussain, Ahmed, did you bring your ID documentation and passports?" Baba asks.

"It's all here, Hamza."

Baba's name, Hamza, was given to him by his great-grandfather, who worked as a poor cobbler in Aleppo. Despite knowing the nervousness behind Baba's voice, the qualms in his words and the dubiety in his undaunted smile, today was the first day where Amira saw Baba live up to his name, Hamza.

He was a lion, steadfast and strong-willed, as was the Prophet Muhammed's Uncle.

It is never a specific event that limits nor classifies who you are, but the attitudes and approach of those involved around you. Amira admired her father. He was the type of man to welcome a defiance with humbleness and a daring, valiant spirit.

"The documents are the most important things to bring. It's difficult proving identities when seeking asylum in a new country," Baba explained to everyone.

"I have them all, Uncle Hamza," Khalid beckoned from behind the men. He was fastening the laces on his heavy combat shoes.

Amira hadn't fully had a chance to take in the conversation Khalid had had the following night about wanting to marry her. She felt a mixture of things; content, tense, eager. She didn't know how to overcome these intense feelings; too much was going at once for her to properly adjust to everything.

Khalid was wearing his usual Syrian football top, black jeans and his keffiyeh scarf around his neck. He was now 22 years old and had grown into a tall, charming young man. He had the kind of looks that stopped Amira in her tracks. All the girls in the town fell for him, but Khalid never noticed, as he saw only Amira.

She greeted Khalid with a nervous smile and he gave her his cheeky wink, something that he hadn't done in a while. It seemed to have elevated Amira completely, for a small gesture gave her a boost of satiating comfort, despite the situation.

"Mira, you coming in my car?" he asked light-heartedly.

"I don't know, Khalid. Shall I?"

"Yeah, come with me...I'll get Baba and Shakil to go in your baba's car so we can be alone," Khalid cheekily grinned at Amira.

"We can take a detour and go the longer route," he teased mischievously.

Amira rolled her eyes and lightly punched his arm.

"Shush, Khalid," she laughed.

"I'm joking, Mira," he chuckled.

"Come on you two, hurry up, we are leaving!" Mama exclaimed from Baba's car.

Amira finished packing the car with her small rucksack of clothes, a hand carrier sack with books, shoes and other sentimental things like her poem book, a few of her favourite novels and old pictures. Amira hesitated for a moment as she contemplated whether she wanted to go back inside the house again, just for a moment or two, to properly say goodbye. The overpowering sensation of grievance and ache began defeating Amira again. She held in her tears as she looked back at her home for the last time, the home that she may never see again, the home that might end up being demolished sooner or later, the home which unforgettable memories resided in.

Everyone sat in their cars. No time was wasted, and within a blink of an eye, they were off.

Uncle Ahmed drove his jeep with his wife Nabeela and daughter Khadijah, whilst Khalid drove Uncle Hussain and Shakil. Khalid led the way, with Baba following and Uncle Ahmed behind.

Irresolutely, Baba drove off after taking a final glance at his home.

Mama sensed the dreariness in Baba's face and she squeezed his hand tightly.

"Hamza, God is with us," she spoke.

"It's for the best..." The words coming from Mama's mouth were just as forlorn as Baba's expressions.

Khalid drove down through the town city centre and the other two followed. It was often hard to catch up Khalid as he drove quite recklessly at times and far too fast. As they all made their way to Idlib, Amira observed the morning sky. Through the glass was the transitional, ever-changing ingenuity of the sky that always seemed to reject the fiascos and disasters that lay only below it. The few white clouds brought unbounded images of infinite splendours and artistry.

Then, Amira looked ahead, around, left, right, behind.

A ghost town, an abandoned city.

It was as if God himself had halted every clock in every home, and stopped time so that the removal of any worldly diversions would illuminate the broken town for what it really was, for what it was now. In that very moment, Amira looked at the broken homes of her town. The walls had long since disintegrated and as replacement towered condensed posts and pillars of blackened wood, crumbling clay bricks and carbonised timber from where the bombing had thrashed the houses. In some places, deeper into the town, before they entered the highway, black, sombre dust swayed in the air. Amira had to close her window as the smell of thick ash encroached on her lungs as she inhaled.

'War, like children's fights, are meaningless, pitiless, and contemptible'.

Amira remembered Ustadh Rumi's quote about war. Amira couldn't have agreed more with this quote.

Khalid's route passed by Shamsa Park. He had done this deliberately. He wanted to visit it, with Amira, one last time. Amira couldn't remember the last time she had been to Shamsa Park when it was safe. Both Khalid and Amira swiftly clambered towards their hill. Many trees had been shelled to the floor but Khalid and Amira found a tree to sit on that overlooked their city. To her surprise, the weeping willow tree that held many memories for both Khalid and Amira was still living and hadn't been destroyed in the attacks.

They both sat on a dead tree, dark ash motionlessly dispersed across the broken swings and slides, and knotted vines embedded themselves between the masses of destruction. The park was silent; too silent. Amira began feeling dispirited as the atmosphere seemed to haunt her.

"We had a lot of good memories here, Mira, didn't we?" Khalid finally spoke.

"And bad…," Amira responded, thinking back to that awful memory of Khalid shooting a police militant.

"Regardless… we grew up here, Mira. I can't help but feel depressed inside to leave all this behind."

"Do you think we will ever come back, Khalid?" Amira asked.

"I really hope so, Amira, I really do...and maybe, just maybe, we will return to this same willow tree if it is still standing."

Sadness overwhelmed Amira and she tried her hardest not to let it overcome her.

They sat there for a few minutes before finally making their way back to the cars.

Amira turned back one final time to gaze upon her childhood park.

As she sank into a deep daydream over past memories, she felt a part of her soul seal itself with an everlasting imprint on the walls and streets of her town, the swings of Shamsa Park, and the weeping willow tree that stood like a protective guardian, for this was the only departing gift she could present to her broken home of Aleppo.

CHAPTER EIGHT
Idlib 2016

The overall journey to the town of Idlib, which is a city located in north-western Syria, took roughly an hour and a half. Amira was in and out of sleep the whole journey. She was awake when they stopped off at Nabhan Pharmacy to get all the necessary medication needed for Mama and general medicine in case of an emergency. The pharmacy was barely standing. They all bought some cheap medication that they could afford for general pain relief.

Amira remembered waking up from her sleep when they were just passing Globe Circle roundabout. When they were crossing through Damascus Aleppo International Way, the families saw a few rebel fighters dressed in full camo clothing with Arab keffiyeh scarves around their faces. They held big guns, guns that Amira had never seen before.

During the Uprising back in 2011, Amira constantly heard that Idlib was the focal point of protesting and fighting during the early stages of the Syrian civil war. Khalid was the main information source from whom Amira learnt of such politics regarding the civil war.

"The war descended into army conflict, Mira, and rebels gained refuge within Idlib," he would tell her.

"It's all about gaining access to certain areas, certain highways, certain checkpoints within both Idlib and Aleppo. Everyone wants a piece of land to control; rebels, ISIS, the government...they want total control of the city."

After the 2015 Idlib offensive that occurred in March, the rebel federation union Army of Conquest, which was led by the group al-Nusra Front and Ahrar al-Sham, prospered in the second battle of Idlib and occupied the city, as well as laying siege to the Shi'a majority towns in North Idlib.

Khalid's friend, Rashad, lived in Idlib. Khalid went to visit him once when he heard of the newly established Army of Conquest group urging people within the city to stay indoors. Later that day, on the 24th of March 2015, Khalid was on his way home from visiting his friend when he heard of the suicide attack near the army checkpoints.

To Amira, the formation of all different groups was often far too complex and confusing for her to understand. It was difficult to fully ascertain the agendas on all the groups within Syria and what their aim was. Although the Free Syrian Army had a main goal of bringing down Assad and freeing people from his regime, people often argued otherwise in terms of their objective.

Everyone stopped off at the small park when they arrived in Idlib and Amira heard two men talking. Khalid, Baba, and both Uncle Hussain and Ahmed had gone to find a hostel to stay in for the night. The women were waiting in the park whilst Shakil and Adam played. Two elderly men entered the park, one smoking a pipe and the other chewing on tobacco.

"The real traitors are the Free Army, I tell you!" one blared.

Amira listened on.

"They turned this war into the mass execution of its own people! They've lost their morale completely and cannot fight!"

The man chewing tobacco replied, "They're just fighting against Assad; they think they are doing what is right. But tell me, what is right in this situation? What exactly is the right thing to do?"

"Assad? Ha!" the other man scoffed.

"This country, I tell you! The only party to contest in the election was the ruling party of Assad's and his damned presidency has and is continuing to turn this country to complete and utter ruin."

Amira stared at the men; both were no more than the tender age of 60. The man smoking a pipe had a fringe of silver, ashen hair around his receded balding scalp. He had a thin, shrunken face and his eyes were like dark black buttons. The other had a meek, feeble look on his shrivelling face that was half-covered by his thick, well-groomed moustache. His wide forehead presented several lines when he frowned or made any sort of facial expression.

"It is like the world war era, brother! Whole cities burnt down, buildings bombed, children killed by phosphorus gas and poisonous chlorine. Where is the shame? The humanity? The entire nation is under attack and Assad will not rest until he brings down his opposition. It isn't just war anymore, brother, it's a massacre, a cleansing of Sunni Muslims," the smoking man declared with intense anger in his voice.

Amira continued to eavesdrop. She couldn't help thinking... 'Assad, killing so many lives? Where was there shame and humanity left in this world?'

"His regime was afraid of losing control and restraint over us. Even in the most peaceful of times during the regime, there were abductions and imprisonments. Women, girls, mothers were abducted and raped during that so-called 'peaceful era'. This murderer has taken the lives of many, all for the sake of presidency and greed for authority and power."

The men walked off in the opposite direction to where Amira and her family were waiting.

She sat on a bed of old, brown grass and waited for the men. After some time, they arrived with bread, grapes and bottles of water.

"Good news! We have found a small hostel to sleep in tonight. We will drive to the airport early morning tomorrow," Baba exclaimed to the women.

"For now, let us eat."

They all sat around the park and nibbled on the stale bread and mouldy grapes and sipped warm water. Amira took a bite of the foul, sour grape and spat it back out. Money was tight for everyone. They money Baba had saved up had mostly been stolen from his pottery shop, Uncle Hussain's bakery was almost destroyed in attacks and raids and hardly anyone ever visited it and as for Uncle Ahmed, ever since the regular attacks within Idlib, Aleppo and Lebanon, he had stopped working altogether. The spare money they all had between them they needed for transportation gas, hostel costs, food and plane tickets to Turkey.

"Is it safe, Khalid?" Amira asked Khalid as they unpacked their cars for the hostel.

The hostel smelled of urine and damp rain. Inside, there was a middle-aged man who was wearing a royal blue and black uniform.

"The hostel? Course it is, Mira, I'll protect you," he replied.

"No, Khalid, I mean everything, all this…Idlib?"

Khalid paused for a moment.

"Mira… what is safe anymore? Just know, that regardless of any danger we come across, I will never let anything happen to you, okay?"

Amira sighed and looked around at her family. She couldn't help feeling despondent and agitated.

When her family all went inside, Khalid pulled Amira by her waist as he hid behind his father's car and tickled her. Amira chuckled and pushed him away playfully.

"Mira, everything will be okay, trust me," he said as he stroked her cheek.

"So…," Khalid stutters.

"I guess you're going to be my wife soon, eh?" he joked.

Amira suddenly blushed and looked down at her hands.

"You…you are happy, right, Amira? That I asked for your hand?" he questioned.

Amira looked up at his loving face and smiled.

"Of course, I am Khalid, is that even something you need to ask?"

Amira was more than excited to be Khalid's wife and to be with him forever. She had idolised the idea of marrying Khalid since she was old enough to understand the seriousness of their relationship and what they both meant to each other.

Khalid felt giddy with sheer excitement. He wanted to shout, run and tell everyone of his joy. He could hardly wait.

"I promise you, Mira, the day you marry me, I will make you forget all your worries. I promise."

■■

Later that evening, Baba, Mama, Adam and Amira all huddled up in their small, dusty hostel room. Mama and Baba had to share a single bed, whilst Adam and Amira took the mattress on the floor.

"Baba, why do Sunnis and Shias not get along?" Amira questioned late at night as she couldn't sleep.

Baba was also awake.

"Nonsense! We are all Muslims. But all these groups have their own identity, their own agenda. Brother kills brother, and a Muslim kills another Muslim," Baba replied.

"Assad wants to get rid of all the so-called 'bad seeds' from Syria. He doesn't want us to ever return back to our homeland."

Assad is a Shia Muslim and many Syrians have suggested his hatred towards other sects is the sole reason for the killings of so many Syrians within Aleppo, Idlib and other neighbouring towns, as the majority population is made up of Sunni sect

Muslims. In his recent speech, he detailed the theory of 'losing the best of the youth and infrastructure'. He also stated that it cost Syria a lot of money and sweat, however, the exchange revealed a victory of a healthier and more homogenous society in the true sense.

"Assad just wants a Syria that shares his traits and his views, that's all. The rest of us...well were just irrelevant," Baba replied, tiredly.

Amira thought to herself, 'Hitler was the same! He wanted an unvarying, uniform Germany, with the specific race, religion and beliefs.'

"Amira child, try to sleep now. We have a long day tomorrow," Baba yawned.

Amira couldn't sleep. For hours, she heard the ticking of the loud clock pinned on the wall. It was 3 o'clock in the morning. The rotting floorboards that Amira lay on creaked every time she moved. Adam, who was beside her, moved every other minute and the noise stopped her from sleeping.

She decided to take a walk.

She got up and put on her grey jumper and boots and left the room ever so quietly, trying her best not to make the floorboards sound too much. She left the door slightly open and went out. The draughty corridors smelt of damp and rainwater. The frosty air was swirling around her feet like a cold tide and the austere wind blew from outside. Amira strolled around the corridor until she reached a small window with a seat beside it. As she sat down, two small spiders scurried into the darkness of the alcoves on either side of the window ledge panels. Their webs were spread around and clinging to the walls.

Amira peered outside the window, onto the road. It seemed silent; apocalyptic almost. The darkness of the night overtook the beauty of the oak trees a few yards away from the hostel. Everything seemed more chilling in the murkiness of the midnight moon.

"Couldn't sleep either, huh?"

Khalid showed up wearing a vest and warm joggers.

Amira blushed.

"No...the floor was making too much noise, and Adam wouldn't stop kicking me," she laughed.

"Tell me about it! Shakil's the same."

He looked out of the window and then at Amira who got up to offer Khalid a seat. He sat down and then grabbed Amira and placed her on his lap.

Amira dug her face into his warm, musky neck and closed her eyes.

"Where is God?" Amira finally remarked, sarcastically.

"He is here, Mira, he is here."

Khalid sat up slightly to face Amira.

"God is everywhere, around us, within us, above us. He is seeing all the injustice, Mira, it is all a test." Khalid's voice suddenly became intense and serious.

"There was never such a thing as Shia, Sunni, Alawaite... It all started from these groups being introduced. We were never just seen as ONE, well, we were, until the death of the greatest men in Islam."

Amira pondered over what she had heard the two men talking about earlier in the park.

For those who saw Bashar Al-Assad as a murderer knew of Iran and Hezbollah's interference in aiding Assad in his crimes and making the inherent and intra-country rebellion into a more complex and sectarian, international issue. The issue could have been solved years ago, but it was more deliberately made a sectarian war by Iran. Amira thought for second of what her life would have been like if she had been born into a Shia home, where she wouldn't have had to flee her home and would have lived within the richer towns of Syria where Iran and Hezbollah and their sectarian militias weren't engaged in executing civilians rather than rebels.

Despite what the media had taught Amira, as well as other Syrians, she knew never to trust the words that escaped from that small, black box. She knew the media never fully stated the truth within the world. She did, however, on her own accord and own opinion, come to one conclusion regarding the war; that Assad's killer regime did nothing other than provide existence and a vital lifeline to nonconformist, sectarian terrorist organisations.

The notion that instilled ideology within the minds of many Syrians was that the Sunni Muslims within Syria were being targeted. This only gave life to recent Islamist groups such as ISIS and Al-Qaeda, who simply wanted to introduce the instilment and establishment of a 'Caliphate'.

Amira hadn't ever come across an ISIS member, despite them seizing large swathes of land stretching from central Iraq to northern Syria. Khalid had.

He had travelled once with his friend to attend a protest where he was confronted by members of ISIS who threatened them if they didn't join their cult and obey the rules according to Sharia Law. They both managed to escape by beating them and running.

"Khalid, there is Assad fighting rebels, rebels fighting Assad, ISIS fighting rebels and Assad. It's all a mess. How did it get to this before our very eyes?"

"Forget ISIS," he scoffed

"You call them Muslims? They haven't read a word in the Quran and they claim to bring back a Caliphate."

Amira listened as he spoke.

"Unjust killing, raping women and marrying them for a few hours, holding young men hostage until they join their fucking cult...There isn't an ounce of religion in them, because if there was, they would follow the so-called 'Sharia Law' that they preach and the ways of our Prophet. He never killed unjustly, nor did he hold anyone hostage! The man treated even captured enemies as royalty, for goodness sake." Khalid was becoming more and more angry as he spoke passionately regarding the doings of such groups.

"The truth is, they are just another fucking group claiming they know what's best for Syria. Makes me sick; bastards!"

Khalid was now silent. Amira could sense the irritation in his voice.

She was stroking his arm when she saw a black inked drawing on the top of his right bicep.

"What's this?" she asked.

It was a drawing of the Syrian flag encircled between the peace sign.

"My new tattoo," laughed Khalid.

Amira licked her finger and rubbed his arm, then her fingers became smudged with ink.

"Ha, if only," Khalid smirked.

Khalid was an exceptionally brilliant artist and drew the most amazing images, portraits and scenery.

"I'm getting one soon, though, when we reach Turkey," he said.

"Err, why would you do that? Besides, it's Haram," Amira retorted.

"Why not? It looks cool, no? And it impresses the ladies."

"Who you trying to impress?" Amira questioned.

Khalid chuckled at Amira's sudden outburst before grasping her into his embrace, his warm, protective arms around her frail body.

"Mira, you know I only have eyes for you…you know my heart beats only for you, to see you smile and happy and you know you're the only girl in this world I want to impress every day."

Amira squeezed Khalid back tightly as the world around her melted away. She lay there, on his lap, not wanting that bittersweet moment to end.

"I love you, Mira, I love you."

▪▪

The following morning, everyone woke up at 8 am, ate the breakfast provided by the hostel and left to continue their journey. Baba took a handful of nuts in his pockets for the journey and Khalid managed to find cheap bottles of juice in a nearby shop. He also picked up some apples, oranges, bread and cheese.

By 10 am they were all ready, dressed and on their way to Lebanon. It took nearly 5 hours to drive down to Lebanon and a further 30 minutes to the international airport.

When they departed on the journey to Lebanon's capital, Beirut, they stopped off at a gas station for necessities and oil. The Rafic Hariri International Airport is located in Lebanon's capital and is where the families planned to catch their flight to Turkey.

At the gas station, they picked up essentials such as plasters, sanitary towels, some almost rotten fruit, dried nuts and fruit and some gas for the cars.

Amira played with the necklace that Khalid had gifted her and scribbled in her poem book. Every so often, she dozed off then wakened again due to Adam's shrilling.

"Adam! Stop all the noise, for goodness sake," Amira snapped out of annoyance.

Baba returned to the car with the bags of essentials, filled the car with oil and set off, following Uncle Ahmed and Khalid in front. Amira caught a glimpse of the trees swaying in the summer heat, dancing with their fresh-blossomed flowers. Despite being chilly last night, the weather the following day was humid and muggy. Mid-May till August in Syria were the months of mild heatwaves and warm afternoons.

They all drove for 20 minutes or so down the M4 in Arihah and eventually reached a roundabout, where they took the third exit onto the highway 60a. After they had driven for a few minutes down 60a, they were halted by a queue of traffic. The traffic jam seemed to have grown in size within minutes. Everyone got out their cars to be told to wait until further notice. Amira sat on the roof of her car to see the commotion at the front of the traffic. There seemed to be a blockage stopping anyone travelling further down the 60a highway. She also saw men wearing combat uniform; Assad's men. She gulped and jumped off the car.

"What's going on, Khalid?" she asked.

"I don't know, Mira; the bastards blocked the roads. Let me go and find out."

Amira clenched Khalid's arm tightly and pushed him back.

"No, Khalid! Leave it, please. Wait here till we find out from someone else," she pleaded, overcome with a disgusted feeling of nostalgia about the incident in Shamsa Park.

"Mira, I'll be two minutes," he promised.

116

But before she even had the chance to reply, shots were fired.

The moment played out in slow motion. Amira remembered seeing a mob of people running in whatever direction they assumed was safe. The uproarious sound of the single firearm shot was followed by 4 more. The noise resonated in Amira's ears and rang out in the distance.

Amira looked around and found herself trapped in the frenzy. People were sprinting in every direction, leaving their cars and running. She caught a glimpse of her baba, who was pulling Mama's arm and holding Adam in his arms. Khalid held Shakil, followed by Uncle Hussain and Uncle Ahmed, his wife and daughter. They ran in the opposite direction to their car, into a small intersection of the highway. Amira followed as she ambled through the herd of scared civilians. Her stomach lurched as she smelled the gunpowder from the shots fired. Adrenaline pulsated around her body as she tried to catch up with her family in front of her, but she was dragged back by her clothes as others pushed past her selfishly.

Finally, she reached her family, who had found a quiet spot on the side of the highway. Amira gasped as she caught sight of Aunty Nabeela. A single white, barbed end of a broken bone carved through her pale ankle and foamy blood ran fast in a thick crimson stream. Uncle Ahmed, Khadijah, Mama and Baba were circled around her whilst Khalid calmed Adam and Shakil. Aunty Nabeela let out an unearthly howl as her husband struggled to help her.

Amira turned to Khalid.

"What on Earth, Khalid?" she shivered.

"She fell and got trampled on. It was a fucking stampede back there," he answered.

"Lucky to make it out alive, especially with these two," he gestured at both boys who were sitting on the floor, panting loudly.

"Her leg, Khalid, the bone is coming out! I can see it! What are we going to do?!" Amira's heartbeat became louder inside her chest and she sensed a panic attack. The screams of pain from her aunty Nabeela further intensified her feeling of anxiety.

Before Khalid could answer, Baba rushed to them both.

"Right, Amira, stay here with the boys. Khalid, come with me and your father to get the cars. We need to get to the hospital as soon as possible," Baba instructed.

Khalid handed over the boys to Amira and ran towards the direction in which the stampede was slowly drifting.

Mama, who was close to tears, grabbed Amira by the arm and let out numerous deep sighs.

"Government forces..." she panted.

"Assad's men, firing shots in broad daylight. Have they no shame?"

Aunty Nabeela cried in disbelief as she stared at her bloodied ankle. Her shrieking made Amira's blood run cold. She looked on as Uncle Ahmed and Khadijah tried their best to comfort Aunty Nabeela, whose eyes were reddened with tears and whose shirt was soaked with sweat. She panted loudly at intervals and tried to reduce her screams inside her sleeve but they became even louder as a slight flinch on her ankle caused her agony.

Khalid, Baba and Uncle Hussain returned with all three cars. They wasted no time and rushed to the cars. Uncle Ahmed and Baba lifted Aunty Nabeela and laid her on the back seat of the car. Khadijah sat on the last seat at the foot of her mother and cried quietly as her mother continued to whimper in anguish.

Amira buckled Adam, Shakil and herself into her baba's car.

"We need to quickly travel to Idlib National Hospital; it isn't too far from here so we can make it before Nabeela gets any worse," Baba panted as he started the car and reached for his seatbelt.

"Oh Ya Allah, please Hamza, hurry up," Mama replied.

Amira kept her eyes on both Khalid's car and Uncle Ahmed's in front of them as they lead the way. She glanced over at Shakil and Adam, who somehow suspected the angst in Baba and Mama's behaviour. Amira despairingly attempted to bury how apprehensive she felt as she sank into her car seat and took regularly deep gulps down her dry neck. She could somewhat control the tremble in her voice to a degree as she distracted the boys.

The journey to Idlib National Hospital took no longer than 20 minutes. The towns on Idlib seemed ghostly almost, with nearly every large building having been torn to the ground by airstrikes. All that remained were spiritless remains of buildings windows, doors, bricks and furniture.

At the hospital, everyone went in to find help for Aunty Nabeela. Her husband, Ahmed, carried her in and checked her in. The check-in took almost 2 hours. The swarm of injured people congested the hospital corridors like sardines in a tin. The river of yelling civilians was all moving in the same direction, to be checked in and given a bed. Aunty Nabeela's bone protruding out of her flesh seemed minor compared to the other injuries Amira saw within the walls of the hospital. Some had their eyes bulging out, others had fingers missing, one man even had the side of his face burnt off from shelling and militant raids. There hadn't been shelling for a few weeks, so Amira asked Baba, puzzled,

"How did they get those injuries? I haven't heard of any airstrikes for a few weeks."

Baba looked into her pure auburn eyes.

"Amira, they have been waiting here for days, since the airstrike on the 26th of May. They still haven't been seen."

Amira blinked. She looked around her into the depths of the hospital's corridors as the injured men and women, children and babies had dark, drying blood crumbling off their skin.

"So how long till Aunty Nabeela is seen and cared for?" Amira queried.

"She is already checked in, my sweetheart, don't worry, she will be fine in no time. The lady at the reception, she checked Nabeela into a room and she is sharing her bed with another woman so it's okay, she won't wait much longer now."

Amira went into the room Aunty Nabeela lay in. Mama was beside her, lulling her to sleep as she was attached to a long IV drip which gave her regular sedation and strong pain relief. The bone in her leg still hosted itself within her purpling skin. Amira looked around the room with disbelief at the sights of urine and blood on the dirty floors, women half-dressed and panting for pain relief top-ups and babies shrieking at the top of their lungs. The timid woman beside Aunty Nabeela had her arm in a sling and her face covered in dried blood. Every so often, she gasped in pain, revealing her chipped teeth and decayed gums. The putrid stench of urine and blood hung in the atmosphere amongst the corridors and rooms and mould and fungi showed signs of monstrous growth along the smutty walls of the hospital. Amira went out of the ward to her father and Adam. The howling of people went on for hours and showed no sign of stopping anytime soon. The noise became too much for Amira at one point so she decided to go for a walk.

The warmth of the summer evening's wind hailed Amira's face as she left the hospital doors. Under the seasonal sun, she felt the last of the heated rays above her as the golden, tangerine sky greeted the city. Amira strolled along the road till she saw Khalid sitting on a bench beside a corner shop. Adam and Shakil played naively across from him with some marbles and sticks, unaware of what was happening around them. She walked over to Khalid, sat beside him and didn't say a single word. Exhaustion and frustration overtook her to the point where words didn't mean anything in comparison to her feelings.

"What you thinking, Mira?" Khalid asked as he watched the boys play with their marbles and sticks.

Amira sat silent for a moment. She shrugged and exhaled quietly.

"She will be okay, Mira, don't stress, eh."

"I'm okay, Khalid," she replied. Her voice was frail and Khalid would hear the slight annoyance in her tone as she replied.

"Smile...?" Khalid joked, trying to lighten the mood.

Amira didn't flinch and continued to stare at her hands.

"Hmm, like that now, is it? Watch, I'm going to make you smile before I reach number 1..." he playfully teased.

Amira knew she was going to end up falling for his silly joke. Since they were young, Khalid's way of making Amira smile was always counting down from 3 and before he reached 1, she always gave in.

"Ready? 3..." he impishly babbled.

Amira turned to face him.

"2..."

He didn't have to reach 1 before Amira scoffed and broke into a light-hearted smile.

"Hah, what did I tell you?! Mira, is there going to ever be a day you let me get to 1 and don't actually smile? Hmm, I don't think so! Do you?"

Amira nudged Khalid with her shoulder.

"Whatever, Khalid," she whispered, as Khalid embraced her tightly so that her head rested on his shoulder.

Amira closed her eyes as she inhaled an immense breath of his soothing scent. She pressed her face deep into the warmth of Khalid's neck and closed her eyes. Khalid held her tight as she rested.

"Mira…" he whispered.

"Hmm?" she replied.

"I can't wait to marry you, Mira…."

For the first time ever, Amira was unfamiliar with the tone in which Khalid spoke. The shyness behind his words, the modesty in his speech and the coyness in his behaviour. She sat up and looked at Khalid, who instantly looked away to avoid eye contact.

"Why…?" she asked, smiling at his modest conduct, something Amira hadn't witnessed before as all she was used to was Khalid's pranks and jokes.

Khalid looked away, trying to distract himself by watching the boys, till he finally made eye contact with Amira.

Her golden eyes were glassy under the setting sun and her lips perched into a slight smile. Khalid watched her lips as she pressed them slowly and touched her face with the back of his hand.

Amira closed her eyes as he stroked her cheek and then untied her ponytail to let out her blonde locks. He had always liked her with her hair down.

"You know I'm no good with words, Mira. But all I can say is, I want to be with you. Ever since we were young, I looked forward to seeing you, and that hasn't changed, even till today."

Amira listened as he spoke delicately whilst peering deeply into her eyes.

"In you, I see everything; my future, my life, my good and my bad. I see the chance for that type of love that others joke about and tell you it doesn't exist or survive anymore. The one that scopes greater than one lifetime. That's what I see when I'm with you and what I feel when you're not around…"

Amira's smile faded into an affectionate glimmer. She always liked when Khalid teased and pranked her as it was his way of showing his love, but she had never seen this side of him. She didn't want him to stop talking.

"There's something in the way you smile, the way you laugh, the way you look at me that reminds me of my better self."

Khalid could see Amira's cheeks glowing a heated rosy colour and she tried supressing her bashful smile.

"You know me, Mira, being this open and telling you all this is not me. Like I said, I ain't good with words like you. You're the poetical one here. But, yeah…I hope I didn't sound too cringey." Khalid blushed and looked away.

Amira looked ahead, still smirking.

"Khalid…" she spoke, shyly.

Khalid looked at her.

"Love you too, Khalid…" she uttered demurely.

They both looked away and watched the boys play, still grinning to themselves.

After a moment, Khalid spoke, being his childish self again.

"I mean how could you not love me? I'm like the sexiest person alive."

Amira chuckled and ran her hand across his head, messing up his perfect curls from his bun.

Khalid grabbed her arm and tickled her till she shrieked with laughter. She tried to run away but Khalid grabbed her by the waist and lifted her playfully.

"KHALID! IM GOING TO FALL!" she yelled.

"Yeah...? Don't play a game if you can't finish it then," he laughed.

"Khalid! Let me down, come on."

Khalid let her down and she mischievously slapped his face.

"That'll teach you for messing up my sexy hair."

"Oh, whatever," Amira scoffed.

Khalid grabbed Amira and kissed her lips quickly before the boys could see. She kissed him back and giggled as he moved away, snickering.

"What's so funny exactly?" she demanded as he flaunted his foolish smirk proudly across his face.

"Nothing..." he said.

"No, go on... What you stupidly laughing at?"

"Nothing…" he said.

"Just, you have soft, juicy lips. Wanted to carry on kissing them," he said, flirting.

Amira smiled from ear to ear and slapped Khalid's shoulder playfully.

Khalid winked at her and went to play with Adam and Shakil. Amira watched as he grabbed a flat football from near the pavement and kicked it to them. For years, Amira had loved Khalid. Falling for Khalid was the purest thing Amira felt. To her, it felt like entering a house and finally feeling as if she were home. The peculiar feeling felt eccentric almost, the feeling of love and being loved. Amira felt it spread through her whole body, overpowering her, making her feel complete.

She gazed around the pavements, at the ruined buildings around her. The once vibrant streets of Idlib that Amira remembered from school trips to the cinema and family picnics with Baba, Mama and Adam felt like a foreign town. The walls were painted with bullet holes and the grey clouds cast a cadaverous spell over the city. Near the hospital was a ragged mountain of rubble, wreckage and destroyed remains of hospital beds.

The boys played on despite the destruction surrounding them, a semi-sweet scene that Amira couldn't turn her eyes away from; the innocence and purity of the game they all enjoyed around the horrific, extinction of life in the city. Amira remembered Rumi's quote at that very moment.

'Never lose hope, my dear heart,
Miracles dwell in this invisible'.

This quote couldn't relate more to how Amira was feeling. Losing hope peaked upon Amira many times, yet it was the sheer sense of belonging and devotion she felt for Khalid, for their life together in the future in a new home and for the affection he showed to her that got her through the most dismal of days. Just like Rumi's quote, the invisibility cloak of companionship and intimacy both Khalid and Amira shared was what never made her lose hope.

Amira whispered to herself...

"Yes Ustadh Rumi, miracles do dwell in the invisible."

▪▪▪

When Amira went back into the hospital, her aunty Nabeela was under heavy sedation and her bone is still in the same position it had been hours ago. Khadijah was sat beside her mother, preventing her from rolling off the bed as every so often, the other woman dug her arm into Aunty Nabeela, and Uncle Ahmed was at her bedside, his head resting on her arm and falling in and out of sleep.

"Mama, how long are we staying here? The boys are getting restless now and hungry," Amira asked.

"Amira, sweetheart, I can't tell, maybe a few days, hopefully," her mother replied.

"A few days, Mama? Where will we sleep? There isn't a hostel or anything for miles around."

Amira began feeling angered by the situation and the pushing and shoving from the other patients didn't help. She snapped at one man who pushed past Mama in an attempt to use the bathroom and ended up nearly toppling her over.

Just then, Baba and Khalid walked in with Uncle Hussain with some bread, oranges and a pot of hummus with a few green olives.

"Good news! We found a small building that used to be a library. They're allowing people to stay there for the night," Uncle Hussain told Amira and Mama.

Amira looked at Khalid, who rolled his eyes out of annoyance. Neither he nor Amira fancied staying the next few nights cramped up with other people in a dusty building.

"It's either there or the cars!" snapped Uncle Hussain, looking at Khalid's face.

"Yes, Baba, as you command," Khalid replied sarcastically.

Amira shook her head and mouthed to Khalid to stop answering back. Khalid sighed and handed Amira and Mama the food.

"Have some, feed the boys and then Amira and I will take them to the building to sleep. They're getting tired now it's almost 10p m," Khalid told Mama.

Adam and Shakil scoffed the oranges down and Khalid had managed to find cartons of apple juice from a local, derelict corner shop. After they ate, Amira left the hospital with Khalid to help take the boys back to rest in the building. It was nearing the end of the day and the glow from the sun was slowly plunging itself into the murky clouds, draining the few rays of light from the day and giving way to the lustrous darkness of the night.

The building, which was once a library, didn't look like much from outside. Before they entered, Amira noticed the burnt bullet holes on the wooden entrance doors, holes that were big enough to see right through to the side. This made her feel nervous. The building that was once filled with books and people now resembled something that had been through hostility. It looked a complete mess from inside. The windows were messily boarded up, the squalid wooden doors were peeling and bolted with iron rods. It almost reminded Amira of a prison as it looked threatening enough.

The hall had no doors nor rooms separating it, so it meant that everyone had to sleep together in their own corners and sections of the hall. To Amira's surprise, there were a few sofas that had survived, although they were occupied by other people in the hall. It was packed and stuffy. There were large families, small families and singular individuals all staying in the building. The hall had barely any light and the only source of light were rays from the midnight sky stealing through the boarded-up windows.

"Mira, it's smelly here," Shakil moaned to Amira whilst treading past the people sleeping on the floor.

"I know, Shakil, but it's only for a few days, I promise. Okay?"

"Nooo, I want to go home," cried Shakil.

He began to tear up and sniff away his teardrops.

Amira knelt down to face Shakil and wiped his tears and embraced him in a motherly hug.

"How about a bedtime story, eh? Would you like that?" she hushed.

Both Adam and Shakil's eyes lit up and they nodded continuously.

"Can we have the one about when Ertugrul Gazi was nailed into his hand, Mira?!" Shakil exclaimed excitedly.

"Of course! Come on, let's find a spot to rest first."

Shakil and Adam both loved listening to Amira's stories. Her poetic way of reciting different stories left them in awe every time.

Khalid found a small, cramped spot, just enough for the boys to lay freely in. It was beside a broken table that had only 3 legs and which had old, hardened chewing gum underneath it.

Shakil and Adam lay on the sheet that Khalid had brought from the car beforehand and rested their heads on a random, unattended cushion left on top of the broken table.

Khalid rested against the wall whilst Amira sat across him with both boys in between them.

"Okay. Shall I start, boys?" she asked.

"Yes, yes, yes, yes!" clapped Shakil and Adam.

"Ertugrul Gazi was a ferocious, mighty and extremely brave Turkish warrior," began Amira. All the boys were glued to her face, especially Khalid, who also loved listening to her stories but never liked to admit it.

"He was the son of beloved Sulayman Shah, who was leader of the Kayi Tribe during the 13th century. Ertugrul's son, Osman, went on to become the founder of the great Ottoman Empire."

"What's Ottoman Empire again, Mira?" asked Shakil, innocently.

"The Ottoman Empire ruled a large portion of the Middle East and Eastern Europe. They ruled for over 600 years!" she told them.

"What! 600?! That's like, so many years, isn't that right, Khalid?" the bewildered Shakil asked Khalid.

"Hmmm, you bet," Khalid replied, eagerly.

He winked at Amira as she continued.

"So anyway, Osman's father, Ertugrul Gazi, was a brave warrior and he was always finding different challenges being thrown at him. He had to do the right thing to always protect his tribe and find peace for his people. So, when they were under the threat of the fire-worshipping Mongols, Ertugrul faced many hardships. Who remembers the name of the infamous, evil leader who hated Ertugrul?" Amira asked.

"Noyaaa, Noyaaa!" shrieked Adam as he grinned brightly.

"Yes, Adam, Noyan!" Amira replied.

"Baiju Noyan was a Mongol commander who was appointed by Ogedei Khan, who was the 3rd son of the malicious leader, Genghis Khan. He was entrusted to expand the Mongol Empire. Now Noyan, well, he loathed Ertugrul. He wanted him dead and once, when his tribe managed to capture him, they took him deep into a dark forest and kept him as a prisoner.

"Why the forest, Mira? Did he live there?" asked Shakil.

"Yes, Shakil. They did. The troops, led by Noyan, retreated to the forest close to the Turkic Tribes because, during that time, there was a major split within the Mongol Empire," Amira replied.

"They took Braveheart Ertugrul Gazi into their haven and tortured him, beat him and caused him so much harm."

"No! Why, Mira? WHY!?" cried Shakil, looking instantly saddened at Amira's words, despite having heard this story numerous times.

"They weren't believers; they didn't fear God. Then one day, they tied the Gazi to a thick, wooden pillar. He had one arm tied to one pillar and the other was free. The wicked leader Noyan grabbed Gazi's free arm and placed it against the other wooden pillar and with all his force, nailed a thick, metal nail right into the middle of his soft hand!"

The boys gasped and even Khalid winced at the thought.

"Mira, no, that's not fair! How could they be so cruel, Mira!" yelped Shakil.

Khalid spoke.

"That's life, Shakil, there are people in this world who are cruel, people who hurt others without fearing God." He looked forlorn in his expression as he spoke and Amira guessed he was saddened by the situation they were all in.

"But it's okay, Shakil, because guess what? Ertugrul freed himself by yanking out the metal nail from his hand and escaping into the forest! He returned back to his tribe and his hand even got healed!" Amira energetically whooped, causing both boys to clap in victory.

Khalid chuckled under his breath at the boys.

"When I grow up, I'm going to be just like Ertugrul Gazi, Adam!" said Shakil.

"Gazi, Gazi," replied Adam, merrily.

"Okay, boys, that's enough for today, let's get some rest now."

Amira placed the thin sheet over both boys as they lay between both Khalid and Amira, sharing a single cushion between them.

Before they knew it, both boys were asleep.

"They're exhausted, look at them," Amira told Khalid.

"I don't blame them," Khalid replied.

"You rest too, Mira, I'll keep watch if anything happens."

"Nah, I don't feel tired, Khalid, in fact, I'm wide awake."

Khalid yawned every other minute and his eyes were bloodshot red.

"Khalid, you sleep, I know you're tired. It's okay, I'm awake for now."

"Hmm..." Khalid murmured under his breath as he rubbed his eyes.

"Mira…?" he called.

"Yes?"

"Read me one of your poems, Mira…" he requested.

Amira grinned.

"Okay, which one?" she asked.

"Any Mira, any. I love them all."

And with that, Khalid placed his head on Amira's lap and closed his eyes. Amira placed her hand on Khalid's forehead and rubbed it gently before clearing her throat and reciting her poem, the poem she had written for Khalid a while back.

> *"If all the tulips in Heaven misplaced their bloom,*
> *And the roses, when pressed, lost all their perfume,*
> *Long after the loyal daylight exits and leaves even paradise forlorn,*
> *And after infinite, celestial twilights are proudly born,*
> *When my lips no longer utter of my devotion and love,*
> *And when the final day appoints for my demise,*
> *I shall sit beside the angels and look down from above,*
> *And guard you closely and redeem your cries.*
> *For my love for you is simply ever-lasting,*
> *As it is buried deeply within my soul,*
> *For such a love like this, has no passing."*

Amira looked down at Khalid as she ruffled her fingers through his hair and caught him smirking to himself as he drifted off into a deep sleep. She smiled and continued to watch him as he breathed gently with his mouth closed and arms crossed over on top of his chest. He murmured and mumbled every so often in his sleep, at which Amira lulled him tenderly. It wasn't long before Amira's eyes began to close and her thoughts began to disintegrate into the silence of the night. She was resting against the wall where Khalid had been whilst she was reciting the story to the boys. Khalid was still on her lap, asleep. After the frenetic evening at the hospital, Amira sank into a composed siesta and rested.

That was, until the bomb hit.

CHAPTER NINE

The messenger of Allah said:
"How blessed is al-Sham (Syria)!"
The companions around him asked: "Why is that O Prophet of Allah?"
The messenger replied:
"O joy to Syria! O joy to Syria! O joy to Syria! I see angels of Allah spreading their wings over al-Sham".

Amira took in the traumatism, physically vision-impaired amidst all the uproar. Slowly, she began to overcome the fuzziness within her eyes which were full of dust and found herself kneeling on the ground, gripping her chest tightly. She looked around to see Khalid holding both Shakil and Adam's hands and dusting off their clothes, whilst also being in a state of frenzy himself. Khalid's eyes were wide open in shock and trauma as he looked around him. He gazed towards Amira, who panted deeply to avoid herself from panicking and having an attack of anxiety.

The ferocious howling that was heard constantly from people inside the building and from the streets was a sound that made Amira's heart sink. As she managed to get herself up from the floor, she looked around to see the furniture upturned and doors and windows free from iron rods and barricading.

"AMIRA!" Khalid yelled as he guided the boys towards the crowd of people near the exit.

"AMIRA, THIS WAY!"

Amira rubbed her dusty eyes and grabbed onto Khalid's shirt. They were making their way towards the door when suddenly, she fell onto a piece of broken window glass and cut her knee. She flinched in pain as hot blood ran down her leg beneath her trousers.

"Mira, give me your hand," said Khalid, pulling her up and making sure she was okay.

"Are you okay, Mira?"

"Yes, Khalid! What is it? What's going on?" she cried.

Khalid didn't answer but instead, gestured her to continue to walk towards the exit doors. As they managed to bundle past the crowd, Amira looked out into the midnight darkness.

Her heart skipped a beat.

In the distance, she saw Idlib National Hospital hit by an airstrike. She felt faint but somehow managed to stop herself from falling. She screamed at Khalid and ran towards the remains of the building.

"KHALID! MAMA, BABA, UNCLE, THEY'RE ALL IN THERE, KHALID! KHALID! PLEASE, KHALID, TELL ME THEY'RE NOT IN THERE!" she yelled at the top of her voice and heated tears ran down her cheek repeatedly. Khalid was also bawling in anguish and he dropped to the ground.

Adam and Shakil were crying and holding onto Khalid.

"Baa..ba.." Khalid murmured, drearily.

His sobbing sounded primal, a sound that made Amira want to sink deep into the ground.

"Baba..?" Khalid mourned, sitting dejectedly on the floor, staring ahead at the hospital.

Amira had never experienced this trauma before; it caused a painful feeling of grief and sorrow deep within her heart. It was as if the pain inside her was physical, as if her heart was being squeezed tightly.

The swarm of people around Amira, Khalid and the boys were all rushing towards the building. Men were chanting 'ALLAHU AKBAR, GOD IS THE GREATEST' as a reminder that God is everlasting and eternal. Men ran towards the site, pushing past Amira and tripping her over.

Amira wiped her face and sniffed. Her nose began to bleed. She grabbed Khalid's arm and helped him up.

"Come on, we need to find them, Khalid, please, come on!"

Khalid rose and took Adam and Shakil's hands. He led the way with Amira following behind them. She tried catching up as every so often a herd of people got in between her and Khalid. She held his shirt tightly until they reached the hospital.

When they arrived, neither the entrance nor the exit was distinguishable in the mammoth mountain of rubble. The only way Amira somewhat recognised where the entrance was by looking at the broken bench where Khalid and she had sat only this morning. It was situated right in front of the hospital.

Without realising, Amira was sobbing uncontrollably. The world had paused around her; she could hear the sound of her beating heart drumming inside her chest and the throbbing pulsation in her ears. The shriek of the airstrike still rang in her ears. She ran towards the site, pushed past others and immediately started digging with her hands through the bricks. She didn't wait for Khalid, nor did she think of anything except drilling her way through the debris to attempt to find them, anyone, Mama, Baba, Khadijah, whoever she could. She picked out bricks and chucked them behind her. Her hands began to bleed from broken pieces of glass and she got splinters from the wooden doors that were left cracked into smithereens. She wept as she set out to find her family and until her eyes had no tears left.

She didn't hear Khalid calling her, nor did she hear the aid workers asking her to move from the area of destruction. The rescue workers from the Syrian Civil Defence wore white helmets which had torches on them. It was dark, and their torches were the only source of light for miles. All other streets lamps had been destroyed.

"Amira, get down from there! It's dangerous!" called Khalid as she travelled higher up onto the mountain of wreckage.

She didn't hear him. She took a step further each time and dug deeper as she lifted brick after brick. She secured her foot slightly higher, not realising the brick was loose. Amira fell to the ground at least 2 feet from where she had been climbing and a deep wound was sliced across her arm. Burning vermilion blood flowed down Amira's arm and across her trousers and shirt. She groaned deeply in pain and pressed her finger against the open wound. The pain got worse and Amira sucked in a sharp breath as the agonising ache coiled around her body.

"AMIRA!" yelled Khalid as she fell to the ground, almost unconscious. He clutched her against his body and wailed like a baby.

An aid worker rushed to them and asked them to remove themselves from the area so that they could begin a search for trapped bodies beneath the rubble.

"Brother, you need to move! We need the area empty so we can bring in the digger to remove the debris," an aid worker instructed him.

Khalid sat there, with Amira in his arms and Adam and Shakil sat on either side of him. Both boys were now becoming more and more anxious around their elder siblings.

Khalid looked up and lifted himself and Amira up to.

"Amira, come, we need to move from here so they can do their work. They will find them, I promise, I know they will." Khalid pleaded for Amira to stay strong.

Amira lifted herself up with Khalid's help and they stumbled to an empty area on the grass a few yards away from the hospital. They took a seat on the ground and Khalid ripped his sleeves off to wrap them around Amira's bloodied arm. She cried in pain and she could just about regain sufficient consciousness.

Every so often, she broke into doleful lamenting and clutched onto Khalid until she fell into a deep sleep. The pain surrounded her body, yet it helped her to fall asleep.

When she woke up, she heard loud noises coming from the rubble. People were all running in that direction as the aid workers began chanting 'ALLAHU AKBAR'. Khalid stood beside the boys, watching what was happening. He turned and his eyes lit up when Amira awakened.

"Amira! Come on! They found a body! Get up, come on!"

Amira instantly jumped up despite the pain in her arm and ran in the direction of the crowd.

People swarmed past her and pushed her but she didn't stop till she reached the front.

She got to the front of the crowd and watched as the aid workers with white-torched helmets were digging. She held her breath as 3 aid workers pulled out a lifeless body from the bricks. A spiritless girl, no older than 4 years, escaped the darkness of the hell beneath her. The workers and people surrounding the scene chanted louder as she let out a cry.

"ALLAHU AKBAR, SHE'S ALIVE!"

Then, more workers arrived and ran towards the building. They found more bodies and began to help with getting them out. The world buzzed around Amira as she stood still, almost paralysed. She thought of her family beneath the hard layers of debris, her aunty with her broken ankle, her baba with his bad back, her mama, and her uncles. They didn't stand a chance. Dread crawled over her like a poisonous snake, leaving an icy spell over her body.

Her heart fell.

An aid worker pulled out a man wearing a green shirt and brown ripped trousers. His eyes were closed and his hands curled. Blood was running from his ear and wetting his shirt.

Baba.

Amira dropped. In that very frozen state of mind, she was thinking only one thing. Baba is dead. Baba is dead, Mama is dead and everyone else is gone. There is no obviating nor eliminating the thought of the unknown fears that lie ahead for Amira.

Khalid ran to Amira as she sat enervated on the floor. She wailed as the workers placed Baba onto a stretcher and covered his face with a white cloth. She wailed till she could wail no more. Her throat ached as unearthly shrieks flew from inside her.

"Amira," Khalid lulled. He didn't have much to say, for no words could aid the sorrow of both of them.

Suddenly, military and what seemed like Russian aircraft flew above the town. Woman and young children screamed in terror and ran to somewhere safe. The aid workers took the bodies somewhere, but restrained others from following them as they got the bodies ready for burial.

"NOO!!! WHERE ARE YOU TAKING MY BABA!!? NO, I NEED TO GO TO HIM, HE IS CALLING ME! KHALID, STOP THEM, KHALID, PLEASE!" Amira was hysterical. Khalid held her down as she tried to run towards the workers taking Baba away.

"AMIRA! We need to go, Amira; there are aircraft flying everywhere! It's not safe, Amira, the boys are getting frightened, please," Khalid pleaded, holding back tears.

People threw stones in the air trying to aim for the planes. The regime and Russia began interfering in the civil war in support of Assad in 2015 and began targeting hospitals and clinics during assaults on opposition strongholds.

"My mum! My MAMA IS IN THERE! SOMEONE HELP! SHE'S PREGNANT! PLEASE, SOMEONE!"

A young girl cried as everyone began running.

She approached Amira and begged her.

"Please, I need to find my mother. She was in there, she was giving birth to my brother. I just went out to sleep in the old library because I wasn't allowed in the ward. Please help me." Amira didn't recognise the girl from the library.

"Come with us," Khalid told her as he stood up and grabbed Shakil and Adam's arms.

Amira got up at the sound of roaring aircraft flying closer to the town.

They all ran for the old building they had slept in. Blood was seeping through the piece of cloth that Khalid had tied around Amira's arm, as she tensed it whilst running for the building. The young girl, who had a slight limp, was struggling, so Amira grabbed her arm and helped her through the crowds of people. Finally, they reached the old building, which seemed to be much more cramped than a few hours ago.

Amira gasped in pain every so often as someone nudged past her injured arm.

As they found a somewhat empty spot, Khalid reached for Amira's arm and unravelled the cloth. She moaned as it really hurt. He got the other sleeve he had ripped off and kept safe in his pocket and placed it over her wound.

"Where is my mum? Is she alive?" asked the young girl. She had jet black, silky hair and innocent light green eyes. She looked around 9 years of age. She fidgeted with her tassels on the end of her floral dress as she spoke in distress.

"Was your mother in labour?" Amira gasped.

"Labour? I don't know what that is, but she was screaming that the baby was coming and I was asked to leave. My father, he was travelling from Latakia to Idlib but I haven't seen him for 2 months. He called us yesterday on my mama's phone and said he would be here in the next few days."

"Do you have his number?" Khalid asked.

"No, I don't. But he promised he would be here. But I need to know if my mama is okay, she must have given birth by now. But the hospital..." she paused and cried.

"The hospital is gone, so where is she now?! Please, help me find her."

Amira looked at the young girl. She drew nearer to her and embraced her gently.

"Shhh, it's okay, I'm sure she's okay." The young girl cried in Amira's arms and Amira cried with her. It was more than just crying; it was the kind of inconsolable wailing that arises from one who is depleted of all hope. The young girl, whose name Amira found out was Alina, sank to her fragile knees and deep into Amira's arms. Amira looked at Khalid as he held the boys, and within that instant moment of staring into Khalid's saddened, sunken eyes, she knew she had to stay strong. For Khalid, for the boys and herself.

Pain ran through Amira's veins like rushing blood and she tried her hardest to keep her tears hidden and silent. Every couple of hours, heavy aircraft howled from above, making Amira's heart skip a beat. The fear of shelling and bombs being thrown on the city again wafted around the old building like a bad smell.

The little girl fell asleep on Amira.

"Khalid, what are we going to do?"

Khalid paused for a second before looking sternly into Amira's eyes and speaking.

"Amira…" he began.

"Amira, I know you're not going to like the sound of this, but just know that what I am about to say is for the safety and good of not only us, but the boys and this little girl too."

Amira gulped.

"The likelihood of any of our parents being alive, including this girl's, is close to zero."

Amira saw a tear fall down Khalid's cheek.

"There will be hardly any survivors. At all. The bomb was too intense."

"But Khalid, Baba? Where have they taken him, Khalid? I need to see him, Khalid, please! You can't make us just leave. How can you? I can't! I won't!" she yelled, almost waking the boys up.

"THEN DO YOU INTEND TO WAIT FOR ANOTHER BOMB TO FALL AND KILL SHAKIL AND ADAM TOO!?" Khalid shouted.

Amira froze.

Khalid had never shouted or raised his voice at Amira. There was something in that yell, a pain behind his voice that Amira knew was aching inside of him. She knew, deep down, his concerns were right, but she was greatly in denial and too afraid to leave behind her whole family rotting underneath the rubble. Khalid's anger was nothing except a shelter for his pain, for he also felt the pain of losing a father too.

Amira wasn't angry at Khalid for shouting at her, but she couldn't help feeling upset that he had raised his voice. Khalid saw her wipe away a tear silently and instantly regretted his sudden outburst.

He pulled himself closer towards her.

"Mira, I'm sorry. I'm sorry…"

"No, Khalid, it's okay. I'm not upset, I just…Baba? And Mama? And they're just lying there alone. I just…" she blubbered with lumps in her throat, barely able to speak.

"Shhhh, I know, Mira, I know. Come here," Khalid whispered.

He held Amira close to him, carefully without disturbing Alina on Amira's lap.

"I know, Amira, I feel it too. If it wasn't for you, Mira, I'd be a broken man right now…" Khalid sniffed.

Amira didn't look up to see his face but felt his tears fall onto her arm.

"I need to stay strong…for you. For the boys…"

Amira inhaled Khalid's scent and closed her eyes. She felt a deep ache from within her as she remembered the last conversation she had had with her father, her mother, her uncle. She knew she needed to stay strong too.

"What are we going to do, Khalid?" she asked.

"The same as we were when we started this journey. We are going to go to Turkey and find refuge there."

"But we don't know the friend Baba was talking about who would help us," Amira said.

"Don't worry, I will figure it out, I promise," Khalid replied.

"Khalid, can I at least see where they have taken Baba, please?"

Khalid sighed and answered.

"Okay, Mira, of course. We need to leave tomorrow; we need to set out because there will be hundreds of people travelling now, especially as the bombs have hit this town. It will become harder now so we need to stay together and alert," Khalid told her.

"What about Alina?" Amira asked, as she ruffled her fingers through Alina's hair.

"I will try and find out if she has family around, but if not, we can take her with us."

Khalid and Amira heard a couple next to them talking loudly.

"They're targeting maternity wards and killing innocent babies!" a man raged as he spoke to his wife.

"Shahid, we need to get away from here. We need to go somewhere safe, please, my wound, it's getting worse by the day," a woman wearing a brown dress and loose hijab replied, whilst panting heavily. Amira cast her eyes towards the woman's bruised and swollen cut on her foot. The cut was deep enough to see her muscle through the skin. She exhaled in painful bellows every so often.

"Are you okay, sister?" Amira asked.

"No dear, my foot, it got caught on a broken glass window when I tried climbing into a hostel for shelter. My husband, he tried helping me but the glass was pierced too deep into my foot. We have been travelling for 2 days now and only reached here yesterday after the bomb hit the hospital."

Amira looked at the woman's foot as she moved it carefully.
"Now, there aren't any hospitals for miles," cried the woman.

Her husband interrupted and angrily yelled.

"The bastard Assad has fucking cut every supply of medication and shelter! Killed all our doctors and nurses! Fucking devil has led us to build hospitals underground where they can't reach us! May God bring severe punishment to the oppressors, I tell you!"

"Our families were in there…" Amira told the woman.

The woman paused and placed her hand over her heart.

"My dear, I'm ever so sorry. Indeed, they have become Shaheed in the name of Islam," the woman replied.

"There's just far too much corruption amongst the government. Too much! And surely, Allah is watching it all. May the day come where there is peace within Syria again," the man morosely told Amira and Khalid.

Khalid turned to Amira and briefed her on what they should do next.

"Amira, I'm going to go back to where we parked our cars and see if they're still there. I think they are. We'll get ready and drive down to Lebanon," he instructed.

He told Amira to watch over the boys and Alina as he tried to find out any information about her and if she had any family alive. Amira stayed in the building as more and more injured people kept swarming in, searching for aid. For hours, the sound of booming aircraft rumbled through the early hours of sunrise. Amira had barely slept as sleeping seemed like a sudden chore for her.

After some time, Khalid arrived in the building and after intense shoving and pushing past the crowd, reached Amira and the children.

"Anything?" Amira asked.

Khalid shook his head.

"No, no one seems to know anything about her or her family," he replied.

The children were all sat up amongst the tumult.

Alina, who had barely spoken, was watching Adam and Shakil as they played with their marbles.

"Alina, do you know anyone in Lebanon? Any family?" Khalid asked her.

Alina seemed somewhat frightened of Khalid as he towered over her. Khalid lowered himself to her height and smiled.

"Don't be afraid of me; I ain't all that scary," he laughed.

From his pocket, Khalid took out a squashed-up piece of toffee in a shiny wrapper. He handed it to Alina and winked. She smiled and took it from him before anyone else could see.

"So, are we friends now?" Khalid asked Alina, warmly.

Alina smiled and nodded her head at Khalid.

"I don't know where Lebanon is, I just know Idlib," she replied, innocently.

Khalid looked at Amira and sighed.

"Mira, I found our cars, I moved all our luggage from the other two into my car. I found the documents too," he told her.

"I think it's best we leave as soon as possible."

Amira nodded her head in agreement and got the boys ready. They made their way to Khalid's car, which was parked just outside the old building. Amira strapped all three children in and explained to Alina about where they were going.

"We're going to find a safe place for all of us, okay?"

"But what about Mummy? And my baby brother?" she cried.

"Alina, my darling, the thing is, they have gone to heaven for now and they're waiting for you," she tried to console her.

"Heaven?" queried Alina.

"Yes, Heaven. They're watching over you, I promise. But for now, we need to go somewhere safe so we can all stay safe...do you understand sweetheart?" Amira tried her hardest to make her understand.

"Hmm...Okay. But, can I go to Heaven soon and be with Mummy and baby brother, please?"

Amira's heart ached as Alina asked her questions.

"Yes, Insha'Allah, we will all go to Heaven one day, Alina" she replies with a croaky shake.

As promised, Khalid took Amira to where the aid workers had taken Baba. A couple of yards away from the hospital was a huge piece of open land. It was only when Amira walked further into the open space that she realised what it actually was.

Deep, ghastly mass graves held piles of horrifying dead bodies. The putrid stench of rotting flesh and blood nearly made Amira throw up. Khalid did try to warn her before going to see where her baba was kept, however, Amira had refused and went anyway.

"Mira, I don't think it's a very good idea if you go...I don't want you to see. Please, listen to me," he pleaded as best he could.

"Khalid, you promised! I want to at least see my baba before I go, to say goodbye" she wailed.

"I can't leave like this, Khalid, I just can't!"

Baba's body was nowhere to be seen.

∎∎∎

In the car, Adam and Shakil slept like babies after they had eaten some bread and cheese that was in Khalid's car. Amira,

Khalid and Alina had all strapped themselves in after packing the boot with essentials for the journey. Luckily, Khalid found everyone's documents from Baba and Uncle Ahmed's cars. Alina was the only one without any papers or identification documents.

"Hopefully, they'll help us out at the airport. Let's just hope for the best, Mira," Khalid said confidently.

Amira was quiet. She didn't feel like talking or making conversation. Her thoughts drifted into spirals of mourning and she tried her best to overcome such a feeling. It was impossible. The trauma of losing not only her parents but her whole family, was something that was impossible for Amira to get over so quickly. Khalid felt the same, though he tried wiping away his occasional tears quickly before Amira caught a glimpse. He didn't want to be weak for her, nor the boys. The reality was that, no matter how hard both Khalid and Amira tried, they had to face the reality that what they both once treasured was now just a memory, a darkness, a shelter enduring deep into the depths of their minds.

"It feels painful, Mira…" Khalid broke down silently as he drove down Damascus Aleppo International Way. Amira looked ahead onto the M5 as he spoke, preventing herself from looking at him and breaking down too.

"It's weird…to lose something that you had only yesterday. It's like an arm, or a leg being ripped from your skin…"

Khalid paused and Amira could hear quiet sniffing. Her heart ached and she flung her arm around his shoulder as he continued to drive. She held onto him as he wept soundlessly into her hair.

"Am...Amira..." Khalid's sobbing became more violent and louder as he threw out his words. Amira sat up and lulled him.

"Shh, Khalid, it's okay. Uncle Hussain is a Shaheed, Khalid."

Khalid began weeping, louder and louder. He had to pull up the car as he couldn't control his tears. His bawling burst forth like rushing water from a waterfall. His chin trembled like a baby as he tried to control his sobbing.

Amira held her tears in till she couldn't anymore. She wept quietly as she tried consoling Khalid. He continued to cry into her shoulder and grabbed her arms tightly as if she was running away. He held on, cried and let out his mournful wails.

"I didn't even say goodbye to him, Amira, before I left the hospital. I didn't even have the chance to say goodbye properly to him. All the times I was rude and shouted and left the house angry, he was always there, and never once gave up on me, Amira," Khalid whined.

"He never once gave up on his son, after all I put him through. I was a stupid son, ungrateful and selfish son, yet he still loved me despite all my flaws."

"Because he was your father, Khalid..."

"He was and still is your father, and that's what fathers do for their sons and daughters. They love them unconditionally and despite their faults," Amira soothed.

Khalid sniffed wordlessly and found comfort in Amira's words and her embrace. He wiped his tears and got up from her arms. He faced Amira, who quickly wiped her sore eyes clear of any tears. He gazed into her deep amber eyes, eyes as undefiled and pure as a child's. Khalid was lifted by a waft of warmth and safety in Amira's eyes and the way her peachy lips formed a small, honest smile. In that moment, Khalid found home.

"Baba is with Mama now, Amira, right?" Khalid asked like a child.

"Yes, Khalid, he is. They are both together now and happy, I promise. And they would all want us to be safe and together too, and strong for one another," Amira pacified softly.

Khalid exhaled and wiped any remaining tears. He started the engine of the car and with that, they were off again.

It was always a little terrifying for Amira whenever Khalid had to stop off for a rest or fill up the car with fuel, mainly because of the fear of airstrikes or attacks from rebels. On their journey to Lebanon, they passed through Maarat al-Numan, which was a north-western city of Syria and south of Idlib. Once described as an ancient city flourishing with history, it was nothing more than a ghost town ruin now.

Amira remembered when Baba once visited his friend in Maarat al-Numan and told her about the vibrant bazaars full of traffic and bustle. He brought back bags of fresh figs and salty pistachios every time he travelled there. Now it reminded Amira of a town hit by an atom bomb, with houses all fallen apart, hospitals bombed, orphaned children running through the grounds and rubble everywhere. Back in 2011, the town was a focus of violently fierce disputing and protesting against the regime. On October the 25th, clashes occurred between loyalists and defected soldiers at a roadblock on the edge of the town. The defectors launched an assault on the government-held roadblock in retaliation for a raid on their positions the previous night. The Free Syrian Army took control from December 2011 till January 2012 and the regime, The FSA, took it back on the 10th of June 2012, however, it was recaptured by the military in August. Finally, the FSA seized the town again in October after the Battle of Maarat al-Numan.

"Khalid, I want to get out now! I want BABA! I WANT BABA I WANT BABA!!"

Shakil was becoming restless and extremely frustrated. They had been travelling for hours and both Adam and Shakil needed to stop and run around for a while.

"Ok, ok, Shakil, another 5 minutes and I'll stop for you. We can play a quick game of football, what do you say, eh?" Khalid replied eagerly in an attempt to keep them entertained for another few hours.

"I want cake; I'm hungry!" Shakil whined.

Khalid was also becoming restless and needed a stretch.

"Cake? Well, I can try my best to find you some cake but can't promise anything...maybe we'll get lucky..." Khalid explained.

"Baaaa, Maammm," Adam yelled in annoyance to Amira.

Amira tried her best to explain to Adam about where Baba and Mama were.

"We will see them soon, Adam, very soon," she'd say again and again. Truth was, she didn't know what else to say or how to make him understand.

"I know how to make cake, Uncle Khalid. I made my baba's birthday cake for him last year. Mama didn't even help, I did it all by myself!" Alina smiled as wide as a Cheshire cat as she told Khalid and Amira about her baking skills.

"What? No way! What a clever girl you are, Alina. Maybe you can bake me a cake for my birthday," Khalid clapped with excitement as he turned to Alina.

"Yes, can I!? When is your birthday?" she asked.

"Next week, Friday," he replied.

"Yes! I will bake it for you, ok? And no one can help because I can do it all by myself!"

Amira giggled as Khalid clapped in enthusiasm at Alina's innocent gesture.

When Khalid parked up on a side road after filling the car with gas, the children all went to play in the small park adjacent to their car.

Khalid took out his baba's wallet and counted the remaining money they had.

"Mira, money is decreasing every day. I took the notes from both your baba and Uncle Ahmed's cars, still, it's getting less every time we buy food and fill the car with petrol." Khalid looked concerned. They still had to buy tickets for Turkey.

Khalid hadn't really figured out the next course of action for when they all arrived in Turkey; instead, he confidently reassured Amira every time she felt doubtful of how things were going to work out.

"We'll just have to buy less food, I guess," Amira suggested.

Amira and Khalid were starving already. They would buy bread, cheese, nuts, rice and sometimes yoghurt from local corner shops, however before they had a chance to help themselves, the kids would devour the food instantly. Their hungry appetites meant that Khalid and Amira had to sacrifice their bellies for the sake of their siblings.

"Khalid, look! Look what I found!" shrieked Shakil.

He ran towards Khalid with a book in his hand.

Shakil gave Khalid the book and ran off to play. Khalid opened it to find a child's passport. He turned to the child's information page in the passport which was painted with dried blood.

He looked at Amira.

"What's his name?" Amira asked.

"Mahmoud Mustafa," Khalid replied.

"His poor family must have dropped it; maybe they were travelling too, like us," he said.

"It's so important we keep these safe, Mira, our passports and birth certificates," Khalid told her.

Khalid stored all the papers in Amira's box, the box that contains her poem book, a few novels she had brought and some old family photos she kept safe inside.

"Whatever happens, do not lose these, ok?"

"Ok, Khalid."

The small abandoned park was deserted. The eerie creeks of the rusty swings made Amira feel nervous, scared almost. It was as if zombies had taken over and left not a single human in sight. Amira remembered watching a zombie movie with Khalid a few years ago. They both snuck into their local cinema and hid at the back as they watched a famous American zombie movie.

"Khalid, is it me, or is it so bloody terrifying here?"

"No, it really is... I feel it too, Mira. It's spooky, in fact, let's make a move. We need to find a hostel or somewhere to sleep and feed these little guys," he replies.

Finding a hostel in Maarat al-Numan was difficult. The dynamic alleys and streets that once abounded with existence stood lifeless and bare. There were no women strolling the streets in their bright clothing, selling handmade jewellery, or fat stall-holders shouting at civilians and tourists to buy baskets of fresh fruit and nuts. There wasn't any laughter left coming from any children, nor were there any games being played in the corners of the alleys. Now, even during mid-afternoon, as the sun was beaming directly onto the empty roads, all that was left keeping one company was the humid wind of the sandy roadside.

The burning, amber sun spouted through the car window, yet Amira's thoughts were grey. Her mood became lower and lower the more Khalid drove deeper into the town.

"This is an abandoned city, Khalid...It's depressing, I can't take it," Amira told him.

"Look over there."

Khalid pointed to what looked to be a small hotel looking building. Outside the courtyard, there were some children playing with a cricket bat and ball. Their scruffy clothing and messy, uncombed hair made Amira realise that they might be orphaned children.

Khalid parked up beside the building and went inside to find out if they could all stay the night. Amira caught sight of a young girl. Her eyes were like hers, hazelnut brown under the sun and her light brown hair was frizzy and long, just below her elbows.

Amira gave her a smile, to which the little girl looked away shyly and stayed sitting on the ground watching the other children play their games. Amira got out of the car to greet her.

"What's your name?" she asked.

The little girl played with her fingers and looked down to avoid eye contact with Amira.

"It's ok...you don't need to be scared of me," Amira told her.

The little girl stopped fidgeting and looked up at Amira. Amira grinned at the little girl's beautiful golden eyes and button nose. She managed a slight smirk at Amira and looked down again.

"You have very lovely eyes, they're like mine...see," Amira pointed at her eyes and the little girl smiled.

"My..." she stuttered.

"My n... nam...name is Rima," she whispered to Amira.

"Wow, Rima! What a beautiful name for such a beautiful young girl. And how old are you Rima?"

"5 years old, but I am going to be 6 in July." Rima's eyes suddenly lit up as she told Amira.

"Oooohhh, what a big girl you are," Amira clapped.

Khalid emerged from the building and found Amira sitting with Rima. Amira got up and introduced the girl to Khalid.

"Rima, this is Khalid, my friend. And Khalid, this is Rima. She is going to be 6 years old in July!" Amira excitedly told Khalid.

"Hello, Rima, aren't you a pretty little girl. Your eyes are just as beautiful as my wife's."

Amira turned to Khalid and blushed. Her cheeks began glowing a deep, rosy coral.

This was the first time that Khalid had even referred to her as his 'wife'. Amira didn't know how to react except smile like a child to herself.

"Huh? Wife? You said he was your friend?" Rima asked Amira.

Amira laughed and before she could answer, Khalid butted in.

"Well, she is also my friend, you see. But wife too. I can have both, right? Friend and wife?" Khalid joked as he lowered himself down to Rima and winked.

Rima giggled innocently and ran off to play with the others in the courtyard.

"Sweet girl, look how lovely her eyes are," Amira told Khalid.

"She's an orphan," Khalid said.

"What? How do you know?"

Khalid turned to face the building behind them.

"This is a small, local orphanage, Mira, they have almost 60 kids inside."

Amira's heart sank as she looked out to Rima who is playing tag with another young girl.

"Back in February, the hospital a few miles away was struck by missiles."

"Oh yes, I remember hearing about it on the news," said Amira.

"The hospital was destroyed, brought down to the ground and all these children lost their parents and family members from it. The building, well it was a local sewing shop, but the owner turned it into an orphanage and now looks after all these children who have no one left."

Amira stood in profound sadness and the feeling of heartache dominated her body. 'Poor children,' she thought as she looked into the distance and saw them all playing artlessly with one another, unaware of the tragedy around them. Some looked as young as 2 years old.

"We can stay tonight," Khalid told Amira.

"The owner, he said we can stay for a night but it's a tight squeeze. I told him were only here a night and then back on the road again tomorrow morning."

"Ok, let's get the boys and Alina freshened up and fed," replied Amira.

"I feel exhausted, Khalid, so exhausted. All I want is a cold bath and some proper food," Amira groaned with utter enervation. Her clothes were dusty from the shelling site and her appearance was wearied. Her sunken eyes and messy hair made her look like she too was a part of the orphanage children. All she wanted was to rest, properly, without fear of shelling, without any grief, without any panic attacks and without nightmares of the day her family died.

Khalid pulled Amira closer and embraced her gently. He sighed and looked into the distance at the children playing, then at the car where all three children were fast asleep in their seats. He placed his hand over Amira's arm where she injured herself. She winced slightly and Khalid kissed her wrapped arm.

"Tell me that Rumi quote, Mira, the one about light entering you."

Amira sighed and looked into Khalid's eyes. Sorrow left Amira's eyes as Khalid touched her cheek and stroked it tenderly.

"I like that one Mira; read it to me again," he requested, chastely.

"The wound is the place where light enters you…" she recited.

Khalid exhaled.

"When we get wounded, Mira, or when we are in trouble and going through a tough time, that is the time when God is closest to us. It's the time we get the illumination and consciousness of his presence…"

Amira listened to Khalid's promising words.

"It's when the bad times come about and when we get hurt by others and the actions of others, whether it be emotional or physical hurt, Mira, that we look up to the supreme one during the darkness and look for answers from him, for only he is the one who can provide that light for us that will help us never give up."

Khalid gave Amira a tight squeeze and kissed her cheek.

"We need to remind ourselves and never forget, that God is with us, in your bad times and good and that is when the enlightenment fixates within us. Just remember, we don't have to look for that light outside, it is inside us, always, Mira. With that light, we will overcome this."

"The light is entering you, Mira... it will all be over soon. I promise."

CHAPTER TEN
Homs 2016

"I have to leave; what other choice do I have?" said Munir, puffing for air as he spoke rapidly.

"It's either stay here and get killed for refusing to join the army or leave and risk your life for survival."

Munir, a 26-year-old man, had slashes and cuts all down his arms and across his bare back. His 'battle wounds' as he called them, were scars from being beaten and whipped whilst in custody. He was migrating towards Turkey with his wife, Sarah. They were planning to settle in Germany with their relatives, away from all the dangers in Syria.

Amira and Khalid met them when they reached Hama, a city in Western Syria that was once famous for serving a vital agriculture market, production site and trade centre for the villages within northern Syria, yet now, was nothing more than a land full of walking ghosts.

Munir was a tall, handsome young man with dark eyes and ginger hair. His wife was equally as beautiful with long, luscious brown hair and fair, freckled skin. She reminded Amira of Mama slightly. Her petite figure and full, pink lips reminded Amira of how Mama looked a few years back when her health was better, before all the migraines. Sarah had a smile that resembled her mama's and to Amira, she seemed to find a sort of comfort around her.

"It isn't just the fighting I'm fleeing, it's the fear of joining it," Munir told Khalid on their way to Homs from Hama.

"I feel trapped, like it's a crime to be Syrian."

Khalid listened as he drove down the highway.

"They left us with nothing! No home to return to after this fucking war, no family, nothing. Left us with absolutely NOTHING except two choices; staying and getting conscripted into the army or leaving our homeland," Munir yelled.

"Shhh, darling, the children are asleep," shushed his wife, Sarah.

Munir quietened down, not realising his voice was raised loud.

"They did the same with my brother, Abdul Sharif. He was only 17."

Munir's voice started breaking, as if he was chugging back tears.

"He was a handful, I tell you, always out till late, messing around with his friends, even got a tattoo across his arm. Hah! The day he came home from getting that tattoo our father nearly had a heart attack," laughed Munir.

He paused for a moment.

"Then, one day, he was out buying our mother's medicine from the Pharmacy when Assad's men grabbed him, tied his wrists with metal handcuffs and bundled him into a bus to be sent off to the army barracks."

Munir was silent and his wife held his hand gently.

"They forced him to kill innocent lives, imprison civilians, all under the 'regime'. For 5 horrid months he killed himself under the oppressors and listened to their every word, how couldn't he? When all they did was threatened to kill him...his family...his friends?" said Munir.

"Then one day..." he halted, holding back tears.

"Then one day, when he tried escaping, they shot him...right through his forehead."

Sarah wiped a tear from her face and held Munir's arm tightly, trying to console him with her touch.

"I'll never forget the day his body was dropped by the army outside my parent's house. His face, the bullet hole, his young, innocent body lying there. I'll never forget that day; that memory will never be able to erase itself from my mind."

Khalid rubbed Munir's shoulder as he drove steadily down the highway.

"Allah is the greatest, Brother, stay strong."

"He is, I believe so with every inch of me," Munir replied.

"Now that my dear mother and father are both with Abdul Sharif, I know they are being well looked after by the Almighty."

He managed a smile at Sarah and winced as he unbuckled his seatbelt, trying hard to prevent his bruised back, arms and shoulders from touching the belt too much.

"I tell you, that was a pretty damn lucky escape yesterday, eh, Khalid?" Munir joked, trying to lighten the mood.

Yesterday, government-held Hama city was a route that needed to be travelled through in order to get to Homs and then Lebanon. Syrian rebels captured the town of Hama and they threatened government loyalist areas populated by minority Christians and Alawites north of the city. The Syrian government forces' checkpoints located in Hama began readily raising the amount of fee imposed on civilians to cross the checkpoints via private cars or public transportation.

Munir was being interrogated by militant forces as he tried crossing over to Homs with his wife. He couldn't afford to pay the fee to cross through to Homs and the militants beat him vigorously as he got lippy with them and lost his temper. Despite his ID cards being thoroughly checked and examined, they refused him entry through to Homs as he hadn't any money to pay the fee.

"Munir, let us take the side alleys routes, please, to avoid any drama," Sarah pleaded with him before they reached the government checkpoint.

"It's too risky, Sarah, not safe, especially during the night. Every day, people's vehicles get raided and women are raped by these bastards hiding in the alleys. I can't risk that," he told her.

"Don't worry, we will be ok, Insha'Allah," he continued.

They reached the checkpoint to be greeted by 3 military soldiers wearing their usual army combat clothing with the Syrian flag sewn across the right arm of the camo jumpsuit.

"Salam, officer," greeted Munir respectfully, as he rolled down his window.

"Bit of a shit car you got, don't you think, boys?" one militant joked to the others.

"We just want to get through, sir, we need to get to Lebanon to visit family," replied Munir, ignoring the militant's joke about his car and trying hard to avoid eye contact.

"Family, you say?" asked the militant.

Munir gulped and replied as calmly as he could without showing any signs of fear.

"Yes, family. They live in Lebanon."

"Where about, exactly?" asked another militant, growing closer to Munir's car.

"In err...erm, Baalbek, sir, yes Baalbek," Munir answered.

"Where exactly in Baalbek?" the soldier continued.

"It's a big place, sir. I can't seem to remember the town."

Munir tried thinking of the town from the one time he visited Baalbek back when he was in university on a trip to see the temple of Bacchus.

"So, you're visiting family in Baalbek in Lebanon but don't know the town's name? Did I ever tell you what us soldiers do to liars, boy?" the first soldier exclaimed with disgust in his voice.

Munir began sweating from his forehead, arms, hands, back and he took several gulps.

"No, no, hang on, I remember, sorry, we're going to Aarsal!"

"Aaaahh, Aarsal, I see. Which road do they live on?" snapped the soldier.

Munir made up a random name of a street and hoped for the best.

"Sharie Karim," replied Munir.

"Karim Street, yes, the one right opposite the football stadium?" asked the soldier.

"Yes, yes, that's the one, Brother!"

"Except…" the soldier paused.

"Except there isn't a stadium on that street. Nor does that street exist…"

Munir's shattered nerves were attacked altogether and in every direction. His sweaty palms were beginning to soak more as he gulped harder each time to swallow the invisible lump in his throat. Fear and dread flooded his body from head to toe and his heart beat faster as if it was to escape any moment through his bare chest.

"Sir…we just want to pass, please, I only have this. Take it all, but please, let us pass."

The soldier didn't answer and didn't say another word.

He grabbed Munir, pulled him out of the car, slammed him to the ground and the 3 of them all kicked and beat him to a pulp. Sarah screamed loudly at them, as they each took turns in beating him.

"PLEASE, LET HIM GO, I BEG OF YOU, HAVE SOME MERCY! YOU'RE GOING TO KILL HIM, PLEASE! I BEG YOU, PLEASE, YA ALLAH, PLEASE," she bellowed louder and louder with burning tears flowing from her sunken eyes.

One of the soldiers went back to their truck and returned with a large whip.

Sarah's heart stopped.

He gripped the whip and spat on Munir's back.

He whipped Munir, whipped him so much till his back was a bloody mass of ripped, exposed flesh and muscle right before Sarah's eyes.

She shrieked at the top of her lungs till she could shriek no longer. She tried jumping on the soldiers and pushing them off her husband, but nothing worked. She was tossed aside and the beating and whipping continued.

The dry clay beneath Munir became soaked with raw, vermillion blood and he groaned in pain as he tried to sit up every time the soldiers moved back.

"Pl… pl… plea…please si…sir, have mer…mercy." Munir fought till his last ounce of strength.

"This will teach you never to lie to a TRUE SYRIAN again!" roared the soldier.

Just as the first soldier went in for a punch to Munir's back, Khalid pulled up.

He wasted no time and grabbed the soldier by his neck and brought him to the ground.

Amira held her breath in sheer horror as Khalid fought the soldier with complete wrath. The other two soldiers watched for a moment before going in for Khalid.

They pulled him back and tried to kick him to the ground, but Khalid delivered a single blow to both their faces, causing them to drop to the ground. The other soldier tried grabbing his gun to shoot him but failed, as Khalid struck his hand with his foot and pushed him to the ground. He placed his leg around the soldier and punched his face 4 times before finally spitting on his bloodied face.

"This is what a TRUE SYRIAN FUCKING LOOKS LIKE, you piece of shit," Khalid yelled ferociously.

All three soldiers lay semi-conscious on the ground, unable to lift themselves up to defend themselves any longer.

Khalid turned to Munir and then to Sarah.

"Can you drive?" he panted and asked Sarah.

"No!" she cried.

Without wasting any time, Khalid instructed Sarah to pack her belongings into his car.

"Your husband is in no fit state to drive; luckily we have 2 seats left in the back on our car. Come with us," he said.

Sarah quickly packed everything into Khalid's car and helped Khalid to lift Munir into the back of the car. Khalid put on his seatbelt as quick as he could before the soldiers could wake up and before they knew it, they were off again.

■■

When Munir regained consciousness, he thought Khalid was a militant, mainly because he was wearing his combat trousers and an Arab scarf around his neck. He sprung up from his seat and began shouting.

"WHO ARE YOU? GET ME THE HELL OUT OF HERE THIS INSTANT!" he shouted.

He lifted his head slightly, trying to find his wife.

"No, no, dear, calm down. This is Khalid. He saved you from those soldiers, and this is his wife, Amira. They're also going to Lebanon. They're taking us with them," she explained to her husband.

Munir looked confused.

"Where's my car? Our stuff? Our documents?" He asked question after question.

"It's ok, Brother, everything is all in here. Your car had to be left behind. You were in no fit state to drive and we were seconds away from being chased by the militants," replied Khalid from the front driver's seat.

"Oh," Munir whispered.

He winced in pain every so often and when he fully regained awareness of the whole situation, he spoke.

"Khalid, is it? Thank you, Brother. I can't thank you enough for helping me and my wife. May God bless you and your family. Shukran, Khalid, Shukran."

"No worries at all, it was my duty," he replied.

"All across Hama, the checkpoint borders are polluted with Assad's rats. You need to be careful. I know it's risky but we took the alley routes and hoped for the best and prayed to God

172

we weren't caught. Only this time we had to cross through this border checkpoint to securely reach Homs," Khalid explained.

"They're everywhere. Not a single day goes by where I don't see at least one of Assad's infested insects," Munir said.

"Well, you're safe now, just rest up and recover," Amira added in, smiling at Munir.

"Shukran Ukhti."

"Here, have some maamoul." Sarah gave Amira, Alina, Shakil and Adam a bag full of maamoul, a traditional Arab shortbread cookie stuffed with a juicy date mixture. Amira felt like a kid again when she saw the maamoul. Her eyes lit up and she smiled at Sarah.

"My favourite, thank you, Sarah."

"My wife's a pretty good baker, Amira; she made a whole batch of these, almost a hundred! Said we might get peckish on the journey," laughed Munir proudly.

Amira took a bite of the cookie and the sugary crumbs instantly melted in her mouth. The aromatic scent of the cookie overpowered every other fragrance in the car and the satisfying crunch from Adam's bite of the maamoul cracked in her ear.

"These are delicious Sarah, thank you."

Amira suddenly felt mournful. She looked down at the half bitten maamoul and then at Adam, who was happily munching on his cookie.

'Always first at the table and last to leave, Amira, I'm surprised you haven't gained any weight with the amount you eat'.

Amira remembered her mother's words as she swallowed her maamoul. She felt sorrow deep within her chest and her eyes shifted from side to side as a glassy layer of tears filled them.

"These…these are just like how my mama used to make them…" Amira snuffled drearily.

Sarah smiled and stroked Amira's shoulder.

"Well, in that case, have another one," she said, offering her another cookie.

The drive through Homs was a depressing one. Munir was struggling to move every so often due to pain, Sarah was distressed seeing her husband in agony, the kids were becoming restless by the minute and on top of that, Amira had started her period but realised that she hadn't packed any sanitary towels. Despite all that, the overall atmosphere could be described as melancholic and ghastly. The streets of Homs were ghastly and bleak. Once dubbed the 'capital of revolution and upheaval' after the locals proudly embraced the call to overthrow the president in early 2011, much of the city fell under the control of the opposition. However, Assad's forces launched a severe campaign to repossess and recapture the opposition fortifications, laying siege to districts once home to tens of thousands of Syrians.

"Khalid…," Amira whispered softly.

"Hmmm?" he replies.

174

"Khalid, I forgot to pack my sanitary towels...my period...its started." She blushed with embarrassment as she told him quietly.

"Ask Sarah if she has some," he suggested.

Amira turned to Sarah and waited till Munir was asleep before she asked her.

"Sarah....do you have any pads? I forgot to pack some and my period has started," she asked Sarah timidly, feeling her cheeks heat up with warmth.

"Yes, I do!"

Amira was relieved. She turned back to Khalid and asks him to stop over at a gas station so she can use the bathroom.

They stopped off at a gas filling station in the town of Jusiyah Al-Amar, a small village area located in the Al-Qusayr district of Homs.

Amira had a few Syrian pounds she found hidden in her box. Khalid gave her a few more.

"Buy some more of those nappy things and also try getting some food if you can," he laughed as he handed her the money. He waited in the car as Amira, Sarah and Alina went into the local shop to buy supplies.

When they entered the shop, the horrible stench of rotten fruit hit Amira's nose and she quivered in disgust. The shopkeeper, an elderly woman, was accompanied by an even older-looking man, whom Amira guessed was her husband.

"Well, hello dear, how can I help you today?" she asked kindly.

"Hello mother, we need some sanitary towels and some snacks," Sarah tells her before Amira can say anything, realising she is feeling too embarrassed to ask. In the past, it was always Mama who bought Amira her necessities, so she never had to deal with the uncomfortable job of asking for pads.

"Of course, how many packets?"

Sarah answered, "Well we are going on a long journey, so for now, 6 packets should do, mother."

The old lady hushed her husband away to the back of the shop while she packed their essentials into a plastic bag.

"Long journey you say; anywhere nice?" she asked.

Nice? Amira thought to herself. Nothing about the journey was 'nice'.

"We're leaving Syria because there is nothing 'nice' left here for us," Amira blurted out.

"No family, no home, no school, no friends, nothing. There is nothing left for us, at all."

The old lady looked at Amira with soothing eyes. Her light brown eyes resembled pure honey and her soft, wrinkly skin was deep and saggy and for some reason, Amira felt suddenly warmed by her graceful, maternal look.

"Yes, child, there is nothing left in Syria...you are right. My son, he left too, 2 months ago. He left for Cyprus, to go and establish himself there and make a life for himself away from bombs and shells and killing," the old woman told Amira.

"Why didn't you go with him?" Sarah asked.

The woman paused for a second.

"Because…"

"Because Syria is our HOME," the old man spoke from behind the girls.

He walked towards his wife and placed his hand over her shoulder.

"We were born here as proud Syrian Muslims, and will die as proud Syrian Muslims. No amount of hatred or fighting will ever force us to leave our hometown."

The old man spoke proudly, with a sense of honour and pride in his croaky voice.

"Our son begged us to leave and go with him. But look at us…we are old now. Our lives are almost at an end. We can't leave…not now," the old woman stated.

"But people are getting bombed and killed every day; it isn't safe here, mother," Amira told her.

"My own parents and family were killed in the hospital bombing in Idlib."

The old woman exhaled in distress at Amira, as she sees a tear fall down her cheek.

"Oh, my dear, come here."

She embraced Amira tightly and gave her a hug that made her somehow forget all her worries and feel protected in the arms of this old woman, a woman she had never met before, but suddenly felt like she had known her forever.

"They have all gone to Heaven, my dear, I can promise you that now."

The old couple allowed Amira, Sarah and Alina to take some dried fruit, peaches, oranges and goat's cheese for free.

"Here, I made this last night for dinner. Take this for your family, my sweetheart," the old woman said as she handed Amira a plastic box of Mujaddara, a popular Arab dish consisting of cooked lentils, rice and sautéed onions.

"This looks lovely, mother, Shukran," both Amira and Sarah thanked her.

They both gave her a hug and left the shop.

"Urgh, this stupid thing!" Khalid shouted at his iPhone as he tried connecting Google Maps to the route he needed to travel.

"Why is there no flipping connection?!"

He angrily chucked his phone on the floor and rubbed his forehead.

"Khalid...? You okay?" Amira asked as she belted herself into her seat.

"This bloody phone! So useless. There's no internet connection working and I need the maps. And my head is killing me, for goodness sake."

"Here...!" Amira handed Khalid a handful of dried pistachios and cherries.

He munched it all in one go. Khalid had been hungry for days now. He tried giving all the leftover food to the kids and Amira when there wasn't enough and despite him always feeling hungry, he continued to sacrifice his share of the food for the others.

"Nice, any more left?" he asked eagerly.

"Yeah, here, have some Mujaddara!"

Khalid grabbed the box from her and found a plastic spoon in the dashboard. He took a large, hungry spoonful of the lentil and rice mixture ravenously. Amira let him. She hands him a bottle of water from the dashboard and opens it for him.

"Thank you, Mira, I was starving!" he laughed.

"It's okay, eat, Khalid."

Munir and Sarah shared the leftover lentils and rice and Khalid saved some for the kids too. They ate amongst themselves in the car for 20 minutes or so before heading off.

"Khalid, Bro, forget Google Maps, take the highway and continue for an hour or so down the N4 till you reach Baalbek Qaa Highway. It's a simple, straight route, don't worry," Munir reassured him.

They set off once again.

"There's been enough airstrikes in Homs recently and on top of that, these fucking extremists are blowing themselves up," Munir said as Khalid drove past a rebel-held area which seemed to be deserted.

"Is this a rebel-controlled area?" Khalid asked.

"It was, a few months ago, till Assad's men captured it."

Amira felt a slight worry in her heart. She prayed that none of Assad's men would turn up and interrogate them.

"There was a suicide car and motorbike bombing recently. Twin suicidal blasts in the North, within the Mukharram al-Fauqani area," Munir told Amira and Khalid.

"Oh yes, the one on the 5th of May last month?" Amira asked.

"That's the one," replied Munir.

"Then on the 12^{th,} just a week later, there was the Zara'a massacre. Forty-two confirmed civilians and 7 national defence forces militiamen killed in the attack."

"What? That's terrible!" Amira cried.

"It was an attack on the Alawite village of Zara'a. It doesn't end there. The same day, around 70 civilians were kidnapped and taken hostage to Al-Rastan. It was only a few weeks ago on the 24th May when The Syrian Red Crescent convinced militants to hand over 49 victim bodies."

Amira felt the disgust in her gut.

"They were transported like animals; the Syrian Army brought them to Homs Military Hospital for identification." Munir shook his head in disgust.

"Syria is an absolute living hell right now," whispered Amira. A sheer sense of repugnance rotated around her belly. For some reason, she remembered Baba Mohammed. She thought to herself, 'maybe it's good Baba Mohammed wasn't here to witness what Syria had become, for the killings, airstrikes and suicidal bombings would have killed him slowly every day, seeing his country fall apart before his very eyes'.

CHAPTER ELEVEN
Lebanon 2016

Driving to the Al-Qaa border in Lebanon took a little over an hour. Khalid followed Munir's directions and drove down the Baalbek Qaa Highway. They stopped at the town called Zira'a for prayers and then travelled North West towards route 4. He then continued onto route 413 before entering Lebanon. Previously, the Lebanese government had preserved the maintenance of an open-door policy towards refugees from Syria, despite the deficiency of formal obligation. There existed no international laws which Lebanon needed to abide by in dealing with refugees, due to them never actually signing the 1951 Refugee Convention.

"Syrians began entering Lebanon back in 2011, but it wasn't until 2014 that the government began introducing all these different rules and policies about the whole immigration issue," Khalid told Munir as they approached the Lebanese border.

"During the 3-year open-door policy, literally thousands of Syrians fled to Lebanon without defined policy or even any legal framework. They got in early, lucky for them. They didn't have to witness all these attacks throughout the years."

"Brother, how are we going to do this?" Munir asked Khalid as he parked up beside the border control.

"Don't worry, follow my lead," Khalid replied.

Amira looked out of the window and saw a large blue-coloured board that read 'You are welcomed to El-Kaa'.

Beneath the white writing, it also showed the distance from Beirut which was 140km.

Ahead of the blue board was a checkpoint guarded by 3 men dressed in uniform. Amira's heart raced faster as they pulled up beside the men. She gulped a piece of rock down her dry throat and croaked quietly.

"Khalid...will they let us through?"

"Shhh, Mira, it's fine. Don't stress."

Khalid got out of the car. Munir insisted on coming out too, but Khalid told him to rest as he still hadn't recovered from his injuries, nor was he in any fit state to walk.

Amira looked on from the window as Khalid approached a middle-aged man. He was accompanied by 2 other men who were seated inside a windowed box.

"Salam Alaykum, Brother," Khalid greeted him light-heartedly.

The man responded and they began talking.

"Amira, do not worry," began Munir.

"They will let us in. In extreme cases, they allow refugees into Lebanon. Last year, they allowed Syrians to stay in Lebanon for up to 6 months automatically, however, under these new measures in 2016, refugees like us need to fulfil certain criteria in order to be granted a visa at the border."

"Visa? But that will cost us money, won't it?" Amira asked.

"Maybe a visa, or maybe they will allow us through if they see our documents," Munir replied.

Amira thought to herself for a second. They all had their passports and documentation papers, all except Alina.

Khalid suddenly stopped talking to the border control attendant and paced towards the car.

He stuck his head through Amira's window and looked at Alina.

"Leena, come with me," he told her.

Amira looked at Khalid in confusion and helped Alina out the car.

"Khalid? Everything ok?" she asked.

"Don't worry, Mira."

Amira left the car door open and listened on.

"This is Alina..." Khalid tells the attendant.

"She is 5 years old, but 6 in August...right, Alina?" Khalid asked.

Alina frowned innocently and corrected him.

"No...I'm 6 in July, silly," she chanted.

The soldier smiled subtly.

"For years now, refugees have made Lebanon their home, ever since the war first began in 2011," Munir spoke from the back seat.

"Rents have risen, wages have fallen, the Lebanese complain of no jobs left as the Syrians keep taking them,"

"There's a constant resentment amongst the Lebanese towards us. They fear us, that our presence of more than a million refugees in their small, fragile country could eventually lead to, or trigger, a renewed civil war," Sarah told Amira.

Khalid, Alina and the Lebanese border control men walked towards the car and Amira suddenly gasped for air. She felt a sense a panic all of a sudden and tried to inhale and exhale quietly to herself to calm herself down. She couldn't help but feel nervous. She always did whenever she saw men in uniform now, ever since that dreadful time in Shamsa Park.

The main militant in uniform, who was leading the others, wore big grey boots that made a dulcet noise against the rumbly ground. His solid and tough build made him look patronizing almost, like a soldier. His face looked brutal, yet had a hint of honesty in his light green eyes. Amira felt hopeful and on edge at the same time.

He reached the car door and with his deep, husky voice, spoke.

"Sarah Mahmoud?" he asked.

"Yes, that's me," she answered.

The soldier looked at his handful of passports and dismissed Sarah's.

Then he called out for Shakil, Adam, Munir and lastly, Amira.

After all their names had been called, Khalid asked him;

"Alina, she is an orphan by the looks of it, brother. We have no knowledge of her father and we know her mother is gone. Please, have mercy," Khalid requested.

Alina was sitting behind Adam's seat and resting her head on the window and looking out into the open land.

The soldier looked at her for a moment then at his watch and then at the line of 4 cars behind Khalid's all waiting to be seen.

He puffed loudly and his hoarse voice spoke.

"The location I gave you... go there," he instructed Khalid.

"If it's Turkey you want to get to, then you can't go anywhere without this girl's passport or papers."

Khalid sighed.

"Go to the camp, and ask for Musa Habib. Tell him Omar sent you."

Khalid shook the soldier's hand and thanked him.

"Thank you, Brother; may Allah reward you for your kindness. I will never forget this favour."

The militant smiled and told Khalid;

"Just don't expect too much from these camps, Brother; the condition they are in, you will want to return back to Syria in a heartbeat."

The refugee camp just 40 minutes from the town centre of Qaa was a sight that made everyone curl up inside. The camp, which was for Syrian and Palestinian refugees, was located in a small village called Labweh.

The village itself was majestic. The beautiful mountains and small, blockwork houses looked like something out of a movie. The sun raged over the hills and the blue sky blanketed the whole municipality.

The camp, however, was the complete opposite.

There was no food, no water, no toilet and nowhere to shower. The other refugees within the camp were either from Palestine, Iraq or Syria. They were all homeless, all after food and shelter. Although the camp provided at least some sort of shelter for the people, it was a living condition which no one would wish upon their worst enemy.

The camp spread for miles, it was as if it was its own little town of broken, barely standing tents. There were puddles of mush, mud and muck in deep potholes across the ground. Amira had to help Shakil, Adam and Alina as they walked across the camp, as there was a risk of them stepping in one of them and getting their clothes dirty. Their clothes were already filthy and needed a wash. They each had a bag of spare clothing, all except Alina, so Amira gave her one of Adam's t-shirts and a pair of shorts that fit her.

Finding food was also difficult. Everyone was hungry and there was nowhere to find food for miles. There were a few charity aid workers helping within the camp, but when food was available from them, it was soon gone before Khalid or Munir could get any for anyone. It was every man for himself in the camp. Every morning, Khalid and Munir would wake early after Fajr Salah and collect food from roads where people distribute donations of clothes and small packages of food. The discontent and regret displayed on Khalid's and Munir's faces a few times when they came back without any food packages broke both Amira and Sarah's hearts every time. They tried their hardest to get by, but the hunger often led the children to cry out in pain of thirst and need. The cries grew louder as the days went by.

One day, Khalid and Munir returned to the camp with a bag of uncooked rice, lentils and mixed beans. Amira almost cried with happiness as both she and Sarah began cooking the rice, lentils and beans for the children. They feasted for 2 full days on the rice and their bellies were full with contentment and gratification.

Finding clean, running water was also an issue. Amira hadn't properly bathed for 5 days. Since arriving at the camp, she had finished her period and needed to bathe. She felt dirty. Her clothes reeked of her sweat and blood and the once lilac-coloured shirt had turned a dingy, muddy colour and her hair was knotted and hadn't been brushed for weeks. The water shortage meant that the small, poorly fitted tube wells weren't allowing enough water to be equally distributed for everyone within the camp. The long queues for the well didn't help, as there was always someone who got the last of the water before Amira or anyone else could get to it. They would wait hours and hours to bring back a few litres of clean water to their tent. They'd collect it in small jars they found lying around the camp.

Amira's family were only in the camp for 2 weeks, yet it felt like 2 years. The sweltering sun burned their necks as they all helped cleaning up outside their tents, keeping them free of mud and clutter, and again when they used the small amount of water they did have for washing their clothes. The mid-June sun scorched their collars, yet they continued, continued to do their best in order to survive.

Musa Habib, the man whom the border control militant told Khalid to find, had taken them all to this refugee camp, where they were told to stay before being allowed to travel across Lebanon to the Beirut Rafic Hariri international airport. Khalid knew that they didn't have enough money to buy 5 tickets to Turkey, just like he also knew that without a passport or proof of identification, Alina would not be allowed to travel across the country to Turkey, but still, he hoped for the best.

"You will need to wait here till I try finding a way to get a passport for this girl. If not, then finding a way for you all to travel together to Turkey," Musa Habib told Khalid.

"How long will that take? We cannot stay here any longer. There's no water or food and we desperately need to leave. It's disgusting and unbearable!"

"Brother, I am trying my best," Musa replied to Khalid.

Then he told Khalid of another option.

"There is something else I can do for you..." he stated.

"What is it? Anything at this point."

"There's this boat; it arrives every 6 weeks and takes refugees across the channel. They don't require passports and ID, so anyone can get on..." Musa Habib tried to continue his sentence before Khalid snapped and finished it for him.

"No, thank you, we are NOT interested in these inflatable boats. We want a flight to Turkey and that's that. As for the money, I will find it from somewhere," he claimed.

"Very well," Musa Habib replied.

"The documents you do have, just keep them safe at all costs."

"Will do," Khalid answered.

On the 11th day of their stay, Musa Habib told Khalid that he had found a way to get a fake visa and documentation papers for Alina. He told him it would cost him, a lot.

"Where do we need to go?" Khalid asked.

"Back to Qaa. There's a man I know; he will make the papers for you but he is asking for money, money which I know you do not have."

"How much?" Khalid barked.

"3000 Syrian pounds."

Khalid sighed and scratched his head.

"Let's go," Khalid said.

Amira looked at Khalid in confusion.

"Khalid? 3000 Syrian pounds? We barely have enough for tickets," she mumbled.

Khalid placed his hand in his pocket and ruffled around till he finally took out a watch. His baba's watch.

"I'll sell this or offer him this watch," he said, miserably.

"But…" Amira stuttered but Khalid quickly replied.

"It's ok…he would want us to be safe, Mira." Khalid became expressionless as he placed the watch back into his pocket and gathered the rest.

"Leave your car here. We will travel in my minibus. It's more believable and makes you look more in need. If they see you have a car, they might question your vulnerability and take other refugees more seriously," Munir told them.

"Vulnerable?! How much more fucking vulnerable do we need to look?! We have nothing! This car is probably the only fucking valuable thing we own!" Khalid shouted loudly, causing alarm to other refugees in the camp.

"Sell the fucking car, then! Flog it for some money! Just get us the fuck out of here and at the airport with tickets!"

"Khalid, calm down…" Amira whispered.

The anger in Khalid's eyes suddenly showed Amira the nervousness and child within him. For weeks now, Khalid had stayed strong for Amira, for the children and tried his best to stay strong for himself. Amira forgot that he, too, was hurting with a deep ache for his dead father, for his mother and for his remaining family.

Amira soon calmed Khalid down and they went to the car to collect their essential belongings and belted themselves into Musa Habib's minibus. They travelled back to Qaa, where they had first entered Lebanon from. It was around 4 o'clock in the morning as the simple 20-minute journey suddenly became 2 hours. As it was the holy month of Ramadhan, a month spent fasting from dawn till dusk, it meant that the town wasn't exactly sleeping. A few Muslims were hanging around the town waiting for the early morning prayers. Although it was predominately a Christian town, it seemed amiable in terms of both religions living in peace together.

There was a long queue of several cars across the road, all waiting to cross over to the other side of the town.

Amira looked outside and witnessed outcry and commotion from further up ahead on the road.

"What's going on now?" she frustratingly asked Musa Habib.

Before he could answer, the sound of a crackling bomb screeched from further up the road.

Adam, Shakil and Alina, who were all asleep in the minibus, were awakened by the terror and screamed in fear. Amira clutched her hands together and looked at Khalid. She began perspiring thick droplets of sweat down the back of her neck.

Crowds of people ran against the traffic and screamed as another bomb exploded. Then once more, after a few minutes, a third bomb erupted and oscillated the minibus. The vibration from the blast just a few yards away made the whole bus rumble from side to side.

Khalid held onto the seats as did Munir, Sarah and Amira. Their hearts twisted and sank each time a bomb roared in the distance. After the third and final bomb, they were all left shaken and in a state of traumatization.

"Wha...what on earth! What is it, Musa!?" Munir shouted at Musa Habib from the back of the minibus.

"Bombing…suicide bombings!" he yelled.

As they all got their bearings, Amira tried to calm the children down before a sudden screaming emerged from outside. She looked out into the road a few yards from her and caught sight of a vested suicide bomber. Before he had a chance to detonate his vest, he was shot down and tackled by Lebanese armed forces, but his vest still exploded, killing not only him, but those surrounding him.

A painful, electrical hurricane current shot through Amira's brain and pained her. She didn't know what or how to feel. The horror behind what could happen next left her numbed to the core.

"We need to go back!" yelled Musa from the front of the minibus.

The windscreen became painted with dust and fine pieces of powder and ash. No matter how many times Musa Habib applied the wipers, the debris remained. Khalid noticed and ran outside as fast as lightning, taking his water bottle with him. He splashed the water onto the windscreen, removing most of the dirt and ran back inside.

"Move it!" he shouted.

"We need to leave NOW!"

But it was impossible. Their minibus was stuck in the longest queue of traffic. Despite it being 4 o'clock in the morning, the town was wide awake, and the minibus they were all travelling in was sardined into a corner with surrounding cars encircling it.

The drivers of the cars were all out, running in the direction of the bombings to see what the commotion was and who had started the bombings, so it was near enough impossible to move the minibus.

"Khalid, I'm scared. I don't want to stay here any longer. What if another bomb goes off!" Amira cried as she held onto all three children in fear. Her body was shaking in reverence and she wheezed in and out intensely to regain her flow of breathing.

"These cars, where the hell are the drivers? We need to move!" shouted Khalid.

They all waited inside the minibus till Musa finally got out to see what was going on near the town centre. He returned after 20 minutes.

He informed the group of what had happened.

"Five people have been killed and nearly 30 injured. There were 4 suicide bombers; they blew themselves up just there in the Bekaa Valley."

"Why? Who were they!?" Sarah gasped.

"We don't know for sure, but I can imagine the blame being placed on the Islamic State of Iraq and the Levant group, ISIS," he said

"They've been situated in the mountains above Qaa for the last several years and the Lebanese army, as well as Hezbollah, have been *'apparently'* fighting them to eradicate their presence."

Amira looked outside at the crowd of people huddled in the distance, probably tending to the injured. A few ambulances drove past in a hurry towards the valley.

"It's a predominantly Christian village, so of course, they'll blame the Islamists. Although these bastards are far from Islam! Shame on them for bringing down the name of Islam!" Munir exclaimed with anger.

"Whoever it is, Lebanon is sure to raise their concerns now, which only means it will be more difficult for us to travel," said Amira, dejectedly.

"We need to wait for the police to direct the traffic so we can leave this area and go back, although the man we need to see regarding the passports is only 30 minutes away...," Musa told Khalid and Munir.

Khalid and Munir look at one another.

'Do they wait and go back or go ahead with the meeting?' Amira thought to herself.

Both options seemed precarious. If they went back, then it would only prolong their journey to Turkey and getting a passport for Alina. If they stayed and continued, there was the risk of maybe encountering another bombing.

"There's a shortcut; if we just cut past these few cars, then we can reach there and back within a few hours safely, Insha'Allah," he told them both.

Khalid and Munir both agreed and they soon made their way to where they needed to go to get Alina's passport.

When they arrived at the man's flat after an hour, he was nowhere to be seen.

CHAPTER TWELVE

The dismal sigh that emanated from Amira's parched, dry lips was listless and slow, almost as if it were slow enough for her mind to accept and process the situation that they were all in. Her tired, heavy eyes were fixated on the queue of traffic ahead going towards the town centre.

It was late evening and the sun was just about to set on the town centre of Al-Qaa, when the group were driving back to the refugee camp. They waited five, long, dreadful hours for Musa Habib's man to arrive.

One hour...two hours...three hours soon turned into five tedious hours of waiting for someone who would have given Amira and her family a way out, a chance to be free, away from danger, away from war, and away from Syria.

But he never showed.

"Are you taking us for a fucking ride, Musa? IF I FIND OUT YOU'RE MESSING WITH US, THEN BELIEVE ME WHEN I TELL YOU THAT YOU'RE A DEAD MAN!" Khalid seized Musa by his collar and as if he was as light as a feather, lifted him off the ground and pushed him harshly against the wall.

"Khalid! Khalid, Brother, I am not lying to you! I don't know where he is! He must have legged it after the bombings, I swear to you and swear on the Holy Quran, I wouldn't lie to you," Musa Habib pleaded.

Amira grabbed Khalid by his arm and begged him to let Musa down as Adam started crying out of fear.

Khalid grunted loudly and pushed Musa away.

"WHERE IS HE THEN?!" he roared.

"Khalid…" Musa stuttered.

Khalid turned to him with a sudden swarm of wrath and fury blazing in his eyes.

"I think…I think he might be back in a few days when the whole bomb attack incident calms down. Maybe he fled out of fear for a while. I would help you find where he is but if he isn't answering my calls then there isn't much I can do, Brother. I'm helping you all I can. I'm not even asking for any money from you as I can see how desperate you all are. Believe me, Brother, I am not lying to you."

Amira looked at Musa Habib.

His ragged beard covered most of his wrinkly face and his deep brown eyes were sunk within his tanned face. For some reason, Amira trusted him. She trusted his words and believed he was truthful in his words. She gestured a face at Khalid to take a deep breath and calm down. When he did, he told Musa Habib to take them back to the camp.

"If he isn't back within 2 days, 2 days, then we're leaving and finding our own way!" he snapped.

"Insha'Allah, he will be here, Brother, Insha'Allah."

With that, they left the flat.

∎∎

"What are they doing, Amira?" Alina asked Amira as she peered out the window.

Just outside St. Elias Church, opposite the statue of St. Elias, mourners grieved their loved ones and tended to the injured. They paid their tributes with candles and lights and gathered around the church.

"They're saying goodbye to their family, and other people who died, Alina," Amira told her.

"I don't like people dying, Amira...Is my mummy dead?" she asked.

Khalid turned and looked at Amira and for a split second, it felt as if they both read each other's minds, for what Khalid replied was the exact thing Amira was thinking in her mind.

"Neither do I, Alina...I miss my mum too...and dad," Khalid stammered with tears in his eyes.

Amira went to sit beside Khalid.

She reached for his arm and rubbed it tenderly. He tried so hard to hold on, to stay strong and to wipe all the tears away from his eyes, and he did exactly that.

"Thank you..." he mouthed to Amira.

The mourners outside huddled up against the minibus, therefore making it harder for Musa Habib to travel across the town centre to reach the refugee camp back in Labweh.

Musa Habib noticed a stall near the town centre, adjacent to the church the mourners were gathered outside of. The man was selling fresh fruit, bread, dried nuts, spices and candied sweets.

"Brother Khalid, Munir, that stall, they're selling food. Come with me - I can buy you some for the kids."

Amira's eyes lit up with excitement. Adam, Alina and Shakil also jumped up in eagerness as Khalid and Munir took them to the stall to fetch some food. Amira and Sarah watched on as they found their way past the people gathered outside the church and towards the stall. A large crowd bustled past and a large space emptied just near the stall. They walked towards the other end of the town centre, where St. Elias's statue was located.

Adam and Shakil soon busied themselves in taking turns to shove their hand inside the white paper bag full of candied sweets and nuts. Alina also shared her bag of sweets with Munir. They jumped around blissfully, unaware of the trauma that encompassed them from local mourners.

The three children drifted off into the crowd, but Amira kept an eye on them from the minibus. They danced around the road and towards the St. Elias Church. Khalid turned to find them, then he caught sight of Amira. She smiled at him and pointed to the kids who were playing with one another. Khalid nodded at Amira and started walking towards them.

As they played amongst themselves, something miraculous occurred which left Amira in tears.

"Amira! Amira, look!"

Amira opened her mouth and stared at Adam, mesmerised.

"Amira, look, sweeties!" Adam sang as he jumped up and down with the sweet bag in his hands.

Amira sighed and smiled like a child. After so many years of trying to help Adam speak and form words, he finally did something she had been longing for.

He said her name, loud and clear, and as fluent as a poet almost.

"Amira!" he continued, laughing with Shakil and Alina.

The ache of missing both her mother and father at this exact moment made her chest tighten with sorrow. How she longed for both of them right now. The ache came and went every so often and returns during such quiet moments. Amira wiped away a tear from her eye and smiled at Adam as he continued to sing and bounce up and down under the street lights that lit up the murky valley. She waved at him and blew him a kiss. He pretended to catch it and eat it. This made Amira giggle.

She mouthed to him and grinned, 'I love you, Adam'.

Then suddenly, amid the bittersweet moment, a policeman emerged out of the crowd and fired a rapid shot at a man. Before anyone had a chance to react or take in what had happened, the man blew up in thin air. Three more men appeared in rapid succession and likewise, blew themselves up in the crowd. The blaring sound rumbled mightily over the sleeping valley of Qaa.

Amira froze, still staring into the crowd where Adam, Shakil and Alina were...where they had been. Dread and despondency began to possess her frail, weak body, pushing, thrusting and urging against her like a secret, hidden typhoon. Her stomach locked up into a knot as she squeezed her locked breath through her neck and nose and she let out a single, haunting cry.

There, in front of her, she saw Khalid, running towards Shakil, then to Adam, then to Alina. All three children lay there, lifeless and bloodied. The crowds rushed around them, some almost stepping over Khalid, almost harming him as she tended to the children. Munir ran to help Khalid and Amira just watched...

She watched...and watched...

She watched the smoke from the suicide bombers' vests as it slowly lifted from the ground into the air, she watched and listened to the sound of howling people as they ran from St Elias's church into different buildings and alleys to find refuge from any more bombs being let off, she watched people being stepped and jumped on amidst the frenzy. A sudden whirlwind of horror stunned Amira so deeply that she felt her paralysed body stand still amongst the delirium surrounding every corner and every direction around her.

She watched until she couldn't anymore.

For all she could see was the remains of people scattered across the floor; a person's arm, another's leg...

And Khalid and Munir, holding onto Adam, Shakil and Alina and running for the minibus.

CHAPTER THIRTEEN

'A time will come when the murderer will not know why he has committed the murder, and the victim will not know why he has been killed'. – Prophet Muhammed (Peace and blessings be upon him).

Cold.

Their bodies were cold, for the life and spirit that resided within them 5 minutes ago and warmed their skins had disappeared from the grounds of this world and they were saved from the pitfalls of this life. No harm nor danger could visit them now, for they had entered the place of peace. Their innocent hearts that were just beating with love, artlessness and mischief were now silent and at rest.

Amira's mind was blank. Her mind that was used to feeling and probing so many sentiments and affections was now hollow, wiped out. Her face was being purified by her warm, gushing tears that blurred her vision with deep, aching woe and anguish. She felt as if she could taste her own mourning and sorrow as the salty tears dampened her sleeves, shirt and face. It was bitter, unforgiving merciless heartache.

"Kha...Khalid...are they..." Amira mumbled like a baby as she dribbled her words out her shivering lips.

"Are...they...are they dead Kha...Khalid?" she asked him.

Khalid had Shakil on his lap and Adam on his arm resting on his shoulder. Munir held Alina.

Khalid trembled like a leaf in the autumn wind and Munir panted heavily like a raging bull after racing.

Khalid placed both Shakil and Adam on the floor of the minibus and so did Munir with Alina.

"Musa, CALL AN AMBULANCE! CALL AN AMBULANCE THIS MINUTE! HURRY UP!" he yelled at the top of his lungs.

"They're coming! Let me get them over to the minibus!"

Amira caught sight of Adam. She saw his face and threw up all over her dress. Sarah aided Amira and consoled her. Her warm vomit tasted like poison leaving her mouth.

Adam's face was burnt to a crisp. His right eye was gone, meaning all she saw was a vacant, hollow eye socket between the burnt, red flesh on his face. The side of his face was bleeding. Shakil's arm was hanging off his shoulder and the whole side of his left leg was naked, showing his burnt skin. In his pocket, she caught a glimpse of his bag of sweets.

Amira didn't know who to tend to, who to help. They all lay there, limp and spiritless. Adam's forehead had a great slash across it and blood oozed out onto his face and down his neck. Amira relentlessly held her hand across the slash and applied pressure to it, however, no matter how hard she pressed, the blood still spouted from in between her shaking fingers and underneath her hand. It began spreading into Adam's shirt.

"Adam, Adam, please open your eyes, Adam. Adam, please, my baby, please Adam!" Amira pleaded and begged Adam to open his eyes and to speak to her, to mumble some sort of gibberish or anything.

"Let me hear you say my name again, Adam, please, Adam...Say my name, Adam, say my name," she wailed.

Sarah grabbed her and she sobbed loudly in her arms. Time itself had become irrelevant to Amira as she gave up pleading with Adam to wake up and speak, to laugh and to smile again just once. The ultimate truth was she was drained of all hope.

■■■

Khalid sank to his knees at the three, diminutive graves, not paying any sort of care for the wet mud that began to soil his trousers. His harrowing tears amalgamated with the dreary rainfall. Amira held onto Khalid and their breathless mourning resounded around the muddy graves that Munir had dug up. A small field near the valley allowed refugee burials; it wasn't owned by anyone, so anyone could bury their loved ones there without worrying about land and burial fees. All three children's graves were together, aligned in a single, swampy line. They didn't have any headstones and were recognisable by the three pieces of spare wood found on the streets.

Amira and Khalid sat there, numbed to the core. Amira found it hard to keep her sorrowful tears silent. She gasped every so often in pain and dug her face into the depths of her wet palm. Khalid just sat there, staring into the graves, like a ghost. Rivers of flashbacks and memories wet both Amira and Khalid's faces. The enormity of ache and despondency displayed in their eyes made them feel helpless, to the point where they felt they just couldn't carry on any longer.

Amira tried not to think too much of her last look at Adam, at Shakil and at Alina. She didn't want to think of their defenceless bodies, the injuries that were plastered across their limbs and the blood that painted their skin. She didn't want to remember them like that; instead, she wanted to remember them all as they were; laughing, giggling to themselves, fighting over sweets, singing and jumping up and down over the stories Amira would tell them. All she thought now was that they were asleep, resting in the ground away from the danger and shameful acts of the cruel world they left behind.

After the suicide attack during the early morning of the 27th June, the terrorists weren't finished with their mission, which is why, after several hours, as Qaa was tending to their wounded and mourning civilians of the village, four more suicide bombers attacked, thus killing and injuring the public, including Adam, Shakil and Alina. The police had somewhat suspected that they had been hiding in a nearby alleyway and when the first man ran out, they were able to shoot him dead, not realising he was attached to a bomb. Then three more emerged in rapid succession and blew themselves up.

Qaa soon became an emblem for the fortitude and boldness of the Christians of Lebanon and this wasn't the first time. During the Lebanese Civil War from 1975 till 1990, Al-Qaa's Christians were the target of sectarian attacks and the overall war estimated approximately 120,000 fatalities. To the East of Qaa lies the Anti-Lebanon Mountain range and beyond is Syria, the direction in which Amira and Khalid came from before they entered the country. Within the mountain area just a few miles from Qaa, there were known to be several hundred ISIS fighters, who were suspected of carrying out the attacks involving suicide bombings, all in the name of Islam. Such attacks and groups could be described as anything but Islamic, or even Muslim. Amira knew that such vile people who blew themselves up and harmed others were nothing but non-believers, for everything written within her Holy book had nothing to do with taking the lives of innocent men, women, children and even animals.

After what seemed like hours, Amira got up. She brushed her dress that was full of dried blood, mud and rain. She desperately needed a change of clothes, a change of undergarments and a bath. She held out her hand and helped get Khalid up. He rose and continued to look at the graves, his eyes glued on the three raised, muddy pieces of hardened soil where each child lay.

As she lifted him up, Khalid fell onto the graves and sobbed hysterically. The manner in which he wailed painfully left even strangers with tears in their eyes as they walked past. He let out agonising howls of grief and heartache and suddenly, the sounds all became a blur to Amira. She heard nothing but muffled crying as she held onto Khalid and cried with him. Not being able to console Khalid was a slow torture to her soul.

"There are risks of more attacks, Brother Khalid…" Musa Habib whispered under his breath as he neared the group after fuelling the minibus with gas.

"I know this is difficult, but we need to keep safe."

Khalid sniffed and didn't show any sign of acknowledgment to Musa.

Amira wiped her face, which was now burning hot and sweaty, and sucked up a deep breath.

"Khalid…" she murmured sorrowfully.

"Khalid, we need to go…we need to keep safe."

Khalid's tears flowed silently in a repetitive stream and he let them.

"I can't leave them; I can't leave Shakil; he's probably cold or tired or hungry, I can't leave him! Amira, I can't leave them, Amira, I can't, I can't!" he muttered miserably.

"Khalid, it's ok, they are resting now. You don't need to worry about them; they are all at peace..." she sniffed.

"They're with Mama and Baba now, both of them. And Alina is with her mama."

Khalid took one final look at the graves as he removed his face from his palms and inhaled loudly. With that, he stood up, held his hand out for Amira and helped her up.

"We have no time to wait anymore, neither am I prepared to wait..." Khalid told Musa Habib.

Amira looked at him, confused as to what he meant.

"Take us to the boats," Khalid demanded.

"Boats?" Amira uttered anxiously.

"The nearest and quickest boats arriving tomorrow are the ones near Mar Elias Refugee Camp, 3 hours away" he replied.

"But Khalid, why a boat? We have our documents for the airport," Amira asked.

"No, Amira, we don't anymore. I lost them in the attack," he replied forlornly.

Amira sighed.

"They were all in my pocket, in my jacket. The jacket is long gone and I looked for it and can't find it anywhere."

Amira tried not to cry, for the idea of riding in a boat crammed with hundreds of other refugees made her heart drop. She had heard stories of refugees travelling by a small inflatable boat across the channels and the thought of being in the dark in the middle of the ocean petrified her.

"We don't have time to waste, not now. The town could be attacked again and we need to keep moving. We aren't finished yet," Khalid told her.

That was the last thing Khalid said for the next 3 hours until they all reached Mar Elias refugee camp. They waited there for 20 minutes before Musa Habib collected them from the camp with a local smuggler. He took them through inside routes to avoid authorities and they ended up near the seaport. It wasn't a regular tourist attraction beach; instead, it was an illegal port.

Then there it was.

Not a ship, not a boat and not even a raft, but a small, old, inflatable dinghy. Amira's heart sank deeper and deeper into the bottom of her chest as they all walked closer to the inflatable.

"Khalid, this cannot possibly hold all these refugees! It will sink, Khalid!" Amira cried.

Around them, there were approximately 60 to 70 other Syrian and Palestinian refugees. They could hardly wait to climb into the boat.

"Khalid! Khalid, please, I can't go on that. We can't. We will drown!"

Munir and Sarah were silent.

Khalid looked at Amira and finally spoke after 4 hours of silence.

"We have no other option, Amira; no money, no ID, no documents, nothing..." Khalid spoke, almost deflated whilst he forced his words out.

"Put these on..." The smuggler, who was a young, bitter-looking man, handed Khalid and Amira two worn-out life jackets.

"Are these even safe or real jackets? They look so old and it's ripped!" Amira shouted at him.

"Listen to me, you! Take it or leave! You should be lucky I'm not making you pay for it, you ungrateful little brat!" he spat out. He was right in front of Amira's face and suddenly made her feel uncomfortable. Before she had a chance to speak, Khalid interrupted.

"Get the hell out of her face, you piece of shit!" he yelled.

With all his might, he pushed the smuggler away from Amira and he fell to the ground.

"Come in front of her again and see what I do to you."

The smuggler didn't argue and simply walked away with an aghast, stunned face.

"Right, put the life jackets on, everyone," another smuggler called out before helping a crowd of people onto the dinghy.

The motor roared and splattered loudly every time a person jumped on and Amira could swear she heard air escaping from the inflatable rubber interior.

"Amira, give me your hand," Khalid called out as they entered the rush of the crowd.

Amira gulped and took hold of Khalid's hand and squeezed it tightly before being pushed and tugged at by other refugees. Shouting and yelling was all she could hear as she approached the boat.

"WOMEN AND CHILDREN GO FIRST!" the smuggler bellowed loudly as he stood at the front of the dingy just beside the motor.

Sarah and Munir were already on the boat and they called out to Khalid and Amira.

"Just don't let go, Amira, I'll pull you inside once I'm in," he told her.

"Ok, Khalid', she cried like a baby.

Khalid placed his right leg into the inflatable and Munir helped him up and Amira was soon pulled into the shaking boat. It was hard to move around whilst wearing an oversized life jacket. Before she knew it, Amira, alongside Khalid, Sarah, Munir and another 60 or so refugees, were on the boat. She watched as the smugglers took money from some refugees to ride the boat. She also watched as so many refugees were being left behind. They tried climbing onto the boat but the smugglers pushed them down before they reach the inside.

"The boat will burst, you fool! There's no space left. Wait till next week when another boat arrives", they told the people left behind.

"You won't even make it a mile before it bursts if you all jump on; how will you reach Cyprus?!"

"Cyprus? But we're going to Turkey, not Cyprus!" Khalid shouted out to the main smuggler who was helping the last few people on.

"Turkey? No, no, this boat is going to Cyprus. You can go to Turkey from Cyprus,"

"Cyprus?" Amira whispered. She had never thought about going to Cyprus, nor even heard of it much.

'What could they do now'? she thought. They had already boarded the boat and were ready to go.

The people on the shore cried and pleaded with the men to allow them but it was pointless and soon after, the boat began to move away from the shore.

Khalid looked around and called out to Musa Habib, who was standing just off the shore beside the other refugees and consoling them. Musa finally caught a glimpse of Khalid and Amira and smiled. Khalid placed his hand on his chest and nodded his head at Musa Habib and mouthed 'Shukran, thank you'. Musa Habib did the same, placed his hand on his chest and smiled kindly.

Khalid then looked down and then at the other refugees. He exhaled miserably and closed his eyes.

"I'm sorry, Baba," he whispered to himself.

"I'm sorry" ...

CHAPTER FOURTEEN
Journey to Cyprus

After only an hour at sea, the overwhelmed motor stopped working and the whole craft upended in the ensuing terror. The sudden rush of panic and fright dispatched several passengers surging into the ocean. They started sinking, and soon Khalid realised that their life jackets were fake ones. They started to sink at first to a point where the shore wasn't visible to them anymore. There was nothing except the water and the sky, both things which seemed to look deadly at the time for Amira.

The boat overturned and many were trapped underneath. Khalid and Amira luckily knew how to swim but Sarah and Munir didn't. Amira and Khalid bobbed to the surface but Sarah and Munir were stuck underneath the overturned boat. Beneath the upturned craft, their life jackets began pushing them up and trapping them against the hull.

People began screaming and chanting 'Allahu Akbar' loudly as the roaring waves began rushing in. Khalid shouted at a few other men to help right the boat and help those trapped beneath it.

"Lift this way, in sync with the waves! The waves will help it overturn and lift up...1, 2, and 3! LIFT!" he yelled to 4 other men who were helping. After the first 6 tries, the boat finally turned over and about 7 people were trapped. Everyone swam and were dragged by others towards the boat and began dropping inside like live fish being caught by fishermen.

Sarah and Munir were panting for breath and coughing out the salty water they had drunk up, as were many other passengers as they entered the boat.

Amira couldn't make out where on earth they all were. All she saw were waves, clouds and the sky, nothing else. No shore, no land and no buildings. She began to regret ever coming on this boat. It was the most dreadful experience.

"Where are we?!" Khalid screamed at the main person who was beside the motor the whole time and was asked to guide the boat towards Cyprus. He knew the route, despite being a refugee just like everyone else on the boat.

"We're still within the Mediterranean Sea!" he yelled back loudly against the violent waves.

"According to my calculations, Cyprus is approximately 3 hours or so away, but because of the stormy weather, it may be longer. We need to ensure the boat is kept safe and no damage comes to it, otherwise, it will prolong our journey and make it difficult for us to arrive on time and together."

"Mira, stay close to me please, we need to stick together; these waves are too fucking fierce."

"Khalid, I'm scared…" Amira began to sob quietly. She could taste the saltiness of her tears against the salty seawater.

"Hey, hey now, come here, Princess," he soothed, grabbing her shoulder and holding her tightly.

"It's ok! Do you think I'm going to let anything happen to you, Mira? Huh?"

Amira sniffed and hiccupped out a few more tears.

"No…" she replied.

"Then stay with me, ok, and when the waves come, hold onto me tightly," he told her.

Amira held onto Khalid regardless, waves or not. She held him firmly as if he was going to run away. The heavy rain fell, like solid, treacherous firing from above. The rain started filling the boat with water, lots of it and Amira could see the panic in everyone's eyes as the boat began getting fuller and fuller.

"We'll sink!" someone shouted from the front of the boat.

"WE'RE GOING TO DIE! OH MY GOD!" a woman holding an infant cried in terror.

"No one is going to die! Grab whatever you can to fill up and start pouring out the rainwater into the sea!" Khalid suggested.

"Anything at all! Your shoes, bottles, buckets, goddammit, even your hands! Fill whatever you can and start to empty the boat! QUICK!"

Some people had baby milk bottles, others used their shoes. Amira, Sarah, Munir and Khalid all used their hands and shoes to fill water in and pour out. Soon, the boat felt heavy and Amira started worrying they would all slowly start to sink into the open sea.

"Khalid, it's sinking, I can feel it."

Khalid looked around him and without any hesitation, he spoke.

"All the men, get out of the boat!" he bellowed.

"Get out!? Have you lost your mind!?" another called.

"Unless you want the boat to completely sink then get the hell out of the boat! All the men, get out and hang against the boat with your legs in the sea! Otherwise, no one will make it to Cyprus alive!" Soon, Khalid began giving everyone orders and they all listened. People were petrified and they hung onto every bit of hope anyone was offering.

"That's it!" he said as they began jumping into the sea and holding the side of the boat.

"Yes! The boat is lifting up! You there! Out, come on!" Khalid yelled at a teenage boy.

The boat lifted extensively higher with approximately 30 men outside of it. It was crazy to think the rubber boat held around 60 people. Amira was baffled as to how such a thing was allowed, how the smugglers got away with it and how upsetting the whole thing was. The fact that so many were made to sit inside a boat just to flee danger from war. To Amira, it felt like danger followed her everywhere she went. No matter how hard she tried to escape it, it monitored and shadowed her like an intruder, imposing on her every move.

Khalid was outside the boat, inside the ocean, hanging tightly to the rubber side of the dinghy. Amira held both his arms from inside the boat. He struggled at first to get his bearings and balance himself so he didn't fall off. She held onto Khalid for dear life. Under the heavy rain, as it poured pugnaciously, all Amira wanted to do was hold onto Khalid and look at him. She peered into his deep, brown eyes and cried mutely. Although it was raining, Khalid could see Amira's tears right through her, just like he saw her pain, her happiness, her excitement and her sorrow. He saw it all.

Amira scanned Khalid's bloodshot eyes. They were reddened with salty seawater and sore. His look gave her a warmth, the sort of warmth you feel when you enter your home after a long day, the warmth you feel when being held tightly by the one you love, the type of warmth you experience when your mother helps you up after you fall and when your father brushes off the dust from your clothes and plasters your wound. Khalid's intense whirls of glassy, coffee coloured eyes captured his every, raw emotion. Amira knew. She knew of his pain, his worry, his panic and of his distress. He displayed it all, yet at the same time, kept it all a secret, hidden from the world, most importantly, from Amira. He ensured his eyes radiated with only spirit and bounce, yet he concealed the grief that positioned a sombre mask that shawled his eyes. When he smiled at Amira, his face lit with happiness at her face and his eyes exuded only contentment and happiness and they did so for only one reason; Amira.

"You know it will all be ok in the end, my Amiraty...my Princess," he spoke softly against the harsh waves.

"How are you so sure, Khalid? How are you saying all this with contentment?" she questioned him sadly, still holding onto his arms.

"Because...I just know."

Amira sighed and closed her eyes.

"Close your eyes, Mira, it will all be over soon..."

Khalid squeezed Amira's arm and managed to lift himself up to quickly place a soft kiss on her hand.

"How about you read me one of your poems…" he asked her spiritedly.

"I can't remember any, Khalid."

Amira's poem book was still with her, as was her small box of books, pictures and other sentimental things. She had managed to keep it with her and she only hoped they weren't getting soaked from inside. She kept it inside her side bag, which was the size of an A4 book.

"Don't ever lose your poem book, Amira…" Khalid muttered.

"I won't…"

"Now, read me a poem, Amiraty."

"Khalid…" she whispered.

"Hmmm?"

"You read one for me…" she requested.

Khalid paused for a moment before he promised her something.

"I tell you what, Mira, I'll make you a promise…" Amira's eyes lit up for a second as she suddenly felt eager to hear what Khalid had to say.

"I promise you, that as a wedding gift, I will write and recite you my very own poem, just for you…"

Amira subconsciously laughed with elation and sheer excitement at his promise.

"You serious!? Say promise, Khalid, you better not be joking."

"Me? Joking? Come on, I don't joke," he laughed.

"I can't wait! It better be a good one and not a silly one like before," she warned him.

"It will be the best poem in the world and I promise you that you will love it…" Khalid held out his pinkie finger.

Amira wrapped her finger around his pinkie and they pinkie promised each other, just like they had done when they were younger.

"It's never been easy for us Syrians and Palestinians who were seeking refuge in Lebanon; you'd think neighbouring countries would look out for each other!" A woman behind Amira who was holding her infant began angrily yelling out of frustration. Amira didn't turn around but heard her conversation with the other passengers. Another woman spoke.

"Lebanon is a divided country! It's got its own history of civil war and political structure based on power, control and influence between religious sects."

The first woman replied;

"At first, they welcomed us, then, when the Syrian Civil war began escalating and showing no signs of ending, more and more Lebanese civilians saw us refugees as threats and a source of insecurity."

"I mean, look at us! Do we look like threats? Do our children look like threats to you?" another woman cried out.

"What if Cyprus doesn't accept us!? Then what? We will have to return back to Lebanon and then there's the pressure of pushing us back into Syria..."

Amira hadn't thought about the possibility of being rejected in Cyprus up until now. She suddenly felt worried that that was going to be the case and they would have to return.

"We have nothing to return back to; no house, no family, nothing. Everything is gone, Ya Allah!" an elderly woman spoke sadly.

As the ladies spoke amongst themselves, an unexpected, enraged wave swayed towards the boat with great vigour, causing the boat to rock bitterly back and forth. Another huge wave ran towards the boat when someone shouted, "HOLD ON TIGHT!"

The wave hit the boat and many of the men outside the boat lost their grip and went spiralling into the water. Khalid lost his grip but was able to swim back in time to grab on again. Amira panted and lifted him into the boat again. Then, a screeching woman wailed piercingly. Amira turned and saw the woman who was holding her infant now bare-handed. Her child had fallen into the water.

"HELP HIM, SOMEBODY! GET ME MY CHILD, PLEASE, OH PLEASE!" she bawled hysterically to the men who were outside the boat and swimming towards the rubber side.

"HE'S THERE! SOMEBODY GRAB HIM! HE CANNOT SWIM, YA ALLAH HE IS GOING TO DIE!!! SOMEBODY GRAB HIM, PLEASE!

Khalid gasped and without any hesitation, he stood up and dived into the water. Amira barely had a chance to stop him before he left. He swam towards the direction of the child, who was wearing a life jacket far too big for him. It began weighing him down as it was a fake jacket and he soon sank into the deep ocean and was no longer visible from the top of the waves. His mother howled louder and louder as the seconds passed and the other women tried consoling her, but it was impossible.

Khalid dived into the sea, moving his arms firmly against the waves, almost as if he was climbing a mountain, yet it was only miles and miles of water surrounding him. Amira's heart was stuck within her throat and she gulped large, hardened rocks every time a wave hit. When a minute passed, it seems almost like an hour. She was filled with panic as Khalid couldn't be seen in the water. He wasn't wearing his life jacket as he had taken it off for it was only weighing him down and wasn't even real. Luckily, he knew how to swim.

"YA ALLAH, PLEASE DON'T DO THIS TO ME TODAY, PLEASE YA ALLAH, I AM BEGGING YOU FOR THE SAKE OF MY SON!" the frenetic woman begged distraughtly.

"LOOK! He's there!" shouted another woman from the other side of the boat. Amira squinted into the distance and finally saw a blurred vision of Khalid. She could tell it was him because of the bright green shirt he was wearing. In his arms, he was holding the boy. As he approached closer, Amira yelled and told him to grab her hand so she could help him up. Khalid's long hair was all over his wet face and he was trying hard to move it from his sight so he could see better. He reached the boat and Amira clutched his free arm and pulled him up. When he was half-way inside, he handed Amira the boy.

The woman cried aloud and Amira handed the child to her. His eyes were closed and his skin was pale, paler than snow. His fingers were pruned like raisins and it was difficult to tell if he was breathing or not.

"SOMEBODY HELP ME!! SOMEBODY HELP MY SON! HELP ME! HELP ME!" the woman's heart-breaking pleading brought tears to Amira's eyes. Her heart genuinely ached with grief and the pain felt electrifying as it spread through her body like a current.

"Khalid! Help him please, he's dying," Amira whimpered. Khalid was now aboard the boat. The other men around the boat were all ok and made their way towards the sides again.

Khalid pushed his soggy hair from his face and carefully stepped towards the woman and her son. He took him from her arms and placed him on his lap on his stomach and whacked his back forcefully three times. He continued again and again and then finally turned him around. He then began pumping his chest vehemently. No matter how hard Khalid tried and how hard he whacked his frail, lifeless body, it was hopeless. He was gone.

Khalid didn't have to say anything to the woman, for she already knew the fate of her 3-year-old son.

"Adnan!" she yowled in pain.

"My Adnan, my beautiful Adnan, my son, my baby, please wake up, Adnan."

Amira cried with the woman and so did Khalid. They both felt the pain of losing a loved child and they both felt the woman's torment.

"I lost your Baba and now you, please Allah help me!"

To see him dead and lifeless in her arms was to die herself.

She held him and wept hysterically into his chest.

From a distance, Amira caught sight of something. She squinted but couldn't make out exactly what it was. It looked like small, insect-sized buildings from afar. She nudged Khalid.

"Khalid, what is that? Look over there."

Khalid rubbed his stinging eyes and squinted.

"LAND! CYPRUS! THERE AHEAD! I CAN SEE IT!" he thundered loudly at the other men.

"ROW! ROW THE BOAT WITH YOUR HANDS! USE THE SPADE TOO! QUICKLY!"

The men all helped row the boat, as did the women. Amira gave the woman words of desperate hope that her son would be ok once they reached land, that they would find help for him and take him to a doctor. But it was pointless.

"He is dead, my child, he is dead."

Amira looked ahead and sighed and helped the others row towards the shore. After a good 20 minutes of rowing and almost 50 hours of battling against the waves, they had reached Cyprus.

CHAPTER FIFTEEN
Cyprus – Nicosia

Due to its geographical positioning within the Mediterranean Sea, Cyprus is one of the most accessible points of entry for migrants and refugees who are in search of a new home outside of Syria. Many chose to travel to either Turkey and Cyprus, whereas others aim further and try to gain access to a home within Europe. The country itself is in the midst of a growing, burgeoning migrant crisis as smuggler networks take full advantage, looking to profit as well as gain from the Mediterranean Island's close vicinity to the Middle East.

There is no current system within Cyprus to deal with refugees who wash up on Cypriot land. Some wait 3 months for accommodation, whereas others wait 3 years.

When Amira and Khalid were washed up on the Cyprus shore, they were greeted by locals.

"Oh, my goodness, are they…? Are they ok? Who are they? Where have you come from? Are you Syrian? Did you really travel from Syria by boat?"

The questions didn't stop.

The chilly seawater circled around Amira's legs as Khalid helped her to shore. The water hissed and fizzled like brine. They finally reached the shore and took their first steps on land, Cypriot land. Their pruned feet inside their shoes pressed against the wet, soggy soles. Amira took off her boots and strode on the warm, grainy sand on Mackenzie Beach in the town of Larnaca. The warmth of the scorching sun beamed down on Amira's neck and behind her, the waves howled in the distance.

Ahead of them, Amira saw tourists wearing bikinis and shorts as they lay on the beach, sunbathing. As they all washed up on the shore and made their way towards the sand, tourists got up from their seats and sunbeds in horror and astonishment to see the women, children, men and babies in life jackets walking towards them. Some began helping them, whereas others just watched.

"Do you need anything? Here, take this, please," an elderly woman who wore a rose-patterned swimming costume handed Amira and Khalid a bottle of water and sandwich box which was unopened.

"Please, eat."

It took a while for all the people to fully leave the boat and gather themselves on the beach. Authorities made themselves visible within 10 minutes of the refugees' arrival.

Amira was overwhelmed at the kindness and help offered by the locals. For her, she always imagined outside countries always 'disliking' *her* people. People of war and colour and Islamic religion. Islam had always been in the spotlight, ever since the horrific 9/11 bombings back in 2001 in America and the religion as a whole had always been scrutinized by the media. Amira felt warmth surrounded by such generous people. People she didn't even know the names of were offering the refugees blankets, food, water, shampoo, sanitary pads and razors. It was truly confounding.

The little boy, Adnan, who had died, was taken to a local hospital to be assessed alongside other refugees who were poorly. Amira saw the last of Adnan's mother as she held onto her dead son's body and entered a minibus and sat miserably against the window seat. She looked into the distance, at the sea and the boat still hovering around in the water with life jackets thrown around it. She gave Amira a final look with her immersed, grey eyes that shifted to her and became polished with a shiny layer of regretful tears and before Amira even had a chance to wave goodbye, the minibus drove off.

■■

A group of aid workers soon arrived at Mackenzie Beach. They took a minibus of 20 people to Nicosia, which housed one of the refugee camps that aided in helping find shelter for refugees either within Cyprus, Greece or neighbouring European countries.

"We are not staying here in Cyprus, Brother, we need to get to Turkey." Khalid tried to explain to an aid worker of his plans to reach Turkey. Luckily, the aid worker spoke fluent English as well as some broken Arabic. Both Amira and Khalid knew English as they learnt it at school when they were growing up in Aleppo.

"Brother, Turkey? You have no money and no ID? You know the only way to Turkey for you…," the aid worker gestured at a life jacket underneath a seat in the minibus. Amira knew exactly what he meant. The only way to Turkey meant travelling by boat again, illegally. That was the only way for many refugees who had lost everything they owned, including their life savings and ID documents.

Khalid sighed and sunk into his seat. Munir and Sarah were behind Khalid and Amira's seat. They were talking between themselves quietly.

"What now, Munir? Are we going to travel further to claim asylum here?" Sarah asked her husband.

"I don't know yet, Sarah, we need to figure this out," he replied.

Amira thought to herself for a moment before she asked Khalid;

"Khalid...Why don't we just stay here? We don't have to go to Turkey, do we? We can start our life here, can't we?"

Khalid stayed deeply sunk into his seat. He was quiet. Then he spoke.

"Mira, as nice as these people seem, I don't think they want us here in their country. At least Turkey is a Muslim country...and it will be easier to find a home there. I don't want to spend a single night in a refugee camp, Mira, neither do I want to put you through that again."

Amira could understand Khalid's concerns. She didn't want to stay in a refugee camp either. Her clothes were soggy and damp, including her undergarments. She desperately needed to shower and put on some fresh clothes. Khalid was right; they needed to go to Turkey, they had to.

Turkey hosted the largest refugee population in the world, with around 3.5 million Syrians living there. The refugees were able to gain access to health care, education and a small allowance. Although refugees do not have the other many benefits such as accommodation and child benefit, they are still cared for much better than in any other European country.

Nicosia was only an hour away. Before they drove towards the refugee camp, Amira saw many refugees, just like her, sleeping in parks and on benches. She saw young kids, no older than 5, playing amongst themselves and in groups. Their clothes were filthy, their hair tangled and their lips parched, yet their faces were full of joy and innocence. She watched them play tag and run after one another with excited shrieking when being caught. Her heart sank deeper and deeper into a black hole as she mourned the presence of Adam, Shakil and Alina. The immense ponderousness of pain from within Amira was felt in every one of her limbs. She tried hard to push aside such a feeling, but nothing could help her from missing her family. How she longed for her baba's arms or her mother's lap. Hot tears ran down her face and she quickly wiped them away before anyone could see, especially Khalid, but he had already seen.

He pushed aside his bag full of dirty clothes, water bottles and a few dried fruits and pulled Amira close. They were sat in an overly-crowded minibus full of other refugees. Some old, some disabled, others injured and many devasted and simply tired of travelling. Not a single person had clean clothes on, nor did they have anything to eat.

"Why the long face, Mira?" asked Khalid.

She didn't reply. She simply placed her head on Khalid's shoulder and wept soundlessly into his neck. She inhaled Khalid's scent, the same scent she smelt when sleeping in his arms, the same scent that made her feel safe and protected. It was a mixture of warmth and musk. Despite travelling for miles and going through dirty seawater and sweating whilst walking for miles and miles through forests and illegal roads, this scent never left Khalid. It intoxicated Amira, as if it were a drug.

"I miss them too, Mira..." Khalid uttered under his breath with despondency and sadness.

He sighed loudly and pulled Amira closer and kissed her forehead.

When they arrived at the refugee camp in Nicosia, a group of Catholic aid workers helped the group of refugees to the camp. The camp was more a tent city, with high extended tents and a walkway full of mud. Despite these tents looking much bigger than the ones back in Lebanon, the atmosphere and surroundings there were just as horrendous, with people waiting hours for the showers that looked worse than you'd find in a prison, children running around barefoot in the potholes full of dirt and wet swamp and women walking around begging for food and clothing.

The aid workers directed Amira, Khalid, Sarah and Munir to a tent, which was already full of a family consisting of 5 children and their mother. She was a Somalian lady who held a baby at her hip and held another child by the hand. The other children were scattered around her.

Amira looked at the old woman. She bowed slightly as she walked around the tent with a small hunchback behind her. The lines on her face were deep and painted across her angry face down to her neck which was sagging. Amira tried smiling at her a few times, to which the woman looked away and simply ignored her. Amira didn't think she would see a Somali family of refugees at the camp, but to her surprise, there were many families she saw who were from Somalia and travelling as refugees.

"They've left their country too," a voice spoke behind Amira as she was undoing her wet laces. She jumped up and turned around. A skinny, blonde-haired boy with freckles and glasses spoke with a swift, fleet voice. He was an aid worker. Amira guessed he was as he held a clipboard in his hand and wore uniform-like attire with a blue badge with the letters 'UNHCR' on it.

"They left Somalia due to political reasons, fighting and conflict. They have no idea where they are," he said.

"What do you mean they have no idea?" Amira asked confusingly.

"Meaning they were put on a boat, left to flee their land and basically had no idea where they were going to end up. All they knew was that they had to escape their country."

Amira looked up at the woman, who was now looking at the boy, hoping for some answers as to what was going to happen.

"Trouble is, she doesn't speak any English, like most of the other Somali refugees here too. I need to explain to her that she is in Cyprus and that we need to find her documents so we can process her through to the refugee scheme."

Amira thought for a second and had an idea.

"Do you have your phone?" she asked the boy.

The boy fished his hand in his pocket and got out his iPhone.

"Here."

Amira took the phone from his hand and opens up Google Images. She typed down 'World Map' into the search bar and opened up a large image of the map of the world. She walked towards the old woman, who seemed to resist and walk back slightly as Amira approached her. Amira smiled once more and showed the woman the picture.

She pointed at Somalia and then fingered the Red Sea. She guessed they had travelled up towards the Red Sea past Ethiopia, Sudan, Egypt and then finally reached Cyprus. Amira finished pointing at Cyprus and gestured the floor, trying to explain to the woman that they were currently in Cyprus. Whilst she explained, the woman's older daughter, who seemed to look around the age of 16, 17, watched Amira's picture and spoke to her mother in their language.

The woman looked at the map again and started to cry. She looked overwhelmed with anger and distraught at the realisation of her location. Amira didn't know how to react and suddenly moved away and hid the picture. She quickly handed the boy his phone back and told him, "Just use Google Translate to explain something to them."

The woman and daughter were crying. The daughter tried to hush her mother but it was pointless. She was profoundly overcome with disbelief. Amira left the tent and looked for Khalid, Sarah and Munir. She wandered around and jumped past all the potholes of mud and dirty water. She managed to change into slightly cleaner clothes which she found in her bag. She also had a 3-minute shower and freshened up, but even then, she felt far from fresh and clean. It felt as if the dirt and filth was tattooed to her skin. She constantly felt unclean.

Khalid had told Amira that he was going to try finding food. She looked around the camp and couldn't find him. She saw an alleyway which was located beside a half-open tent. She walked past the tent to find a bunch of children inside laughing and playing with paint. She curiously took a peep inside to find Sarah and Munir, alongside a group of young teenage charity workers painting on large canvases with the children. Amira smiled and entered the tent.

"What's going on here!?" she exclaimed excitedly.

Sarah turned to her.

"These are all orphaned children, they're looked after by charity workers. Every day they bring arts and crafts for them to busy themselves with," she told Amira.

"Aww, that is so fun! Look at this little one," Amira pointed to a small boy who was wearing a Palestinian football shirt with black shorts. His light brown hair swayed from side to side as he ran cheerfully up and down the tent with green paint all over his palms. He finally stopped at a white canvas board and stamped his hands on the clean space. When he lifted his hands away, his eyes lit up with joy as he saw his handprints imprinted in bright green paint. He jumped and bounced up and down, with not a care in the world.

Amira laughs to herself and can't stop giggling at his cute mischievousness.

"Oh, Khalid was just here; he went literally 5 minutes ago towards the hill," Munir told Amira.

Amira left the tent and walked towards the hill area in front of her. She decided to walk down the alley to reach the hill as it seems less congested than strolling past other people constantly moving in and out of the camp area.

As she entered the alley, it suddenly seemed dark. She looked above her and saw pieces of roughly sewn plastic sheets covering the top of the alley. The alley itself was a place between tents all full of people. She quickly strolled down the alley until she heard a sound. It sounded like a pebble being thrown from behind her. She got a sudden sense of déjà vu and before she had a chance to turn around, Khalid jumped up and scared Amira. Only this time, she prepared herself.

"RAHHHHHH!!" Khalid bellowed loudly, grabbing Amira by her hips.

He paused, confused as to why she didn't jump up in horror.

"What!? You serious?" he laughed.

"You didn't get scared? Oh man!"

"Nope, you don't scare me anymore, Khalid," Amira giggled.

"Oh really? Hmmm, interesting..." Khalid replied, slyly.

He placed his arm around Amira's shoulder and pointed his other hand towards her shoulder.

Amira turned around and saw a hairy, brown spider scattering down Khalid's hand towards her shoulder. She screeched loudly and panicked. She pushed her arm away from Khalid and ran down the alley, flapping at her shoulder. Behind her, Khalid fell to the floor in hysterics and fresh tears rolled down his face. He laughed and laughed till his belly ached and Amira just watched from afar.

"KHALID! HOW COULD YOU DO SOMETHING LIKE THAT!? YOU KNOW I HATE SPIDERS, KHALID! DON'T SPEAK TO ME EVER AGAIN! I NEVER WANT TO SPEAK TO YOU!" she cried as she shivered in disgust.

Amira had always hated spiders. She wiped away her tears and fat rolls of sweat from her forehead and sighed. She looked at Khalid, who snickered and chuckled to himself in the distance. She couldn't help but smile after she gathered herself together, but didn't want to show Khalid her smirk. She hadn't seen Khalid laugh like that in a while, and it warmed her heart to see his face full of joy and happiness, even if it did last only a moment.

Khalid started walking towards Amira.

"You better not come here if you have that ugly, disgusting creature in your hand, Khalid! And don't think I'm joking; I am NOT speaking to you again!" she spoke sternly.

Khalid smiled.

"But...but I thought I didn't scare you anymore, Mira? What happened there, huh? I mean, to me you seemed pretty damn scared," he joked.

"Hmm!" she exclaimed.

"Look, look!" Khalid pointed to his hand.

"Look it's gone, I promise, Mira, my princess."

Amira looked at his hands and couldn't see any spider. She folded her arms and faced away from Khalid, showing him her annoyance.

Khalid couldn't help smiling to himself and when he reached Amira, he placed his face deep into her warm neck. He closed his eyes and breathed in her smell. She seemed to have soothed and alleviated Khalid more than he expected and before she knew it, his strong, pacifying arms were around her waist, wrapped snuggly around her stomach. He kissed Amira's neck slightly and bit it. She inhaled and closed her eyes, for she didn't want this moment to end. She felt safe around Khalid, with his face in close proximity to hers and his protective arms wrapped around her body.

After a while, Khalid moved away and faced Amira. She tried her best to hide the smile on her face, but even before Khalid made eye contact with her, she was smirking from ear to ear.

Khalid laughed.

"Oh, Khalid, just shush!" she whined.

"Ha! I thought you weren't talking to me ever again?"

"Whatever!" she pushed him away and he came back and hugged her tightly.

"Oh Mira, my beautiful princess..." he exhaled.

"You know I love you...like SOOO much, right?" he asked, playfully.

"Hmmm, no, not really," she replied.

"No? Ok, well let me tell you now, I love you...My Amiraty..."

Amira giggled shyly and punched Khalid's arm light-heartedly.

"When we get married Mira, I will give you everything! I'll give you the whole world at your feet, I promise..."

"Khalid, I don't want everything, I just want you and me and somewhere safe to live," she uttered in a low voice.

Khalid stared into her loving eyes and stroked her pink cheeks. He stared into her cordial, kind eyes before stroking her lips with his finger. He leant in and closed his eyes. He gently placed his parched lips onto hers and kissed her. Amira shivered with butterflies in her belly and goosebumps all over her arms.

Khalid looked at her and said, "I know, and I promise that too. But you just wait and see Mira, I will treat you like the proper princess that you are. I'll take you to nice restaurants in Turkey, and buy you roses and always keep scaring you," he chuckles as he spoke and couldn't contain his excitement. Amira did the same and looked down at her feet. Khalid lifted her face and asked, "What's wrong, Mira?"

Amira sighed and hid her tears. She choked on her tears as she uttered, "I miss them..."

Khalid embraced her tightly and stroked her hair. He held onto her for a few minutes before whispering, "It's ok, it's almost over, my princess."

When Amira and Khalid got back to their tent, the charity worker who was inside was leaving as they entered.

"The family in there…" he began, "They're quite sensitive at the moment. They were deceived by smugglers."

"What do you mean?" asked Khalid.

"Meaning, the smuggler told them and promised them that the boat was to be taken to Italy, where their families were waiting. Unfortunately, that wasn't the case. They were also told a smuggler would stay on board and help with the journey, however, he fled as soon as the boat was off."

"The bastard!" Khalid snapped, angrily.

"Not even half-way into the journey, the engine started playing up. Didn't end well…many died at sea, whereas others died on board." The charity worker sighed and tensed his brows.

"They'll just have to wait here for now, till we find a secure place for them to stay before they somehow make it to Italy to be with their family," he said.

"They can seek asylum, no?" asked Khalid.

"Well they can, but it will be difficult; they barely speak English, nor do they have any documents…" he replied.

"We will help them through the process and once they apply for asylum, they'll receive an identity document that will allow them to work after a month."

"Where can they seek asylum?" Khalid asked the charity worker.

"Cyprus has two reception centres where newly arrived asylum seekers wait to be registered, one near the southern city of Larnaca and the other is in the village of Pournara."

"Hmmm, I see."

"But Brother, you have to remember, Cyprus doesn't grant refugee status to Syrians and instead, they are classified under 'subsidiary protection status,'" the worker tells him.

"Meaning?" Khalid asked, confused.

"Meaning, the classification offers fewer rights and doesn't allow you to travel onwards."

Khalid got agitated and sternly asked, "So how do we travel? We need to get to Turkey as soon as possible."

Khalid knew the answer, as did Amira.

"The expectation is that once the situation in Syria stabilizes, Syrian refugees will go home."

"HOME!? HOME!? WHAT HOME!?" Khalid began getting red in the face and Amira grabbed his arm to calm him.

"We have no fucking home left!? Where do they expect us to go? To what home?"

Amira's heart sank deeper into her chest as she thought about the idea of returning to Syria.

"It isn't like the war is showing any signs of stopping..." Amira added in.

"I know, so for now, you can seek asylum and stay here till it does, but even then, too much congestion of refugees may force authorities to send you back."

Khalid gathered himself and exhaled loudly.

"I'm sorry, Brother, it isn't my call," the worker told Khalid.

Khalid shook the worker's hand and thanked him for his help.

Inside the tent, the woman is sat with her children around her. She didn't look up when both Khalid and Amira walked in, but instead stays still, staring at the floor with her hand resting on her forehead. Her children all sit around her, some asleep and others sat, powerless.

Amira looked at Khalid and he gave her a nod. She walked over to the woman and sat beside her. The stench of saltwater and damp came from each and every child, and also from the mother. The woman took no notice of Amira as she sat down beside her and didn't flinch in surprise. Amira felt anxious for a moment for she had this sudden fear the woman would get angry at her for sitting near her family.

She gulped and took a deep breath, and lifted her hand to hold the woman's hand. The woman winced slightly and moved her eyes to meet Amira's. She studied Amira's face with her ashy, dark grey eyes that reminded Amira of the colour of the ocean. They were a mix of dark grey and blue. In those eyes, Amira could somehow read the woman's pain, for it was simply displayed in her look and the way she glanced at Amira. Amira gently squeezed the woman's hand and smiled in a friendly manner, to which she managed a slight, faint flinch of her lips. It wasn't exactly a smile but it wasn't a frown either. After a minute or two, the woman's children started playing amongst themselves.

Amira looked at the woman again and spoke, "Amira," she said, pointing at herself. She tried to make the woman understand what she was trying to do. She pointed at herself again and said her name clearly. She then pointed towards the woman to ask for her name. The woman sat up suddenly and spoke.

With her fierce, yet comforting voice, she rumbled, "Ilhaam…" She pointed towards herself again and repeated her name to Amira, and to Amira's surprise, she gave her a broad, warm smile.

"Ilhaam."

Amira extended her arm towards Ilhaam as if she was going to shake her hand. Ilhaam did the same and they both shook hands.

"Asalamu Alaykum, Ilhaam," Amira giggled.

Ilhaam chuckled and replied to her greeting.

"Wa'alaykum Salam, Amira."

That evening, when Khalid and Munir went to find food, Amira introduced Sarah to Ilhaam and soon, they were all trying to communicate with hand gestures and sounds. Amira felt a sort of contentment in making friends with Ilhaam, for she saw a positive outcome for her children who were all smiling now and busy in play. Amira felt as if this was because of their mother smiling and giving them that simple sense of complacency.

The boys returned with some food that they had found on a stall. They had some bread, olives, apricots, a small jar of raspberry jam and a small packet of uncooked lentils. Amira and Sarah both boiled some water and cooked the lentils and the whole tent was satisfied with a hearty meal of warm, soupy lentils with bread and apricots for afters. They all filled their bellies until there was nothing left.

After eating, Khalid began having a conversation with Munir.

"I'm stuck, Brother..." Khalid spoke dismally.

"Why, what's the matter?" Munir responded, slurping the last of his lentil soup.

"My heart is telling me to go to Turkey, and make my home there just as my Baba wanted, but..." he paused.

"But?" Munir asked.

"But my brain is telling me that getting on another boat will just fuck up the situation even more...Ahh Ya Allah, what do I do?" Khalid groaned and took a long, dreary sigh. The sigh was desolate and drained and it displayed a frustrated declaration of the end of deliberate exertion. Khalid was tired, tired of trying to figure everything out alone, without Baba. Although he had Amira beside him, he desperately longed for his father to guide him, as a father does.

"Life won't be easy here if you were to stay, and imagine we get sent back to Syria? Then what?" Munir stuttered under his breath.

"The language difference is already difficult for refugees who can't speak English. I mean just think about it...work opportunities are bound to be restricted to manual labour tasks like cleaning or factory work."

"Hmm, your right. Look around at how many older men there are here; they won't be able to do such labour, I mean it isn't fair on them," Khalid replied.

Amira and Sarah listened.

"They'll exploit our people. Both men and women are already being sexually exploited for a bed or shelter, an aid worker down by the market told me. They're pushing innocent refugees into corruption in order to merely survive. I mean, look at the migration policy! That's where the fault lies and problems arise. How can they tell us that eventually, we will have to go back to Syria?" Khalid shouted angrily.

"They haven't seen what we have; they haven't lost loves ones or seen bombs erupt in front of them. What do you expect? They're heartless," Sarah uttered faintly.

"It's the policy that's flawed and that's what's causing the asylum seeker crisis, not the refugee crisis itself," Amira added.

The group sat in silence for a while. Ilhaam was fast asleep, alongside her children. There weren't any proper beds inside the tent, only dirty, thin mattresses. There were 2 remaining mattresses left. Sarah and Munir slept on one after they cleared away the food and Amira lay on the other. Khalid went towards her mattress and sat up beside her. He sat there for a while. Amira was in and out of sleep when she was awakened by a noise. It was Khalid.

He was moaning and puffing angrily every so often and when Amira rubbed her eyes, she found him still sat up beside her. His back was slightly turned to the side so she couldn't see his face. She saw him sitting there, with his legs crossed, scribbling something onto a piece of paper. When she sat up, she found him writing something on a torn sheet of paper from her poem book. He had torn it ever so carefully so that the book wasn't ruined. Her box of books, pictures and poem notebook was in front of him.

"Khalid…?" Amira puzzlingly murmured.

Khalid immediately got up and hid the paper behind his back, unaware that Amira had woken up.

"Mi… Mira… Sorry, I just…I just needed a paper from the book, your poem book. Don't be angry…I just need one, I promise. Actually, or maybe 2…" Khalid was stuttering more than usual like he did when he was caught out. He used to do the same when Amira would catch him going to a protest back in Syria and taking part in marches.

"What you doing?" she asked.

"Are you annoyed?"

Amira chuckled. "No, Khalid, it's just a piece of paper, of course, I'm not annoyed. But what are you doing though?" she asked again.

"Phewww, man, I thought you were gonna be screaming your head off!" he joked, then took the paper from his hand and waved it in Amira's face.

"What's that?"

"Well… it's my very own poem…" he replied proudly.

"Poem?"

"Yup, remember my promise? This is my poem that I am going to give to you when we get married," Khalid said with a hint of a glimmer in his eyes as he proudly folded the paper and placed it inside a plastic zip-lock bag and then into his inside jacket pocket.

"No way!" Amira shrieked quietly.

"Show me! I want to read it!" she said eagerly trying to snatch it from him.

"Ha, ha, nice try! You aren't getting this just yet, Mira. I'm still working on it...but it's so hard, man! How do you do it? I've been reading your poems and trying to get some inspiration, but you're just an expert, I mean how can I compete with you?" Khalid laughed and started clearing away the stuff he had taken out of Amira' s box and shut the lid tightly.

"Owwww! not fair Khalid. At least let me read what you've written so far...come on..."

"Nope, not even a word! Patience is a virtue, you know," he sniggered as she got annoyed at his sarcasm.

"Ughhhh! Ok, ok...fine, I'll wait." She folded her arms like an upset child and frowned.

"What a cute little frown... here...let me try turning it around."

Khalid tickled Amira's belly and left her in a fit of silent, muffled laughter. Tears rolled down her cheeks as she couldn't help feeling ticklish.

"Better?" he asked, once she had pushed him away with her legs.

"Shush!" she snapped, still giggling quietly without waking anyone. Then all of a sudden, loud, rumbling snoring came from behind Amira and Khalid. They both turned around together to find Munir snoring away. They couldn't help but laugh into their pillows.

"Shall I chuck my sock at him?" Khalid asked Amira.

"No! Don't be so silly, Khalid."

Amira went back into her space on the mattress and Khalid joined her. He placed the light sheet of cloth over her first, then himself. They both looked up at the roof of the tent, which was coming apart due to heavy wind.

"Imagine a bird flies past and poops on your face while you are sleeping," said Khalid.

"Why on earth would I want to imagine something so stupid?" she answered back.

Khalid's parched, dry lips formed a wide smile. His goofy sense of humour always left Amira giggling to herself.

Soon, Amira could feel her eyes shutting. She tried opening them but they became heavier and heavier every time she tried. She shuffled closer to Khalid, who was now also falling asleep. She placed her head on his chest and one arm around him. He lifted his arm to embrace her and they both fell asleep in each other's arms.

CHAPTER SIXTEEN
Leaving Cyprus – July 2016

Cyprus, having a residential population of approximately 850,000 civilians, witnessed asylum applications rise dramatically by 56 percent by mid-2016. It had provided security and protection to many refugees, whilst many others were simply left with their application with a 'pending decision' status. The ongoing number of rising refugees being swept in from neighbouring borders resulted in tensions growing amongst the country as a whole, as well as straining the reception system, leading to more and more homeless refugees who began getting forced into being trafficked and sexually exploited in return for food, shelter and clothing because they were vulnerable.

There was a constant, hindering pressure on the island's main refugee camps and soon, Khalid and Amira were told to begin looking for private accommodation.

"You what? Private shelter? And where exactly shall I get the money to pay for my private accommodation, dear friend?" Khalid gawped at an aid worker who was managing the charity.

"I can understand your frustration, sir, but…"

"But nothing! We were here first and now you want to kick us out because there is no space for new refugees? Am I right? How is that fair, tell me!" Khalid snapped.

"Look, sir, there's just nothing more we can do, we are overcrowded as it is. I mean you can see the situation for yourself."

Since they had all arrived in the camp almost 2 weeks ago, the number of refugees being placed in the camp had increased drastically and the camp was slowly becoming majorly congested. Ilhaam was still in the tent and wasn't sent away, but a few friends that Amira had made from neighbouring tents were all being sent away, one by one, to find their own accommodation.

"I knew they would kick us out eventually! How do we not look desperate enough?" Sarah moaned to Munir.

"They're kicking all the young and 'able' people out and prioritising women and children and those injured," he replied.

"Haa! Private accommodation! That's fucking impossible. We barely have money for food, so how can we afford rent for accommodation?" said Khalid.

Khalid found a job cleaning a nearby restaurant and he had been working there for the 2 weeks they had all stayed in Cyprus. Munir did the same, but instead of cleaning the restaurant, he was asked to work as a security guard. Both soon had a small wage at the end of every day to feed themselves and buy new clothes and general necessities, but there was no way they could afford the expenses of private accommodation or even a simple shelter house fee.

People began resorting to sleeping in parks on benches. They made their own tents from fabric or old clothes and slept in parks, empty grassy areas and any spare piece of land they could possibly find. Women, children and vulnerable men, all cramped up in small spaces along different parks was something Amira did not want.

"We can't stay here," Khalid turned to Amira.

"We need to leave."

Amira gulped.

"Things will only get worse if Syria weakens even more and the war continues to extend. I don't want to wait around for that to happen and then Cypriot authorities telling us we need to go back. They will begin resenting us, especially now there are more and more of us arriving every other day at the border," Khalid spoke to the group.

They listened on.

"No, we need to leave." Khalid turned and left the tent. Munir followed him and Amira waited with Sarah.

"I don't want to leave, Sarah, I'm scared. I'm so, so scared." Amira began to whimper and from behind her, Ilhaam approached her and embraced her tightly. Her motherly hug consoled Amira for a moment but nothing could remove the intensity of fear and anxiety she felt squeezing her chest every time she breathed.

"It's okay, darling, we will find a way out, don't worry," Sarah reassured her. Ilhaam kissed Amira's forehead and gave her a maternal, soothing smile.

Amira felt all sorts of emotions. She felt a sudden mourning for her family, for her baba and mama and little brother. She started recalling every conversation she ever had with them all. She remembered her father's daily antics about poetry and writing novels and her mother's telling off. She began remembering it all.

'Do not feel lonely, for the whole universe is inside you'. She began to recall all the quotes and poems she ever wrote with her baba and all the things he used to say in response to a new poem she had written. She remembered the time her mother was ill and Amira stayed up all night to tend to her. She sat beside her bed and massaged her legs and gave her regular sips of water and honey. She also remembered Baba Mohammed and his soft, frail voice when he would give Amira advice and recite new poems to her.

She rubbed her chest for the pain hidden deep inside her ached her every vein. She felt helpless and deeply regretful. She tried desperately to find a way out of this pain. She tried thinking of a happy or funny memory, focusing on something else and busying herself with the children in the play tent, but it was impossible. She still felt the same, until she opened her box and took out her poem book and began to write...

That evening, Khalid and Munir returned from work. Khalid entered the tent and looked straight at Amira with desperate, apologetic eyes.

"Pack up, Mira...We're leaving."

∎∎

Saying goodbye was never easy. In the same way, not saying goodbye had an equal measure of regret. Amira often thought about how she never had a chance to say goodbye to her parents, to Adam and to the rest of her family and friends. She thought about the time she last saw Baba Mohammed at the market after the shelling back in Aleppo, and how she had said goodbye to him, not realising it was the last goodbye she would ever utter from her lips to him. Now, standing in front of Ilhaam, Amira didn't feel like saying goodbye.

Ilhaam had prepared Amira and Sarah some brown rice with lentils and chickpeas. She also made a simple yoghurt mixture with lime and some leftover onions from the night before. She handed Sarah the pot. Amira looked at Ilhaam. She walked towards her and threw her arms tightly around her. She smelt of burnt onions and rice and her smell soothed Amira somehow. Ilhaam stroked Amira's hair and lulled her as she wept into Ilhaam's shoulder. She missed Mama, dearly. All Amira wanted was her mother's hug, her mother's screaming, her mother's laughter. She ached for it desperately. Ilhaam kissed Amira's forehead and gave her a last smile before they all exited the tent, forever.

This time, there wasn't a large group travelling with Amira, Khalid, Sarah and Munir. Instead, the group consisted of only 8 other refugees travelling to Turkey. To Amira's relief, a smaller group meant an easier journey whilst at sea, however, she still had her doubts and worries about the whole thing. The group travelled with a smuggler. Khalid and Munir managed to find a local smuggler within Nicosia who arranged for the group to travel to Turkey. Khalid ensured that he provided the group with working, real life jackets, a proper engine that was fully functioning as well as a pilot to guide them towards the coast of Turkey to safely reach Alanya. They had to drive towards the Cypriot city of Kyrenia.

The drive towards Kyrenia was horrifying. The group were placed inside a container. Although the drive was only an hour long, every second was terrifying.

"Khalid…Khalid, I can't…I can't brea…I can't breathe, Khalid…" Amira was panicking and her pulse rate exceeded its normal state. Her whole body started to sweat and the tightness in her throat caused her to gasp loudly for air.

"Mira! It's okay! You can breathe. Breathe with me...come on." Khalid synced his breathing to help Amira calm her nerves. They sat inside the container with nothing around them other than darkness. She could not see Khalid beside her, nor Sarah and Munir in front of her and not even her hand raised in front of her face. Sheer pitch-black darkness encompassed her and encircled her every move. Amira placed herself slowly on the floor of the container as Khalid helped her inside. Munir used his torchlight from his phone to make it slightly easier for everyone, but soon, after a few minutes, his phone battery died. Khalid placed himself next to Amira and held her close.

"Mira, you okay?" he asked, as he wiped his sweat from his brow.

Amira felt far from okay. Her lungs felt elastic and springy as she forced deep breaths out from her mouth, but the straining and struggling led to more and more breathlessness. The darkness that is supposed to aid one to fall asleep in peace was now that same darkness that felt lethal. The stench of sweat wafted in and out of Amira's nose and the humidity and heat from inside the container was impossible to escape. Salty beads of sweat intruded into her eyes and Amira wiped them away continuously.

Khalid pulled Amira closer to his chest and hummed rhythmically to calm her down.

"How long, Khalid? I need to get out of here. Why are we even in here? Can't we go in a normal car?"

249

"Not long, Mira, I promise you. We can't be seen; were not citizens in Cyprus so they will realise were trying to escape and travel... We can't risk it and be sent back to Syria."

"Oh, Khalid! I can't bear anymore! I can't bear any more of this," Amira pleads with Khalid. He started to rock Amira slowly, reaching for her face carefully without poking her in the darkness. He stroked her cheek and hummed quietly.

"Mira...?"

"Yes, Khalid?"

"Read me a poem, Mira."

Amira shuffled in her spot and paused at Khalid's request. The only time Khalid asked Amira to read him a poem was either when he was happy or when he was anxious or stressed. Amira remembered when Khalid was beaten up by a militant back in Shamsa Park and he was in grievous pain when he asked Amira, "Read me a poem, please." Khalid must have also been feeling anxious about being in the container. Amira felt guilty almost, as she felt she had abandoned the needs of Khalid and forgotten that he too was a part of this haunting journey.

"Which poem shall I read you, Khalid?" Amira asked sweetly.

"Any...they're all good."

"I made one about you..." she said.

"Let's hear it then, my Amiraty."

Amira cleared her throat and peacefully recited her poem to Khalid.

"Whenever life gets hard and the road seems a little rough,
My eyes search for yours, for they make me tough.
You wipe away my tears and grab my hand firm,
And as the days pass, there is always something new we both learn.
I love you today,
As I have from the start,
And I'll love you forever,
With every inch of my heart.
When I look at you,
My whole world is filled with pleasure,
For every moment with you,
Has been my greatest treasure" …

"This is why I love you Mira…" whispered Khalid into her ear. She closed her eyes and patiently waited for the journey inside the container to come to an end.

When the container stopped moving, Amira waited for someone to lift the metal opening above their heads to release them from inside. A minute went by, then another and soon Amira felt as if she was waiting for hours. After 10 minutes, the smuggler opened the rounded metal door from the top of the container.

"Acele et, hurry! Before polis see you. Acele et!" The smuggler spoke in broken English and Turkish. He hurried the group along to swiftly exit the container without being caught. The blinding sunlight slapped Amira's face and the warmth of the Cypriot sun kissed it better.

To Amira's surprise, she exited the container with Khalid's help and found herself standing in front of an extraordinary colossal castle. The walls were made up of different-sized stones. They varied in size, shape and colour as some were light brown whereas others were slightly darker. From afar, it seemed a uniform colour but as Amira and Khalid walked closer, she saw the intricately mosaicked rocks all piled tightly together to form the huge walls of the castle.

"Wow!" gasped Amira, as she fingered the walls of the castle.

"How beautiful, Khalid! Look!" She pointed at the top of the castle where the chambers were.

"I know, right, imagine living here," he joked.

From behind them, the smuggler spoke.

"This...Kyrenia Castle," he pointed at the castle as he explained.

"Built by Venetians, during Ottoman time."

"Hmm, Ottoman Empire...interesting," Khalid muttered.

Khalid was pretty fond of history and he knew exactly what castle this was and the history behind it.

"I know this place. It was this castle that got surrendered to the Ottomans and it remained in their possession for 3 centuries. Then, when the British colonised and controlled it, it was used as a prison and police school," Khalid said.

Amira was shocked at how much history Khalid actually knew.

"Wow, Khalid, I didn't know you knew all that," she joked.

"Come on! I'm like the next Einstein," he replied.

"It is a beauty, though," he told Amira as he looked up towards the castle.

The castle overlooked the coast of Kyrenia and Amira was in awe of how magnificent the sea looked. The sea that frightened her whilst travelling through it, was now looking ever so regal and magical. The sparkling, clear blue water shone like diamonds and crystals under the beaming sun and the sparkle of the water pinched her eyes. It was truly breathtakingly astonishing and for once, Amira felt happy being in a foreign country, as if she didn't want to leave, not yet.

"This way, Brother, this way," the smuggler instructed the group to hurry along the edge of the pavement and walk towards the boat.

"We cannot be seen, come on," he said.

Apart from Khalid, Amira, Munir and Sarah, there were only 8 other refugees being smuggled out of Cyprus. From what Amira could gather, there were 2 families.

From a distance, the group's boat hovered in the sea as the calming wind blew swiftly in the afternoon sun. Amira watched the pink and yellow flowers planted along the pavement as they swayed from side to side in the summer air.

The boat they were travelling on was much sturdier-looking than the one they had been in a few weeks ago. It had tough, hard plastic encompassing the engine motor and the inside of the actual boat looked clean and unused before. Amira had some hope that this time, the journey would be far less traumatic and smooth. She suddenly started feeling better and hopeful.

The smuggler, Tariq, was a thin, grey-haired, middle-aged man who wore thick boots and a black rain jacket. His face was starting to wrinkle up and his large forehead formed wrinkle lines every time he spoke. He helped the refugees in one by one till they all sat comfortably within the boat. He made sure not to make too much noise and he didn't want the locals to alert authorities regarding the illegal escape from Cyprus, as well as being caught as a smuggler. Munir and Khalid both worked extra shifts at their jobs for a few days to raise some money and to be able to pay the smuggler. It wasn't much, but Tariq accepted it.

As the motor started, a loud clacketing sound emerged from inside the boat and Tariq looked around continuously to see if they had been seen or heard. Luckily, they hadn't. Tariq began turning the boat around and started the motor again at a higher speed and just like that, they were off.

It was roughly 4 pm, late afternoon, and the weather was just as warm and comforting as it had been for the past few days. Amira thought to herself 'at least it will be a warm journey with hopefully no rain'. She sat beside Khalid, clutching her box by the handle. She looked at the castle as it became smaller and smaller in appearance and also noticed a few people standing by the edge of Kyrenia looking towards them. They just watched and after a moment or two, they disappeared.

"At least we're not all cramped up like last time," said Munir to Sarah.

"Still, I can't help feeling anxious, Munir," she replied.

"It's okay, be positive, my love," he reassured her.

"So…" smiles Khalid as he looked at Munir.

"How did you two meet, eh?" He chuckled.

Munir gave Khalid a goofy smile and then looked at Sarah.

Amira giggled at Sarah.

"Well, I saw her one day in the market and well, I just fell in love, really. I mean, come on, I hadn't ever seen someone so beautiful walk past me in my life."

"Leave it out, Munir!" Sarah laughed as she slapped Munir's leg.

"What? That's what happened, though."

"Yeah, it actually did. I used to work on my father's pottery stall when it was his day off. Munir was walking past one day and started talking to me and showing off in front of his friends," she told them.

"Pottery shop? My father also worked in a pottery shop!" Amira exclaimed proudly.

"I fell in love, I guess…" Munir sighed.

"Madly in love with such a kind, caring and respectful woman,"

"I asked her dad for her hand and well, next week will mark 6 years of marriage, Alhumdulillah." He smiled at his wife and held her hand.

"Mashallah, Brother! Mashallah! Inshallah you will celebrate your anniversary in a new country with wonderful new memories," said Khalid.

"We are also getting married Insha'Allah. As soon as we reach Turkey! I made a promise to her father as well as mine. As soon as we reach Turkey, I'm marrying my princess," Khalid spoke boldly, as if he wanted everyone on the boat to hear of his promise and excitement. He felt proud to hold Amira's hand and call her 'his'.

Amira blushed in her seat and shuffles shyly as he spoke.

"She's my best friend, always been there for me, and always will be."

Munir and Sarah looked at both Khalid and Amira and gave them a kind, warming smile.

"I pray Allah keeps you both together forever," said Sarah.

The other passengers on board didn't pay much attention to Amira's group and instead busied themselves sorting out their bags of shoes and clothing. A few of them were asleep. Tariq, the smuggler, shouted every now and then when the wind blew a little too harshly.

"Hold on!" he roared over the sound of the waves, which were now becoming more and more violent as the sun slowly descended into its hidden cave.

They had been travelling for just over an hour now and the sun was slowly setting over Cyprus.

"Are we still in Cyprus?" asked a small child to his father.

"Abi, where are we?" the father asked Tariq.

"Still travelling across the sea, Mediterranean Sea," he replied.

"Abi, wind is picking up. Look at the waves, they're becoming harsher, no?" said another man from the back.

"Hayir, Hayir, no, no, it is okay, Brother," replied Tariq.

Amira became somewhat apprehensive and fidgety in her seat. She looked out onto the water and at the waves in the distance. They started to gradually roll in closer and closer to the group and Amira nudged Khalid every so often as they came only a few metres away from them.

"Khalid, I feel like there's a storm coming, look." She pointed to the sky, which had begun to form hues of dark blue and grey above them and then there were the crashing waves.

"Read your dua, Mira, it's ok, I got you," he reassured her.

Amira wasn't the only one who had begun to get troubled and tense at the sudden weather change from being a cool summer's day in Cyprus to a stormy turbulence. The women in front of her start voicing their concerns to their husbands and then to Tariq.

"Look! Look, everything ok," Tariq pointed at the boat's motor engine and indicated that it was fully functioning.

"Storm come, we will be ok. Engine strong!" he shouted loudly as the wind blew more furiously against the boat. A child's cap flew off his head and fell into the water as another course of harsh winds blew.

"BABA! MY HAT!" he cried.

"Shhh, Zain, I will buy you a new one in Turkey," his father assured him.

His cap was long gone by the time 2 more waves overlapped near the boat.

The waves kept rushing in, each time rougher than the last. Amira felt a drop on her nose. She wiped it off and then she felt another splat on her ear. She looked ahead and to her horror, the sky had transformed into deep, black rows of thick fog and unrecognisable clouds. The heaviness of the rain began increasing readily from the obscure sky.

Amira's heart sank.

The dismal intuition in Amira's head slowly began devouring every bit of hope and belief she had left. She started to question the unknown, started to question every event that had occurred. 'Why am I here? Why am I living? What did I do to deserve this?' Such thoughts encircled her mind until finally, she couldn't find the answers to her repetitive questions and the dread began to develop into arduous panic.

Storms gathered on the cold, dispiriting horizon. Amira starting sinking deep into her seat, uneasy at the sight and realisation of what was about to come. She gripped Khalid's hand tight, as if he was a child about to cross a dangerous road. He looked at her, expressionlessly.

"It was so warm and sunny just an hour ago," Amira whimpered to Khalid, who, subconsciously closes his eyes in deep regret.

Booming thunder began to growl in the distance and the sudden glimmer of lightning crackled across the sky. Amira watched the reflection in the water and started praying silently. The rain became heavier by the second and soon, the rapid torrent showed no sign of stopping. The commencement of the storm had only just started.

"OH MY GOD, ARE WE GOING TO DIE!?" screamed a lady from behind her husband. She shouted at Tariq and demanded answers.

"YOU SAID THAT EVERYTHING WAS GOING TO BE FINE! LOOK AT THE STORM COMING THIS WAY!"

Another woman cried out aloud, "What are we going to do now? Please Ya Allah, help us."

Amira's heart pounded harder and harder against her frail ribcage and her pulse increased.

To her horror, a huge wave was thundering towards the boat. She panicked and froze. A gust of wind intervened mid-way to push the angry wave towards the boat.

"HOLD ON TIGHT!!" yelled Khalid.

Everyone held the side panels of the boat or the seats they were sitting on. A few violent waves rocked the boat ferociously from side to side, yet no one fell off. Tariq tried rushing to hold onto a seat but slipped on the soaking bottom of the boat deck. Munir helped him up.

The boat lost direction and soon, it was impossible to distinguish where they had travelled from, or where they were heading towards.

"Which way are we going?!" shouted Munir at Tariq, who had cut his arm on the wooden plank of the seat.

"Abhi, where's my compass!?" replied Tariq, patting his pockets.

The group began to sense fear in Tariq's voice and started to become increasingly anxious. Another 3 deadly waves crashed against the boat and Munir and Tariq fell out. Sarah screamed in dread and called for her husband.

"MUNIR! MUNIR, THIS WAY! SWIM THIS WAY, PLEASE!" she wailed.

Tariq managed to swim to the side of the boat but Munir began drifting further and further away from the boat until he was just a faint silhouette in the distance.

"MUNIR!! OH MY GOD, MUNIR, PLEASE!" Sarah howled insanely and begged for help.

"Please! Someone!"

Without warning, Khalid leapt into the wild waters of the sea and began to swim. Amira watched in fear as he too became a distant silhouette. Khalid reached Munir within a few minutes and helped him back to the boat.

"Oh, thank God! Thank you, Khalid, thank you. Shukran, Shukran!" cried Sarah as they reached the boat and pulled themselves inside. Sarah kissed Khalid's hands and helped her husband.

Amira clutched onto Khalid when he sat down and she began to cry.

"Khalid, don't keep leaving the boat every time, please, I can't lose you, Khalid, I can't, I just can't."

"Mira, I'm here. Look, the waves are getting bigger, please, hold on," he told her.

Khalid pressed his eyelids together, preventing any tears from falling. In that very moment, everything felt unfair to Khalid. No matter how hard he strived to make the right decision and help his loved ones, he felt pulled back by any invisible hand. His taunting regrets emerged into his thought process and he was losing hope. He had lost hope that maybe this time, just this once, his mind might be satisfied and contented with his decisions, but it wasn't, and like an inexorable, pitiless ghost, it would be back tomorrow, and the day after and the next, for it would haunt their memories again and again.

He looked over at Amira, whose eyes were stinging with saltwater and red with pain. He stroked her face amidst the frightful turmoil and shouted to Munir.

"MUNIR!"

"Khalid?" Munir panted, still regaining his breath.

"Munir...Read our Nikah."

Amira looked at him, confused. 'Why is Khalid saying that? What's gotten over him?'

Another huge waved crashed against the boat and almost tipped Amira out. Khalid pulled her close and held her arm tight.

"Read our Nikah, now!" Khalid demanded.

Amira looked on, still puzzled at Khalid.

Another wave was thundering towards the group and a crack of lightning shrieked from above. Amira looked onto the scene and then it hit her. It hit her why Khalid was telling Munir to wed them both.

Munir began reciting verses from the Quran, loud and clear. He prayed Surah Fatiha, the opening Surah in the Quran and called for another man to be present during the ceremony.

Khalid looked at Amira, his eyes enchanted by hers. Since the very first day, her beauty had remained the same. Falling in love with her was so easy for Khalid. Her smile, her laughter, her touch, it was all natural to him. He found himself missing her when she was away for a moment or two; he craved the smell from her hair, he longed for her embrace and above all, he felt content around her. Even now, as the waves and thunder crashed every minute, he saw nothing except her deep, golden eyes that were filled with love. The whole world stopped around them. Munir continued.

"Amira, your father's name?" he asked, panting loudly.

Amira looked straight ahead at Khalid and whispered, "Hamza Mahdi."

"Khalid?" Munir asked him the same question.

With a proud, jubilant voice, Khalid SHOUTED, "HUSSAIN KARAM!"

Munir cleared his throat and began asking Khalid the question that was about to change his whole life. Sarah took her soaking wet scarf from around her neck and placed it on top of Amira's.

"Khalid Hussain Karam, son of beloved Hussain Karam, do you accept Amira Hamza Mahdi, daughter of beloved Hamza Mahdi, as your wife who you will love, cherish and grow old with in accordance to the Sunnah of our beloved Prophet Muhammed, may peace be on his soul?"

"Khalid?" Amira whispered, now crying. Another crackle of thunderous lightning hit the water.

"Khalid, what are we doing?" she sobbed.

Every dream Amira had of her wedding, the gown she would wear, the cake she would eat, the songs she would dance to and the people she would have around her, all those dreams were slowly becoming a distant recollection of senseless fantasies, for the thought of ever getting married on a boat, with a group of strangers all in the midst of a noxious storm was something that had never crossed either Khalid or Amira's mind.

"Amira, I made a promise to you and our fathers!" Khalid yelled over the wind and thunder.

"I made a promise to you, that as soon as we reach Turkey, I would make you my wife and marry you. I never break my promises, but I don't know whether this storm will mean us getting to Turkey alive, so in front of all these witnesses, I want to make you my wife!" Khalid said.

"Munir! Munir, I ACCEPT!" yelled Khalid, now beaming with a large smile across his face.

Amira wiped away her tears, looked at Khalid and forgot everything, the thunder, the storm, the treacherous journey, and was bewildered into a frozen daze. Everything seems so hallucinatory and overwhelming; was this really happening?

"Khalid Hussain Karam, son of beloved Hussain Karam, do you take Amira, daughter of beloved Hamza Mahdi, as your wife, to comfort her during times of need, grow with her as a Muslim and help her to become a better person?" asked Munir a second time.

"I accept, Qabul!" he yelled again, now laughing.

"Hurry up and ask me for the last time, Munir!" Khalid laughed.

Another violent wave thrashed towards the boat, almost flipping Tariq into the sea.

Munir asked Khalid the same question for a third time.

"QABUL! QABUL! QABUL!" Khalid jumped for joy and patiently waited for Munir to ask Amira the same questions.

Amira wore a mystified yet animated expression on her face. Her eyes gleamed with warmth yet her mind was everywhere. She didn't know how to feel, or what to say. Khalid looked at her, eagerly waiting.

"Amira Mahdi, beloved daughter of Hamza Mahdi, do you accept Khalid Hussain Karam, son of Hussain Karam, as your husband who you will respect, honour and cherish?" Munir asked.

Amira looked at Munir, then Sarah, who was smiling yet still in fear of the waves that were continuing to crash against them every other minute, and then at Khalid.

"But..." she stuttered.

A whoosh of severe wind smacked the side of the boat, nearly toppling Amira into the ocean. Khalid grabbed her wrist and pulled her back.

"But…but Khalid…" she babbled.

Khalid looked confused.

"But Khalid, my wedding dress, I'm wearing these ugly clothes. Khalid, I don't even look nice and my hair is a mess!" she cried innocently.

Khalid cackled with a mischievous grin, beaming right at Amira. She sighed and placed both hands on either cheek and laughed.

"Qabul! I accept!" she stated.

Munir asked again while another wave rocked their balance, but they manage to hold on and continue. A rumble of thunder boomed loudly in the distance and startled the boat's passengers. By now, everyone was watching what was happening and witnessing their marriage.

"I accept."

He asked a final time.

Amira inhaled and recited 'Bismillah'.

"I accept" …

Khalid froze for a second and then erupted into an eager jabber of laughter. He was intoxicated with happiness and a sense of pride. Amira's eyes twinkled and she grinned from ear to ear at Khalid, who was now jumping up and down and shouting at the top of his lungs.

"MEET MY WIFE, MRS AMIRA HUSSAIN!! YOU THERE, LOOK AT ME, I JUST GOT MARRIED! WOOOOOOOOOOOOOO!" Amira couldn't help but giggle and blush at the same time. Sarah hugged Amira tightly and congratulated her. The other women on board were in a state of confusion at both Khalid and Amira, but Khalid didn't care. All he cared about now was being Amira's husband. He ran from one side of the rocking boat to the other and once he was done parading with joy, he sat down beside Amira.

Amira's focus was shattered into a million thoughts. She was filled with coy and timid anticipation so that she became slightly giddy. She tried hiding her smile when Khalid looked at her and she couldn't even hold a conversation without smiling like a child.

"So..." Khalid whispered directly into Amira's ears.

"Hello, wife, Mrs Hussain...How you doing, princess?"

Amira closed her eyes and without warning, embraced Khalid with immense force and sobbed silently in his arms. She was overcome with feelings, all at once. Scared, nervous, excited, overwhelmed, her feelings seemed to be never-ending all of a sudden, as she was taken aback by everything.

Khalid leaned closer to her ear and whispered something. She pushed him aside as she felt ticklish and shy listening to his smooth, quiet voice in her ear.

"Mrs Hussain, my princess, my Amiraty...I love you..."

CHAPTER SEVENTEEN
Lost at sea - July 2016

The storm didn't end. It only got worse. For three hours the group had been stuck at sea now, and the storm showed no signs of stopping, nor did the rain. The sky was dark and full of rage and it only reflected its emotions onto the surface of the ocean. Amira and Khalid had been clinging onto one another for hours and praying for a halt to the storm. Despite all the havoc, there was one thing they were both certain of, they had lost their way and neither Tariq nor the group knew where they were heading.

"We don't know where the hell we are going! We've lost all direction; we're going to die here!" shouted a woman at Tariq, who by now, was panting whilst sitting on the side of the boat and trying to control the motor to prevent it from breaking down due to too much water exposure. Then, without warning, complete obscure darkness dominated the sky as the clouds expanded and started clotting together. A sense of chilling dejection filled the air. The wind, which hadn't calmed down in the meantime, was rising more and more ferociously and began pushing an angrier-looking surge of flow that soon transformed into mountains of enraged waves.

Amira gasped as she saw a monstrous wave flow in their direction and she held onto Khalid.

"I got you!" he yelled.

Inside the boat, there was no sitting still, nor was it guaranteed that the boat wouldn't turn itself over with the force of the wave, and that is exactly what happened next. The boat turned over on itself and everyone fell out, including Amira and Khalid. Some people, just like last time, were trapped underneath the inside of the boat. Amira found herself panicking and gasping for air as she hid beneath the boat alongside Sarah and some other people. The children cried aloud and screamed for help. Some couldn't swim and so were struggling. Amira took off her lifejacket and put it on a child she saw crying hysterically. Amira began panicking as they all tried lifting the boat but failed. She heard the men on the other side, including Khalid, shouting and trying to help lift the boat.

After some attempts, they finally managed to lift it up with great difficulty and help those trapped underneath. Amira quickly swam towards Khalid and threw her arms around him, sobbing.

"Khalid! Khalid, stay with me, please! I'm scared!" she wailed.

"I'm here, Mira, I'm here. Look, help us turn the boat around. I'm here okay?" he comforted her.

They all tried again and again to lift the boat and after what seemed like an hour, they succeeded. Khalid helped Amira onto the boat and then dragged himself up. Amira felt a sudden sense of dread as she looked around and couldn't find her box of poems and pictures. She started panicking and looking around desperately until Khalid jumped inside the boat.

"Easy girl, I have it, look," he said, holding her box. The box was made from thick, rigid cardboard and was slowly wearing away from being in the water for a long time. Amira had tried her best to preserve what was inside for as long as she could.

She opened it and saw her things inside, only slightly soaked. She felt relieved.

The weather showed no clemency nor compassion, only vicious vehemence for hours until soon after, the storm began to quieten down for its departure was near. The fog that had formed created a misty, thick smoke of fear surrounding everyone and by now and the sun had gone down. The deep ocean ahead looked completely haunting and there wasn't anything in sight aside from water. There was no sound, no other people on boats or ships, not even the sound of eerie winds to accompany them. Even the light they all yearned for to warm up their cold, shivering bodies was absent and replaced with nothing more than slow, deadly spells of icy breezes.

Everyone was shivering and clattering their teeth every time the wind blew past. Amira was soaked from head to toe and the damp clothes on her felt like a burden. She was beyond uncomfortable. Chilly water seeped from her shoes and socks and her face was dripping in salty, stinging water. They had been travelling for hours now, and soon, night started to fall fast upon the ocean and the sky that was stained in the morning with hues of sapphirine and azure blue with glitters of saffron yellow and orange had now miserably departed and wilted its beauty, leaving behind nothing more than a murky, lustreless, black panorama. There were no stars in the sky, no birds, no clouds and no hope. Darkness was the only thing that existed apart from the raw, biting wind.

Khalid saw Amira shiver and shake uncontrollably and removed his jacket, although it was also soaked, and placed it around her.

"Don't go peeking in my pockets…Wouldn't want you finding a poem or something…," he whimpered in the cold.

"He…hey…hhheyy, you said you…wou…wwwwould give it to me…as a…a…a…wedding gift!" she trembled, wiping her running nose and suddenly feeling embarrassed.

"Soon, it's almost finished, I promise," he replied.

The group tried to get their breath back and recover from the storm. Tariq, who was trying to fix his smashed compass, sat on the edge of the motor, which to everyone's surprise, was still running. He clapped the palm of his hand against the shattered screen of the glass compass and then fingered the pieces of glass, but it was useless now, for a broken compass was no use to anyone in finding their way out of the nameless unknown. Floating on the surface of the sea with nothing to go on, no direction, no help and no other people around, felt frightening.

"Tariq!" Khalid called loudly, "Brother! Get us the hell out of here, come on! You said you knew the way," Khalid began getting annoyed. His voice was stern and Amira could tell he was close to losing his cool. She looked at the others, all drenched in seawater, their eyes stinging with pain, children crying. Sarah and Munir were huddled up close together and Sarah was almost drifting into sleep. Munir held her tightly.

"Mira, you want to sleep? Come and rest," Khalid asked Amira, noticing she was also feeling exhausted.

"How can I, I feel so uncomfortable. I'm soaking wet," she replied.

"It's fine, come on my lap and sleep, I'll make sure you're comfortable, Mira."

Amira shuffled on her seat and tried to get comfortable. She placed her head on Khalid's wet lap and moved it continuously to find a comfortable spot. It was not long before she found a spot and felt a gradual heaviness embrace her whole body like a duvet, but not a duvet filled with duck feathers or any warmth, but a duvet stitched with ice. However, somehow, it began making Amira's eyes feel and become weary and heavier by the second, as if the whole world was resting on them. Her eyelids began to close as Khalid stroked her hair away from her face and warmed her neck with his hand, gradually, causing her to fall into a dreamless, uneasy sleep.

Except, she did dream.

As her attention dwindled into another dimension, her mind descended into free-fall, churning and swirling into the allure of a new dream.

She dreamt of warmth and contentment, as she found herself strolling through Shamsa Park. Despite the weather whilst they had been in Cyprus being gleamingly warm, it felt as if the journey had taken all the sun and warmth away from every corner of the Earth. After what felt like she had lived so long without it, she was amazed by the heat glowing on her neck from the sun's rays. She wore a pink and white knee-length dress with flat pumps, the one's her friend Maliha had once let her borrow. Her hair was tied up in a high pony-tail with locks of golden curls bouncing behind her as she breathed in the sweet smell of daisies and freshly cut grass. Birds tweeted and sang above her, dancing in the slow breeze alongside the swaying trees that seemed to greet her as she passed.

She looked around at the empty park and for once, she didn't feel fear. She didn't feel fear of one of Assad's men approaching her, nor the fear of bombs falling from above her. She felt solitude, the same tranquillity and escapism she felt when she would perch herself against her favourite weeping willow tree and bury her head deep into a book or busy herself with writing her poems. It was her place of absolute stillness and comfort.

The park was serene and peaceful, and the only rustling to be heard was the faint whisper of the leaves as they swayed in the wind. As Amira roamed around the park, she caught sight of the old wall that once had the graffiti spray-painted all over it, only this time, it didn't. It was a perfectly painted cream wall that read in bold, red letters, 'WELCOME TO SHAMSA PARK'. Amira knew fully well that she was dreaming, yet it was a dream she didn't want to wake up from, ever.

The weeping willow tree.

It stood there, prouder than ever, like a king of the lands amongst all the other trees, yet this tree was the proudest of all. Then, to her surprise, she saw Baba sitting there on a white and red checkered picnic blanket, and so was Mama. Amira's eyes filled with tears as she sprinted faster than an Arabian horse towards them. She found herself shouting, louder than ever at the very top of her lungs. She galloped down the hill until she finally caught their attention. She had forgotten that she was dreaming, for everything looked and felt so real.

"BABA!! MAMA!! IT'S ME, AMIRA!" she cried and sobbed with happiness.

Baba looked up and smiled.

"Amira! There you are," he said.

Mama got up and walked towards her and Amira threw herself on Mama.

"Easy, girl," Mama laughed.

"Where have you been? We've been waiting ages for you, silly girl," Baba asked.

Amira walked towards Baba, sobbing continuously, yet for some reason, neither Baba nor Mama could see her tears or her pain. She hugged Baba tightly, not wanting to let go. She held him close, afraid he might disappear, when suddenly, she heard a voice behind her.

"Miraaaaaa!!!" shrieked a voice, coming closer and closer towards her. She turned around and found Adam, holding a paper bag, running in her direction. Amira's heart filled with joy and her eyes filled with sweet, mirthful tears. She ran to Adam and squeezed him in her arms and cried into his soft, woollen jumper. He smelled as he always had, of sweets and buttered candies. She pulled him away and looked into his innocent, lively eyes and hugged him again, for she didn't ever, ever want to let go.

"Adam, I've missed you, Oh Adam, why did you leave me?" she whimpered, but yet again, Adam could not see her tears.

"Sweety?" Adam held out his paper bag full of the same sweets he had when they were in Lebanon. Amira laughed and pulled out a sweet from his bag.

She picked out a juicy piece of sticky malban, a fruit jelly made with grape sugar and molasses, jelled with starch and flavoured with sweet rose water or orange blossom. The piece Amira picked out was stuffed with crunchy pistachios and sprinkled with desiccated coconut. She put the whole thing in her mouth and crunched on the nuts. She swallowed the first piece and went back in for another. This time, she picked a ruby red-coloured one that was covered with amardeen, a succulent apricot paste, and walnuts. She devoured it within seconds. The nostalgic memories of her past came flooding back, just as the harsh waves, as she remembered the times Baba would bring a whole box of malban back after every month's wage he earned. She would always get first pick and always took the best ones. As she got older, she started leaving the best ones for Adam.

"Come, eat, you two, your ice cream is melting!" Mama spoke from behind them. Amira held Adam's hand and walked towards the picnic blanket and sat down. She looked at both her parents, sitting beneath her weeping willow tree, in peace. She didn't want to take her eyes off them, nor Adam. She smiled to herself like a child and deep from within her, she felt warm; the warmth you feel when you come home after a long day and your mother holds you; the warmth you feel when you fight with your sibling but they make up with you by offering you their sweets and the warmth you feel when you lay your head on your father's lap and he reads his poems to you.

"I hope you saved some ice cream for me, dear," a voice calls out in the distance; a husky, frail voice that sounded soothing to Amira's ears. She didn't even turn to see who it was for she already knew. Standing there, with a smile as large as the moon, Baba Mohammed looked down humbly at her. He looked as old as he did when she last saw him, yet she could still see a younger version of himself yearning from within him. His skin was pure honey, glistening with luminosity and his beard was whiter than ever. His smile radiated in Amira's heart and she felt elated with gaiety.

"Of course, there is, come take a seat, Uncle," replied Baba as he ruffled a cushion beside him for Baba Mohammed to sit on. Baba Mohammed sat beside Baba and Amira.

"How are you, my dear?" he asked Amira.

"Any new poems? I haven't read one in ages, goodness..." he laughed.

Amira wiped away her tears and chuckled.

"Baba, no, I haven't written any recently, but please...I'm dying to hear one of yours," she replied.

"Oh, I see," he sniggered.

"Well, let me see if I can remember one."

"Pass this around, Amira, before it melts," said Mama, handing Amira small plastic plates of fresh, syrupy Hétaliyé, a creamy, stringy ice cream that had the complexion and texture of a melted marshmallow. Amira took a bite from her plate and slurped the melted syrup at the bottom before scooping her spoon upwards to add some of the creamy bit. She took a bite and her mouth danced with the flavour of sweet rose and milk, with the crunch of toasted almonds and walnuts. Again, she had a sudden sense and feeling of warm nostalgia.

"Lovely!" Baba praised Mama.

"Have some, dear…" he passed his spoonful to Mama.

"No, no, dear, you know I'm on my diet," she replied.

"Ha! Diet? Please woman, you are the most beautiful lady I have ever laid my eyes on!" he teased her.

Mama smiled and chuckled.

"Fine, maybe just one bite…" she laughed.

Baba fed her a spoonful lovingly and gave her a tender smile.

Amira watched, for she didn't want to miss a thing.

"Ok!" exclaimed Baba Mohammed loudly, after finishing his plate of ice cream within a few seconds.

"I have this one poem, although it isn't any good, especially compared to yours, Amira."

He coughed faintly and began to recite…

"The ground itself rose above her, causing her to topple and fall again and again,
Yet despite the pain, anguish and loss, she rose once again.
She longed for stillness and desired the forgotten place of peace again and again,
Yet life took its toll and she fell once again.
She took another step, walking closer and closer to the light of hope, and ran its way before it faded again,

And as she continued her journey, she kept falling again and again,
Till she realised that soon, that she was home again."

"She kept falling, Baba, but she kept rising, again and again...surely she must have given up sooner or later?" Amira started asking her usual questions as she did every time Baba Mohammed read her a new poem.

"If you keep falling again and again after trying so hard to be strong, not only for yourself, but others too, then surely you are bound to feel downhearted when it all goes wrong?"

Baba Mohammed sighed and gave her a long, soothing look. His eyes displayed so much life, life that gave Amira life too.

"My dear..." he spoke, softly.

"Come with me."

Amira got up and took a walk with Baba Mohammed. She waited for him to speak, but he didn't. She looked back often, to see if her parents and Adam were still there, for she didn't want them to go. They all sat there, Mama handing Adam more ice cream, Baba pushing his reading glasses back and burying his head in a book and Adam, sweet Adam, dancing to the sound of the birds. This didn't feel like a dream to Amira, it felt like paradise.

Baba Mohammed halted. Amira didn't realise they had reached the very top of the hill. She looked down at Shamsa Park, which was looking cleaner and more tranquil than normal. She saw the expanse of the light green, emerald grass that blanketed the ground, the pebbled pathway lined with magnificently elevated trees and beds of inharmonious, kaleidoscopically coloured flowers. From the hill, Amira could faintly see her parents and Adam, still sitting there below the willow. In the far distance, she made out the silhouette of the market place, still standing. Amira looked at Baba Mohammed.

He pointed down below.

"What do you see?" he asked her.

Amira tried to make out what it was exactly that he was pointing at. She soon realised that it was the willow.

"A tree…" she replied.

"Which tree?"

"A weeping willow tree."

"Ah! A weeping willow. Now tell me, do you know why it is called a weeping willow?" he asked.

"Because the curved branches hang from the tree and when it rains, it is as if the tree is crying and dripping with tears. It also resembles a woman, facing her head down and weeping with her hair over her face, which is hidden underneath her hair."

"Hmmm, well done," he muttered.

"Look at the tree, the loneliest of all, standing all by itself and the saddest looking one out of all the others. Yet tell me, did you ever see any other trees in this park that get as much love as this one?"

Amira thought for a moment, and she remembered that every time she went to Shamsa Park with Khalid, it was always the weeping willow they wanted to sit beneath, never any others. On a few occasions, they also saw others sitting beneath it and it was always a favourite tree, not only for them but other people too. Khalid would always feel a little jealous when he saw that someone else had sat beneath it for he owned it as 'their' special spot. They would both always wait for their spot to be freed, even if it meant waiting hours.

"Such a beautiful, lonely tree, yet so much love," he continued.

"Now, the answer to your questions…" he mumbled.

"If you ever feel disheartened and alone, and feel as if you are losing everything, then remember this tree, Amira, Princess…"

Amira looked at the tree and was slightly puzzled as to what Baba Mohammed meant. She waited for him to continue.

"This tree will soon lose all its leaves and branches, for every year winter will visit her, yet it will remain standing here, taller than ever and with pride, waiting for better days to come…"

Amira didn't notice the tear that ran down her cheek, but Baba Mohammed did.

She sobbed painfully and turned to him.

"Please, Baba, don't go…don't leave me here. I miss you; I miss Mama and Baba and Adam and everyone. Please don't go again."

Baba Mohammed wiped away her tears and smiled.

"Oh, but my dear, who will keep my seat warm up there?" he laughed.

"I don't want to wake up, Baba, please...don't go." Amira snuffled and hiccupped and sobbed.

"This sadness inside me, I want it to go, I want it to end, Baba. It's like a deadly seed of agony and depression, and it won't stop growing inside of me. I feel it every day, it pokes at my heart, it pokes at my mind when I try to be strong, it keeps me awake at night...I want it to die!"

"My dear child, it is these challenges that are helping us...you will realise this soon. And remember the words of dear Ustadh Rumi, 'If you are irritated by every rub, then how will you be polished?'"

Amira sniffled and hugged Baba Mohammed tightly as if he was about to disappear.

"Do not grieve... anything you lose will come around in another form," he said.

Amira continued to hold on, as she could feel her consciousness causing her to wake up. She hugged him even tighter and pressed her face into his robe that smelled of woody musk and almonds.

"Don't go," she wailed.

"Don't leave me alone."

"Tell me one more quick Rumi quote..." Baba Mohammed requested. His voice was breaking and becoming further and further away as he spoke.

"I...I can't...rem...remember any," Amira cried.

"Stay with me! I don't want to be all alone."

"Do not feel lonely, my dear..." he whispered, even more faintly.

Amira sobbed and finished his sentence.

"The whole...the whole world is inside you."

With that, Amira woke up to the sound of gentle waves and seagulls chirping. She jerked up from Khalid's lap and startled him.

"Mira? You okay?" he asked.

"Khalid! Where is he? Where's Mama? Baba? Adam? They were all here just now, now they're gone! Khalid, they were here, I saw them!" she entered a state of frenzy as she spoke and started to panic. Sarah helped her and calmed her down while Khalid rocked her in his arms.

"Shhhh, Mira, it's okay, I'm here, it's okay."

Amira hugged Khalid and sniffled. "I saw them, Khalid, they were all so happy."

"I know, my princess, we will see them soon, I promise you," he told her.

Amira rubbed her eyes and the sunshine cast itself affectionately on her skin. Amira looked around and wondered if anyone else had noticed how astonishing the weather suddenly was with the baby blue skies illuminating the sea below. She wondered if they saw the serene equanimity of the clouds in the sky that floated by. She wondered if they noticed the small fish in the ocean swimming by with their scales shining like diamonds under the clear blue water.

"LAND! THERE, LOOK!" shouted Tariq. He was pointing towards a small piece of land that he had caught a glimpse of.

"How long have we been lost for?" Amira asked Khalid.

"Altogether, nearly 11 hours, Mira."

"How long was I asleep for?"

"Almost an hour," he replied.

It felt like longer to Amira.

"Ok, everyone, row with your arms towards shore," instructed Tariq, already with half his body out of the boat. Although the motor was still working, he wanted everyone to row to get there faster. In the distance, Amira could see a small island.

After 10 minutes, they had reached the island. Amira did not know where to look and she hardly blinked, for she was in awe of what she saw. When she stepped outside the boat and placed her bare feet on the warm sand, her feet dug deep into the grainy pebbles. The sand was glittering like it was gold itself and the shimmering water behind her was crystal clear and sparkled under the radiance of the sun.

Just like last time, the tourists witnessed their arrival. This time, however, with disgust. No one helped them up or out of the boat. They simply stood there, in shock and horror and some even recorded it on their phones. Amira felt like an alien. She felt as if all eyes were on her and the group. She didn't even know where they were or what country they'd been washed up on.

Khalid, Amira, Sarah and Munir walked towards the beach until members of the authority reached them. Two men dressed in police uniform approached them and when Amira caught sight of their badges, her heart sank.

They weren't in Turkey at all.

CHAPTER EIGHTEEN
Heraklion, Crete - August 2016

Situated between Rethymano and Lasithi, on the eastern lateral of Crete, Heraklion is known as the greatest domain in Crete, that holds the highest popularity amongst tourists for its beauty and beaches. It is also the capital of Crete and the fifth-largest city in Greece, which has succeeded in maintaining and conserving traces of the ancient Minoan civilisation. It was also the resting place of a famous writer, Nikos Kazantzakis, who wrote a book Amira had once read called 'Zorba the Greek'.

The chronicle of the city started in the Minoan era, as was explained and shown by the ancient, historical town of Knossos, which happens to be the most developed and drafted of all Minoan towns in Crete. The town had been hidden under ashes and was excavated to reveal a flourishing ancient town with a remarkably impressive palace.

"It was found under ashes because apparently, scientists believe that all civilization was destroyed by a nasty volcanic eruption in Santorini," said Khalid to Amira, as they made their way to the town of Heraklion in a minibus.

"You know a lot of history, Khalid," Amira murmured.

She gazed around her as they left the beach on which they had been washed up. The sweltering sun shone like a golden disco ball in the sky, causing her neck to burn up and her hair and clothes to dry. She inhaled a deep breath of fresh air from the beautiful seaport city and watched the waterfront from the window of the bus. The waterfront was packed with modern-looking ferries, as well as smaller fishing boats with different names on them.

Tobrouk Beach, where they had been washed up, was a well-organised, clean beach that was located approximately 10km away from Heraklion Town. Amira counted how long it took to reach the main city and it was around a 15 to 20-minute drive.

Amira felt annoyed. A mass of infuriating rage overwhelmed her, mainly because of the mere fact that, yet again, they had not reached Turkey but instead, had ended up in Greece. It only meant trying again to find some sort of accommodation or looking for a way to leave and travel to Turkey. She tried not to think about it, nor did she feel like speaking about her anger to anyone, especially Khalid, for he too was overwhelmed with fury. He tried staying calm, despite burning inside. All they both wanted was to safely reach Turkey and finally be at ease, yet now, they were sitting on an overcrowded minibus on their way to a police station to be questioned, which was something none of them were looking forward to.

Khalid tried to distract Amira, as he could sense she was not happy.

"You know, after the Minoan era, Heraklion prospered again as a vital haven of the Byzantine Empire. After Crete's fall to the Venetians, the town itself developed gradually in terms of economy," he told her.

Amira really did not feel like talking, but for Khalid's sake, she did.

"Hmmm…Why was that?" she replied.

"Because of trade."

"What about the Ottomans?" she asked, now slightly intrigued to see if there was any Muslim history behind the city.

"Ahaa! Well, during the Cretan War, Venice was pushed out of Crete by the mighty Ottomans! Most of the island fell drastically in the first years of the war," he boasted, feeling proud of his explanation.

"I see…" murmured Amira.

"Tell me more about the Ottoman Empire, Khalid, it's interesting."

Amira secretly liked listening to Khalid talk about history; not only did he educate her in Islamic history, but it would also touch her to see Khalid speak about things he was so passionate about. He had always been brilliant at two things, art and history, and so for Amira to watch him speak for hours and hours about these two things was very satisfying and she would find herself staring at him for hours as he rambled on.

"What shall I tell you?" he asked, feeling rather shy at her request.

"Anything, just keep talking." She placed her head on his shoulder and listened.

"Well, when the Christian Roman Empire fell, Syria became part of either the Eastern or Byzantine Empire, but in 637 A.D., Muslim forces successfully defeated the Byzantine Empire and took control over Syria."

The minibus, packed with people, kept stalling, causing everyone to jerk forward, then it would spit loudly and sputter to life once again, making a blaring, dreadful sound resembling a smoker's cough.

"Then what happened, Khalid?" Amira asked, trying to ignore the racket surrounding her.

"Then…well, then the Islamic World spread like wildfire! Throughout the whole region, and its different groups slowly rose to power!" Khalid spoke like an excited child, his voice giddy and full of colour.

"The Ottomans achieved a lot, didn't they? They ruled for so long and in so many different countries." Amira was purposely asking a lot of questions, as she wanted Khalid to keep talking; talking so that he would lose himself in his own words for a moment, and not think about what was coming next.

"You bet! They started off as simple, nomadic Turks. They originally were from central Asia, and were converted to Islam by the Umayyad conquerors in the 8th century."

Amira sat up now to face Khalid as he continued.

"Led by Braveheart Uthman, they established a whole empire in 1300, amidst the ruins of the nasty Mongol-wrecked Seljuk Empire in Northwest Turkey."

"Uthman, he was the son of Ertugrul Gazi," Amira remembered from her stories, the stories she had told both Adam and Shakil. They would sit for hours and hours, listening to her recite stories about famous Ertugrul Gazi, who was the chief leader, after his father, of the Kayi Tribe in which he lived.

"Yes, he was…," said Khalid, faintly, almost undistinguishably. He had gone quiet all of a sudden.

287

"Khalid...?" Amira whispered.

"What's the matter?"

Khalid was looking out the window, and his eyes became watery. He inhaled a deep breath.

"Sometimes...sometimes, a single word or song or phrase is all it takes to remember someone...," he murmured.

"Do you remember how excited Adam and Shakil would get listening to your stories?" he asked.

Amira looked down and forced a smile, for Khalid.

"Yeah!" she laughed.

"Always wanted a story about Ertugrul or Noyan or Ibn Arabi...always the same ones. They never got bored, did they?" she giggled.

They both sat there, their breathing synced in unison and Amira could hear Khalid's sniffles. She held onto his hand and kissed it tenderly.

"Such beautiful, yet painfully bitter memories, Mira..."

"Every memory is like a new chapter in a storybook. I do not want to let go of these memories but then again, I do. I want to leave them tucked away on a high shelf, so they gather dust for years and years, then when I need them, I can open them up to whichever chapter I want to read and remember, and then put it back again."

"A book also has some empty pages...where you can make new memories, Khalid. You will never forget the old ones, they'll always be there. You won't forget them...him."

Khalid gave Amira a soft, warm smile and stroked her cheek. Amira shivered in her seat at his touch and closed her eyes. He kissed her forehead, lovingly, and she placed her head on his shoulder again.

"So, carry on," Amira remarked, playfully.

"What other countries did the Ottomans conquer?"

Khalid jolted up and cleared his throat, cheekily.

"50 years later, Uthman's successors invaded Europe and conquered Constantinople in 1453 and in the 16th century, succeeded in conquering all of the Middle East."

"Imagine if the Ottomans were here today, how they'd help us," Amira muttered.

"You bet; you think they'd let anything happen to us Muslims? HAA! No chance! Especially us Syrians! We have brave blood inside us, Mira!" Khalid became passionate as he spoke.

"They'd never let Syria perish! We hold the tomb of the great Khalid Bin-Waleed, the greatest soldier of Allah! We hold the great Mosque of Damascus, Umayyad Mosque, not forgetting the amazing bazaars and souks we have! Find them anywhere else, they'll never be more vibrant as ours!" Sarah and Munir, who were sitting a few seats down from Amira and Khalid, heard him speak and turned around. Khalid caught Munir's eye.

"TELL ME, Brother! Will you find such amazing bazaars as the ones in our Syria?! Or find another town like Aleppo? The parks, the streets, the people! The people, I tell you! Will you find good-hearted, compassionate and benevolent people like

289

us!?" Khalid yelled across the minibus, now causing the attention to be on him. The other refugees listened on.

"NO, KHALID! YOU WILL NEVER FIND SUCH PEOPLE ON THIS EARTH! NOWHERE EXCEPT MY SYRIA!" Munir roared back, smiling proudly.

Khalid nodded his head in agreement and smirked.

"Quite right, Munir," he grinned to himself with pride.

He reached over to his chest, where the football shirt that he had on had a small Syrian flag badge stitched on it. He reached down and kissed the flag and then turned to Amira.

"Our Syria, Mira, ours."

▪▪▪

The police station was dull and grey. It had a strong stench of coffee and plants and the humid air inside the building was muggy. As Amira and Khalid, followed by Sarah and Munir, strolled down the hallway towards the interrogation room, the sound of soft clicking from the policewoman's shoe hit the marbled floor. The wallpaper on the walls was peeling away at its edges due to dampness, and the plants on the window sills look like they hadn't been watered for decades. The hallway was wide and patronisingly uncomfortable with windows of offices, and it led to a main office right at the bottom of the passage. Amira felt as if everyone is watching her, secretly. All eyes were on Amira as the group walked towards the main office. The policewomen and men behind the windowed offices along the passageway all peeked out of their windows; some even moved their plastic blinds up to get a better view.

The women working at the police station, which looked more like an office building site, wore tight suits with their legs bare and had their hair tied up in tight buns. They wore subtle, but stunning makeup and high heels. The men wore smart suits with shiny dress shoes. Some were in police uniform and had guns attached to their belts. The woman who was leading the group to the office wore a light grey skirt with a white shirt. Her hair was bright yellow and done up in a high pony-tail. Amira looked down at herself. Her ragged, damp clothes stank of seawater and were stained with green seaweed and crumbs of sand. Her hair was loose and tangled at every curl. She had never felt so insecure before, especially after seeing other people around her dressed in such attire. She tried to cover herself with Khalid's jacket that she still had on. She buttoned the front and held Khalid's hand. Finally, they reached the office.

The inside of the office was painted an egg-yolk yellow colour. There were chairs against the damp walls and the same dying plants on the windowsills. On the big office desk that sat directly in the centre of the room, lay stacks of paper and folders. A cup held some rulers and pens and there were random paperclips floating around the desk. Amira and Khalid sat down on the chairs opposite the desk. Sarah and Munir waited outside.

The woman sat on her swivel chair and chewed on her pencil whilst peering at her computer. The large bookshelf next to Amira had rows and rows of thick, fat books. She couldn't make out what books they were as they were all in Greek.

"Passport? No ID?" the woman finally spoke. Her voice was piercingly high-pitched.

291

She looked directly at Khalid, as if Amira were invisible to her.

"Documents, sir! No ID? Then who are you? We don't know," she spoke again.

Her accent was thick, so it was difficult at times to understand her words.

"Lady, we have come all the way from Syria. I had it all, passport, identification papers, everything. But there was a bomb blast..." Khalid's voice became weaker.

"The bomb blast, it killed our family...we lost everything, including the papers. I kept them so safe, but I lost them at the same time as we lost our brothers."

The woman sighed, showing no compassion whatsoever in her voice.

"Then what shall I do, huh? I cannot submit anything, no shelter, no accommodation."

"Please, Sister, give us a place to stay. I will work, we both will. Me and my brother outside, we will work; give us anything and we can try to get ID somehow by contacting someone back in Syria."

Amira listened to their conversation, patiently.

"What can we do?" the woman said, raising her voice slightly.

"Greece is still suffering from the effects of a decade-long economic crisis."

"I know, I understand, but..." Khalid was interrupted.

"But what, huh? When refugees like you turn up on our island, tourism decays gradually. Just look at the news; politicians are always fighting and arguing that the migrant crisis has scared people away."

Khalid sighed. He rubbed his fingers on his temples and squeezed his eyes shut. He was getting a migraine. Amira rubbed his leg. She then looked up at the woman, desperately.

"Miss, we have nothing...look, this box is the only possession I have left. My clothes, shoes, our papers, money, everything... it's all gone. We are helpless and desperately asking for your help." Amira spoke kindly, with a soft voice. Her voice seemed to have soothed the woman's heart. She sighed loudly and ruffled through some papers on her desk. She then left the room briefly.

"Khalid, what are we going to do now? You know for sure these people won't allow us to stay here for long. If anything, they will keep us in some camp and sooner or later send us back to Syria," Amira rambled on, worried.

"Turkey seems so far away, so impossible. Why is it so hard to just go to Turkey?! It was the first place we wanted to go and now it seems like the last."

"Turkey is still an option, Mira," Khalid mumbled under his breath.

"Again? On a boat again? Khalid, I'm done with these boats; look how dangerous they are. It's so terrifying getting on and not knowing the course of the journey. Say we end up in another country other than Turkey? Then what? We're back to square one again."

"I'll figure it out, Mira, I promise, Amiraty."

The woman entered the room again and plopped herself down on her swivel chair.

"Ok, look. This hostel here, you see…" she pointed at a piece of paper in her hand with a map and directions.

"The authorities can allow you shelter here. Only for a while, not long-term. But you will need to work and pay a small rent for the hostel. The rest, you can keep for food and clothing. We will give small amount too to help you," she explained.

Amira and Khalid's eyes lit up.

"In the meantime, you find some way to find documents."

She passed the booklet to Khalid and stood up.

"My colleague outside will help you and your family."

Amira walked towards the woman. "Thank you! Thank you, Sister," she exclaimed happily.

They left the room and told Sarah and Munir the plan.

"Mira, we will find a way to go to Turkey, okay? I promise you. For now, let us work for a few weeks and raise some money. I'll try my best to find a way, and even if it means going on a boat again, then it might be the only option to reach Turkey."

Khalid felt forlorn as he explained this to Amira. He wanted to keep her safe but also fulfil his promise to not only his father, but Amira's father, too. He desperately wanted to be in Turkey and restart his life with Amira.

Since January 2015, more than one million refugees in search of international protection and security were mainly travelling from countries such as Syria, Afghanistan, Iraq and Pakistan. They were coming into Greece for the whole year of 2015 and the number of illegal, sea-borne newcomers arriving totalled a staggering 856,723, while for the first 6 months of 2016, it decreased drastically to a total of 155,989. Nearly 57,000 refugees remain within the country. Greece was not expecting a high number of refugees arriving and were not ready to respond to such a high influx of people seeking protection from war-ravaged countries. The Greek state responded belatedly and the Greek authorities had been struggling to manage the registration and reception of new arrivals, especially in key entry points such as Lesvos and Chios islands. Despite the high number of people entering Greece, until recently, only very few of them applied for asylum in the country.

Another worker in the police station took Amira, Khalid, Munir and Sarah to the hostel.

As they left the station, Amira saw all the other refugees from the boat waiting in the hallway waiting area. She avoided eye contact with them, in case they felt that they were being treated as inferior to the rest of the group, however, that wasn't the case. They also were being taken to a refugee family unit.

The hostel was only 15 minutes away from the station. The roads were clean and smooth in Heraklion, and the skies blue. The tourists and residents in the city didn't give off that same sympathetic response that the ones in Cyprus had. There was a waft of arrogance that lingered in the atmosphere that not only Amira but everyone else sensed too.

"Why are they looking at me funny?" asked Amira, peeking out the window at 3 elderly men smoking outside a café. She felt uneasy in her seat and wanted to sink down deep into it so they couldn't see her. They all gawked at the group in the car from where they were seated. The driver had stopped at a traffic light, that unlike a normal 60-second traffic light, felt like a 10-minute one instead. One of the men, who hadn't batted an eyelid the whole time, was muffled inside a raincoat and wore thick leather boots. His face was wrinkled deeply and every now and again, he puffed out a thick waft of smoke. He didn't take his eyes off Amira and stared right into her eyes, as if she were an alien and he was trying to figure out what planet she had come from.

"Oh my God, is he still looking?" asked Amira, sinking into her seat.

"Yeah, ignore him, Mira," replied Khalid.

Khalid looked over Amira's shoulder and saw them still staring. He stuck his tongue out at them like a child and with that, the traffic light turned green.

"Khalid!" Amira whacked his arm, but he just laughed.

"Look, I think that's the hostel, Mira." Khalid pointed at a run-down looking building.

"It looks like there are only a few bedrooms inside; its small isn't it?"

"Hmmm, yeah, does look small. I hope the rooms aren't too cramped up, but at least we'll have a decent bed to sleep on tonight," replied Khalid.

The receptionist inside the hostel was a tall, skinny woman with several moles on her neck and arms. She reminded Amira of her old maths teacher, Mrs Kauser. Amira hated maths and hated Mrs Kauser. She would make Amira sit right at the front of the class, alone. That was because Amira and Maliha did nothing else in maths lessons except chat. They both hated maths and didn't see the need for them to attend the lesson.

The receptionist, who wore a name tag that read 'Gabriela', spoke to the driver. The driver told her the situation and Amira could have sworn she heard the man say 'after 3 weeks, they won't be your problem anymore'. Whilst all this was happening, she didn't know how to feel. It was a weird feeling. She didn't feel at home, she didn't feel content, or happy in the least that they had found shelter. It was as if there was something in the back of her mind telling her that something might go wrong soon. She tried being positive and just went with the flow.

The driver didn't say anything to the group, nor did he even look at them when he left. The receptionist was the same. She got a worker to show them their rooms. Luckily, Amira and Khalid had a separate room to Munir and Sarah. Amira felt slightly apprehensively coy, thinking about sharing a room with Khalid. Now that she was married, and his wife, she knew the certain duties she had to fulfil for him, and likewise, 'Was Khalid thinking the same thing? Was he waiting for something to happen tonight? Was he as nervous as her?' She asked herself question upon question until finally, she tried not to

297

think about it too much, for it made her feel nervous to the core.

The room itself was a decent size. It had a double, scruffy, spring bed, an off-white rug beneath it and a window that overlooked the field in front. The bathroom and shower were outside the room, shared by others in the hallway. There were only 2 toilets and 2 showers available, as one toilet was out of order. Munir and Sarah's room was down the corridor from Amira's. Inside, Khalid plumped himself on the bed.

"Argghhh, I tell you, Mira, it feels good sleeping on a bed again," he said, as he closed his eyes and exhaled loudly. Hands behind his head, he looked at Amira. She had a face of disgust on her.

"What's wrong?" he asked.

"Khalid, what's that smell? Can't you smell it?"

"Hmmm, no…," he replied.

She walked around the room, sniffing every corner. A picture frame of Medusa hung beside the door. Amira took a long breath in and exhaled in repugnance.

"OOOORH!" she yelled.

She lifted the frame and saw a huge patch of rotting damp behind it. She gagged and almost puked. It smelt like rotting banana skins that had been left in the sun for weeks.

"Oh, come on, are you serious?" Khalid got up from his bed and walked closer. He froze as his nostrils got a whiff of the scent.

"Ahhh, fuck, man!" he laughed.

"That is disgusting, Khalid! Can we change the room, please, or tell them to remove the damp?" asked Amira, hopefully.

"I don't know, Mira, let me ask."

Upon his return, Amira already knew they weren't moving rooms. Khalid returned with a pack of floor wipes and a black bag.

"Erm...yeah, so we aren't moving rooms, unfortunately...apparently they're all booked."

"So, who gave you those?" asked Amira.

"The receptionist, hardly spoke 2 words, stupid woman. She just handed me these wipes and bag. 'Clean yourself', she said."

Amira sighed.

"Okay, well, beggars can't be choosers, I guess," she said, taking the wipes from Khalid and removing the frame from the wall.

The large damp patch was almost a circle. It was a filthy black and ebony colour with bits of grey and dark green mould forming around its edge.

Khalid laughed behind her as Amira wrapped a cloth around her nose and went in to clean it.

"Wooooow, looks like another planet. Hey, Mira, do you think an alien is going to come out of it?" he joked.

"Khalid, please, if you're not going to help then please, don't distract me. I need to concentrate!" she snapped.

"Ooooooh, concentrate, ok, are you doing an exam that you need so much concentration?" Khalid snorted in laughter and pushed Amira slightly in her back.

"KHALID!"

"Ok, ok, sorry, sorry...shall I help you?"

"NO, JUST MOVE OVER THERE!" Amira pointed to the window, which was located on the other side of the room.

Khalid giggled silently, scared of Amira hearing, and then lifted the black bag off the floor.

He walked towards her and opened it wide.

"Here, I'll help."

He held it open wide and Amira used many wipes from inside the pack to clean the mould off. She gagged a few times but managed to clean most of it off. The smell still lingered in the room, so Khalid found an air freshener in the bathroom and sprayed the room.

When they had finished, Khalid took the black bag full of dirty wipes and left it outside the room.

"There!" he clapped, "Home sweet home!"

"Home? This is far from home," replied Amira, huffing and puffing for air.

"Home, Mira, is wherever you are."

Amira blushed.

"Is that so?" she flirted.

"Yup, right now, home is this lovely room with a cracked window, broken doorknob, mouldy wall, and you...just you, Mira."

Amira smiled at Khalid and he winked back, teasingly.

"Anyway, I don't know about you, but I am shattered. Here's what we'll do. Munir has some money left from Cyprus, and I have a few Euros too in my jacket. We're going to go find some food and I'll try finding a stall or something that sells clothes. We need fresh clothes, Man, I smell like a dead rat," he laughed.

"But you just said you were tired, Khalid. Come rest for now?" she asked.

"No, no, you rest, Mira, have a shower too and wait here; I'll bring you your clothes and then I'll shower. Then I'll rest."

"But..." Amira interrupted him.

"But nothing; I don't want you feeling all uncomfortable and dirty. Let me look after you; I am your husband after all, no?" Khalid scoffed as he spoke and Amira could feel the meekness in his voice. He cleared his throat, kissed Amira's cheek and left the room.

Amira waited outside the shower room for her turn. She clutched a small pink towel, a bottle of shampoo and a bar of soap, all bought by Khalid and Munir. The hostel only provided the very basics such as toothpaste, towels, tissue paper and small soap squares.

Finally, after 20 minutes of waiting, a large, bulky woman opened the shower room door. Hot steam slapped Amira's face and the only thing she could think was 'I bet she's used all the hot water'. The woman, whose face reminded Amira of Miss Trunchbull from the movie Matilda, had rolls of fat on her arms and legs. She had covered herself with an oversized towel, yet half her legs were still visible. Her neck was hidden and her hair was up in a messy, wired bun. As she left the room, she gave Amira a piercing, dirty look. Her eyes, like daggers, gave Amira a shiver down her spine. She looked away, at the floor, until the fat lady left, for she didn't want to make eye contact again. The lady grunted something indistinguishable and very slowly ambled away to her room. At the same moment, Khalid ran up the hallway stairs and caught a glimpse of the lady entering her room. He held his laugh in and Amira couldn't help but giggle. He blew air into his cheeks and teased Amira.

"Here, take these." He handed Amira a bag. Inside, there was a fresh set of clothes; a blue shirt, black leggings and undergarments.

"Where did you get them?" she asked.

"A stall; wasn't much but I haggled…although all the euros are finished now, but I think I might have been able to find a job already. Down the road, there's a car wash. I'll try there, first."

"Thank you, Khalid," Amira grinned.

"No problemo, wife," laughed Khalid.

"I'll wash these dirty clothes in the shower and hang them on the window sill to dry, that way, at least we can wear them again once they're clean," Amira told Khalid.

"Good idea; wash my jacket too, please!" He took his jacket off and slipped his hand inside the inside pocket.

"Let me just take this…" he smirked, playfully.

Amira knew exactly what it was, even though Khalid was trying hard to hide it.

"I already know it's the poem! Why are you trying to hide it? We're married now! You said you would read it to me."

"I know, I know, but I just want it to be perfect, come on. Besides, we're married…you've got the rest of your life to keep asking me for this," Khalid chuckled teasingly as he pulled himself closer to Amira.

"No! I'm giving you another week, then the poem has to be done. I'm dying to read it."

"Ok, we'll see…maybe not a week, though, maybe 2…or 3…"

"Khalid!"

"Ok, ok, gosh, so many demands already, wow."

Amira smiled and stuck out her tongue at Khalid. He rubbed his hand on her hair and gave her a loving, calm look.

"Anyway, go have a shower, you smell like fish," snickered Khalid.

Amira slapped his arm gently and entered the shower room.

The shower room was steamed up like a hot sauna when Amira entered. There was a shower attached to the wall and a small sink opposite. There was also a mirror, that was cracked, and a small wall cabinet. Inside, Amira found old razors, tissue paper and empty bottles of cream.

She undressed and placed all her dirty clothes on the floor. Amira looked at herself in the cracked mirror. She'd lost so much weight from not eating and vomiting out seawater. She looked at her thinning thighs; a big purple bruise had painted itself deep into her skin. She'd got several bruises from the boat journey when she kept getting knocked about by the waves, but the one on her thigh is particularly painful. Some more deep violet and dark blackish-blue welts and scratches were scattered all across her lower belly. Amira took a deep breath in, but even breathing hurt her. She'd been in pain ever since the first boat journey to Cyprus and now, it had only gotten worse. She hadn't told Khalid, nor did she want to. But now, she wondered if Khalid himself would see her bruising tonight. How would she cover them? She didn't want to worry him, but more importantly, she felt embarrassed. She didn't want Khalid to see her like this.

The steam in the room cleared slightly and Amira, very carefully, avoiding any slips, walked towards the shower. The shower had loads of different options to choose from when regulating the speed or setting of the water. Amira twisted the dial and to her surprise, hot water actually poured out. She gave a sigh of relief and stepped inside. The water poured like rain, dripping by her sides as she placed her head directly beneath the showerhead. She withered into a deep calmness and closed her eyes. The warmth of the water on her head, neck and back felt heavenly and all she wanted to do was sleep beneath the hot water and imagine she was standing under an endless waterfall. She kept her eyes closed and slowly leant her body against the cold tiles. The smacking of water droplets against the tiles, the shower running at full speed, the car horns loudly blaring outside, all the noise, disappeared in an instant. Amira was amidst two realities, one where she pictured herself inside a huge house, with a garden and flowers growing on the bushes, and fresh pancakes and nutty barazek cookies being baked in the oven, and the other reality was here, now, under a shower, in a hostel, with no money and no family except Khalid. A perfect reality against an actuality. How she longed for herself to be a part of the first.

Amira showered, washed her hair twice, and cleansed her body with thick olive soap. By the end of it, she felt cleaner than she ever had. She washed her old clothes, as well as Khalid's, and left them to dry on the window sill in her room. Luckily, the clothes Khalid had bought fitted her like a glove and she finally felt clean after such a long time. After her, Khalid went in for a shower and returned feeling the same.

"Ah, man! Feels good to feel so clean and fresh," Khalid sighed after finishing his shower. He walked into the room bare-chested and with a towel around his hips and legs. Amira blushed to herself and looked away, trying not to look too much and too often in case Khalid noticed. She didn't know why she felt so shy; they were married, after all. She pressed her lips tightly, inhaling deeply as he walked around the room so aimlessly and unbothered. Water droplets dripped down his long flocks of hair and slid down his chest, then his perfect abs. He, too, had lost weight, but his broad shoulders and abs still remained. The water did well in defining every muscle from his back to his abs. Khalid began drying himself with another small towel. He went for his hair first and spent a good 5 minutes drying his long locks of thick brown tresses. When it was dried, he placed it into his usual bun and then put on a new shirt. He wore a green, slightly woolly shirt with a pocket on the breast and he slipped on his grey tracksuit under his towel, then removed the towel.

He finished and jumped onto the bed.

"Careful, Khalid, you'll break the bed," giggled Amira.

"I'm not that fat, am I?" he replied.

"Only a little."

"Oh really...?" Khalid smirked and grabbed Amira by her arms and tickled her. Amira burst into fits of laughter and pushed him away.

"You're messing up my hair, Khalid!" she yelled, still laughing.

He then grabbed her legs and Amira suddenly screamed in pain.

"Khalid!" she screamed, holding her breath due to the sharp, sudden pain down her thigh.

"What? What's the matter?" he jumped back in shock as Amira winced and flinched in pain.

"Did I hurt you? Amira, talk to me?"

"Its...its fine, Khalid, it's just a small cut. It's nothing," she groaned.

"How? What happened? Did someone hurt you?!" he asked question after question and became more agitated by the second.

"No Khalid, it's just a small cut from the boat."

"Show me..." Khalid instructed.

Amira resisted and told him she was fine, but he insisted.

She tried to lift her leggings to reach the top of her thigh but they were too tight to go all the way up. Khalid got up and pulled her leggings down slowly, trying not to cause her too much pain. Amira's cheeks began turning pink and she felt her ears turn red hot with nervousness. She didn't want Khalid to see her bruise, in case it disgusted him. She felt highly insecure and coy.

Khalid's hand was warm and chary, shaking with caution and he reached for her bruise. He fingered her dark purple bruise and she winced slightly. Anger and rage overcame Khalid as he felt hot lava swirl inside his veins. He couldn't stand this, seeing Amira in pain. The fact that she was standing there with a monstrous bruise on her thigh and whining in pain only infuriated him. He felt as if he had failed.

"Oh, Mira..." he sighed.

"Khalid...honestly, I'm okay," she whispered, trying to stop herself crying.

Khalid stroked her bruised thigh and placed his lips against her heated leg. He rubbed his lips and nose against her skin and his stubble pricked her. She flinched and closed her eyes as she felt his hot breath against her painful bruise. He kissed it gently and helped pull her leggings up again.

"Be careful, okay, Mira? Look after it and I'll find some cream for it, okay? I promise," he told her.

"Okay, Khalid," she smiled back at his worried face.

"Come, let's lie down, Khalid, I'm tired."

It felt like a luxury almost, laying in a bed after so long. The bed wasn't even that comfortable. The springs bounced loudly every time Amira or Khalid turned, the mattress was stained and smelt damp and old and the wood beneath the mattress was wearing away, yet it felt like resting on a cloud. Amira softly ran her fingers across Khalid's arm as she lay her head on his chest. She pressed her warm cheek against his cool, soft skin and slipped her legs into the sheet duvet. She slid into it, eased to rest her exhausted feet and placed a leg around Khalid, intertwining with his.

Khalid and Amira shared their first night together as husband and wife.

In that moment, that split second before Khalid touched Amira, every nerve in her body felt intoxicated, electric. She felt nervousness with the foreboding of being alone with Khalid, as his wife, in a manner which exceeded further than any words could explain.

In that moment, in that instant and in that heartbeat, Amira loved Khalid, as did he love Amira, with their eyes as much as just their physical bodies, hearts fusing and connecting in quiet moments between action and quiescence.

Khalid breathed hard, and his heart pounded inside his chest like a banging drum. He looked down at Amira, who was succumbing to the call of sleep. Her eyes, opening and closing gently, her slight golden freckles twinkling from the small ray of sunshine coming from the shut curtain and her pomegranate pink lips, parted slightly as she breathed calmly onto Khalid's face. He stroked her hair and held her close. A tear rolled down his cheek onto her nose and he wiped it away. The bruise on her thigh, the small scar on her arm, her freckles that she despised, all the blemishes she was insecure of, were all the things that enticed and captivated Khalid. In all those insignificant, meaningless imperfections was where Khalid found someone who was perfect. When he looked at her, he forgot about his past, his pain and all the mistakes he ever made. Everything vanished with a simple look, a simple touch.

"Your eyes, Mira...," Khalid whispered into her ear as she drifted in and out of sleep.

"Your eyes, they see right through me."

Amira shuffled and mumbled something in her sleep.

"You look past my every flaw, my anger, my mistakes..."

He stroked her cheek fondly and kissed her parted lips and enveloped himself in a tranquilising, sedating sleep.

CHAPTER NINETEEN
Heraklion, Crete - September 2016

"I want to announce some good news."

Khalid and Amira strolled through Heraklion Archaeological Museum, hand in hand. The museum was fairly empty, with a few guards securing the area wearing smart uniforms and heavy boots that squeaked every time they moved. The marbled flooring was slippery. Amira and Khalid were in room 6, admiring the historic findings from cemeteries at Knossos, Phaistos and Archanes. The room held intricate clay figures and gold jewellery, all displayed behind glass shields.

A few other people in the room roamed around aimlessly, taking pictures, writing notes and chatting quietly amongst themselves. Amira and Khalid simply wandered curiously around the different figurines. People eyed up both Amira and Khalid and whispered to their families. Security guards also kept a close eye on them both, as if they were up to no good. Neither Amira nor Khalid paid any attention to them.

A television in the corner of the hallway, just outside the room, blared in the background. It caught Khalid's attention quickly as he realised it was President Recep Tayyip Erdogan, the President of Turkey.

"I want to announce some good news," he spoke sternly, yet his voice was kind and understanding. He spoke about Syrian refugees living in Turkey.

"We are going to help our Syrian friends by offering them the chance, if they want it, to acquire Turkish nationality. The

Interior Ministry will shortly announce how the citizenship procedure will work."

"Khalid? So, does that mean We can find help in Turkey, then?"

Khalid looked on at the blaring TV and smiled.

"Yes, Mira, we can!" he said ecstatically.

"And with the money we have saved up, we can try and get our papers and documents sorted too."

"That's great news!" Amira clapped happily.

After his speech, Erdogan experienced a high level of criticism for allowing Syrian refugees to stay in Turkey and gain nationality. Ankara had refused to grant refugee status to Syrians who fled the devasting war across the border since 2011, referring to them as guests. Only a small group were actually granted work permits and residency. A trending hashtag spread like wildfire worldwide across all social media platforms; #ÜlkemdeSuriyeliİstemiyorum (I don't want Syrians in my country). This was all a result of Erdogan's new plan for Syrian refugees.

Although it was a positive step by President Erdogan, many Turkish citizens thought that the process would not be easy to make it solely and exclusively simpler for Syrians to gain citizenship. There were others in need such as Georgians, Armenians and other foreigners who were located within Turkey for economic gain as well as other reasons. It wasn't clear whether such people would also be included within the scheme or not, and whether that would cause conflict amongst refugees and others trying to gain access to nationality. Aside from this, many also assumed that opposition in Turkey might see this plan as a bid by the President to import voters and help him strengthen his grip on power.

"It's a sense of pride for them, having this open-door policy for us. We're brothers," Khalid told Amira as they wandered around the room.

"But you hear these stories of people arriving at the border and then not being allowed to cross."

"I can only imagine life being a struggle in Turkey too, Khalid, just like here…" said Amira. They had been staying in Heraklion for almost 2 months now, and life wasn't easy, despite having a roof over their heads. Khalid, Amira, Sarah and Munir were moved to a different hostel twice. The boys found work at a local meat shop slaughtering chickens and the girls found a poorly paid job cleaning a café kitchen for 3 hours a day. They were paid next to nothing, but it meant saving enough money to sort out their documents to travel to Turkey in a plane.

"Life's a struggle everywhere, Mira. The Syrians in Turkey at the moment, they mainly live off odd jobs here and there and they barely earn enough to feed their families, not forgetting the fact that the country is also hosting around 300,000 Iraqis who have fled ISIS over the years."

"At least Turkey is looking more and more achievable, Khalid…" she replied.

"I know, Insha'Allah we will be out of here soon."

"I hope so," replied Amira.

"Anyway, so how do you like your birthday gift, eh?" Amira teased.

The 23rd of September, today, was Khalid's 23rd birthday. Whilst working as a cleaner for the past 2 and a half weeks, Amira had managed to save just enough money to put aside to buy two tickets for the Heraklion archaeological museum. Khalid was fond of history, so Amira thought it would be a nice birthday present for him.

"Are you crazy? It's the best gift ever, Mira, thank you" Khalid replied, hugging her close.

Although all 4 of them worked, money was tight. They got paid less after working hours and hours doing labour, and it was barely enough to survive on. They had saved some to buy food for the day, clothes, essentials and put the rest aside to slowly raise enough for a flight to Turkey as well as documents. It seemed like a lifetime away, but gradually, they persisted.

"Wow, I'm 23! Soon I'll be 50! Will you still love me when I'm old and grey with a walking stick?" he laughed.

"I mean, I've seen you in the mornings, so I guess seeing you at 50 won't be so bad," she replied, giggling.

"Ahhh, ok, ok, very funny… don't forget I've also seen you in the mornings, too."

"Yeah, and? At least my hair doesn't look like a rag roll in the mornings."

Khalid was now 23. His hair had grown considerably longer into thick, luscious locks of chestnut brown waves that were as wild as a jungle. As the wind blew mildly, his hair danced to its own rhythm against the breeze. He had started to grow his beard slightly, and it covered most of his face. It suited him well and Amira thought he looked handsome with it. His skin was tanned due to working in the sun often and his build was gaining some shape to it again, as both Khalid and Munir helped one another to train with some old, used weights.

"I'm sorry I couldn't get anything else..." said Amira, in a low voice.

"Don't be silly, I love it...There's so much history here!" he replied, pulling her towards another room.

"Did you know, this city was actually founded in 824 by the Arabs under a man called Abu Hafs Umar? He was expelled from Al-Andalus by Emir Al-Hakam and had taken over the Island from the Eastern Roman Empire."

"Really...? How do you remember all this information?" asked Amira playfully.

"I have a big head, you know, it can store all this knowledge," he laughed.

"Okay, birthday boy, carry on...tell me more," she replied.

"So, the Arabs built a moat around the whole city for protection and named the city Rabd al-Handaq."

"Castle of the moat...," translated Amira, "Interesting."

As they were talking, a middle-aged man approached them. It took only one glance for Amira to sense the burning resentment and hatred igniting in the man's narrowed, beady eyes. His mouth, slightly parted, was clenched tight, as if he were about to go in for a blow and his fists were gripped tenaciously.

'That's the thing with anger', Amira thought before the man even opened his mouth to speak. It's like a muted hawker mincing in the midnight air, always ready to strike when one least expects it. It looms over one, like the early morning fog in September, darkening one's judgement and perception. Its goal is to deceive whoever and whenever it wills.

"YOU! YEAH, YOU! UGLY SCUM IMMIGRANT REFUGEES!" the man bellowed with a mighty yell.

Amira watched as the whites in his beady, bespangled eyes turned sombre a black colour and his irises took on the colour of flaming molten lava. His virulent stare felt harrowing and it pierced right through Amira's body, as if his repulsive glare pricked every hair on her neck, giving her stinging goosebumps.

"GET THE FUCK OUT OF OUR COUNTRY, YOU SYRIAN REFUGEE SCUMS! TAKING ALL OUR FUCKING HOUSES AND JOBS, GO ON! GET OUT!" His voice is boorishly crude, like two large pieces of volcanic rock crushing against each other. Khalid held onto Amira, before taking a step closer to the man, with Amira behind him. The man wiped his lead-grey, cable-like hairs from his ruddy face and fixed a loathsome glance at them both.

"Your country? I mean, I didn't know you had your name on this country..." Khalid spoke, calmly, yet Amira could taste the rage in his voice.

"YEAH! MY COUNTRY! NOT YOURS, OR YOUR BITCH HERE! GET THE FUCK OUT AND TAKE THE REST OF THEM WITH YOU...YOU'RE POLLUTING OUR LAND WITH YOUR SMELL. MUSLIM SCUM."

This wasn't the first time. They had heard it before, the racist remarks, the cursing, the discriminating. Amira experienced it with Sarah when they worked, cleaning the café. Women would smirk and laugh at them, their clothing, their language, them. It wasn't their fault their country was going through a civil war, nor was it their fault that they ended up in Greece, a country they didn't want to turn up in anyway. Theoretically, that's all racism was; hijacking and defrauding the unknown fear centre of the mind. People were taught hatred and animosity just like they were taught to brush their teeth or tie their shoelaces, it was a norm.

"I beg your pardon?" Khalid gritted his teeth and his eyes narrowed until he was almost squinting.

"Khalid, leave it...seriously, let's go, it's not worth it," Amira begged. She could hear the tension and anger in his tone.

"YEAH, YOU HEARD ME, TERRORIST! TAKE YOUR BITCH AND GET BACK ON YOUR BOAT TO SYRIA OR IRAQ, OR WHEREVER THE HELL YOU'RE FROM!"

There was a sudden idle stillness on both sides. If the malice and disgust was perceivable in the atmosphere, the air would have been besmirched with the staining of vermilion red. It lasted no more than 5 seconds before movement emerged with so much force in every blow. Khalid threw several punches to the man's gut and then his face. He exploded, exploded into a rushing volcanic storm that had been boiling up inside for weeks and months. He saw red, everywhere. Amira begged him to stop, begged him to leave the man and just walk away, but Khalid heard nothing except the language of ferocity and vehemence.

"Please, KHALID! LEAVE HIM! JUST LET HIM GO!" she cried, at the top of her lungs.

"You're going to kill him!"

The man groaned loudly after every punch or kick, and soon he passed out on the floor. He was a bloody mess, his eyes swollen, spit drooling down his chin and blood rushing from his lip and nostril. He moaned in pain. Khalid, standing right above him, grunted and exhaled harder and harder, as if he was unable to catch his breath. The deep, regretful sigh that escaped Khalid's cracked, dehydrated lips was slow and rueful, as if he wasn't instantly remorseful of his actions. His glazed eyes were fixated on the floor at the moaning man, and his head dropped low, like a sorry soul.

Amira gasped, panicking, as she caught sight of 3 policemen running towards them.

"KHALID! We need to go, Khalid, come on!" She pulled him by his arm but he couldn't hear or feel anything.

"Khalid!!" she yelled, as they got closer and closer.

It seemed unjust, cruel even, that no matter how hard and how much Khalid committed himself and strived to be the man his conscious desired him to be, it would continue to mock and scorn him with his mistakes, his past failures and his weaknesses. Each new occurrence, the regrets and sorrow would resurface on the simple look on Khalid's face.

The policemen, dressed in thick navy-blue uniforms, arrived. The man remained on the floor and none of the men knelt down to help him. Instead, they went for Khalid. The rest was all a blur...

■■■

There was something unsettling about the cemented, boxed chamber that Amira and Khalid were placed in. The room itself was empty; no bed, or chair, just four grey walls with sharp corners and a single, perfectly cut-out window with uneven metal bars and a large metal door. The putrid stench of urine mixed with blood lingered in the air. In the background, away from the chambered room, sounds of chains clicking, men shouting and prisoners yelling abuse grew louder and louder and more constant.

"Ahhh...Owhh," Khalid groaned in pain, lifting his arm slowly and using it to lift his battered body from the floor. Amira jumped up from beside him and helped him lift himself up.

"No, Khalid, don't try to get up," she whispered, as if she was scared of someone hearing her.

Khalid had been unconscious for the whole time they were inside the cell. The policemen, who had handcuffed both Khalid and Amira, first beat Khalid to a rotten pulp. They used thick, metal batons and whacked his chin, punched him as he tried to resist the beating and finished by finally handcuffing him. Amira tried her best to help him, but it was impossible, for she too was handcuffed and could not help Khalid.

"Whe...where are...we?" Khalid whimpered. His chest tightened and ached as he spoke and he spat his words out with great difficulty. The pain had a sickening warmth to it and it quivered at every nerve in Khalid's body. It was followed by cramps of nausea and dizzy spells. Amira grabbed Khalid as he

318

tried to get up, but he only fell again as his legs were too weak to control his body's weight.

"Stay still, please," Amira replied. She tried to hold back her tears when looking at Khalid struggling and moaning in agony.

"We're in jail, Khalid. They took us in that van... don't you remember anything?" she sniffed.

"What van?" he asked. He was completely oblivious to what had happened after the policemen beat him.

"They handcuffed us and brought us here," Amira raises her hands to show Khalid where they handcuffed her. She had slits of cuts on her wrist where the handcuffs were pulled and dragged. The blood had dried around the cuts and all of a sudden, Khalid's eyes lit up, almost protruding outwards.

"WHO DID THIS TO YOU!?" he yelled, forgetting his pain and anguish and sitting up straight, away from the wall. He moaned as he spoke, yet he asked over and over till Amira replied.

"TELL ME!"

"The...the police, Khalid...and now, we're stuck in here. They just threw us in here and we haven't been seen or spoken to for almost 3 hours."

Khalid rubbed his eyes slowly and looked around the room. He grunted angrily and clenched his fists.

"FUCK'S SAKE!" he roared.

"Now they'll definitely fucking check up on us and our status, even send us back!"

Amira froze.

"Back? Back where?" she questioned, nervously.

"To Syria," Khalid replied with a forlorn, solemn voice.

Amira sank to the floor. That single, 5 lettered word sent Amira's brain into a blurred stutter. Every limb in her body recessed and brought itself to a subconscious halt whilst her thoughts tried to catch up. She turned to Khalid, looking at his bloody face and tired eyes in hope of some reassurance.

"Syria? But...but the war...it's still going on!" she stuttered.

"I know, I know, listen, it will be okay. We won't go back," Khalid replied, although he didn't sound very convincing.

Amira fingered the necklace round her neck, the same one Khalid had gifted her for her birthday. She couldn't help but feel disappointed, nettled. She wanted Khalid's birthday to be a special one.

"So...guess what...?" Amira teased Khalid back in the hostel after he returned from work.

He was exhausted and immediately threw himself on the bed, almost cracking the wood underneath.

"Erm...You're pregnant?" Khalid laughed.

"No! Don't be so silly!"

Khalid chuckled and rested his head on Amira's lap.

"Imagine..." he said.

"Imagine what?"

"Imagine a little me and you running around playing football and driving us mad," Khalid's voice suddenly lowered, as if he didn't want anyone to hear his conversation, despite the room being empty.

Amira smiled at the thought and brushed Khalid's hair with her soft fingers.

She had never really thought of it, but now that Khalid had mentioned having children together one day, she felt giddy and excited at the thought. The reality, however, was it wasn't going to be anytime soon. All Amira could think of was having a permanent home and then having a family in a safe environment for them to grow up in.

"I think you'll be a great dad one day, Khalid," she shyly whispered.

"You think? I'd teach my son to play football like a pro."

"Son? And if you have a daughter?" Amira giggled.

"Yeah? Then I'll teach her the sickest football freestyling and she will also be a pro!" he replied, eyes beaming with excitement.

"Insha'Allah Mira, one day..."

"Insha'Allah."

"Okay, now guess, Khalid," she said as she jumped up.

"Erm...I don't know, tell me."

"So...it's your birthday tomorrow..." she began speaking in a low, loving voice.

"Oh snap, it is as well. I actually forgot, wow," he replied, stunned.

"And…" she teased.

"And…?" Khalid repeated.

"And I've saved some money over 3 weeks and got us both a ticket to visit the Heraklion Archaeological Museum as a birthday gift…"

Khalid sat up.

"You did what?" he asked, moved by her words.

"We're going to a museum; it's got lots of history in it… just what you like," she replied.

Khalid's eyes met Amira's. From beneath her messily tied, honey-coloured ringlets of thick curls, her eyes peeked through, shining a beauteous colour of chestnut brown diamonds. The deep curve on Amira's lips radiated her beauty even more and it was the sort of smile that brought back a million memories in a single second. It was the kind of smile that made Khalid feel like he was home.

"Oh, Mira…," Khalid wrapped her in a warm embrace. He didn't want to leave. For that moment in time, where so much pain, regret and confusion followed their life like a lost puppy, it all felt invisible in her arms.

"I wrote a poem too, for you, just a little one, though," she sang in excitement.

"Poem? Go on then…read it to me," he replied eagerly.

"Nope, later. Once we finish with the museum...when the moment is right...," said Amira.

Just then, as Amira was reminiscing on this moment from only yesterday, a sudden clacking sound came from the metal door in the cell. Amira's heart sank and twisted with nerves as she waited for the door to open.

"Read it now, Mira..." Khalid's voice was disjointed and faint. His request made Amira's heart shatter into a million pieces, each piece making a crushing noise within her. How she had longed to make Khalid's birthday special this year...

"Khalid...not now...," she cried, holding onto him as the person behind the door jingled through his metal keys, trying to find the right one to open up.

"Please, Mira...read me the poem."

Amira wiped away her warm tears and stuttered and hiccupped like a baby. She took a deep breath and whispered in Khalid's ear.

"I can't think of a way,
That I could ever live a day,
Without you...
I mean...what would I do?
Being without the one I adore,
Yes, it is true...I love you more.
Keep on loving me, Khalid, the way that you do,
And I promise you, wherever and whenever you need your Mira,
She will be standing right here, waiting for you..."

She grabbed onto Khalid's arm and pulled herself close to him and suddenly, an icy breeze rushed from beneath the door as it opened slowly. It reminded Amira of a winter she once experienced back in Syria. It was a chilly winter's morning in December 2013. She remembered staring out of her window onto the thick blankets of pearly snow embedded across the streets of her city, Aleppo. It was truly magical. Magical because when she gazed up at the perfect, clear sky that shone proudly over the city, she felt the clarity and pureness of the pristine clouds carving their way to a new day. This, however, was much different. Every minute felt like hell; the sounds, the shouting, the echoing, and now, the person behind the door, who ultimately, was about to determine both Khalid and Amira's fate.

CHAPTER TWENTY

Ibn Umar reported:

The Messenger of Allah, peace and blessings be upon him, said, *"**Be in this world as if you were a stranger or a traveller along a path.**"*

A believer has two attitudes toward this *Dunya* (world).

The first, is that of a stranger in a strange land that does not belong to him. No matter how hard he tries, or how hard he tries to make it his, it does not belong to him. Ultimately, it isn't his home for him to feel welcomed or entirely content in. His desires, mind and heart can never be connected nor bound to this land, which definitively, is nothing more than clay from which he was created. Everything and everyone within this world will either pain him, let him down or betray him, one way or another. Rather, his heart and mind should be working in conjunction on finding a way to prepare and return back to his home. Time, effort and struggle are all occupied with this purpose. His time is not spent wasted on forming such love and connection with this world, for it too will end, alongside every other thing he owned. One is not to invest himself so profoundly within this world to which he does not belong and ultimately, forget his goal and purpose of being.

Fundamentally, these are the simple attributes and characteristics of a stranger when he is travelling to a foreign land. He isn't happy or at ease with his days unless he feels that during his days spent within a foreign land, he has accomplished something that will someday lead him, with guidance, back to his home. Moreover, he keeps to himself and doesn't focus on competing or opposing any of the locals within the foreign land, both their interests are completely polarized. Essentially, everyone is on their own journey.

Winning the praise, respect and validation from others is something a traveller does not seek during his time, as his heart is merely yearning to return to his home. Born in Medina, 642, Al Hasan al Basri (Rahmatullah), an early Muslim preacher, ascetic, scholar and mystic narrated the comforting words:

"The believer is in this world like a stranger. He does not become unhappy from its humiliation, nor does he compete for its honour. He has one purpose and the people have another purpose."

For that reason, a believer will not care to compete as a rival against others in this Dunya. Many times, a man will be considered 'strange' and 'alien' to others, however, such a thought will not concern or hurt a believer, for he will most definitely be a stranger to such people as his concerns and aim in life will be much more polarized from theirs.

For a Syrian refugee, the absence and lack of identity documents is more than just a slight inconvenience. It was like an alien, from a completely different planet, was given a task of trying to prove not only his identity, but also that his presence in another country is actually legitimately lawful. In some parts of the world, aliens without their documents and identification papers are often subjected to severe detentions and often, summary deportation. Measures of this nature are exceptionally serious for refugees as it means there is a risk of being sent back to their place of origin, often a country going through war.

They sat there, silent. The walls around them felt more and more suffocating by the minute, as if they were enclosing around them within the invisible blur of darkness that crawled into their surroundings. The same darkness that only those who had lost a loved one saw, the same darkness that was seen only by those afflicted with such pain and suffering to last them a lifetime, the same darkness that wasn't seen by just anyone.

She knew she was scared. Scared wasn't even the right word to use when Amira thought of how she felt. Such a feeling couldn't be defined with a simple dictionary word. It could be described as memories, all placed together in a bubble. The fearful memories, all playing in front of her. The roaring of heedless shells dropping on a whole town at a time, the howling of babies and mothers in anguish and hysteria, the dead, defenceless bodies of children, the last conversation she had had with her parents, the way her baba was dug out from rubble and thrown into a pit of bodies, the face Adam made when he finally said Amira's name, the face he then made when he was brought to her, dead. All these images, all these memories were replaying in front of Amira. Why? Because of a seven-worded, simple sentence that was nothing more than a statement, yet to Amira, it meant everything.

"We are sending you back to Syria," stated the man in the blue and grey uniform. His eyes, a chilling ocean-blue colour, pierced right into Khalid's, then Amira's. He was emotionless, in his speech, his voice, his face. He felt nothing. The wrinkles around his eyes were deep and still, for he showed no sort of facial expression whilst talking.

"Your name?" he asked, sternly at Amira first, then Khalid.

Amira gulped down a large boulder in her throat, that felt like it was stuck and almost choking her to death. She tried again and her airway seemed to have cleared. She timidly replied to his question.

"A...Amira," she croaked.

"And you?" he pointed towards Khalid whilst looking down at the paper on his desk.

Khalid sat silent and didn't answer.

"My friend, you will make this difficult for yourself," said the man, still looking down at his papers. His voice and tone were stoically impassive, like he didn't care about the fears Amira and Khalid had, as if he was a robot, not capable of feelings. 'How can you just ruffle through your papers and act like everything is normal?' thought Amira. 'Do you not care? Care that we will have to return to a country that's in the middle of a whole civil war? Where people are dying every single day? Where we most probably will soon die too if we return? Do you not care? How is it so easy? So easy to act cold-hearted and passionless?'

"We are not going back to Syria," Khalid said, adamantly.

"Say all you like, but the truth is, you cannot stay here. To be honest, you're lucky you were here for this long in the first place," snapped the man in the uniform.

"The way you behaved towards one of our citizens, well, you're lucky we don't lock you up in a detention centre."

"My behaviour!? What about him? Shall I just accept a man insulting my wife? Accept his racist remarks!? Shall I?"

"Was that enough to beat a man to a pulp?" replied the man, sarcastically, with a grin on his face.

Khalid clenches his jaw and lifted himself from the chair until Amira swiftly placed her arm over him to ease him. She spoke in Arabic, so the man could not understand.

"Min fadlik Khalid, Tahada," she whispered, "Calm down."

Khalid took a large breath and exhales loudly.

The man, who was proudly smirking, lifted his eyes from his papers.

"So...name?" he spat out.

"Khalid!"

The man scribbled on his paper.

"So, what will happen now is you will go back to your hostel with an accompanied member of staff, collect your things and be taken to the airport. You will wait there for the next available flights and that might be awhile seeing as your country is in the middle of a war. The flights aren't as regular. Maybe they'll send you to Lebanon first, who knows."

"Do you not realise that if we are sent back to Syria, we will end up dead sooner or later?!" Khalid exclaimed, with tears in his eyes.

"There are still fucking killings every day! Multiple airstrikes, especially after Trump and Putin announced their plans for a nationwide ceasefire! More people have died after this. There's hardly any aid or hospitals available where we live, delivery of aid convoys is constantly hampered." Khalid's voice was becoming weaker and more staggered as he whimpered lifelessly in his chair, sinking each time he spoke.

"Just last week, the city of Dayr al-Zawr was struck by US airplanes," cried Khalid, holding back solid tears.

Dayr al-Zawr, an Eastern town in Syria, was somewhere Khalid often visited with his friends. He had taken Amira once, too. It was approximately 5 hours from their home town, Aleppo. The wondrous town was located on the right bank of the Euphrates River. Khalid loved visiting this town for it was enriched with heavy history. He educated Amira on their day trip to the town. He told her about how the Ottomans built the whole town in 1867 to control the nomads of the Euphrates area. Under the Ottomans, the town was the capital of a bureaucratic, administrative district, the seat of the governor and the site of outposts maintaining and policing the country. Occupied by the British after the Ottoman retreat in 1918, the town was then captured and controlled by Faysal, son of Husayn Ibn Ali, King of Hejaz, for a short period before the French occupation began in 1921. Then, during the years from 1941, when the World War 2 era approached, the town was captured by a British force to prevent Syria and Lebanon from falling to Axis troops. Eventually, in the year 1946, the town became part of the Republic of Syria.

"It doesn't stop; every day there's a new target, a new airstrike, a new family killed. Understand! Please! Do you not realise, WE WILL DIE?!"

If one had looked into Khalid's eyes, they would have seen he was broken. He bore the declaration on his face of someone who was nearing the end of all hope and faith and beginning to realise that maybe, there wasn't a light at the end of the tunnel.

The man sat up, chucking his pen on the desk. To describe his facial expression would have been like describing a brick wall or a piece of blank paper. It was an expression of complete and utter disdain.

He rolled his eyes, sighing in annoyance, before finally replying to Khalid's plea.

"And do you realise..." He paused, pokerfaced with irritation.

"That we simply have no place for you here?"

....

"What do you mean we are being sent back to Syria?" Munir's voice was raspy, like he'd just been shot with a bullet through his chest.

"Who is this man?" he stared at the man in uniform supervising both Amira and Khalid as they packed.

"Munir, they're sending us back," replied Khalid.

Then, he spoke in Arabic. He gave Munir a look, and in that look, Munir understood.

"Laqad han alwaqt litanfidh alkhutat alty naqashnaha 'iidha kan hdha sayuhduthu. 'Atasil bialmuhrab, 'ukhbiruh 'anana mstedwn khilal eshr daqayiq."

Amira's heart sank, as it did back in Syria, back in Lebanon and back in Cyprus.

She listened to Khalid's stern instructions to Munir and with every step, died a little inside.

"It is time," he said sharply, his eyes fixated on Munir.

"It is time to go through with our plan we discussed if this situation were to occur. Call the smuggler, tell him we will be ready in ten minutes."

■■■

Khalid made the man in uniform wait outside their room.

"She needs to change! Wait outside!" he snapped in aggravation.

"No, you outside," he pointed at Khalid.

Khalid grunted and pushed him in anger. The man clutched his handgun and ground his teeth.

"I said, wait outside! She needs to change!"

The man came close to Khalid's face, baring his nicotine-tarnished teeth that were are all either rotting or contorted. Snarling loudly, he swallowed his anger and turned to leave the room. Amira watched as he lifted his hands away from his gun, which was fastened tightly to his side belt.

Before he left, he gave both Amira and Khalid a piercingly repulsive stare, the kind of stare a hunter gives before he shoots down a deer, or the kind of look a rival gives his opponent in battle before he pitches his arrow at his heart. It was the kind of look that made Amira apprehensively tense.

"Five minutes! You understand? I'm counting." The man left the room, slamming the door shut behind him.

Khalid rushed from one side of the room to the next, he packed everything he owned into his duffle bag. Amira stood there, watching.

"Amira! Come on! What are you waiting for!" he whispered cuttingly.

Amira didn't answer.

"Amira! COME ON!" Khalid spoke more irately this time, then suddenly felt bad for raising his voice.

Amira numbed to the sound of his voice. Subconsciously, a salty tear escaped her eye and ran down her burning cheek. Khalid sighed and drops the duffle bag.

"Oh, Mira…"

He pulled her close and she could hear his beating heart drumming like thunder inside his chest. She didn't sob, or wail, but instead, the tears just escaped in a continuous spout.

"Please don't cry, Mira, it will be okay."

"Why? Why can't I cry, Khalid? These tears are what keep my soul alive in this misery, and remind me that I'm still human," she spoke coldly, with no emotion except inertia, as if she were in an immovable daze.

"What smuggler, Khalid? When did you plan this? You didn't even tell me anything."

Khalid sighed and looked away.

"Amira, I had to have a plan. I knew something like this would happen sooner or later. I had to stay prepared, for both our sakes. Do you want to be sent back?" Khalid asked.

The muscles in Amira's chin trembled like a leaf before she burst out.

"Then why did you have to lose your temper, Khalid?! Why did you beat that man!? Everything was going fine for now! WHY!?"

Amira bawled frantically, as if the aggressiveness of it might turn back time; as if by the utter strength of her grief and deeply sunken heart, the news would be undone.

Sheer regret and remorse were written all over Khalid's face as he took in Amira's words. Although she spoke out of anger and worry, the deep regret re-emerged before him, despite him trying to forget his mistakes. Whenever it dawned upon him, he would assiduously scrutinise them again and again, in search of some sort of contentment where his mind would suddenly be comforted or convinced with his self-proclaimed guilt, but it never really was, especially after listening to Amira's outburst. Like a pitiless, unsympathetic wraith, it would be back tomorrow to haunt him all over again.

He looked down to his feet, shoulders sunken back and eyes closed. He didn't know what to say, for he knew she was right. Two frail, whimpering words escaped his lips.

"I'm sorry..."

Amira said nothing, lifted her hands to her eyes and wiped away her tears. She took the duffle bag from Khalid's hand and placed in it her box of poems and books. She walked to every corner of the room, hastily, and collected her things.

"Amira, I'm sorry, Mira, please..." Khalid begged from behind her.

Amira didn't hear him; not that she was ignoring him deliberately, but because all she heard were waves. Thick, deadly waves crashing against her body.

Khalid walked in front of her, now sobbing like a child.

"Mira, I'm sorry, please forgive me," he cried.

In that moment, they both cried, reaching out to one another for help and comfort. Khalid hugged Amira tightly, refusing to pull away. He embraced her warmly, leaving no air between them, as if that hug would keep her safe forever, away from any harm or pain.

"How did this all happen, Amira? Why?" he cried into her hair.

His gentleness was trawling Amira into a swift trance. He smelt of woody musk, the sort of spray a car wash would use after they finish cleaning a car. In that embrace, as always, and for as long as Amira had been Amira, and Khalid had been Khalid, all bad thoughts and worries were blown away like dead, autumn leaves in the wind.

"I'll make it okay again, trust me..." he told her, still clinging onto her tightly.

Before Amira could reply, a sudden, thundering knocking sound thumped from outside.

"HURRY UP!" yelled the man outside, still waiting.

Amira began to panic and they both quickly pulled away and packed the last few remaining pieces of clothing. Amira put on Khalid's jacket.

"We need to leave, NOW!" instructed Khalid.

"Munir is waiting for us near the petrol station, and so is the smuggler. He will drive us to the port, near Rocca a Mare Fortress. The boat will be waiting for us."

"Is it just us four on the boat?" Amira asked anxiously.

"I think there is just one other family of five."

"And the smuggler? Is he coming too or are you paying him?"

"We need to pay him. Munir and I have enough, just about, anyway, so we will negotiate with him."

Another loud thump came from outside, making Amira jump with fright.

"Oh, Khalid! He's coming!" she shivered.

"Let's go!" Khalid ran towards the window behind their bed. It was mainly covered by the headrest of the bed, but they both managed to squeeze through without having to move the bed away from the wall. As they were only on the first floor, they escaped the room and landed safely on the ground. Khalid carried the bag of things, whilst Amira clutched his free hand.

They both ran.

Outside.

Khalid was still aching. Every so often, he experienced sharp pains below his ribs and if he moved too quick, the wound on his hip would bleed and seep through his shirt. It was seeping now. But he couldn't stop to wipe and clean it, or stop to take a breather, for behind them, the man who was waiting for them peered his head out the window from which they had both escaped and ferociously shouted,

"OI YOU! COME BACK! NA STAMATISEI!"

"AMIRA! RUN!!"

The ground beneath Amira's feet blurred before her as she felt a sudden rush of adrenaline. Her knees wobbled like jelly as she tried running with Khalid. All she heard was the distant shouting of the man from behind her. She turned back to see. He was still there, at the window.

"AMIRA, COME ON! DON'T LOOK BACK!" yelled Khalid. He took a hold of her arm and pulled her along. The man in the window was no longer there. The persistent thumping of her footsteps echoed in her ears and thick beads of sweat rolled down her forehead.

"He's coming…" Amira whimpered to Khalid.

"Then come on! Munir is waiting, let's GO!"

Amira nodded in assertation and followed Khalid's pace. The warmth of the humid, damp air made her feel suppressed in a tight suffocation. Her trousers, shirt, vest and hair all clung to her sweaty skin. She looked forward and ran, without looking back. Khalid breathed loudly and grunted stridently at people to move out of their way. People cursed back and some even tried to stop them from running as they caught sight of the man in uniform not far off behind them, running in their direction.

They zoomed past the people around them, shoving as they went. The street was busy, with people shopping at small fruit and spice stalls.

They passed stalls, small houses cornered off from others, large buildings and a small café, all aligned into sectioned streets. Khalid noticed a small intersecting alleyway. It was familiar to him as it was the same alley in which a small mosque was located. He went there a few times with Munir and made friends with some of the local brothers.

"This way," he pulled Amira by her wrist and down the alley.

Outside the mosque, which was called Mosquee Heraklion, people stared at both Khalid and Amira with apprehension. They ignored everyone around them and ran into the mosque.

Inside, the smell of woody oud hovered around the rooms. In the main, carpeted hall, there were around 10 to 12 men. Some were praying, some sitting against a wall and others reading the Quran. From the corner of her eye, Amira caught sight of a small side room in which 2 young boys were doing their ablution, washing before prayer.

Khalid and Amira panted vigorously like they'd just climbed a mountain. It was the type of breathing where one has run for hours and loses his breath mixed with the heavy breathing of panic and fear.

"Is...is everything okay? Brother?" asked an elderly man with a pure, white beard. He reminded Amira of Baba Mohammed for a moment; even his voice sounded slightly like his. She was surprised to hear him speak fluent Arabic.

"We...we need...we need to leave," Khalid puffed, trying to catch his breath.

"The police, they're after us. We...we...can't..." Khalid pauses and winced in pain.

"Can't what?" the man asked, worriedly. The other people now turned their attention on both Khalid and Amira.

"We can't go back," Khalid struggled as he spoke, as if his tongue had been held to ransom.

"Back where, child?"

"Syria! We can' go back to Syria. Please, let us stay here for a moment. We will be out of your way soon..." Khalid pleaded and begged as if he was convinced of the man's answer before he even spoke.

Then, all of a sudden, Khalid bent over as abruptly and sharply as if he had just been winded by an invisible soul. Three, thick droplets of crimson blood splattered onto the cream-coloured marbled entrance of the mosque. Khalid coughed and 3 more drops flowed from his mouth.

"KHALID!" Amira cried.

Khalid lost consciousness slightly, as he stumbled whilst bending over. His eyes rolled back as he lifted himself up, so Amira helped him. He suddenly dropped and Amira went down with him.

"Ya Allah, SOMEONE, HELP!" the elderly man cried out to get someone's attention in the main prayer hall.

"Khalid! Khalid, are you okay!?" Amira rubbed his forehead and pleaded with him to answer.

"Khalid, please! Talk to me!"

Khalid grunted and mumbled something under his breath. Blood and spit ran down his neck and Amira wiped it clean with her sleeve.

Two other men came running towards them both, one holding a glass of water, the other, a towel.

Amira took the towel and cleaned the blood off his face and neck.

"Sister, is he okay?" asked the first elderly man.

"Please, help us. He's coughing blood. He's been coughing every day since…" she paused as Khalid mumbled again.

"Mia…Miaa," he tried to form something but was unable to. He tried again.

"Mir…Mira…"

"Yes, yes, Khalid, I'm here! You're okay, I promise. Come on now, stop scaring me."

"Mira…jacket…the pock…the pocket…"

Amira wiped her tears and sat up slightly. She was confused. 'What was Khalid talking about?' she thought.

"Khalid, what is it?" she asked.

"Inside the pocket, read the poem…," he murmured.

Amira realised she was wearing his jacket and he was referring to the wedding gift poem he was meant to give to Amira weeks ago, but hadn't finished.

"Khalid, this isn't the time for a poem...please, sit up and have some water," she snapped.

"Sister, here..." A man handed her a glass of water and she lifted Khalid's head.

"Why is he bleeding?" he asked her.

"It's ever since we got here, we haven't had any proper medical attention or medicine. He's had a nasty cough for weeks. All that dirty seawater and cold winds...he's probably got a chest infection that hasn't been seen to, and it's only getting worse." Amira wiped the sweat off Khalid's forehead as he gulped down the water. He lay there, still as a rock as if he was resting.

"Let him rest, he will be okay. Sister, I will get you some medicine; wait here for me," the elderly man who resembled Baba Mohammed offered his help and Amira was touched. She sniffed and thanked him gratefully. He left the mosque.

The other men inside hovered around for a while until they left Amira to it.

Khalid was breathing gently in Amira's arms, his eyes occasionally opening then closing, drifting in and out of consciousness and mumbling something every time. The world seemed a blur, and random images appeared to levitate purposelessly in the lagoon of Khalid's thoughts. An occasional rub or soothing touch by Amira momentarily brought him back to the real, outside world, despite him being in a pool of drowsiness.

He soon woke up. It took him only 15 or so minutes to sit up and be his normal self again, although to Amira, it felt like almost an hour.

"Oh, man, my hair is messed up," he laughed, brushing his thick locks.

"Khalid...are you okay?" Amira asked, hugging him tightly as he lifted himself up.

"Me? What's going to be wrong with me?" he joked.

"Did we lose him? The man?" he asked.

"I think so, but Khalid, you literally blacked out. You were bleeding from your mouth."

"I'm okay, I'm okay, sorry if I worried you. Look, we need to leave..." he said, lifting himself upwards and using the handle beside him to help him. Amira got up in a hurry and interrupted Khalid.

"But Khalid, we're safe here for now. There's a man, he's gone to get you some medicine for your cough..."

"Mira, we can't stay here forever. Munir and Sarah are waiting; what if they leave without us? The authorities are bound to be after us; if they reach Sarah and Munir, they might leave without us."

"At least wait for some medicine, Khalid, please." They don't wait long. After 2 minutes the man arrived holding a pharmacy bag of different painkillers, cough syrups and plasters.

"Dear child," the man ran to Khalid, happy to see him awake.

"Are you okay, young one?"

"Yes, I'm okay. Thank you for these, you really shouldn't have gone to all this trouble." Khalid kissed the man's frail, wrinkled hands.

"It was no trouble at all; you are my brother, my son," he replied humbly. Khalid smiled and gave the man a hug.

"Our Prophet Muhammed taught us, help your brother in time of need and Allah will help you during your time of need," he narrated.

"I am grateful," Khalid said.

"Me too," Amira added.

The old man smiled. There was a kindness in his wrinkly smile, a delicate benevolence. His small, grey eyes were filled with compassion and his face radiated a glow of sincerity.

"Are you Syrian?" the man asked.

"Yes," Amira replied timidly, "we are…"

The man rejoiced, as if Amira had told him that he had just won the lottery.

"Ahhh Syria! What a place, I tell you!" he cheered.

Amira laughed like a child at his excitement.

"Yes, Syria… Have you been?" she giggled.

"Been? I lived there for almost 34 years, my child. It was my home. My life…"

"Thirty-four years? Wow! Where did you live?" Khalid asked.

"The great city, Damascus."

"No way! You didn't live far from us…We're from Halab, Aleppo," said Khalid.

"Masha-Allah!" he said.

"Why did you leave Damascus, Uncle?" Amira asked, intrigued that this man was actually from Syria.

"Well, my dear, my parents were from Iraq. They had lived there for their whole lives, until the war…"

"What war?" asked Amira.

"Ottoman Iraq was attacked by British-Indian troops in late autumn 1915…"

Khalid spoke.

"Oh yes, that war. After having taken control of southern Iraq, British-Indian forces marched up the Tigris but were intercepted in the battle of Ctesiphon in November 1915 and after a prolonged siege in Kut al-Amara, they had to surrender in April 1916."

"Bravo, boy, I'm impressed with your knowledge," said the old man, smiling widely.

"I love a bit of history…" Khalid replied.

"So why do you live in Greece now?" Amira asked, curious.

"Well after my parents moved to Syria for a better life, I was born in June 1937…"

"Wait, so that means you must be...82 years old!" gasped Amira.

The old man chuckled humbly.

"Well, I do tell myself I am still 16," he laughed.

Amira grinned politely.

"So, when I was born, I lived in Syria for 34 years. I had the best time, until 1971. I was 34 at the time, my wife, 30. Syria changed in that time..."

"1971, hang on, that's the year the Assad family came to power..." said Khalid.

"Right you are, boy. Since then, ethnic and sectarian minorities began facing discrimination, freedom of expression was suppressed and simple things like public gatherings of more than five were banned. My wife and I, we just didn't feel at home anymore, I guess. That's the best way to explain the feeling...it wasn't home anymore. A home is where you can be yourself and not worry about anyone judging you. Syria, it wasn't our home to live in anymore." Amira studied his face, sad and regretful with coldness in his speech as he spoke of his past. His eyes, fixated on the floor, were like windows, and inside all Amira saw was woe.

"Nothing's changed there, then," scoffed Khalid as he listened to the man.

"My wife and I, we moved to Greece. Our children all moved away to the USA or Europe. But my wife and I have lived a wonderful, peaceful life here in Heraklion ever since, and for once, even though this was also not our home, we felt like it was."

"Did the Greek people not despise you? Did they not rant in your faces or make racist comments? They don't like us, Uncle, no one does…" Khalid says.

"At first, we did experience some, but gradually and slowly it became less and less. It's not that they don't like us, child, people are just ignorant about what they don't know. They will see someone new and already have an opinion and judgment on them. Remember one thing, children, Allah the Almighty is the ultimate and only judge."

"You're right…so right," Amira agreed.

"So, you have never been back to Syria since?" asked Khalid.

"I did go once, in 2000, when Assad took over from his father. He too failed to improve basic human rights and we already know what a darn good job he's done in Syria," the man sarcastically mocked.

Amira looked at the man's face. She felt a security around his voice, like a protective shield. His wrinkles on his face carved and engraved many stories of a regretful yet happy life, a bittersweet life. The man smiled at Amira, his tired, resentful eyes squinting slightly and his skin pure, yet grey with weariness.

"You remind me of my granddaughter," he spoke warmly.

"Do I? How?" Amira's eyes lit up at his words.

"She's a gem, a diamond! Her eyes are light like yours and her hair is the exact same colour. As for her character, well, she is as fierce as a tigress, I tell you. Always up for a debate."

Amira laughed and looked at Khalid, who was stretching his stiffened neck.

"Is she a little annoying too, like Mira?" Khalid joked.

"Shush you!" Amira giggled.

"MashaAllah, may Allah shower his every blessing upon you two..." the man whispered.

"Adhakkalahu-Sinakk," he recited. "May Allah always keep you smiling."

"We need to leave..." Khalid got up and wiped the last of the blood from around his chin.

"Khalid? How? Just wait a bit..."

"We can't; Munir and Sarah are waiting for us."

"Son, how will you get to Turkey? It is too dangerous by sea...these smugglers ask for thousands and they rip you off with fake lifejackets and boats that barely work..."

"Khalid...just not now. Wait, till you are better at least, please."

"How, Mira? Where will we stay? Who will take us in now without asking the same bloody questions again and again about who we are, or where are our papers?" Khalid's voice became edgy, anxious even.

"Me...," the old man murmured.

Amira and Khalid looked at him, his eyes smiling with humbleness.

"Pardon?" whispered Amira.

"I can look after you…you can stay with me until you are fit to travel again."

"What?" Khalid spoke.

"But…We couldn't, it's too much to ask for…" he continued.

"Nonsense! I have a spare room, a bathroom, a kitchen, everything you need. Until you are better, Son, you can stay with me as long as you wish. Since my beloved wife passed away, I have been so lonely, so I don't mind the company. You are my children; I cannot turn you away in this state. I wouldn't be able to live with myself."

Khalid and Amira both looked at each other, lost for words. Inside, they both felt a sense of relief, as if the world's largest and heaviest boulder had been lifted from their chests.

"I…I don't know what to say…thank you, Uncle…" stuttered Khalid.

"Your friends? Sarah and Munir, you say. Do you want to go to them and tell them to come too? Then you can all go together to Turkey," the man suggested.

"Yes, they are waiting at the port, near Rocca a Mare Fortress."

"Okay! I can drive you there; let us go," the man replied.

Khalid and Amira were deeply humbled by the man's offer, so much so, that they didn't even know how to repay him with their words. Not enough 'Thank yous'" or 'We are grateful' could ever come close to the way they felt.

When they sat in the car, Amira looked around. She felt severe paranoia, as if the man who was chasing them earlier on was lurking around somewhere close by like a bad smell. Her heart thumped louder by the second as they got in the car, belted themselves up and drove down the alleyway to the main road. It felt strange looking out from the car window. Khalid sat in front whilst Amira sat behind him in the rustic, old Reliant Scimitar. People outside, they didn't even look like humans. They were more like oblivious zombies, walking around totally unaware of the hurricane of thoughts and feelings Amira felt.

The drive down to the port wasn't long. They arrived within 15 minutes and as the old man parked up, Amira and Khalid found themselves standing in front of the most magnificent fortress.

It was in the shape of a square, with the heavy structure consisting of strong, thick walls.

The gate entrance to the fort was at the edge of the western pier and was significantly guarded and protected. Three robust wooden doors were on the vaulted roof and a ramp ran down steeply which led to an inner port. As they got out of the car, both Khalid and Amira strolled towards the fortress.

"It's just like back in Cyprus...we saw the beautiful Kyrenia castle before we left," said Amira.

Khalid took his hands from his pocket to place an arm around Amira.

"Yes Mira, it is. Shall I tell you a little about this fortress?" he said.

"Go on, Mr know it all…"

"This fortress was named Koules fortress. During the Venetian rule, it was known as Rocca a Mare or Castello a Mare, meaning fort of the seas."

Amira asked, "So why was the name changed?"

"Because the name that finally prevailed was 'Koules' from the Turkish name 'Su Kulesi'. In the first years during the Venetian rule, the fortress served the purpose of protecting the harbour and the city, which was of great strategic importance in the region. The original structure was poorly built and so during 1303, it was destroyed by an earthquake."

"I'm guessing later it was rebuilt and repaired?" asked Amira.

"Yup, and during the 21-year long siege of Candia, Ottomans easily neutralised the fort's firepower. They eventually took the fort in 1669, after the Venetians surrendered the entire city."

"Hmmm, interesting… Still don't know how you remember all these dates and events," Amira mocked.

"I'm super clever you see," Khalid joked.

The old man, whose name they discovered was Fadel, was waiting near the road in his car. Khalid and Amira began walking closer and closer towards the edge of the port, the scent of salty fish and rotting seaweed quivering their nostrils. The ocean zephyr whispered in their ears, placing salty pecks on their cheeks and meddling through their loose hair.

"It's hard to see from here; let's go closer and down these steps," suggested Amira.

Munir and Sarah were nowhere to be seen. They both strolled forward, nearing the end of the port. By this point, they had walked pretty much all around the fortress, until they reached the long pathway.

"Where are they?" Khalid was beginning to get worried by this point. They had been searching for 10 minutes now, but even a single minute that passed seemed to be elongated by another 10.

They neared the edge of the pathway, when Khalid saw something in the distance. He told Amira to wait at the pathway as he jumped over onto the large rocks that surrounded the footpath. As he climbed down, he stumbled a few times.

"Khalid! Careful please, the rocks are unsteady…" yelled Amira from behind, loud enough for him to hear. He kept looking forward, fixing his eyes on something. It was only then that Amira realised what he was looking at.

She closed her eyes to the hypnotic singing of the sea, breathing in its pungent salty breath. There, in the ocean, was Munir and Sarah on a rubber dinghy with 7 other refugees, drifting further and further away from land, and deeper and deeper towards the horizon.

CHAPTER TWENTY-ONE
Heraklion, Crete – January 2017

"Sometimes it is hard, Amira, child... you need to remember one very important thing. Often, when you trust in Allah the Almighty's plan, it is the best thing he had chosen for you, your fate has already been written..." Amira could listen to Uncle Fadel for hours without getting bored. He had the same effect on her that Baba Mohammed had, and her baba. His voice, soporifically soothing and delicate, reminded her of the way Baba Mohammed recited poetry and read novels to her. He drank his sweet black tea and made a faint slurping sound with every sip. Amira, who was also drinking some black tea, sat across from him, legs crossed into a neat, respectful cross.

"Allah's plan is what is best for his believers, even if it means it might the most painful thing that you ever experience...there is always a reason behind it," he slurped the last of his tea and looked at Amira, her sparkling amber eyes bouncing around.

"When God pushes you to the absolute edge of quandary and hardship, that is when you place your full trust in him. One of two things will happen, my dear, either he will catch you when you fall or..." he paused and smiled at Amira. She already knew the next sentence for it was probably the 5th time she had heard this quote.

She grinned shyly and replied, "Or he will teach you how to fly."

"Ahhh, exactly dear, exactly."

"I'm…I'm scared…" Amira whispered under her breath reluctantly, almost as if she was afraid to tell Uncle Fadel about how she really felt inside.

"Of course, you are…" he replied.

"That just shows you are going to do something very brave! You are not scared of 'Zalaam', are you? The darkness? No… you are just scared of what is inside it. Similarly, you are not afraid of heights, just of falling. That's the reality of fear, Amiraty. Don't let it overcome you; you are much stronger than a simple four-lettered word."

Amira listened, silently.

She shuffled around on the cushion she was sat on, fingering the small woollen pieces that were tearing off. Behind her, the warmth of the subtly crackling fire burning artfully from the fireplace started casting dancing shadows in front of her. The flares swayed and spiralled, flickering in every direction. Uncle Fadel watched the fire like he was in a sudden state of hypnosis, then spoke.

"Khalid Bin-Waleed! What a great man he was…your Khalid has the exact same characteristics and personality as the Prophet's Sahaba, fierce, fearless and above all, brave!" Amira sheepishly tried hiding her little smirk at the compliments she heard of Khalid.

"That's Khalid for you…" she giggled.

"Let me tell you a story, Amiraty…" Uncle Fadel cleared his throat and placed his empty cup beside him. His eyes, a deep brown colour under the flames from the fire, were looking directly into Amira's. She knew this was going to be a good story.

"Khalid Bin-Waleed was a valiant, courageous man. He was dauntless! Every battle he took part in, he stepped into it with great boldness and heroism. He was nicknamed 'Saif-Ullah, the sword of Allah'. But tell me something...do you think he was just born a Braveheart? Fearless? Do you think he never felt pain? Or worry and fear?"

Amira saw where this was going.

"No..." she answered.

"My dear, when Khalid Bin-Waleed embraced Islam, he already knew that his dear father was destined to be thrown into the depths of Jahannam, hellfire...but he converted to Islam regardless! You think his heart didn't break every time he read the verses in the Holy Quran that cursed his father, or when others recited it and he heard them cursing his father?" Amira listened, waiting in sheer anticipation to hear more of his words that sounded like eloquent, poetic verses of wisdom.

"Allah knows how he must have felt...just like Allah knows how you feel. Khalid Bin-Waleed didn't let that affect his relationship with his deen or his Lord; instead, he went on to become one of the greatest warriors of Islam! The world will never forget him or his courageous conviction." Uncle Fadel roared with pride as he spoke of Khalid Bin-Waleed, as if he had known him personally.

"Khalid suits his name, doesn't he...," she muttered modestly.

"Of course! He is just like Khalid Bin-Waleed! The name itself is synonymous with gallantry, valiance and above all...victory!"

"He was so patient...and strong," Amira replied, amazed at the bravery and diligence of the Sahaba.

"This is it! You see, my dear, this is what rising above pain can do to a person...this is what 'sabr' can blossom into; a fruitful life of living only to please our Lord and having the conviction that no matter what, he is there."

Amira listened.

"Do you know what Khalid Bin-Waleed said to Roman champion warriors Kulus and Azazeer when they threatened to kill him during the conquest of Damascus?"

"No, Uncle...tell me," replied Amira.

"Let me tell you a story...the story of the conquest of Damascus..."

Suddenly, Uncle Fadel had slipped on his Hakawati voice and began narrating a poetic narration.

"Damascus, my dear child, was widely recognized as the sweetest fruit from Paradise itself. It was certified as the utopia and wonderland of Syria."

"Why, Uncle Fadel?" asked Amira.

"Well, for one, it was a magnificently spirited capital that inhabited everything needed to make a city imperially grand! It had wealth, sanctuaries, warriors, troops and culture. Our Prophet himself narrated: 'Damascus is one of the most blessed cities of al-Sham'."

Amira didn't blink an eyelid and continued to be fascinated by Uncle Fadel's mollifying story-telling.

"Anyway, at the time of the Syrian expedition, the Roman commander in Damascus was called Thomas. He was the son-in-law of Emperor Heraclius. The general who was in operative duty and in charge of the command post was a warrior named Azazeer."

"I think I remember Khalid telling me about this man years ago..." said Amira, pondering on the different historical stories Khalid had told her in the past.

"Azazeer was a skilled, disciplined soldier who had spent the majority of his lifetime crusading in the East, gaining fame in fighting against the Persians and the Turks in many battles. He was full of pride and arrogance at the fact that he had never lost an encounter or a battle."

"So, he lived in Syria?"

"Yes, as he had served in Syria for many years, he also knew Arabic pretty well too. His military barracks consisted of around 12,000 soldiers! Now that may sound like a huge army, however, the city of Damascus had neither planned nor adapted for a siege. They knew mighty Khalid Bin-Waleed was coming! Although its walls and fortification were in decent order, there were no provisions made for food storage and shelter. Such a task would have taken months, time which they didn't have..."

"Why? That was a bit careless of the Romans, don't you think?" said Amira.

"Well, ever since the defeat of the Persians by Emperor Heraclius in the year 628, Syria hardly saw any major threats, so they sort of, relaxed, you might say. Since they had come to know of Khalid Bin-Waleed and his forthcoming siege of Syria, Heraclius began working from a central base located at Antioch and started to prepare the city of Damascus for a siege. Having organized and systematically ordered those who remained in the army of Ajnadein to delay the Muslims at Yaqusa, he sent a force of many soldiers from his headquarters in Antioch to support the army of Damascus. Kulus, a warrior who was in charge of this army, boasted, "I promise you, leader Heraclius, O mighty one, that I will not return till I bring back the head of Khalid Bin-Waleed on a stick!" In the background, Thomas worked frantically to prepare the city for the siege. After all the right provisions were put into place, the city did nothing else but wait anxiously for the arrival of our mighty warrior, Khalid bin-Waleed!"

"So, they were scared? Even though they hadn't ever met Khalid Bin-Waleed face to face, they all feared him?" asked Amira. She was so deeply embedded into this story that everything around her stopped and the only noise heard were the compelling chronicles escaping Uncle Fadel's lips.

"Feared? They would cower before him in his absence for all the stories they heard about him were full of victory and triumph. They didn't know of his plans. Khalid had already coordinated and classified a strong military team. He formed armies from different Muslims all over the Middle East. From all the regions he had once fought in, Arabia, Palestine, Iraq and Syria, he collected men from such countries and they all worked together in collecting information for him by questioning agents regarding the military positioning and locations of the Romans. Nothing was kept hidden from him, nothing!"

"Tell me more, Uncle...tell me more." Eagerness glowed in Amira's eyes.

"From Yaqusa, Khalid Bin-Waleed galumphed with his troops towards the city. After a few days of marching, they arrived at Marj-us-Suffar, a few miles away from Damascus. It was here where they were greeted by Roman forces blocking their way. The army, led by Kulus and Azazeer, had been instructed by Thomas to fight a battle and drive away the Muslims. Marj-us-Suffar, which means 'the yellow meadow', spanned south from Kiswa, a small town 12 miles away from Damascus on the present road to Daraa."

"Daraa?! You mean Daraa as in the same town where all these protests and demonstrations began? When those young boys were arrested and imprisoned? Surely it isn't!" Amira was taken aback at how the town of Daraa was the same town in which mighty warrior Khalid Bin-Waleed had once been.

"Right you are, my dear, the same Daraa. Soon, the battle commenced with Muslims and the Romans assembling their troops for the battle of Marj-as-Suffar. Khalid Bin-Waleed strategically brought in his devoted champions first to fight."

"Like who?"

"Abdur-Rahman bin Abi Bakr, Shurahbil and Dhiraar. There must have been more, I'm sure. They all rode out from the believers' frontal, anterior rank and went right in for their enemies. NEARLY EVERY ROMAN WAS KILLED!" roared Uncle Fadel with a victorious cheer.

"They taunted and challenged one another until finally, Khalid Bin-Waleed made his entrance at the center of the battlefield."

Amira was on the edge of her seat as she breathlessly listened on.

"I AM THE PILLAR OF ISLAM! I AM THE COMPANION OF THE RASOOL! I AM THE NOBLE WARRIOR, KHALID BIN AL-WALEED!" Uncle Fadel bellowed, thundering those chilling words.

"Poor Kulus had lost his bravery somewhere in the battlefield, for he declined Khalid Bin-Waleed's challenge and rode away to the back of the army with his troops. Khalid managed to catch Kulus and jerked him off his horse effortlessly and soon, he was carried away by two other Muslims and kept as a prisoner."

"And Azazeer? What about him?" asked Amira.

"Khalid Bin-Waleed came closer to his opponent, Azazeer. With sheer arrogance, Azazeer spoke.

"O Arab brother, come closer so that I can speak with you." Khalid replied with disgust, "Come near me yourself, oh disbeliever, or shall I come closer and take your head?" How much pride Azazeer manifested within him, Amira, dear child. He rode closer to Khalid Bin-Waleed and spoke with nothing but superciliousness and egotism.

"Are you not scared, oh Arab brother? Soon, your army will be without a leader," he said.

The sword of Allah replied, "O enemy of the Almighty! After seeing what we have already done to some of your troops, you fear not? By Allah, if I were to give them my permission, they would easily destroy your entire army with the help and guidance of Allah the Almighty! Men who are with me, they regard death as a pure, blissful blessing...this life, it means nothing to them."

Azazeer replied, with smugness and cheek, "I think you do not know me, for I am the Champion of Syria, the killer of Persians and the destroyer of the Turkish armies!"

"What is your name?" asked Khalid.

"I am named after the angel of death himself! I am Israel!"

The sword of Allah laughed and mocked the man, "Oh, Israel, I fear that whom who are named after calls for you hastily, to throw you to the pits of Jahannam!"

"What happened to him in the end, Uncle?"

"Khalid Bin-Waleed dismounted his horse after conversing with Azazeer and strolled towards him, sword gripped firmly in his hand. Azazeer himself sat comfortably on his horse, relishing the fact that he was mounted securely whilst Khalid Bin-Waleed was on foot. 'I have Khalid Bin-Waleed, the mighty so-called warrior of Islam exactly where I want him', he thought to himself, smirking with uncouthness. As Khalid arrived within striking radius, Azazeer raised his sword and made a quick swipe in an attempt to aim for Khalid Bin-Waleed's head."

"Was he hit!?" asked Amira, worriedly.

"It was inches away from getting torn right off his shoulders! Khalid made a resistant slash at the Roman leader's horse, from which he came tumbling down. All bravado and gallantry escaped his quivering body as he fell to the ground.

Khalid grabbed him before he could run off and marched him right back to the Muslim army, where he joined his fellow commander, Kulus."

"What happened to them? Did they escape?"

"Escape! Ha! Never. Khalid Bin-Waleed had both Kulus and Azazeer chaperoned in irons near the East Gate..."

"Why the East Gate, Uncle?"

"Because, dear, it was at the East Gate where both commanders were in full view of the Romans on the wall. Now, Khalid Bin-Waleed was merciful, and offered the both of them for a way out. He offered them Islam."

"And did they accept?" she grilled anxiously.

"No...they rejected. Then, in full view of the Romans, both were executed by warrior Dhiraar, and, well, that was the end of them."

"Uncle Fadel, look how brave the Sahaba were back then. They feared nothing, nothing but the Almighty, for even death was a sweet prize for them during battle," spoke Amira, subconsciously smirking at the heroic character of Khalid Bin-Waleed and pairing it with Khalid's heroism

"But Amira, do not be fooled, my dear. It wasn't just the men who were such brave hearts, who had such noble and valorous traits."

"What do you mean?" she replied.

"The sword of Allah's stalwart warrior, Dhiraar, was captured and injured by the Romans. The loss of his presence had a mournful effect on the rest of Khalid's army. He was

361

taken prisoner by them. In the midst of the battlefield, just as the Muslim's spirits are impending slowly, a lionhearted, dauntless Muslim rider flew past Khalid Bin-Waleed and ran towards the Roman front. Confused and curious, Khalid Bin-Waleed rode closer to the rider, who was dressed in black and covered from head to toe. He wore a breastplate and held a large stick in his hand as well as a sword. Before Khalid could speak to him, he was gone further into the battlefield. A thin scarf was wrapped loosely around his face, concealing his facial formation and he wore a green turban. Only the eyes were visible. When Khalid Bin-Waleed reached the Roman front where the Muslim rider threw himself into the madness of the fight fearlessly without a single hesitation, he asked the rider, "O warrior, show us your face!" Dark, gallant eyes pierced back at Khalid's and without a second's wait, the rider rode off again into the middle of the battlefield to strike another Roman. Khalid caught up with him again and asked, "O noble warrior, your commander calls you and you turn your face away from him! Show your face and tell us your name, for you shall be properly honoured." Again, the rider rode away, as if he wanted his name and identity to be secretly concealed from everyone. When Khalid Bin-Waleed caught up with him a final time as he fought venturesomely against a new Roman every time, he spoke exhilaratingly, "You have surely filled our hearts with admiration; tell us, who are you?"

"Who was he?" questioned Amira, inquisitively scratching her head, curious as to whom it could have been.

"Khalid Bin-Waleed, a great solider of Allah almost fell off his horse when he heard the person's voice..."

"Huh? Why?"

362

"He heard the reply of the daringly spirited masked rider, but it was the voice of a girl!"

"WHAT? A woman?" said Amira, shocked.

"O commander of Allah, I only turn my face out of modesty and respect for you. I shall stay behind the veil, but fight like this as if my heart is on fire!"

"WOW!" grinned Amira, holding her hands to the apples of her cheeks.

"The commander replied, "Who are you?" "I am Khawlah, sister of Dhiraar. My brother, he has been captured and taken as a prisoner and I need to fight in order to set him free."

Amira looked into Uncle Fadel's eyes, overcome with astonishment and sudden happiness.

"A girl...fighting in a battle, dressed as a man? I mean...where did she find such valour, such endurance and bravery?"

Uncle Fadel smirked at Amira, giving her a look of contentment, for his eyes shimmered with a chilling sense of peace, the peace of mind and gratification that Amira was desperately after.

"Amira, my sweet princess. You know what Ustadh Rumi would have said to you, if he were alive today?" he asked her.

Amira looked down at her palms, radiating an innocent smirk for she already knew the quote which Uncle Fadel was about to recite to her.

"You have seen your own strength, Amira. You have seen your own beauty, and you have seen your golden wings…Why do you worry?"

Amira and Khalid had been staying with Uncle Fadel for almost 4 months now. Ever since September last year, all Khalid had been doing was finding different jobs and working any role in order to save money to leave Greece. The first few weeks he worked for a dumpster collection organization, then it was selling fruit and veg at a stall until local authorities started sniffing around, and then it was working at the port catching fish for local fishers and helping them sell them at fish markets. Although the language barrier was difficult at first, Khalid's hard work and dedication paid off as he was seen as a strong worker who always got the job done.

Uncle Fadel, despite being an elderly man living by himself, lived a very simple life. He had a small house with 2 very small bedrooms. When his wife was alive, they had shared a room whilst the other was always used for their children whenever they came to visit. He cooked simple, easy meals that he had learnt from his wife, did his weekly grocery shop every Friday afternoon after Jummah Salah and cleaned once a week. His children often sent him money, but he also had some savings that he used for food and other necessities. It was truly a blessing that he met Amira and Khalid in the Mosque in September last year, for it had allowed Khalid to work and save enough money to travel to Turkey.

Uncle Fadel and Amira were so deeply engrossed in their conversation that neither realized that Khalid had walked in with a bag of groceries. He tip-toed behind Amira and gave her a fright.

"Oh Khalid, you're back!" she sat up, eyes gleaming with happiness.

"Stopped off at the local market and brought some groceries...I'm craving some Kibbeh today, Mira, the ones you make with mince and onions..." he replied.

"I'll make some today then," Amira said, eager to cook for her husband and also Uncle Fadel.

"Uncle, today I saw some policemen roaming the fish markets, I heard people talking. Apparently, they're finding illegal immigrants every other day and deporting them back to their homeland," Khalid told Uncle Fadel.

"Ahh, yes, well, you need to be careful. You know better than me how these men in authority use their power to degrade people like us."

Amira took the bags from Khalid and began unwrapping the small newspaper which contained a very small portion of minced meat. She chopped up some carrots and diced a small onion into a pan of warm oil. Recently, everything Amira did reminded her of her family. She would chop up some vegetables for a hot soup recipe on a cold, rainy day for Khalid and Uncle Fadel and suddenly remember the way her mother used to hum to 'Umm Kulthoom's song, Enta Omri whilst washing the dishes, or the way her mother would sway her hips slightly when her favourite Fahd Ballan song came on the radio. Amira would be writing a poem, when suddenly she would recall all the times she sat on her father's lap as a child, his strong scent of musky perfume lingering in the air as she would fall asleep listening to his poems. She'd be sleeping beside

Khalid, ruffling her fingers through his hair and remember the times she would put Adam to sleep in the same way…

The regular visits down memory lane, reminiscing on the happiest of times where life was simple and carefree, caused Amira to yearn for a hug or a kiss from her loved ones… a stroke of their hand against her cheeks or a smile, even.

"Mira…?" called Khalid from behind her as she fried the onions in a small pan.

"Hmmm?" she replied.

"Mira, you okay?"

"Yes…why? What's wrong?" she asked.

"Nothing…it's just…you know, tomorrow…well…I know you're scared…" Khalid stuttered nervously.

"We've been talking and preparing for weeks now, but I mean…even I can't help feeling nervous."

Amira stopped stirring the browning onions and turned to face Khalid.

She sighed.

"Yes…" she exhaled, "You know I am."

Khalid stroked Amira's cheek with his thumb and gave her a sad smile.

"It will be okay, my Amiraty…I won't let anything happen to my princess now, will I?"

Amira grinned, "No Khalid, you won't."

She groaned loudly unexpectedly and clutched her belly in pain and discomfort.

"Mira?! What's the matter?" Khalid became anxious at her sudden outburst of pain.

"I'm...I'm okay, just a sudden jolt of pain went right through my stomach." She wiped her forehead as thick beads of sweat ran down the side of her face.

"Sit down, Amira, take a seat, please!" Khalid begged her.

"No, no, I'm fine, honestly..." she lied. For weeks now, she had been vomiting every morning, feeling nauseous at every mealtime and suffering from severe migraines and restless nights, all without Khalid's knowledge.

"I'm fine Khalid, come on, let's finish up." She handed Khalid a paper towel.

"Mira, you sure?" he asked again.

"Yes!" she joked, lightening the mood.

Khalid started drying the plates for serving and helped Amira to plate up the food.

"Love you, Mira...so much," said Khalid, drying the last plate.

Amira looked up at him and kissed his cheek.

"Love you too, Khalid."

That night, Uncle Fadel, Khalid and Amira all feasted on the food Amira had prepared. They banqueted on spiced, baked Kibbeh, dipping them in mint yoghurt alongside grape leaves stuffed with mince, yalanji and crumbly falafel. For dessert,

Amira attempted to make halwat al-jibn, a fragile piece of pastry rolled and stuffed with creamy, thick milk cream and drizzled with a honey syrup called 'atr'. Both Uncle Fadel and Khalid's eyes lit up at the sight of glorious home-cooked food that felt like they were back in Syria.

"Good Lord, this is too good, child!" declared Uncle Fadel, wiping the yoghurt sauce drizzling down his finger.

"Mira, you've got magic hands, I don't remember your food ever tasting this good," said Khalid, chomping on his 3rd Kibbeh.

"Slow down, Khalid," laughed Amira.

If he could have opened his mouth wider, he would have scoffed the whole kibbeh in a single bite. Amira watched as they both enjoyed their food, smiling at their hungry faces devouring the meals, then, exhaling a sigh of deep anguish. She looked at Uncle Fadel, slurping his water and held back tears, and then at Khalid, wiping his lips with a napkin. They ate and ate, enjoying every bite off of their plates as well as every crumb until they were finished their very last meal together.

■■

'Why?'...

Why was it, that refugees, whether from Syria, or Yemèn, or Somalia or even Iraq...? Why was it that they would pay smugglers thousands to board an overcrowded, life-threatening rubber boat and entrust their lives to a barely working engine rather than simply using that money to board a flight to their destination?

There was no choice…there never had been. It wasn't a perfect and simple world where Amira and Khalid were presented with two different travel options. It was much more complex than that.

"I don't understand why we can't just go to the airport, Khalid. We have enough money for the tickets and our new documents, too." Amira begged Khalid, begged him to find another way.

"Amira, you know why." Again and again, Khalid would say the same thing to her.

"It doesn't matter about the documents anymore. If we go to any airport in this city, we will get stopped. Airlines get fined for allowing people like us on a plane, despite these stupid papers. Who do you think will allow us, huh? Will they risk their jobs or their pockets to help us? They don't care about us, none of them do. They all turn a blind fucking eye when it comes to dealing with refugees." Amira knew it all, yet she would insistently repeat the question, hoping for a new and different answer each time.

"If anything, at least these documents and papers will show who we are when we arrive in Turkey," said Khalid.

Khalid had worked for months now. He had managed to earn and save almost 2400 euros. With that, he paid for new documents and identification papers. A visa, however, was much harder to make, or even to find someone to make it. Heraklion was a small place, and Khalid had just about found a man to help with the new documents.

Uncle Fadel had also saved some money aside for Khalid and Amira. In total, Khalid had 3500 euros.

"I cannot take this, Uncle, it is too much," Khalid told Uncle Fadel as he handed the envelope of notes back to him.

"La! Nonsense, it is merely paper, son. Please, just take it, I insist."

Khalid took the wad of notes from him and embraced him in a long, heart-breaking hug. Amira watched as he held back his tears from the world, from her.

He grieved secretively on the inside, yet every time he convinced himself that he buried and veiled his sorrow from others. He was one of those people that, despite believing they were invisible in their sadness, were, in fact, the complete opposite and easily read. Amira could see it in his eyes, his motions and gestures, the way he sloped his back when he stood up or his sagging stance when he walked.

"I can't think of a way that I can ever repay you for everything. You have done so much for us, treated us like your children, and fed us. As Allah is my witness today, on the day of judgement, I will sing your praise to the Almighty." Khalid wiped away a tear as he pulled away from Uncle Fadel. Amira, who was also weeping quietly, gave him a long hug.

"You both will always remain in my heart; just keep me in your duas, children, that is all I ask. We will meet again, for sure." Uncle Fadel gave them both a wrinkly, heart-broken smile.

It was all happening again, like history repeating itself... The goodbyes, the tears, the anticipation of waiting for the smuggler, paying him the money, fastening the life jackets and then, at last, sitting inside the rubber boat.

"You know, my dear, there is no separation between us; this isn't goodbye... you know why, Amira?" asked Uncle Fadel to Amira. He knew she knew of the answer, for it was Rumi's words.

She sniffed and finished his sentence, for it was the only thing promised her happiness again. Happiness and anticipation to meet Uncle Fadel again, as well as Mama, Baba, Adam, Shakil, Maliha and everyone else she ever loved and desperately longed for.

"Goodbyes are only for those who we love with our eyes..." recited Uncle Fadel.

Amira finished it off.

"Those we love with heart and soul..." she tearfully snivelled and continued,

"Those we love with heart and soul, there is no separation".

CHAPTER TWENTY-TWO

Leaving Heraklion, Greece – January 2017

'The most dangerous heart disease; a strong memory' –
Nizar Qabbani

There isn't a person in this world who doesn't feel trapped at times, who doesn't feel the fear or aversion of being tightly closed in, without any way of escaping the darkness, and fears the horrors or demons who imprison us with the notion of 'fear' itself. Those same demons, who liquidate our minds and remind us daily to cower before others who present themselves as superior to us, or remind us that we must fear the darkness or ignore the noises we hear within our own heads telling us to stay strong and not lose hope, those same demons then grovel and bow before you when you learn the adroitness of transforming such monsters into worthy pieces of art. When painted with the colours of the sun that rises above the pain every morning, and dressed with its warmth and radiating rays, one can then understand how to value the beauty of triumphing against such battles fought with oneself within the most discreet and silent of dens within the soul.

The container was filled with frozen meat. Boxes and boxes of it. Not that Amira could physically see the frozen meat, for all around her was pitch black, but it was the rotting smell of dead flesh. It felt as if, despite standing in the warm, setting, Greek sun only a moment ago, both Amira and Khalid had stepped into a walk-in freezer. They sat there, cornered into the back of the container between two large, damp boxes of meat. Amira, wrapping her arms tightly around Khalid's, shuddered in disgust as the scent of the putrefying meat whiffed past every now and again. Like before, there were other refugees in the container, although much fewer than last time. They all hid, trembling and sweating with distress and fear of the authorities finding them. Every time the container took a sudden halt and braked harshly, everyone went silent. The mothers hushed their children; some even held their hands over their babies' mouths to stop their babbling or crying.

"Why have we stopped?" someone whispered from the far corner of the container.

"Shhhhh!" another snapped, "Keep your voice down, for goodness sake!"

The container would begin moving again and everyone would let out a sigh of relief.

"Are you scared, Mira?" Khalid asked, tugging at her arm gently, sensing that she might be anxious.

Amira took a deep breath and closes her eyes. She rested her head against Khalid's shoulder and took in his familiar scent of warm musk. She pressed her face deeper into his neck now and rubbed her face softly.

"Khalid..." she whispered.

"Did you know, there was a tough, fearless warrior during the time of the Prophet Muhammed who was a woman...?"

"Really?" Khalid already knew who Amira was talking about, yet he continued to act oblivious in order to keep Amira talking and thus, distracted.

"Who was she?" he asked, stroking her hair.

"Her name was Khawlah bint al-Azwar. She went on to become a military leader and was known as one of Islam's greatest female warriors."

"Really?" Khalid went on, "tell me more."

"Once compared to Khalid Bin-Waleed himself, she was known for her fierce character on the battlefield whilst fighting against enemies. She was the sister of Dhiraar bin Al-Azwar, the soldier and commander of the Rashidun army."

The container jerked from side to side, as if it was being driven up a rocky mountain. The other refugees within the container sighed and inhaled fearfully. Amira paused for a moment, until Khalid took her hand and squeezed it reassuringly.

"Carry on," he requested admiringly, trying to keep her attention focused on her story.

Amira continued.

"She fought alongside her brother in many battles and did you know, Khawlah also fought in the Battle of Yarmouk in 636 against the Byzantine Empire?" she exclaimed.

"Hmmm, interesting. What a strong woman," said Khalid.

"Khalid...If a woman like Khawlah, who fought side by side with stronger and bigger warriors than her, didn't give up hope...then who are we to?"

Khalid sighed quietly and Amira felt his chilly breath on the side of her neck.

"You are a strong woman, Mira, you always have been."

"I haven't, not until recently, until all this, until the war, until everyone dying..." she murmured painfully.

"That's the thing about strength, Mira, my Princess. It grows, blossoms and blooms during those moments when you are convinced you cannot go on any more, yet you do anyway. It's not until we are faced with our greatest weaknesses that we recognise and understand our very own strengths," replied Khalid.

Amira pondered upon Khalid's words for a minute. He was right. Amira didn't realise just how much she had bloomed over the past few years and just how strong she had become, or more so, she had had to become.

"Mira, this is almost over."

Amira moved against Khalid's face, trying to find his cheek in the darkness. She placed a cold kiss on his cheek and replied, "And once it is, everything will be okay."

Amidst the gloom and darkness of the rotting container, light emerged. Not the kind of light that leaves your eyes squinting with sudden blindness after you awaken from a long nap, nor the blue light that blinds you at the dentist when he hovers in and out of the shadows over the dental curing light. It was the kind of light that Ustadh Rumi would use to guide you all the way home once it entered your heart, the kind of light that he said stayed lit, regardless of anything, just like the moonlight does when it doesn't avoid the night time. That's when it hit Amira. It hit her that sometimes, against all odds and in obscure moments, when one felt shattered by this world, there was only one thing that made one carry on: -

Hope.

This was the kind of hope that Khalid displayed in his subtle, subconscious ways when he held Amira just a little closer when they drove over large bumps, causing vast and vicious quakes inside the container, or when he hummed her to sleep, stroking her hair gently as he whispered, "It will all be okay soon, my Amiraty". It was when Amira knew that Khalid had entered a sudden daze of nostalgia and mournful regret when he began missing his brother Shakil, or when he saw other boys with their fathers within the refugee group, that she would plant a simple peck on his forehead and ask him to read her some historical tales of the past. In this way, they both, earnestly, wholeheartedly and selflessly exchanged vows of hope, for they knew that even a single 'It's okay' would be enough to prosper some hope when all seemed hopeless.

■■■

"Leave in twos! No more than two people to leave the container! DO I MAKE MYSELF CLEAR?!"

The Greek smuggler spoke with haste as the refugees exited the container in pairs. Like a conveyor belt, they quickly left the putrid container that had left them all chilled with frostbite on their fingers and toes. As instructed, Amira and Khalid left last, in a pair and followed the smuggler's next instructions.

"You see that Venetian harbour? Along the pathway? Quickly, very quickly you need to go there and meet the other man at the boat. NO STOPPING, YOU HEAR ME?!" The smell of burnt ashes and scorched cigarettes escaped his mouth as he roared. His grubby hands, hidden behind the fat rolls along his arms, were dirty and dry. He shouted once more, as if both

Amira and Khalid were deaf and didn't understand his orders the first time.

"HURRY UP! ALONG THE PORT!" he yelled.

"Sir, we haven't turned deaf during the past 30 seconds since your last instruction; do not worry, we are headed for the port", replied Khalid mockingly with a cheeky grin.

Amira chuckled, tugging at his arm.

The smuggler gave him a ghastly stare before advancing towards Khalid. He spat out yellow phlegm and snorted, "Why I ought to... Think you're being funny, do you, boy?!"

His hands clenched into a tight ball as he neared both Khalid and Amira.

"What you going to do? Punch me? I ain't afraid of people like you," said Khalid dauntlessly, not being intimidated at all by the fact that the man was almost twice his age.

"You want to go in for a punch, go ahead, but believe me...I can punch harder," he joked.

The smuggler, taken aback by Khalid's humour, was left speechless at his courage to speak to him in that manner, for other refugees were all too scared to even make eye contact with him, let alone talk.

"Just get on with it, boy!" he replied, overwhelmed.

Khalid winked at Amira and they both walked quickly towards the port where they saw the other smuggler waiting.

"Why do you do that, Khalid? You purposely provoke them," said Amira.

"Naaaa, just having a bit of fun. Gotta piss them off before you go," he laughed.

Another misty, clouded evening toured in and screened the remains of the crepuscule, gloomy sky. The silver greys and ashen, sombre clouds started concealing the sky, hiding even the most ignited, luminous stars. Soon, they became non-existent, and the only illuminations visible were from the port, floor lights and the moon.

"This is exactly where we saw Sarah and Munir last, remember Khalid?"

Khalid looked onto the boat in the darkness of the night. They passed themselves steadily across the crumbled rocks just above the sea, as they helped one another to sit comfortably inside the rubber dinghy. Amira almost slipped twice as the bottom of the boat swirled with cold water.

"Yes, Mira, it was. I hope they are safe, wherever they are," he replied.

"I don't think they meant to leave us on purpose, Khalid. They must have waited for us. You remember that day? You were unwell and Uncle Fadel took us as quick as he could in his car. They probably thought we had left them or something."

"Yes, maybe..." Khalid replied, breathlessly.

The icy wind near the sea always left them both gasping for breath, despite being surrounded by nothing other than sea and air.

"Payments! Get out your payments!" the new smuggler prompted.

Khalid took out 1500 euros, the agreed price that Khalid said he negotiated with their old smuggler, Tariq. It was the price for both of them to travel.

He handed the notes to the smuggler, his face frowning.

"1500? Boy, are you joking?" the smuggler's hair was barely combed back into the messiest ponytail with specks of mud dried randomly across his whole body and clothes. His ripped jeans were wet from the knees downwards as he had one foot in the water and the other on the rocks where he balanced himself against the boat.

"Yes, 1500...problem?" said Khalid emotionlessly.

"Damn right there is a problem, boy! I need another 500 euros, or hurry up and get it out!".

Khalid gave the smuggler a single look and Amira knew there was going to be trouble.

"Listen!" Khalid began. His eyes were narrowed, rigid and full of rage.

"Tariq agreed on 1500, so that is all I am paying, got it? Now if you would like to confirm with Tariq then, by all means, go ahead, but I should remind you we are very close to authorities who could come snooping any minute. Your call!"

The smuggler stared at Khalid, giving him a wild-eyed glare that sent a shiver down Amira's spine.

"Well?" incited Khalid, almost with a sense of playfulness in his voice.

The smuggler grew angrier, "YOU LITTLE..." He took a sudden, tight grip of Khalid's shirt. Immediately, Khalid grasped his hands around the smuggler's wrists and with a forceful push, shoved him backwards. He lost his balance and a few rocks crumbled beneath his feet as he fell into the water. The other refugees looked on, anxiously.

"Don't ever touch me again," spat Khalid into the sea.

He sat in the boat where his seat was beside Amira and gave her a flirty wink.

The smuggler grunted loudly but by now he was more and more conscious of both the time and also of authorities who might have been lurking around.

"Fucking cheeky immigrant," the smuggler mumbled under his breath as he got up.

"That I am, brother," laughed Khalid.

"Khalid...shhh," said Amira, tugging at his arm.

"It's fine; he won't do anything, look at him," he replied.

The smuggler collected everyone else's money and without hesitation, he pushed the boat deeper into the sea and started the motor. The motor spurted loudly for a second, then ran smoothly without any hassle. As for the life jackets, they were all thrown in the bottom of the dinghy and everyone placed one over their heads and secured it tightly. Whether they were fake or real, no one knew or could tell. The other refugees sat still on the boat as it sailed further and further away from the Venetian port and deeper into the sea.

The boat wasn't too packed this time round; however, it was still daunting. The children in the boat looked terrified of seeing strangers all being placed into a rubber boat.

"These darn, selfish smugglers! They barely provide enough fuel to make it to international waters and then abandon the boat and all of us to our fate! Where are we even going?! No directions! No compass! Nothing!" A middle-aged, bearded man holding onto his sleeping daughter voiced words of criticism as he watched the smugglers both walk off into the distance and back into their container with nothing more than a fat grin on their faces and pockets full of cash.

"They'll be laughing all the way to the bank!" he yelled.

Greece, being a small, touristic island, had neither prepared for nor envisioned the phenomenon of the refugee crisis, nor had they built the infrastructure or facilitating services to approach and tackle the basic needs of the people that arrived illegally on their island, like Amira and Khalid. This placed a massive strain on the island's communities. In 2012, when the Syrian civil war began, Greece attempted to control the rising numbers of illegal crossings by creating a security fence on the border with Turkey. However, since the civil war progressed rapidly without warning, the number of sea-borne newcomers began to increase. In 2013, the number of refugees and migrants arriving on the Greek islands had more than tripled from 3,600 to a staggering 11,400 and furthermore, almost quadrupled again in 2014 to 43,500. Almost 40,000 Syrian-originated immigrants arrived in Greece in the first few months of 2015.

'Why?' one would ask.

Why was it that, after understanding that travelling in such a manner would put their lives at immense risk, refugees would still opt for such a dangerous method of travel? The majority of refugees and migrants arriving within southern Europe travelled there with the intended hope of travelling onwards. The countries of northern and western Europe, such as Sweden and Germany, are recognised as contributing and offering more effective and safer protection, improved support for asylum-seeking applicants and easier prospects for alliance and integration. For Khalid and Amira, Turkey also offered a similar response. Millions of Syrian refugees live in Turkey, although Turkey is not fully registered up to the 1951 Refugee Convention, which is a key legal document approved and established by 145 State parties. The Convention details the term 'refugee' and outlines the rights of the displaced, as well as the legal duties of the State in order to protect such individuals. The nucleal tenet is non-refoulement, which alleges that a refugee should not be returned to a country where they face serious threats to their life or their freedom. This is now perceived as a set rule of customary international law. However, this isn't always the case. Migrant rights and aid agencies within Europe, working alongside charities to support refugees, say that often, illegal immigrants and refugees are commonly subjected to police brutality, detention and severe beatings within European countries. Cases of men being held in cages, waterboarded and handcuffed to beds by detention centre guards and women often groomed and raped have been widely reported throughout the crisis years. The U.N High Commissioner for Refugees has since then openly publicized and voiced concerns over the actions of the EU. Experts fear that these reoccurring breaches may lead to the rule of non-refoulement being surrendered and losing all its value and importance in the near future.

For Amira and Khalid, the option of travelling to Turkey was still a good one. Although in Turkey they would be able to access many benefits, such as health care, education, resettlement, status determination and a chance to co-exist with local communities, they would not receive the many benefits that refugees in the EU get, such as child benefit and funded accommodation. Despite all this, Turkey was still providing much safer refuge and asylum for many than other countries in Europe.

The oscillating gusts of the wind against the oceanic sprays soon adopted a steady current of gradual ripples and rolls in the seawater. The perfume of salty water and the fizzing of waves surrounded the boat, hissing at every surge. Once again, fear found Amira. It chanted to her in its snarling, insolent voice. It told her fingers to fidget and curl up with anxiety, her gut to wrench and twist with disgust and her legs to shake with chilled terror. As the boat started picking up speed against the waves, Amira snuggled her face into Khalid's arm and held him tight. Khalid gulped and held her close, sensing her hidden, suppressed apprehension. Likewise, Amira also heard the thumping knocks from inside Khalid's chest when she pressed her face deeper into his arms, detecting also his suppressed worries.

"Read me a story, Mira...," he whispered into her ear.

He gulped another bouldering rock down his dry, drained throat and breathed in her warmth. He looked at her, eyes full of distress.

"Please," ...he whimpered.

CHAPTER TWENTY-THREE

The boy with 'emerald jewel eyes; Alzamard jawhrat sa'

"Many years ago," she began.

"How many years, Mira?" interrupted Khalid, as he always did when Amira began a new story.

"Already starting with the questions, Khalid?" she sighed, rolling her eyes.

"Ok, ok sorry. Carry on," he shivered in the cold.

"Many years ago, there lived a young boy in the great city of Dimashq, which today, as you know obviously, we call Damascus." Amira narrated the story beauteously, with hints of romance in her gentle voice. She noticed a small girl, huddled up with her mother, begin to listen to her story.

"This young boy, who was maybe 15, or even 16 years of age, was known for his captivating, glorious, green eyes. Everyone in his town knew him as the boy with 'emerald jewel eyes; Alzamard jawhrat sa'. They were hues of the summertime forest, wreathed with shadowy plant leaves; the sort of earthy green that restores the meadows and grassland after a long, ferocious winter. His eyes, well they told a story, his story....

At the tender age of 7, both his parents died during the second Mongol invasion of Syria that took place in October 1271. The young boy became an orphan at a young age and had lived with his grandmother ever since. His emerald jewels that shone like newly picked diamonds form the ground held such rage, danger and magnificence all at once. At times, he was like a wild beast, a lion, untamed, uncontrollable and impulsive, yet, despite it all, unquestionably bewitching. The pain he had felt, since a young age, of losing both parents, gelled itself with him, like thick honey. No matter how hard he tried, especially as he grew older, he could not let go of his anger.

"I hate myself!" he would cry to his grandmother, who like anyone, was worried about this boy's behaviour and actions during times of red rage.

"Everyone hates me! My friends have all left me! I cannot do anything without feeling angry all the time! Every single time I feel like I am moving forward and progressing, the anger takes over!" For hours, the boy would sob to his grandmother about his insecurity. Some days, he would smash plates against his bedroom wall, or yell at anyone who walked past, and often, he would also hurt himself and others.

His grandmother, who was an old, dying woman, would advise him on ways to deal with his anger.

"My boy, what did our Prophet say to us? The strongest among you is the one who can control his anger during times of rage."

"But I cannot help it! Anger flows through my blood, I was born with this curse, Ummi, and there is nothing I can do about it."

There was a long river, just a few minutes' walk from the boy's home. It was called Barada River and it was the main river of Damascus. The water was murky and green. Against the melodic chirping of the songbirds and chants from the mockingbirds that always commenced a new day, the soft whistling and whooshing of the river was what the young boy came to listen to during his times of frustration and upset. There was a large, friendly weeping willow tree that he would lean against and speak to. It was 'his' tree, for the tree knew all the boy's hidden secrets, his desires, frustrations and pain. He spoke to the tree more than he spoke to any human. He always admired the tree, as if it were his guardian or protector. The branches that swayed in the late summer afternoons would shield him from the burning sun and the trunk itself had the most astonishing, flawless skin. Hues of rich henna, chestnut and deep, dark chocolate painted themselves along the thick tree trunk.

"Oh, dear willow tree, you have seen every tear that has fallen from my face and landed at your roots since I was a boy. You have seen me grow into this monster, this barbaric animal that cannot control his anger. Why? I didn't want this life; I didn't ask for it. I wanted a normal life, like all the other boys in this town. I wanted a home, a warm home with a mother and a father and maybe a brother or two, yet fate took its turn and left me all alone in this world with nothing except my rage." The boy would question his existence and his fate and often, God too. For hours and hours, he would sit there, talking to the willow tree. For years, the willow tree had been steeped in the boy's sorrow and pain.

One autumn evening, as the falling leaves bid farewell to the summer days, the boy was strolling through his local market. He was off to buy bread and cheese for his grandmother who was preparing supper for both of them. He went to his local shop and purchased a small loaf of talami bread and a block of goat's cheese. On his way home, it began to rain. Thick, sparkly droplets of muggy rain clouded the boy's vision. As he jogged down the alley leading to his home, a young boy ran across in his direction. The boy accidentally splashed his tiny feet in the large puddle, causing the boy's bread and goat's cheese to be soaked with dirty rainwater from the ground. The boy with emerald green eyes turned to the young boy, who was overcome with such a sudden sense of fear that he began to weep. The whites of his eyes turned a frightful black and his teeth gritted with vehemence.

"HOW DARE YOU! ARE YOU BLIND THAT YOU DID NOT SEE ME?!" the boy roared as loud as the thunder above, staring directly at the small boy.

"I...I...I'm sor...sorry," he whimpered, shivering in the cold.

Before the small boy could say another word, the boy threw his bread and cheese to the ground and grabbed the small boy's wrist tightly. He swerved him across and clenched his soaking shirt at the neck. Without thinking, he gave the small boy a single blow to the head and killed him. He dropped to the floor, bleeding from his temple, lifeless and still. The boy saw him lying there, motionless in the thundering rain that showed no signs of stopping, and he too dropped to the ground.

"WHAT HAVE I DONE?!" he cried, hands covering his eyes. He sat there, watching the boy lying dead on the ground and sobbed to himself like a baby.

"Oh, Allah! Why have you made me such a fool, an ignorant fool?! And now, a killer!? Why ya Allah, why?"

Suddenly, the sound of men approaching came from an intersecting alley. The boy knew if he was caught at the scene, then he would have been killed for murdering a small boy, even if it was out of anger and not intended. The boy jumped to his feet and ran for his dear life. He took a quick look back, wailing silently. "I'm sorry…" he whispered to himself, as he saw the boy silent on the ground. He ran as fast as his legs could carry him and ran for his tree. His willow tree.

The willow tree had hardly any leaves left on its swaying branches. The boy sat against the trunk of the tree and violently howled into his hands. Salty tears escaped his emerald eyes, which now looked a dark grey under the ascending moonlight.

"Oh, willow tree, dear willow…," he mourned.

"I've done it again…I killed a boy. A small, young, innocent boy who did nothing more than jump in a puddle. Oh, willow tree, when will I find peace in my life? When?"

The boy's hysterical bawling was more violent than the thunderous gale swirling around him from high above and he felt a deep torturous sensation within his heart. Every bone in his body, every artery filled with burning blood and every hair on his body screamed in unison with his wrath and regret.

As he sat there, frenzied, the earth below him rumbled. The roots that took in the boy's tears hollered and growled beneath him. The first thought he had was 'is this it? Is it judgement day?' He looked around to see if anyone else was around. He saw no one. Again, the earth shook with thunder and rumbled mightily. The pitter-patter of the rain against the river stopped, as did the sound of the gunshot droplets that fell from the skies. Then, a loud voice came from above.

"Oh Azeez, son of Haider Mohammed..."

The boy jumped in fear and horror. The voice echoed deafeningly and shook the boy with fright and panic.

"Who...who's there?" he stuttered anxiously.

There was silence.

"I said who's there!?" he spoke, louder this time.

To his astonishment, the voice thundered even louder this time, a voice deeper than the ocean itself.

The boy fell to the floor, not out of fear, but because the ground below him shook and quaked harshly, causing him to fall over a root of the tree.

"Azeez, son of Haider, it is I, your dear old friend," said the booming voice.

"Fr...fri...friend? I don't have any...friends...," replied the boy, staring at the sky.

"Who are you? And, where are you? And how do you know my name?" he questioned, stammering with fear.

The voice replied, "My child, you lean against my trunk every day and cry and water my roots, yet you have forgotten who I am?"

Azeez, the emerald-eyed boy froze in shock and astonishment. He looked up at the weeping willow tree in amazement.

"Willow tree?" he whispered.

"But how? Trees cannot talk," he said.

"It is I, Safasaf; Willow."

Azeez wiped away his tears with the back of his hand and stroked the trunk of the tree. Moss and damp rain filled his hands.

"But how...?" he asked.

"I see you are in trouble again today, Azeez...tell me, what is the matter?"

Azeez, frozen in complete bewilderment and awe, finally took a seat and leant against the trunk of the tree.

He began...

"Oh, willow tree. I tried not to, although I think I tried...but I couldn't help it. My anger, it takes over daily. I didn't mean to kill a young boy, never, but I see red and black and nothing else. I do things I regret the second I do them. People in this town, they hate me and despise my existence. I despise my existence!"

Azeez didn't realise, but he was whimpering and sobbing unconsciously to the tree.

The willow tree listened and listened for hours, as Azeez mourned his mistake and spoke of his everlasting pain.

When he finished, the tree spoke, this time, in a gentler tone.

"My child, do you know what your name means?" asked Safasaf.

"No...," he replied.

"My child, your beautiful name is derived from the Arabic language and means strong and powerful! It is one of the glorious 99 names of Allah the Almighty! How valuable your name is, yet you tell yourself otherwise?"

Azeez sat there, leaning against Safasaf, pondering over her words.

"But Safasaf, I have this unforgivable, untamed temper that I cannot control. Please, help me get rid of it," he begged her.

Safasaf paused for a moment before answering Azeez.

"Indeed, you have something very peculiar and abnormal about you, Azeez. Show me...."

"Show you what, Safasaf?" he asked confused.

"Show me your temper, the anger that blows in your blood, the rage that burns beneath your skin and makes your veins darken with wrath... show me," she asked.

Azeez shook his head in confusion and looked up at the willow tree.

"Well...I can't really show you right now..."

"Why ever not?"

"Well, because it just arises suddenly, out of nowhere."

Safasaf began to laugh humbly, bringing back the thundering noise from the ground.

"Then, my dear, it cannot be your own true nature, for if it were, then you would have been able to easily show it to me at any given time…"

Azeez looked down at his hands, where specks of dry blood from the young boy lingered across his palms.

"My dear…why are you allowing something that isn't even yours to afflict your life?" Safasaf's voice was motherly, soothing to the ears, as Azeez listened to her calming, hopeful words.

From that moment, Azeez, the emerald jewelled-eyed boy, promised himself as well as Safasaf that whenever his temper was to arise, he would remember the words of his dear friend, Willow.

"Safasaf, I promise that from this day onward, I will never become angry again," he promised her.

"The hollow gap I have had for years of missing out on having a mother and father has prevented my heart from ever being happy again and thus, allowed rage to take over," he explained to Willow.

"No matter how difficult life gets, I will always remember your words," he eagerly pledged to the trunks of Willow.

"Are you sure, Azeez? Distress, separation and loss are always around the corner…do not promise something which you may not overcome," she warned him.

"I promise you, Safasaf, I am a changed person."

Azeez thanked Willow for her advice and ran home to his grandmother.

To his outrage, he saw his old grandmother, dear Ummi, laying on the ground, dead.

He looked at her, eyes welling with salty, thick tears and sighed. He took a deep breath in and remembered Safasaf's words...

'Separation, loss and distress are always around the corner, for it is a part of life that no one except Allah can control'.

Azeez wiped his tears and recited words of the Holy Quran, seeking refuge in the Almighty. He whispered in Ummi's ears and held her close.

"Ummi, I won't fail this test, I promise..."

Amira saw the young girl who had been listening to her shift her eyes away shyly as the story came to an end. She gave her a motherly smile, which seemed to quickly bring her eyes back to Amira, as if she had been waiting for it.

Khalid lifted his head from Amira's shoulder, sighed regretfully and spoke, his words sounding like mournful drivel. His voice was full of sadness and heavy with sorrow, the same manner in which his guilt and remorse weighed down on his shoulders.

"That boy...," he whispered.

"He sounds just like me..."

CHAPTER TWENTY-FOUR

The ocean seemed to have adopted its own rage within her heart. It was as if, just as humans felt fear or anger or sadness, the blue heaven beneath Amira, surrounding her from every corner, had felt the same. At times, the water swayed sadly against the slow winds, like she had just been parted from her long-lost lover and sent thousands of miles away. The sadness she felt displayed itself as she indolently teetered along with the sound of empty skies. Other times, she cried brutally, thwacking her waves violently against the boat. Passionate wrath lived deep inside her, as if her lover had betrayed her in the most tragic way and left an indentation in her soul. And sometimes, only very rarely, she felt fear. It was the same fear Amira felt. Fear of loneliness and regret; despite being the magnificent ocean herself, the beauty of the universe, the soul of the world and custodian of all aquatic kinsmen, she felt it all. Happiness and contentment were things she felt too, but hardly ever showed it, for it was too much of a threat to reveal her emotions to anyone again for all she thought about was the feeling of being betrayed and alone again. When she did show small signs of it, she would dance joyfully, her surface rising and descending with tuneful comfort. Nevertheless, it was the most innocent and innocuous of things that often caused the most turmoil.

Just like the ocean, Amira also began to feel a sudden fear of loneliness. There was a time, not long ago, when Amira loved being alone. She would sit beside her willow tree in Shamsa Park, crunching sugared cashews and almonds, with no one beside her except her two loyal friends, her poem book and a pen. She idolised the notion of finding a sense of serenity and peace within her own company, yet now, just as the winds had changed their tune, the clouds their colour and the water its rhythm, Amira too had changed. She no longer wanted to be alone, no longer craved that feeling of being sat somewhere, despite having her two loyal friends in her bag, alone, with no one.

How? How was it that after almost 7 years since the Syrian civil war first began, Amira had changed? It had changed her personality from a witty, bubbly young girl who loved craving a moment's peace, and she had now become someone who was afraid of loneliness. In the past, for hours and hours, she would sit alone and ponder upon her life, her aspirations and her dreams, she'd lose herself intensely in a good book or a new poem, yet now, she had developed a sudden, extreme case of everlasting isolophobia. She thought back to the days she would debate for hours with her father about why she loved being alone so much.

"Let me tell you something, Amira, my princess," he continued, playfully. "We, as humans, we aren't designed to be alone. You hear me? The worst thing in life is ending up alone with no one around you. Is that what you want? To push everyone out? To be isolated forever," he'd say every time.

"I mean, I can go if you like, Mira...and come back later when you finish your poem writing session," Khalid would joke.

"Or I could just hang around here, till you finish," he would tease her as he hung playfully from the only branched arm of the weeping willow tree that he would reach.

"Don't hang on that Khalid, please. You will fall one day and break your neck," she would reply.

"And no, you can stay here…as long as you just don't ask me a million questions."

Many hours had passed since Amira and Khalid started their departure from Greece. A single cloud that had been lingering since dawn, obscure and adamantly stubborn, drowned the winter sunrise.

She was angry again.

Only an hour ago she was fine, singing a tuneful song with her waves. It didn't last long.

The thunderous blasts of whirlwinds that bulldozed harshly against the small boat showed no attempt nor regard to diminish. The air, just like the people in Syria's tears, became thick with salt, conveyed by a temper typhoon that only danced to a single move. It was yet another storm that warranted a vow. A dreadful vow of nothing but miserable menace.

"I'm cold, Khalid…" shivered Amira, quivering in the numbing cold.

"Here, put this on." Khalid took off his jacket and placed it around Amira's shoulders. She slipped her arms through the jacket and snuggled up close to Khalid.

The jacket, as always, smelled of Khalid, his warm, musky scent.

"Don't go sneaking in the pockets," he joked, despite the heavy waves trouncing over them.

The little girl, who had been listening to Amira's story before, sat silently in her father's lap as he angrily tried to get a hold of Google Maps on his iPhone. His grubby, chunky fingers were no use when trying to open anything up on the phone, for the plastic bag he had placed around the phone to keep it from getting wet, was far too slippery.

"Damn these phones! Useless pieces of crap!" he roared, heatedly.

"Brother, how are you receiving signal out here?" shouted Khalid over the blasting waves.

"I don't. It comes and it goes; I'm trying to work this stupid phone so I can see where exactly we are," he replied.

"Let me try," Khalid suggested.

"Khalid, please, just stay here," begged Amira, worried that the booming waves would overwhelm him and drag him into the water.

"It's fine, I'm just here, Mira."

He got up and stepped towards the little girl's father. Every time he lost his balance and almost tipped over the edge, Amira's heart stopped with sheer uneasiness. Again and again, she would recite different Surahs to protect him, the four Quls, Aytul Kursi, and Surah Fatiha, anything that came to her mind. Khalid made it to the man and started looking at his phone.

"WHAT IS THAT? LOOK!" shouted an old woman, maybe in her 50s. Everyone turned to where she was pointing and there, in the midst of the adversity and plight, was another boat. To Amira's utter stupefaction, the boat was nothing like the one she was on. This boat, that was similarly full of refugees, had the capacity for approximately 30 people, however, there were more than just 30. Their sinking boat, like a tinned can of sardines, was filled with more than 70 refugees.

"They're coming this way! HELP THEM!" yelled Khalid.

"HELP? ARE YOU MAD? WE BARELY HAVE SPACE FOR US! NO! WE CANNOT ALLOW ANYONE ELSE ON THIS BOAT!" replied the little girl's father.

"Have you lost your mind?! HOW CAN WE NOT HELP THEM? WHERE IS YOUR MERCY? YOU'RE NO BETTER THAN ASSAD AND HIS KILLERS!" Khalid was beginning to become angry as the man spoke more words of ignominy.

In her heart, Amira's brain was steering more towards what the man was saying, but then she quickly shook off her bad omens as she felt guilty for possibly thinking of leaving innocent people who were in desperate need. She couldn't turn them away, nor could Khalid.

Khalid got up from his seat near the man and travelled towards Amira's bench where she sat, troubled and fretful.

"Mira, when they come, help me, please," he panted, almost out of breath. The course of the guttural and rowdy waves was becoming more bitter by the second.

"Help all the women and babies first...you know we can't just leave them," he huffed.

"I know Khalid, I know," she replied.

"I'll jump into their boat and help them to pass over onto here, then you pull them through, ok Mira? We got this, princess, it will all be okay."

"Khalid...," she cried, "just be careful please".

Khalid gave Amira a soothing, playful wink and gave her a flash of sudden optimism and hope.

"THEY ARE NOT BOARDING THIS BOAT, DO YOU HEAR ME, BOY?!" the man yelled loudly over the waves and his family seemed to become more and more distraught. This wasn't the time nor place for such a bitter quarrel and it proved his wife and small children were becoming afraid.

"FEAR GOD!" Khalid shouted, before reaching over the edge of the boat, diving into the waves and reaching into the other boat.

"ALL THE MEN OUT! GET OUT AND HELP!" bellowed Khalid from the water.

Only 4 men and a young boy, maybe 14 years old, dived into the water to help Khalid. The man with the iPhone stood stubbornly on his seat, gritting his teeth hard with fury.

"Bloody fool!" he grunted.

Amira gave him a chilling, piercing look and then paid him no more attention.

Amira looked on as Khalid and the other men swam towards the sinking boat. It was overcrowded, waiting to sink. It wasn't long before the boat tumbled over and began descending into the water with great speed.

"Take my baby, please! Someone save my daughter!" cried a woman who was holding onto her child firmly as she floated in the water.

Another small girl, no older than 9, held onto another child.

"Please, someone take my brother, please save him," she cried hysterically, screeching as she spoke.

Another held onto a dead baby, his face blue and purple with quietus.

"Please give my son a proper burial, for the sake of Allah, take him," she sobbed, mournfully.

Amira, speechless with defeat and grief, began to whimper in her seat, trying hard to fight back stinging, acidic tears of pure sadness.

She held out her hand to the women and children and babies in the water, floating, and frantically waiting to be saved and pulled aboard Amira's boat.

"GIVE ME YOUR HAND!" shouted Amira, as loud as her lungs could without being swept away by the gusting wind.

"ALL THE MEN, OUT OF THE BOAT! STAY OUTSIDE THE BOAT! OTHERWISE, IT WILL BE TOO HEAVY TO FLOAT AND WILL SINK!" cried Khalid, ferociously, whilst spitting out seawater that he kept taking in. One after the other, Khalid helped a new person exit their boat and Amira pulled them over.

"This boat is still okay only if a handful of you stay on it, no more than 15 people, otherwise it will sink and it is already sinking gradually. You all stay in here and stay close to our boat, then we will all travel together and guide one another in direction. You there, use your phone and see if you can use Google Maps for directions!" Khalid began giving everyone orders, instructions on what to do and without hesitation or conflict, they all began listening.

She grew more powerful by the minute, taking down more and more people with her, who tried their best to swim back before the next wave overturned them again. Caliginosity prevailed as the obscure smog and murky clouds thickened with storm and wrath. The wind began forming intense mountains, overpowering the refugees in the boats as they continued to morph into vehement waves. The sharp wind began slapping the faces of people and the hailstones falling from the sky felt like tiny pebbles being thrown at their bodies. Trepidation and fear of the unknown sat on Amira's chest like a suffocating cushion, choking her airways. Although she was breathing, despite it being tremendously difficult as the wind was almost breathtakingly stupefying, it left her struggling in the boat as she tried to help others. She felt the boat, which was now becoming much heavier and not as fast as before, sinking slightly. There were no holes or punctures in the boat, yet due to the vast amount of people who had climbed on board, it was suffering a gradual decline in efficiency.

Khalid, who is in between the other refugee's boat and his, stayed in the water whilst hanging from his original boat. Amira shuffled herself over, after an immense struggle, and leant against the edge of the boat, where Khalid was floating in the water.

"Khalid! Khalid, are you okay?" she panted. The people behind her, who were mainly women and children, pushed her hard against the edge of the boat. She screamed suddenly out of pain and hissed as the tough plastic motor beside her dug into her ribcage.

"MIRA! Be careful," shouted Khalid, still battling the mountainous waves that kept visiting every few minutes.

"YOU'RE A FOOL, BOY!" the man bellowed from the far end of the boat, still clutching his daughter in one arm and his iPhone in the other.

Amira and Khalid both ignored him.

"Khalid, please, come onto the boat now. There's space, look…" Amira pointed to a small space on the boat where she knew he wouldn't fit.

Khalid didn't bother looking at the space beside her and replied, "Look, Mira, I'm okay…I think we are almost there. I heard a man in that boat tell me his phone worked, and we are close to Turkey." He sounded reassuring, yet Amira couldn't help but feel helpless and guilty for allowing Khalid to float for god knows how long in the cold water.

Amira welled up, looking at Khalid fighting the waves. Each wave left the occupants of the boat shaking with terror as they all grabbed onto one another and the edges and sides of the dinghy to prevent themselves from falling into the ocean. Khalid, alongside a few other men outside the boat, was constantly challenged by the ferocious waves. A few times, Khalid let go of the side of the boat where he had hung his arms over and scurried a few meters away. He quickly hurried back, swimming swiftly before another wave overwhelmed him again.

"Talk to me, Mira," Khalid begged. Sensing an impression of feeling powerless, Amira began talking to Khalid. Surrounded by monstrous waves, with bullet-like hailstones falling from the sky and almost 100 refugees, some wailing and others moaning, Amira talked to Khalid. She talked to him as if they are sitting in Shamsa Park, under the willow tree, eating caramelized peanuts and pistachios. The only difference was, no matter how hard she tried, she kept subconsciously welling up with thick, painful tears strolling down her wet face.

"I...I miss them, Khalid..." she cried, silently.

"I wish I was in Syria, sitting on Baba's lap, listening to his poems, or eating Mama's Kibbeh, or playing hide and seek with Adam...I miss them, Khalid, so much."

The desolation Amira felt after suddenly missing her dead family was tearing her apart. In this heartache, this sadness and anguish, it felt as if the sun would never shine again upon her face, the birds wouldn't sing the merry tunes of the early winter mornings, the laughter of children wouldn't be heard in homes anymore and the memories would never fade.

"Mira...," Khalid finally spoke, spitting out repulsive seawater.

Amira looked deep into his eyes, which were blood-red and inflamed from the stinging of saline.

She fell for him again, for his eyes showed nothing but pure and honest love; the type of love that feels strange almost, for it stretched and ran through all of Amira's body, confounding and wondrous, yet still making her feel complete. Having no limits, bounds nor depth, it was unsullied, absolute.

"You are so...beautiful," Khalid sighed with great pain in his heart as he spoke.

Khalid spoke, then grunted as he continued.

"There...there isn't...any," he whined, as if in immense pain.

"Khalid? What is it?" Amira quizzed, worried at his sudden change in tune.

Khalid grunted louder and said, "There isn't anyone, ANYONE! in this world as beautiful as you, Mira, and you have no idea how proud I am to call you mine."

Amira looked at Khalid, confused as to why he was suddenly saying such things and spitting out his words quickly, as if he wanted to say the words before something bad happened.

"Why are you talking like that, Khalid?" she asked.

"I once had a thousand desires, but in my one desire to know you, all else melted away…" he replied, almost whimpering like a child as he spoke.

Amira gave Khalid a grievous look of ruefulness and whispered almost silently, "Rumi…"

"Khalid…?" she wept.

"Falling in love with you was so easy, Mira…" Khalid held out his hand for Amira to grab onto as another wave threw itself at both boats. When it did, Khalid growled louder.

"What is it, Khalid? Why are you moaning, what's happened?" Amira started crying, deplorably. She held onto Khalid's arms and with one hand, he touched her face as he did whenever he felt love towards her. He stroked it, gently, wiping away every tear that raced down her cheeks.

"Tell me, Mira…tell me once more…" said Khalid. His eyes started rolling back, as if he was entering a sudden stupor.

"Khalid! Wake up!" she cried. She tried pulling him over the edge of the boat and asked someone to help her. She was surrounded by women all holding their children and small babies, so no one came to her aid.

"Please, Khalid! Get up and jump on the boat, PLEASE!"

Someone from the other boat aggressively addressed Amira, but she ignored him, not listening to what they had to say.

"Say it to me…" he said again, this time, more eagerly.

"Say what, Khalid?" whimpered Amira, not caring about the people shouting at her from behind, nor listening to what they are saying.

"You know…" he replied, opening and closing his mouth, repeating himself, "You know, Mira…"

A man bellowed from behind her, as did another old, haggard-sounding woman, yet Amira heard nothing. They kept yelling loudly, but Amira completely disregarded them and looked lovingly into Khalid's eyes before they closed again. A final time, Khalid gulped and echoed, "Say it…"

"I love you, Khalid! I LOVE YOU!" she sobbed hysterically.

Khalid gave her a weak, halfhearted smile and replied, "I can survive anything, Mira, as long as I have your love…" He wiped away another tear that sat on Amira's eyelash.

Suddenly, something tugged at Khalid from beneath the water. He groaned louder and more violently in complete agony.

"KHALID!!" screamed Amira.

Another tug and Khalid's grip on the edge of the boat loosened.

"SOMEONE HELP!" she screeched, burning tears streaming from her eyes. She tried reaching out for his hand but failed repeatedly.

"SOMEBODY HELP HIM!" She continued to wail and beg for help. Whilst speaking to Khalid, she hadn't realized that within those 3 minutes, there was only him left outside the boat, for the other few men had all jumped on either one of the boats that were only meters apart.

Another tug dragged Khalid deep into the ocean.

"KHALID!!!!!! KHALIDDD!!! SOMEBODY HELP!!" Amira shouted as loud as her lungs could manage and she felt her throat burn with spasm. She tried jumping into the water but was pulled back by an elderly woman.

"LET ME GO! LET ME GO, MY HUSBAND IS DROWNING!" she yowled violently, insanely.

She pushed the woman away and tried again. She managed to get one leg into the water before another woman pulled her back.

"Daughter! Please! It is too dangerous," the woman said.

"Dangerous! HOW?! HE IS GOING TO DIE IF I DON'T HELP HIM! HE WILL DROWN, HE'S FAINTING!" she yelled angrily, her voice almost dry and hoarse, strangling her from speaking further.

That is when she knew.

She knew, and finally realized.

She realized the reason people were all shouting and aggressively speaking behind her when she was talking to Khalid. She knew the reason why all the other men who were dangling their bodies against the boats had suddenly jumped into them instead and she knew the reason why Khalid, despite being the fastest swimmer, was carried away by the waves and drowning.

"THERE! IT'S THERE!" bellowed someone.

"SHARKKKKKKK!! THERE, LOOK!"

Amira's blood ran cold and amidst the cruel iciness, a single bead of sweat trickled down her stone-cold face. She sat there, powerless, crippled and dumbfounded in sheer torture, not knowing what to do, or what to think, how to think, too scared and too agonized to think.

"Everyone, get your hands and feet inside the boat! The shark is right there!" wailed another person.

Even in the crepuscule, the gushing blood from Khalid's leg that the shark had bitten into was beaming crimson red under the brightness. It spurted into the fizzing seawater so that, with every blink, Amira flinched. In the distance, she saw him. His skin, pale as snow and eyes growing duller and duller. The pain that was just burning like a blazing flame from a hot fire inside Amira's aching chest, bleached into a blood-curdling paralysis. The world had stopped, as had the waves and the wind and the life within her. Numbing opacity crowded the corners of her visuals and an overpowering sense of anaesthesia suffocated her airways, leading to the only sound drumming in the atmosphere being Amira's thundering heartbeat. She took a breath, a deep one and it furtively escaped her quivering lips with jagged and seedy gasps.

Khalid was now indistinguishable, his face deeply imbedded into the aquatic realm of death.

"You promised..." whimpered Amira, her tears falling into the sea and joining Khalid.

She closes her eyes and dreamt.

She dreamt of waking up from a long, frightful night, looking to her side and finding it empty.

"I'm having the wall side!" Amira would tease Khalid about sleeping on the wall side of the bed.

She dreamt of his muscular, protective arms wrapped tightly around her as she slept peacefully, to the scent of his musk suddenly not being there any longer for her to run to during times of need. She dreamt of flowers growing from 'their' weeping willow tree, painted with multicoloured, pulchritudinous pigments then suddenly dying as a dark, gloomed cloud rose above them, killing all plants and blooming blossoms in sight.

She dreamt of peace.

She dreamt of fairness, justice and love...

She dreamt that one day, the children in Syria would smile and laugh again, just as they used to, that they'd go to school and learn to grow to be strong and brave. She dreamt of Eid-Ul-Fitr, where she wore her favourite sequined, amethystine gown made of soft satin, loose and frilly, tied at her waist. She dreamt of eating her mother's yearly Eid sweets that she made hours before anyone would awaken for the festive day. Baked, powdered kahk filled with walnuts and sticky zileibi, a delightful sweet dish eaten on Eid. She dreamt of biting into the crispy fried sweet as it dripped with sugary syrup, and then licking her fingers afterwards. She dreamt that the nation's favourite flower; the Jasmine, would grow in abundance with it's sweet, comforting scent.

She dreamt of the last moment she looked into Khalid's eyes, his big, toffee brown eyes that made her forget all her worries. She dreamt of his last touch, as he gently wiped her tears away with a single stroke, his last kiss that he placed on her lips, the last embrace, the last time they ever made love and the last words he ever uttered to her before she failed to save him from his destined fate...

"I can survive anything, Mira, as long as I have your love..."

And once the storm was over, when the ocean decided she wanted to dance with sudden rapture and excitement, Amira didn't remember anything. She didn't remember how, after battling with herself over the fear of loneliness and mourning, she made it. She didn't know how, after seeing Khalid being washed away in the prodigious ripples and waves, she survived. She was confused, feeling drugged and sedated almost. She didn't know whether the storm was really over. She looked around. It wasn't fair that the ocean only decided to dance now with happiness. Why was it that when Amira was in time of need and pure desperation, the ocean wanted to demonstrate her performance of raging wrath, yet now, when all was done and said, when loved ones had fallen into the depths of the world and lives were endlessly, eternally shattered, she decided to sing and dance with elation and triumph, as if her lover had returned or apologized for the betrayal and confessed his urging love for her?

The waves capered merrily and she closed her sunken eyes to the gentle hypnotic cradlesong of the sea whilst breathing in its intensely piquant breath. Everything seemed serene, peaceful even, so was the storm really over? Or was it just blooming deep inside of her soul, growing into something bigger than she ever imagined?

Amira knew one thing for sure...

Whether the storm was really over or not, she knew that she would never be the same person she was before she walked into it.

Ever.

CHAPTER TWENTY-FIVE

'I choose to love you in silence,
for in silence, I find no rejection.

I choose to love you in loneliness,
for in loneliness, no one owns you but me.

I choose to adore you from a distance,
for distance will shield me from pain.

I choose to kiss you in the wind,
for the wind is gentler than my lips.

I choose to hold you in my dreams,
for in my dreams, you have no end...'

Ustadh Jalāl ad-Dīn Muhammad Rūmī

Amira sniffled and whispered into the marine air and breeze of the descending ocean, her trembling eyelids quivering shut as she inhaled the brackish odour. She looked back to where the boat now swayed in the steady water. Ruffling her toes, she stroked the tender, sugary sand that was still sopping wet from the withdrawing current. With every listless, slow step she took towards the crowd in front, the sand beneath her toes shifted. It was like strolling through a winter wonderland at Christmas time, with newly fallen snow blanketing everywhere. The only difference, however, was unlike the crystallised snow that falls and gives one severe frostbite when trodden on with naked feet, the sand would do the opposite. The sand under Amira's feet gave her nothing but assuaging warmth.

People in front of Amira, and behind, all hurried along the shore towards the coastguard rescuers. Two helicopters flew over Amira's head. The refugees ran towards the rescuers, crying, wailing and some falling into sujood out of gratefulness for arriving back on land alive. They all raced one another, fleeing almost in a scurry as if they had been told to go back or they would be left alone if not met by a coastguard in time. Some limped, for their limbs had been cut, some sprinted, others ambled as they held onto their dead children, hoping there still might be a chance for their survival; all but Amira. Despite the heat, she felt frozen. She stared, emotionlessly, at the refugees all going in the same direction, some falling and tripping as they went. She watched them, frenzied and hysterical, lost in complete desperation and cataclysmic sorrow. Her gaze fell upon a small girl, holding a stuffed penguin toy which was soaked in seawater. She had beautiful, thick black hair, which was also soaking. As she limped in pain, her hair cascaded down her pure, white skin. For some bizarre reason, her hair reminded Amira of the night time waves that she had seen only hours ago. Clenching her damp penguin toy tightly, the little girl opened her shivering mouth to call for her mother. Her words, scared and grievous, came out spasmodically, the sounds half-strangled by a desolate blubbering.

"Mam...mamma...MAMAAA!" she shrieked, louder each time. In her fright, she was wailing too much to be comprehensible.

Amira strolled towards the little girl to help and comfort her, despite her being in need of reassurance from others. She had only taken a step or two before the little girl's mother emerged from the crowd. Her mother screamed to her and sprinted towards the child as fast as her legs could take her.

"MY BABY! MY BABY NADIYA! NADIYA!" yelled her mother, delirious.

They both embraced one another, sobbing uncontrollably. The father of the small family also emerged after a moment and was carrying his son on his shoulders. They all fell to the ground, clasping one another firmly. The father, a tall, wearied man with wrinkly eye bags, held onto his wife and let her cry. She cried, depressed deep into his arms and said nothing and Amira, still standing in the warmth of the sand, watched as the woman placed her cold, maudlin kisses on her husband, daughter and son's warm cheeks.

Just like the tear that glides swiftly down Amira's cheek at the sight of the family reunited amongst the frenzy, diamonds too have a similarity to her precious, anguishing tears. Tears, that were filled with nothing but painful memories, terror, sadness and mourning, just like diamonds, were created and borne from pressure. All diamonds were, were rocks of coal, powerful and rigid just like Amira, who, after experiencing all that she had, was stronger and braver than ever. On those days, the most excruciatingly laborious and unbearable of all when the world resided itself upon Amira's shoulders, just like a precious diamond birthed under the weight of mountains, she flourished into what God moulded her into; a warrior, a diamond, Amira. Princess Amira.

One by one, the coastguard rescuers helped the refugees as they waited in a messy, barely distinguishable line.

"Your name, please? How old is your child? Do you have your documents? Are you alone?" Amira can hear the bombardment of questions as the rescuers and coastguard refugee volunteers went through each person or family. During the storm, most of Amira's documents, the fake ones made back in Greece, had been soaked with seawater as she had forgotten to place them within a zipped plastic bag. They were still, however, intact and readable, once dried. The small box she once owned that was home to her poem book, her pictures of her family and other sentimental things, had been transferred into her sturdy drawstring bag.

A sudden gust of ocean breeze splattered small sprinkles of light mist on Amira's face, leaving her lips salty to the taste as she licked them. She shuddered in the chilly breeze that lingered for a minute or two. Forgetting that she was still wearing Khalid's jacket, she snuggled her face inside the large collar. Her heart filled with dysphoria and pain as she caught a whiff of Khalid's smell. Subconscious, soul-crushing tears flowed from her eyes and she took off Khalid's jacket and placed it over her face. She shut her eyes to his scent, ambrosial musk, and painful memories dispersed before her, almost as if she was dreaming. The compelling recollections, the joyous reminiscences and the profound memories; they were like the penguin toy the little lost girl held onto, only, it was made of shattered glass shrapnel – the closer and firmer you cherished and clung to it, the deeper it cut. The dreams, hopes and aspirations Khalid and Amira had both planned and spoken of, the adventures they once fantasised of embarking on and the fire that burnt within them with passion and love for one another, now could only be described as a painfully, everlasting heartache on Amira's part. The heartbreak she felt was like a rapacious, hungry fire that blazed viciously within Amira's body, torching all the oxygen in her and leaving her lackadaisical and hollow. She inhaled deeply the fragrance of her dear love, her soulmate. She took another breath as the memory of Khalid first teaching Amira how to ride a bike when she was 7 overwhelmed her spirits, the deeper she breathed in his smell. Another breath in, she remembered the time Khalid made a snowman during a winter's afternoon. A few more inhalations, she began to reminisce the way she felt when Khalid first laid eyes on her as her husband, his heart full of love and nothing but love and devotion for her. He surrendered so much adoration and love to Amira, the love that killed all her doubts and ensured she never felt lonely in this world again, the love that allowed Khalid to see every damaged and scarred part of her, whether internally or externally, and still sang their praises and made them sparkle like bejewelled gems, and the love that gave Amira the sweet, treasured glimpse of heaven.

Amira stood there, weeping achingly into his jacket, taking in as much of his smell before it gradually would one day wither and fade away.

"Oh, Khalid…" Amira whispered, thick droplets of tears escaping her eyes and soaking into his jacket.

"Every moment I've spent with you, they're all such painful memories now, Khalid", she mourned. "Come back to me please Khalid, please".

She felt Khalid's jacket getting progressively wetter with her sorrow. She was purely grief-stricken, fighting with herself, trying to stay brave, just like he learnt to do, but the throbbing ache in her barely beating heart was sharp, cutting right through her as she thought of Khalid. Even the sweet, exultantly euphoric moments they shared were like deadly knives, stabbing at her already broken heart.

People around Amira still cried and recollected themselves as they, one by one, were questioned by the volunteers. Amira was in such a daze inside Khalid's hypnotic scent, that she didn't even know where she was.

Was she in Egypt? Or Tunisia? Or Cyprus again? Did they even reach Turkey? She did not know, nor did she attempt to find out any time soon, for she was benumbed. All she wanted to do was stand there and stay with Khalid's smell before that too left.

As she crumpled his jacket closer to her face, she stroked it across her cheeks. She heard a synthetic, plasticky sound coming from inside his pocket. Ignoring it once, she heard it again as she rubbed the jacket now across her other cheek. She moved the jacket away from her face and felt in his pockets. She dug her hand deep inside the first pocket, where she found his ponytail that he tied his long hair in, a toothbrush and his pen. Amira found it strange that he carried a pen around. It was only until she reached into his other pocket, that she realised why he carried his pen.

From the pocket, she took out a perfectly sealed, plastic bag that seemed to be encompassed with many zip lock bags, as if it were protecting something extremely valuable.

'What would Khalid have been trying to protect and conceal so cautiously?' The thought suddenly came to her mind, something that sent an instant shiver through her weak, tired body.

Her heart began to drum inside her chest and her hands trembled as she opened the sealed zip lock bag. She found another zip lock bag inside the previous one and she continued to open the bags. After 6 zip-locked sealed bags, she found a piece of paper.

Amira fell to the floor with remorseful lamentation and agony as her glacial eyes skimmed the double-sided piece of paper. She gasped, sounds of tragic sobbing escaping her pursed lips. After wanting to hear this poem for so long, she finally had her wish granted in the most brutal, cruel manner. She read the poem written by Khalid, his messy, scribbled out writing, doodles on the edges of the sheet and his words, almost as if he was speaking and reading it out himself...

She read the wedding poem that Khalid had written for her.

My dear Princess Mira...

I want you to know, that I have always loved you. I have loved you since we were young with snotty noses and really bad hair days and oh, the disgraceful outfits our parents made us wear as children. I loved you when you first came crying to me, I think you were probably 9 or 8 years old and a boy had ripped up the poem that you wrote in Shamsa Park. I fell in love with you when you secretly saved me the extra piece of Kibbeh on Eid when everyone devoured their feast and I arrived a little late to supper. I fell in love with you, when you smiled at me, giving me the maddest goosebumps. I don't know...there was just something about your smile, Mira; you gave me so much relief and contentment in just simply smiling. I'm not so good with words, but what I'm trying to say here is that...Always, Amira...I have always loved you.

If you are reading this, then it means I am no longer with you, but hey! Don't worry, because guess what...I promised you, didn't I? I promised you I would write the best poem in this world just for you...and I also promised you that everything will all be okay soon. I never break my promises, Amira. You've reached safely onto land, haven't you? People are helping you? They'll probably take down your name and age and documents and soon, they'll keep you safe. My first promise, I've kept! Second promise, well, let's just say this poem is going to bring back that gorgeous, beautiful smile that I fell in love with.

Listen to me, Amiraty, my wife...Soon, very soon, it will all be okay...I promise (and we both know I don't break promises), so just hold on a little longer, my sweetheart.

Amira read the first side of the paper, laughing at Khalid's handwriting, crying at his words, almost hearing him speak as she read on and on. She didn't want it to finish or come to an end. She sniffled, wiped her tears and turned over the paper.

'Every road I turn seems empty without your face hiding amongst the crowd of people who come and go,
Is it any news to you that wherever you walk, is the direction that I am yearning to forever follow?

There is a special peace and tranquillity I find whilst buried deeply in your arm,
It is as if someone is whispering to me 'Khalid, this is where you will find no harm'.

418

Your warm, bewitching smile is what made me fall completely and won my heart,
21 years of laughter, tears and memories, where did it all start?

In the beginning, I'll be honest when I admit, that I didn't really know what love was or what it meant,
But as time went on, all I understood of it was feeling of being purely content.

Watching you grow and admiring your soul,
The fulfilment and happiness I felt, was richer than gold.

The devotion and love I feel for you is more than true,
So please, hold onto it, as I have held onto you.

For all the times we have held each other through the darkest of rain,
And all the times we have comforted one another to ease away the pain...

You've accepted me for who I am and treated me like I've never sinned before,
And made me feel complete with a simple embrace, that always leaves me craving more.

The people in our town would always laugh and tell me;
 "Are you crazy? You' re just a boy" ,
And then they' d say ⋯
 "You have your whole life to think about marriage! Why the rush?" ,
And sometimes, they' d even say,
 "You don' t even have a proper job; how do you expect to provide for your wife?" ⋯

One day, we are going to grow old together Mira, for this the promise I have proudly made,

Because quite frankly, you already know that I don't give a shit what 'they' all say!

All I want, is to carry on loving you, like I already do every second of every minute of every day,

Then continue to sleep to the sound of your soothing voice, as you recite your poems to me, for they'll keep me intact and never lead me astray,

And then Insha' Allah, by the will of my Almighty, hope to become a better husband, person and father someday⋯

How'd you like my poem, eh? I hope you liked it, I put a lot of blood, sweat and tears into this you know! Well, maybe not blood...or sweat, but maybe a few tears.

Hold tight to my promise, my Princess...
Everything will be okay, and like Rumi said...

'Do not feel lonely,
The entire universe is inside you'...

And when that universe is born, I know she'll be a girl, I just know it! Do me one favour, and call her Khawlah, so that she grows up to be strong and brave and fearless! Just like her mother!

I love you, Mira, always.

Khalid x

"I love you too", Amira blurted, laughing, then crying, at Khalid's words.

The rays from the sun caressed the back of Amira's neck, warming her back to her senses. She stood up, clutching hard to Khalid's letter, staring at the descending line of refugees. She inhaled deeply and exhaled in sync with the singing birds and swaying waves behind her. A woman, who was dressed in coastguard rescue uniform and wearing a bright neon high-viz vest, approached Amira with a warm, welcoming smile.

"Hello, my dear," she said.

"What is your name?"

"Amira...Amira Hussain," she replied, weakly.

"And your age, darling?" asked the woman, writing down the answers to her questions on her heavily stacked clipboard.

"21," replied Amira.

"And are you here alone?" the woman finally asked.

Amira looked at the woman and gave her a faint, subtle smile, a smile that diminished with her last tear that quickly trickled down her cheek and got wiped away with a courageously valorous stroke of her palm. She giggled, thinking back to Khalid's words in his letter, his silly handwriting that never seemed to have improved since school and his poem. Still holding onto the paper, she placed it inside her pocket and placed both hands on her slightly inflated belly, thinking back to the time she would wake up during the early hours of the day and spend an hour in the bathroom, vomiting. Khalid would rub her back gently, consoling her with words of solace and support. She stroked her stomach, ever so tenderly, grinning blissfully to herself, before looking up to the woman and softly uttering...

"I am not alone, I have the whole world inside of me" ...

To be continued ...

ABOUT THE AUTHOR

'Nazahah Zahid is a 24-year old aspiring author and grew up in the heart of East London in the borough of Waltham Forest. Post completing her A Levels in College, her career began working within the education sector and has worked alongside Primary, Secondary and College-level pupils. At present, she works full time within an all through school in East London.

She began writing her debut novel 'Princess Mira' purely on the basis of 'telling a story'. The Syrian Civil War is now entering its 9th year. A big portion of Nazahah's inspiration for this novel was the goal of spreading awareness of the tragedy and despair experienced by the thousands of Syrian children who lose their families on a daily basis and are forced to live in a war-zone or flee. Too often their cries go unheard and Nazahah advocates for the help and support of all those affected by the ongoing war.

Amira and Khalid, though fictional characters, represent the fear and danger of all the Syrian's having to find a way to survive in circumstances so out of their control. Nazahah stepped away from fictional writing and in publishing Princess Mira, has chosen to address the raw realism of war. Looking forward, she intends to focus her next works on more true stories, in an effort to catalyse the same thought-provoking response from readers and she hopes this one will.

Nazahah is a fond reader and especially enjoys the works of her favourite authors; Khaled Hosseini and Elif Shafak.'